THE EPIC OF HAVEN
TRILOGY

BY R.G. TRIPLETT

BOOK ONE
THE GREAT DARKENING

BOOK TWO
THE RAVENOUS SIEGE

BOOK THREE
THE COMING DAWN

Itxaro Mountains
Western Wrea
The World of Aiénor
as recorded by the Citadel of Haven
N
W
E
S
Greywood Forest
Isle Dušana
Herald Tower
Dardanos
Hekate' Mountains
Aerebus
Dark Sea

t   h
Terriah
Hilgari Mountains
Northern Altar of the Priest
The Retreating Forest
Petros
Pool of Eiluned
River Abonris
Mt. Aureole
Piney Creek
The Capitol
Westriver
Haven
Black Mountains of Cair
Abondale
Meinir
River Ichelтом
Halvard
Lake Riene
The Outlying Lands
The Talsfyn Pass
Bright Harbor
Maris
Bay of Eurwen

THE RAVENOUS SIEGE

R.G. TRIPLETT

EDITED BY MELODY FARRELL

THIS BOOK IS PUBLISHED BY LOST POET PRESS

Text copyright © 2016 by Robert G Triplett

Jacket art by Rob Stainback copyright © 2016 by Lost Poet Press

Map art by Rob Stainback copyright © 2016 by Lost Poet Press

Illustrations by Amanda Farrell copyright © 2016 by Lost Poet Press

Published in the United States by Lost Poet Press

First paperback edition.

www.epicofhaven.com

www.lostpoetpress.com

ISBN 978-1-944470-02-9

Library of Congress Control Number:

2016912076

Lost Poet Press first edition paperback, August 2016

For the dreams and the dreamers
who have tasted the bitterness of exile...
this is not the end.

Contents

THE
RAVENOUS
SIEGE

PRONUNCIATION GUIDE

CHARACTERS

Abaddon (A-bah-dohn)

Ádhamh (AH-dahm)

Aius (AHY-uhs)

Alon (AH-lahn)

Amaian (ah-MAHY-ahn)

Angrah (ANG-grah)

Ardghal (AHRD-gahl)

Armas (AR-mahs)

Astyræ (A-stir-ay)

Bakaren (BACK-ah-rehn)

Benhiram (BEHN-ha-reem)

Blodeuwedd (BLOW-day-wehd)

Brádách (BRA-dak)

Branwen (BRAN-wehn)

Caedmon (CAYD-mohn)

Calarmindon (cal-ahr-MIN-duhn)

Celrod (KEHL-rahd)

Chancellor Chaiphus (KAHY-fus)

Clivesis (CLAHYV-zees)

Črotmir: (CROHT-meer)

Deryn (DAYR-ehn)

Edur (ee-DOOR)

Éimhear (ahy-MEER)

Eógan (YOU-gahn)

Faolan (FAY-ow-lan)

Farran (FAIR-ahn)

Fryon (FRI-ohn)

Goran (GOR-an)

Gormlaith (GORM-layth)

Gvidus (GVEE-duhs)

Haizea (Hi-ZAY-ah)

Harmier (hahr-mee-AYR)
Iolanthe (ee-oh-LAN-thay)
Isme (EES-may)
Johnrey (JOHN-ree)
Julen (JU-lehn)
Kahri (KAH-ree)
Keily (KAHY-lee)
Kemen (KEE-mehn)
King Cascarie (KAS-kah-ree)
King Illium (IHL-ee-uhm)
King Kaestor (KAY-stohr)
Klieo (KLEE-oh)
Linnaea (LIHN-ee-ah)
Llinos (LEE-nos)
Meledae (MEL-eh-day)
Moa (MOH-ah)
Niniané (nih-nee-AH-nay)
Nogcwren (NOCK-ren)
Oren (OH-rehn)
Oskar (OH-scar)
Oweles (OOLS)
Payam (PAHY-yam)
Portus (POR-tuhs)
Pyrrhus (PAHY-ruhs)
Remiel (reh-mee-EHL)
Roshan (RO-shuhn)
Šárka (SAR-kah)
Seig (SEEG)
Shameus (SHEY-mus)
Soren (SOAR-ehn)
Tahd (TAWD)
Timorets (TIH-moor-ehts)
Wielund (WAHY-lund)
Yasen (YEAH-sehn)
Zuriñe (zur-EEN)

PLACES/LANDMARKS/THINGS

Ágoni gi (Ah-GO-neh-gee)

Aiénor (ahy-NOR)

Argine (ahr-GEEN)

Arianrhod (AY-ree-an-rud)

Asier (ah-SEER)

Bay of Eurwen (YOOR-wihn)

Clarus (CLAY-ruhs)

Dardanos (DAR-dah-nohs)

Enguerrand (EHN-ger-uhnd)

Falls of Sarangrael (Ser-ahn-grey-EL)

Fionnuala (fee-oh-NOO-lah)

Gwarwyn (GWAHR-wihn)

Hekate' (Heh-KAH-tay)

Hilgari (hihl-GAR-ee) Mountains

Isle Dušana (doo-SAH-nah)

Islwyn (IH-sehl-wihn)

Itsaso (it-SAH-soh)

Kalein (kah-LEEN)

Maris (MAH-rihs)

Melania (meh-leh-NEE-ah)

Menashe (meh-NASH)

Mount Aureole (AH-rohl)

Petros (PEH-trohs)

River Abonris (AB-ohn-rihs)

Shaimira (Shahy-MEER-ah)

Sleth Aodh (slehth ay-OHD)

Talfryn (TAL-frihn) Pass

Terriah (TAIR-ah)

Viðarr (vee-OHR)

Preface

The need to wish, the desire to hope, and the compulsion to dream—good and honest dreams—is not just for the pure of heart. For within us all, the emigrant and the exiled, the savage and the civilized, the virtuous and the corruptible ... there exists a native, instinctual gravity. This primitive force within pulls us all together and points the truest parts of our souls towards the grandeur of the greatest story.

A story

Of songs and prose and tales of great courage,

Of beauty and rescue and longing hearts,

Of deeds done well and passionate embraces,

Of vanquished enemies, victors, and victorious graces,

Of mercy and magic and merriment made,

Of darkness defeated, and dawn's glory displayed,

Of legends and lore and the most lucid of dreams,

Of redemption and reward, and of restoration at the end of all things.

By their very nature, our weary and wounded hearts cannot help but hear the whisper that beckons us to revel—indulgently and yet profoundly—in the light of something much bigger than ourselves. It is in these epic reveries and poetic rebellions that men may, daily if we dare, glimpse the reflections of both our former and our future glories.

Prologue

THE HOOVES OF THE PALE, speckled gelding pounded the stone pavement with anxious urgency as both horse and rider wove through the streets of the city's square.

"Come now, boy!" the rider shouted to his steed. "We cannot be late for the council of the elders—not when we have such news to bring!"

The young man's long, dark hair whipped and bounced in the rhythm of the horse's gait. Kemen willed his mount to move faster and faster until finally they arrived at the grand Palladium at the heart of the city of Asier. He leapt from the panting horse, running with great haste up the winding stone steps until at last he reached the House of Wisdom, which overlooked the square of the river city. As he strode in through the great entrance and past the ornately sculpted vases and luxurious muslin curtains that flowed lazily in the breeze, his broad chest heaved as his lungs gasped for air. Kemen felt it out of place to disturb the serenity of the Palladium with his desperate panting, but this noble House of Wisdom was at a great altitude, and he had not ascended its stairs with such urgency in a long, long time.

When at last Kemen reached the middle chamber of this great structure, he paused at the curtained entryway, trying to catch his breath and compose himself before he slipped into the gathering. Inside the chamber stood the elders of Asier, already engaged in a heated debate. Kemen eased into the room and pulled the curtain closed behind him.

"What would you have me do? Huh?" Julen, Lord of the amber city asked with great anger in his voice "Abandon all that we have labored for? Give up all that our fathers and their fathers before them gave their backs and blood to build?" The questions echoed off the high pillars that surrounded the room.

"The other tribes and townships are moving southward, seeking solace in the light of the sorceress," said Soren, chief of the watchers. "My sentries and scouts have seen many a banner displaying fealty to her as they journey through the Greywood."

"Nonsense! Why would they trust the sorceress? That is both folly and madness! How do we know that it wasn't she who poisoned the great tree across the sea to begin with?" the white-bearded Zuriñe argued.

"What does that matter now, Zuriñe?" Bakaren said dejectedly. "You know the truth as well as I do. The light we have come to rely upon will not last forever. This first dimming is only a sign of things to come ... her offer is one that we cannot simply ignore!"

"That is exactly what we should do. Ignore it altogether. The Asierian people have little need for trade or wars or alliances. We are a self-sufficient people and we can continue to provide for ourselves right here along the River Argiñe!"

"But what if what she offers is true? What if it is the answer to our worried prayers?" Bakaren asked as she wiped away the tears from her wrinkled face.

"They are all lies! All nothing more than tricks of her conjurings!" shouted the appalled Zuriñe. "Mark my words, that ... that *Raven* will have the whole world kneeling before her, and then she will pluck out their eyes with her damned poisoned beak, all without a word of protest!"

"Let them kneel! Let the blind fools *kneel* if they like ... but we will not,"

Lord Julen said between gritted teeth as he pounded his gloved fist upon the carved, wooden table. "Our walls are strong enough, and the *Giver of Light* has given us plenty to live by."

"But what happens when He takes away His light for good?" Kemen asked aloud, interrupting the heated argument. "What if there is no more light?"

The room went quiet at the asking of the most terrifying question of all.

"This darkening is not the first one our people have endured. When the Jacarandas were stolen from Aiénor, our world lost its brilliance forever. But there was always the bright amber and silver light across the dark waters of the *Itsaso* to hold our deepest fears at bay," Julen said steadily.

Kemen spoke up. "But now ... now it would seem that the *Giver of Light* is removing his gift from this world, and perhaps it would be prudent if we were not so exposed to the impending darkness."

"What do you mean ... *boy*?" Julen asked with great suspicion.

Kemen eyed the twenty-one pairs of eyes of the twenty-one elders, who stared in return with great curiosity, waiting to see just what it was that this young hunter proposed. "What I mean is that we-"

Kemen's words were cut short as a tall, ashen-faced nobleman stepped through the doorway and interrupted the convening council, seizing their attention. "Elders of Asier, my name is Isme, herald of the Raven Queen," he said with slight bow.

"The Raven Queen?" Zuriñe blurted out. "She fancies herself a *queen* now? On whose authority does she derive such titles?"

"You are most *unwelcome,* herald of the sorceress," Julen demanded as he stood to his feet, his offense evident to all. "We will have none of your forked-tongued council here, sir!"

"You will count yourself wise to hear the good tidings I have to bring on this dark, dark day, Asierians," Isme continued. "For the Raveness has called forth a new light for all our kind, and we will never have to fear the darkness again. If you lords would but bend your allegiance to her *benevolent* will, like so many of your neighbors have already done, then you would have this light for yourselves." Isme spoke while staring down the long-haired hunter.

"Bend our allegiance ... and then what?" Soren asked. "Gifts—magic or otherwise—do not come without a price!"

"The Raven Queen but offers a new light, a light that needs no flames, no trees, no fickle giver. And it is by this light alone that all who choose will see their destiny."

"And what if we don't take it?" Bakaren asked nervously. "What then?"

Isme looked up towards the ceiling, and a sickly, green glee seemed to burn from deep within his eyes as a sinister grin crept across his gaunt face. The muslin curtains began to whip wildly in the wake of an unforeseen storm. The red-bricked pillars started to shake and rumble, and the very structure that held them all threatened to collapse underneath the intensity of the pressure.

"What is that? What is the meaning of this *devilry*?" Julen nervously demanded.

The eyes of the council darted back and forth in frightened horror as torrents of pounding wind ripped through the grand Palladium, sending paper and goblets scattering across the tiled floor.

Kemen reached for the arm of his uncle Zuriñe as he whispered his worries against the wind of this witchcraft. "We are not safe here any longer, Uncle!"

"Agreed, my boy."

Isme's eyes burned with a sickly, green fire as he surveyed his terrified audience here in the river city. "A new light has come for us all, on the benevolent *wings* of the Raveness' good will. It would ... behoove you citizens of Asier to receive her gift; that is, whilst it is still offered."

"Why?" Bakaren asked. "Why is all of this happening? Why is she forcing this ... *gift* ... upon every city on the Wreath?" she begged, with frightened tears upon her wrinkled cheeks.

The pounding wind stopped and the ground below their feet shook with a succession of heavy crashes. The herald's smile grew wider and his green eyes glowed all the brighter in the satisfaction of the moment. Kemen held his spear at the ready, trained on the unwelcome servant of the sorceress. Julen reached for his two-handed sword that rested across his table, feeling the same, instinctual response as all who were gathered: war.

"Because ... *darkness* is coming." Isme's words took a sinister tone as he spoke his farewell. The herald disappeared behind the wind-beaten curtains and then, in an explosion of unexpected fire, the rafters of the grand

Palladium burst into flame.

The elders grabbed what they could and fled from the flaming pyre that was once their grandest hall. Smoke was thick upon the evening air, and the people of Asier ran out from their homes, standing in the streets to watch the green flames consume the revered structure atop the hill. Some of those who witnessed this devilry ran to the aid of the elders and the watchmen, doing what they could to quell the fire that threatened their city.

"We cannot contend with that kind of power," Kemen said to his uncle.

"That is precisely what she wants us to believe!" Zuriñe said as he tossed a bucketful of water upon the unnatural flames.

"Our homes are no longer safe," Julen admitted. "How can our city contend with this ... this damned vile magic?" He spoke with defeat on his face and in his voice as he, too, tossed a useless bucketful of water into the burning hall.

"Why does she care if we take her *new light* or not? Huh?" Soren asked as he wiped the smoke from his wet eyes. "We have never meddled in the wars of these lands! Never once has Asier given aid to her enemies."

"I fear that evil needs no reason to lust for more power. That is its nature: to reach, to grab, to control whatever the might of its appetite and the strength of its reach can afford to consume," Zuriñe offered.

"Even so ... I would rather see our city burn than succumb to the bite of her ravenous hunger," Julen said defiantly.

"And so you may! Look, it burns even now. What other choice do we have, my lord?" Bakaren argued. "Can't we at least discuss her offer before we surrender all that we love to the flames of her fury?"

The elders watched as their people worked, desperately and to no avail, to put out the green flames that maniacally burned, spreading further and further down the hill and towards their city. All the while, the weight of Bakaren's question hung heavier and heavier about them.

"We could fight her!" Julen proposed. "Stand defiantly, with spears brandished, and choose to defend our freedom."

"Or, instead of watching our sons and husbands fall needlessly, we could receive her *gift* and forego the impending darkness," Bakaren insisted.

"Fight and die! Surrender and die!" Zuriñe argued. "Neither of these choices are worthy of much thought ... if you ask me."

"Well, what then? What do you propose?" Soren asked in reply.

"We could ... we could hide," Kemen offered.

"Hide?" Julen asked.

"Hide ... yes. We could make a new city, a new life ... one hidden from the sight of the sorceress and her *gift*," Kemen continued. "Perhaps we could find a sanctuary somewhere, where we might recover strength enough to rise again."

The elders thought quietly for a moment before any dared to speak.

"This would mean ... this would mean the end of life the way we know it," Julen said.

"Look around you, my lord," the white-bearded old man offered. "That time ... that life ... has already passed us by."

"This is lunacy!" Bakaren said. "We will become nomads, wandering enemies of the sorceress with no way to protect ourselves or our people!"

"Do you know a place, hunter?" Soren asked.

Kemen surveyed the eyes of the elders before he spoke. "I do."

Chapter One

HOLLIS, CHIEFTAIN OF THE WOODCUTTERS, surveyed the barren forestland with a wary and grim expression. The red, unruly eyebrows of this crestfallen hero furrowed as his eyes narrowed in calculated observation, straining to see by the dull, amber light that flickered leagues away from him. He squinted hard against the suffocating darkness that threatened to swallow up the encampment of woodcutters.

He had done his best to retain some semblance of order and purpose here in the North, calling upon the fortitude of the woodcutters who had not been sent to harvest and colonize the Wreath. Timber carts had been sent back to the city as often as they could be filled, but the timber of the northern territory had finally been consumed. Now, with the last of the trees brought low by the holy axes of these holy men, Hollis and his woodcutters could do nothing but wait nervously in the dark. There, in the hopeless aftermath of the now-dead forest, the North grew darker and tenser since the felling of yet another branch from the great tree.

There had been no further assault by the green-eyed evils since Hollis and the woodcutters had returned north, but the great chieftain and his men lived with the understanding that no moment was truly safe from them. In fact, the vanishing of the raven-fletched arrows and traceless disappearance of their shadowed assailants was perhaps more unnerving than their presence, for each and every northman could wonder only one thing: *Where had they gone?*

Whispers in the wind and fogs in the air brought unrest to the brave, fur-clad chieftain, and though there were still nearly one hundred and fifty of his mighty axe-men remaining out here in the far north of the kingdom, he sometimes felt as if he were utterly alone.

"Brádách?" the old chieftain called out. "Where in this damnable dark are those timber carts? Was it not seven or eight days now since we sent them south to the city? Should they not have arrived already with word from the Citadel?"

Brádách looked down from the watchtower and eyed the fiery-haired chief. The surrendered look on his bearded face told Hollis what he already knew. There was no sign of the timber carts.

The old woodcutter, who had been relegated to the tower due to the fact that he limped more than walked these days, began to make his way down the ladder to speak his mind. "I haven't seen any sign of them for days, Chief, and," he looked to see that none were listening in on his hushed, paranoid words, "if I may speak plain, I don't think we ever will."

"You think they have deserted?" Hollis thundered. "Why would our comrades leave us stranded here in the shadows? Huh?" He spat in disgust. "My men are better than that, Brádách."

"Aye, Chief ... they are. I don't mean deserting ... I don't mean that I think that they would *leave* us," Brádách said, nervously stumbling over his explanation.

"Then you best tell me exactly what it is that you mean!" Hollis said through gritted teeth.

The woodcutter shifted painfully back and forth from his good foot to his wounded one, trying to collect his words before he dared to speak them.

"Well then? Out with it, Brádách! Before I bury a blade in your other boot!" growled Hollis.

"Have you noticed just how quiet it has been these last four days, Chief?" asked Brádách. "Not one bird or beast in the wild has been spotted or heard. Even our own livestock have gone nearly silent. I've hardly heard a snort or whimper in almost a week of days."

Hollis stopped to think as he listened to the eerie quiet that hung in the air. He could hear the sounds of the settlement—hammers working the forge, blades being sharpened, a few hushed conversations here and there —but not a single sound from the beasts of the camp.

"And there." Brádách pointed southward. "The light from the tree dims more each day, though the last branch still remains. I can barely make it out through the shadows! Here, see for yourself," he said as he handed Hollis the brass spyglass that hung around his large neck.

Hollis raised the monocle and squinted his eye. What he beheld made his mouth as dry as desert sand.

"It grows by the day, Chief," Brádách said, obviously wishing that he had different news to report. "It's that same ... that same black fog. It has cut us off from the city, and now it cuts us off from the light of the great tree."

Hollis lowered the spyglass; his stern face did not betray the ever-growing panic that rumbled in his bowels. "Aye," he told his comrade.

"Even if orders *were* sent to us ... or even if the timber carts did manage to make their way back ... I do not see how they could have reached us here. Not with that damned, black fog, and whatever hells it hides," the woodcutter reasoned.

"Aye, I see the meaning of your words now," Hollis replied.

"How are we supposed to send the last bit of timber to the city without our carts and riders? What is to become of us? Surely the fog will be upon us soon?" Brádách asked in earnest.

Hollis raised his bushy, red eyebrows in a moment of incredulity. "I do not think that the delivery of timber is of much concern any longer, Brádách, nor do I believe that we are the object of that black fog's intention."

Brádách's face was lined with confusion as he listened to his old chief.

"Whatever green-eyed evil it is that hides in that fog, it has not come to cut off our timber lines from the city. The timber is gone, brother. It has come for the city itself." The great chieftain looked around his camp, letting his eyes linger on a pile of axes that lay in a heap. "The days of the woodcutter are over."

Brádách stood there in disbelief. The thought of any force daring to challenge the might and the brightness of Haven itself had not crossed his mind as a real possibility.

"Are ... I thought ... are you saying ..." Brádách stumbled over his words as he tried to make sense of it all. "Are you saying what I think you are saying?"

"Gather the men, Brádách," Hollis said with a disproportionate calmness. "Be quick and be quiet as you do. The city is besieged, and we might be the only ones who even know about it. Whether the Citadel chose to listen to my words of warning or not, the woodcutters of Haven will not stand idly by and see this ... this darkness prevail. We still have strength, do we not?"

Brádách nodded as he took in a deep, steadying breath.

"And our strength, it is found where it has always been found ... in the resolve of our spirits and the bite of our blades. I have wasted too many amber days as it is, licking the wounds of my bleeding pride, cowering in the shadow of this green-eyed doom." Hollis pulled at his braided beard as he spoke. "No more, Brádách, no more; not while our brothers still draw breath, and our hearts still beat with conviction. Gather them, brother, for there are deeds yet undone for us."

"Aye!" Brádách said warily as he limped off into the encampment with as much haste as he could muster.

Hollis stood tall, the white fur of his cloak whipping in the wake of the cold wind as he stared towards the unnatural darkness that swelled just a half-dozen leagues to the south. He fingered the fabled blade, Viðarr, his most trusted companion, and he brooded over the doom that waited for him and his men.

"I told you, Armas," he spoke into the darkness. "Didn't I tell you, old friend? Didn't I try to warn you?" His words turned to shouts. "And they named ME the crazy one! Me!" The angered words of the woodcutter echoed into the darkened forestland.

"Hollis?" The pregnant silence that hung in the shadowy air was interrupted by the sound of a thin, bewildered voice. "Hollis ... what is the meaning of this assembly that Brádách is speaking of? And where are the timber carts? I should hope that your final days as a woodcutter of the

Citadel would be singularly focused upon the holy task at hand."

Hollis turned to face the small, robed frame of the Priest assigned to his camp, and his mouth turned to a grimace. "What is it to you, Priest? From the looks of things, your days are numbered as much as mine are."

"I have traditions and assignments that I must uphold, and no laziness or irreverence or random assemblies will deter me from my responsibilities. Tell me plainly what you intend here, that you would see fit to interrupt the righteous work of the THREE who is SEVEN?" he said with obvious annoyance dripping from his words.

"You are a damned fool. All of us, the whole lot of us ... *fools*." As Hollis spoke, a mix of defeat and disgust colored his words and washed out his face.

The Priest just stared back with a suspicious scowl, offended and silenced at the insult hurled by the chief of the woodcutters.

"There are no more carts, Priest. There are no more trees to fell, and no more carts to fill with their timber." Hollis reached up to the flint that hung around his burly neck, and with one violent tug he snapped the leather thong. "All of my life I followed your flintish ways. All of my days were in service to the Citadel and to my city ... hoping beyond hope that my deeds would somehow assuage the wrath and anger of the THREE who is SEVEN." Hollis looked back towards the growing darkness. "But we have failed, Priest. Our service, our sacrifice, our piety ... it is not enough!"

"Blasphemy, woodcutter!" the Priest shouted back in defiance.

Hollis held his large, calloused hands up. "Oh, save your offense, Priest, and look out there at that fog. I'll wager that whatever green-eyed devils lurk within that darkness wait only to destroy our city."

The Priest looked confused as the gravity of the words took a moment to settle down upon his understanding.

Hollis flung the flint and thong toward the dumfounded Priest. "I suggest that you put down that precious flint of yours and pick up a blade if you ever hope to see our city in one piece again."

Chapter Two

IT HAD BEEN NEARLY A score of days since the men of the first colony landed on the sandy shores of the Western Wreath. Their voyage had come at a great expense, for though the expedition had set sail from the Bay of Eurwen with two bright, strong vessels, only one had arrived at their long-anticipated destination. Seig, governor of the first colony, had set his men into a flurry of motion as soon as their feet reached the dry land. Scouts were sent to survey the terrain nearest the shore, and guards were posted as the company of Haven staked their claim on the Wreath. Some had been given the task of ferrying the stores and supplies from the hold of the grey ship to the newly constructed shelters. The guardsman stockpiled a great wealth of weapons and water, tools and tents, here upon this foreign soil.

The governor had seen fit to make his stronghold near to the shoreline, deciding it prudent to let the still, silent waters of the Dark Sea serve as guardian to their eastern flank.

The woodcutters, under the guidance of their comrade and chieftain, Yasen, went to work straightaway, setting sharpened steel to the virgin forest. The hero of the North commanded his men with prowess and fervor. Their blades were faithful to their cause, though their allegiance rested firmly with their leader. Watch fires had been set ablaze by the spark of the men of the flint, and the rhythm of progress and determination woke the long-abandoned coast with the light of life. Palisade walls, hewn from the large pines that dominated this part of the Wreath, were quickly erected to offer these brave colonists some sense of safety here in the ever-dark wilderness. The newly fashioned defenses stood nearly as tall as two full-grown men. At their peaks, the timbers had been cut to a deadly point so as to deter any Wreathers from scaling them.

At both the western and the southern points of the circled stronghold, two watchtowers had been hastily constructed. They stood nearly fifty hands high, providing the guardsmen a safe vantage point into the dark woods that expanded beyond the scope of their sight. Each tower was crested with its own large, metal brazier. The fires continually burned atop the towers, casting a welcomed light into the busy settlement. Day and night, without fail, the watchtowers were occupied with the nervous men who made up this new colony. Wells were dug, gardens were planted, and stable yard sprung to life there in the relative safety of the wooden walls. The men began to settle into the routine of their new calling, spurred on by the knowledge that their mission must succeed.

The light from the great tree upon these wilderlands was nothing but a faint glint of illumination. Though it still existed beyond the black water of the Dark Sea, its influence on their colony was little more than a rumor and reminder that they were living in the last days of the last branch of the great tree of Haven. Each morning by the light of the watch fires, the men would wake to the round, earthen sound of the woodcutters' horns. Cutters and guardsmen alike would don their furs, collect their weapons, and gather in the center of the stronghold to speak and hear the words of the Priest. The colony had but one Priest remaining after the perilous voyage had claimed the life of his counterpart. This young, determined man of the flint had taken it upon himself to win back the favor of the THREE who is SEVEN by way of ritual and piety. None—neither governor nor groomsman, guardsman nor woodcutter—were exempt from his rigorous resolve in this matter.

And so, before they broke their fast each morning, the men of the first colony listened to the fiery charge of the lone Priest.

"This new day, born from within,

Was predetermined victory.

The choice for life now begins

As you subdue this darkened territory."

"We, by the THREE who is SEVEN," the men of the camp would echo in reply.

Flints were kissed, bread and ale were passed among them, and day's work would commence. The woodcutters would take up their blades and pass through the timber gates to make war with the darkness of this world, while the few remaining guardsmen continued their frenzied efforts to fortify their stronghold.

Governor Seig observed the activity of his men while he sipped from his flagon of warm ale as it steamed in the cool, morning mist. Standing in the center of the stronghold, with fires burning brightly around him, Seig could not help but allow a smile of self-satisfaction to stretch across his proudly punctuated features. Glory for both his name and his station were within his reach, and his brief reign as lord of the first colony was well on its way towards receiving the renown and victory that he singularly longed for.

"Captain Tahd!" the governor called as he beckoned his second in command to come to conference.

The short, silver-haired man saluted as he approached. "Yes, Governor?"

"Tell me, Captain, of what news can you report this morning? Are we nearly ready to begin harvesting for the sake of the city?" Seig asked pointedly as he savored the warmth from his drink. "For I am indeed eager to report back a bright victory for our Priest King. Soon, Jhames and all of Haven will be indebted to our work here upon the Wreath."

"I should certainly hope so, Governor," the captain replied. "It would seem that nearly all of the defenses are adequate enough for the moment, though I would soon prefer to reinforce the timber walls with stone." Tahd was more than eager to please his arrogant commander. Although Seig seemed rather oblivious to the way his decisions truly affected those under his command, the short-statured captain could not help but continue to kiss the boots of his shortsighted leader.

"All in good time, Tahd. All in good time," Seig said with a condescending smile. "We must not forget the intention of our work here is not to merely fortify our position. The Citadel expects a load of timber, and we cannot afford to delay any longer."

"Yessir ... though I must say that we should not grow too comfortable in our routines and defenses just yet. For we do not know what kind of enemy lies beyond the coastlands," Tahd said tentatively with a wary glance into the forest.

"Is that fear I detect in your voice, Captain? If so, you had best be rid of it. We shall remain on guard ... with that I agree. But I would not risk the well-being of our city for your speculations of phantoms out here in the shadows of the Wreath. The light is dying, and Haven needs the timber. Do not for a moment presume that I will take good, strong backs from our true mission, just to quarry rocks in appeasement of your worries." Seig scowled at the little man in front of him.

"Of course not," Tahd said, shrinking away from the menacing presence of the governor. "Your bravery is enough to fuel our men with courage of their own. I only mean to suggest that we ... I mean, *you* ... might consider ordering a scouting party to search deeper into this wilderness. There is no need to distract the woodcutters from their assignment, *of course*. I know our guardsmen number fewer than any of us would have expected. Perhaps we can task some of the other members of our colony for this particular mission."

Seig stared at his captain for what felt like an eternity before he spoke. The steam of his drink danced and swirled about his dark, bearded face, deepening the already silent tension. "*Very well* then, Captain. Send your scouting party ... but you will *not* diminish our already thin defenses by sending what few cavalry we have left on this errand. Send some men that we can afford to spare."

Not forty paces from the center of the stronghold, a young, blonde-headed groomsman was busy seeing to the colony's herd of horses with a care and a deep ease that seemed almost out of place. His way with them was a bright pinprick of light in this otherwise dark, industrious outpost on the edge of the world. He brushed their coats and shod their hooves; he oiled their leather saddles and worked at softening their cart harnesses, all the while singing poetic tunes to their nervous ears.

"There you go, girl," Cal spoke softly to the large draft horse. "Your coat is coming in nicely, huh? This cold chill of a wind won't be bothering you much now."

The large, sorrel-colored horse nodded her head in agreement, showing her gratitude for the attention he had so lovingly bestowed upon her. "Here, girl, eat up," Cal said, giving her an extra scoop of milled oats. "There is much work still to be done. You are going to need your strength."

His grooming was interrupted mid-stroke by the thin voice of the captain of the colony guard. "Groomsman?"

Cal looked up from behind one of the chestnut cavalry mounts. "Sir? Captain, yessir, how can I be of service?"

Tahd examined the line of well-kept horses, nodding in approval. "Groomsman, the governor has a new assignment that you will need to see about carrying out right away."

"A new assignment? Does the governor require me to swing a blade as well?" Cal rested his hand on the horse's flank as he walked out from behind the animal. He looked to the sorrel-colored beast, then approached Tahd with a concerned look on his face. "I am honored to serve the colony, but if you assign me to fell timber, I will not have the time to care for the animals. With all due respect, sir, they deserve—"

"What?" Tahd interjected, a bit annoyed at the rashness of this groomsman's speculation. "No, no one is taking you from these horses. In fact, you will have a chance to put your equine knowledge to some other uses here in this wilderness of a land."

The worry on Cal's face shifted to intrigue. "So you say ... my apologies. I just thought-" Cal began to speak, but Tahd cut him off again before he wasted any more of his time.

"The governor and I believe that it would be prudent to explore the surrounding area," the captain said. "You are to take one of these horses here and see about scouting the lands beyond the tree line." Tahd continued to inspect the horses as he spoke. "You shall keep your groomsman duties in order as well, but I need a swift rider to discover who else it is that calls these wild lands their home."

Cal took in the words of the captain for a moment, hardly able to contain his excitement. Since arriving upon the shores of the Wreath, his days had been spent tirelessly in the service of the colony, with no time to pursue the true purpose for which he had come.

"Yes, Captain, I would be glad to," Cal said eagerly, his breath catching in his throat as the possibilities of what he might find began to fill his mind.

"I have no way of knowing what kind of dangers are out beyond the safety of our stronghold," the captain thought aloud. "You do have a blade, don't you?"

"Yes ... yes sir, I have sword," Cal answered him.

"Very well, then," Tahd said. "Keep a keen eye about you, and keep that blade of yours at the ready."

"I will, Captain," Cal replied. "You can count on me, sir." The eager glint in Cal's eyes was complemented with a resolute courage that could not be overlooked.

Tahd examined the strong, golden-haired groomsman. "Yes, I believe I can."

"What is it that our governor hopes I will find out there in the forestlands?" Cal asked. "Is he not satisfied with the timber fields here?"

"Well, that is just it, isn't it, groomsman?" Tahd replied. "We are not sure what else makes its home here, and I would rather not be taken by surprise to find out. If Wreathers inhabit the forest nearby, they may not be willing to share their shelter, or their timber, or their home," he said with a faint snarl of disdain.

Cal looked out beyond the safety of the stronghold through uneven gaps of the palisade wall. "I will see to it, Captain," he replied with an anticipatory smile.

"Very well, then. Report your findings directly to me, groomsman," the captain ordered before he turned to take his leave and return back to the oversight of the encampment.

"A scouting mission, huh?" asked a familiar voice.

"It would seem so, Wielund," Cal replied, sizing up the strong, lanky blacksmith that approached. "Hey ... would you want to ride with me?"

"Don't you think you should ask one of the others?" Wielund asked, his forced nonchalance not lost on the groomsman. "I'd wager that the cook or maybe old Captain Means would like to see something more of the Wreath. Besides ... I am not the swiftest of riders, and I have a mountain of work still ahead of me, and I would hate—"

"If the captain had wanted a cook or a sea captain to take up this task, don't you think that he would have asked one already?" Cal interrupted. "No. He asked me, and, well ... I am asking you."

Wielund stood there, his mind racing for a reason to decline the invitation.

"I can't just sneak off, Cal. What if they catch me?"

"A risk worth taking! There is a reason we were brought to the Wreath, and I do not believe that it is timber alone. Come on now, brother, ride with me on this assignment. You will be safe enough."

"What of my duty? What of *my* assignment?" Wielund argued. "I have seen the stocks that Pyrrhus and his men just finished, and I am the one who forged the bars for the prison hold." He wiped at his sweating brow with a dirty rag, leaving a worried smear on his pale forehead. "I do not wish to encounter whatever enemy those are intended for, nor do I want to find myself closely acquainted with them."

"Just this once, alright?" Cal reasoned. "It's not like I am asking you to wage a war ... just to discover if there is, well ... anything we should be *concerned* with. And think of what we may find! What if we ..." Cal's voice trailed off as he reveled in the awareness of his grander calling.

"Cal?" Wielund said reluctantly.

"Come on then, that settles it! I'll ready your mount; you go see about some mail and maybe something sharp to ward off your fear," he said with a teasing grin.

Wielund slowly walked toward the smithery from the small stable yard, dumbstruck at what had just happened. Cal busied himself with tack and saddle, readying one of the chestnuts for his friend the smithy, and the dapple-grey, Farran, for himself.

Inside the seclusion of the stable, the small, strong voice of Deryn the Sprite called out to him from the rafters of the roughly constructed barn. "What great providence we have been shown, my friend!" The blue-winged sentinel dashed swiftly and silently down from his dwelling place and hovered excitedly in front of the face of his friend.

"Yes, indeed, Deryn! What if today ... what if today is indeed the day we find what we have set out in search of?"

Deryn landed atop of one of the wooden stall railings, watching Cal cinch the saddle on the large chestnut. "That may be ... though my heart tells me that our Great Father's light is not merely laying idle and undiscovered, even here in the shadow lands of the Western Wreath. No, Cal ... I suspect this charge of yours to seek His new light will take us both to the bleakest edge of darkness before it relents its hidden brilliance."

"Well, that may be so, but one can still hope, right?" Cal said playfully in reply.

"Indeed, one can," Deryn said with a placating shake of his tiny, blue-haired head.

Cal brought out his bronzed, feathered chest guard that had been a gift bestowed upon him from the Poets of Kalein. He had kept it safely tucked away in his small quarters inside the stable. Here in the torchlight, the ancient piece of armor shone with such an out-of-place majesty that even the Sprite was taken aback by its brilliance.

"You are going to wear this gift of yours?" Deryn asked him.

"Yes, I am," Cal replied as he fastened the three leather thongs on the right side of the chest piece.

"You look like a King of Terriah," Deryn said wistfully. "A rather young king, I suppose, but a king nonetheless."

"Cal? Cal! Where are you, groomsman?" Wielund shouted in a rather grumpy tone of voice from outside the stable entrance. "Are you ready to get this frightful task over with yet?"

"On my way, Wielund! Quit your complaining and prepare for an adventure!" Cal shouted back at him.

Cal slipped on his leather cloak, and Deryn shot inside the fold of its inner pocket. The groomsman secured his ancient blade in its white leather scabbard, then took the reins of the two horses and led the mounts outside.

"Alright then," Cal said to the nervous smithy. "Let's go see just what kind of wilderness this is that we have chosen to call home, huh?"

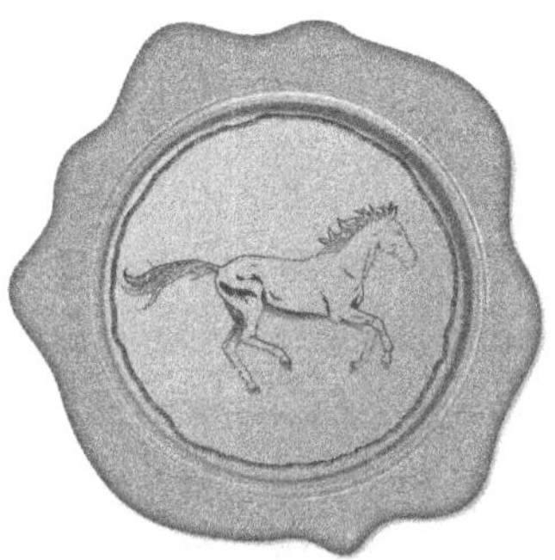

Chapter Three

THE TWO YOUNG MEN RODE astride their mounts. Cal's eager eyes searched the tree line as they passed unceremoniously through the timber gates of the colony's walls. The forest's edge towered roughly half a league from the newly constructed stronghold. The bright watch fires of the mighty woodcutters blazed a safe distance from the pine border, illuminating the encampment and warding off whatever dangers might be lurking beyond what they could see.

The sound of blades biting birch and pine, oak and cedar was both a welcomed and familiar cadence to the ears of the riders. There was safety—or at least a presumed safety—in the chorus of forty axes, and the enormity of the Greywood seemed somehow smaller whilst their notes rang out upon the air. For weeks, the woodcutters had been commissioned with the task of providing timber for the construction and the establishment of the colony's garrison. Finally, with the stronghold complete, their collective strength could now be focused on a harvest for the great city of Haven herself.

Cal smiled brightly as he and Wielund spied the northmen in the dim shadows on the edge of the forest.

"And just where are you off to on this fine day, groomsman?" a large, bald, mountain of a man shouted out to Cal between the swings of his axe. "Hunting, I hope?"

"Goran! Why is it that the only thing that seems to be running through your mind is food?" Yasen shot out in feigned annoyance.

"Well, it's more pleasant to dream of stewed rabbit and spitted boar than the endless growth of this damnable darkness!" Goran replied matter-of-factly.

"It must be more than dreams, brother. It appears that the darkness is not the only thing growing around here!" Yasen said, pointing the blade of his axe toward Goran's plump midsection.

Goran's cheeks reddened with the beginnings of laughter, and he affectionately patted his large belly. "Ha ha! Perhaps I have been doing a bit more than dreaming! Well played, North Wolf, well played indeed."

Cal and Wielund joined in the laughter of the woodcutters, and there in this shadowy wilderness, the brothers of the North relaxed the rhythm of their burden for a moment of lightheartedness.

"So if you are not hunting then, what are you doing? Why do you ride out here in the Greywood?" Goran returned to his question of Cal.

"Scouting," Cal said. "I've been given the task of searching the woods that surround our stronghold. Somebody has to make sure that you poor, defenseless woodcutters are kept safe out here!"

A wry smile split the beard of the large man, and soon a deep and good-hearted laughter erupted once again. "Oh, if Oskar were still here!" Goran said, shaking his head and wiping the laughter from his eyes. "He would have ..."

"He would have liked that one, eh?" Cal finished the sentence for his friend.

"Aye," Goran nodded, still humored by it all. "Well, watch yourselves out here in these wilderlands, boys. It wouldn't do to diminish our company much further. We have already lost more than we can spare." Goran patted Cal's horse gingerly as he peered into Cal's eyes with meaningful intent.

"We will return safely and soon enough, don't you fear," Cal said kindly.

"Well then," Yasen spoke up. "We must be back to work. Mind that you two keep a sharp eye about you." The North Wolf turned to survey the thick, dark shadows that hung heavy in the undergrowth of the Greywood. Though he wore a leather patch over his wounded right eye, he still possessed a keenness of sight both in his vision and his intuition. Though I do not feel any danger at the moment, Cal ... I do not believe that we are alone," Yasen told him.

Just then, the silver-coated Farran let out a loud whinny, piercing the stillness of the forest with a jolt. Wielund spooked with a violent fright, not expecting the sound to erupt from the animal. His abrupt movement startled his own horse into action, and the large chestnut jumped forward, nearly throwing the young blacksmith from the saddle.

"Never you fear, brothers, for I have brought with me the brave Wielund to accompany me on my quest!" Cal said with exaggerated formality.

The woodcutters joined in laughter once again. Goran nearly doubled over in throes of amusement. "Indeed you did, groomsman! Indeed you did," he bellowed.

Wielund struck Cal's arm with a brotherly blow. "Alright then, you have had your fun ... just remember who it is that sharpens your steel and shoes your steeds! Huh?"

Cal shook his stubbled face at the embarrassed smithy, and a moment of mutually understood camaraderie passed between them. Although Cal knew the calling he had from the Oweles, and still felt the pull and gravity of his ultimate purpose, it was good to not be alone out here on the edge of the world. "Come on, then," he told Wielund. "Let's be on our way."

They bade goodbye to the woodcutters and the two young men rode off; the pounding hooves of their mounts littered the air with dirt and grass as they rode out of sight of their friends. Cal and Wielund went deeper and deeper into the Greywood, away from watch fires and woodcutters, away from the sounds of the stronghold and the singing axes at the tree line. This ancient forestland was a sight to behold, here in the outer shadows of this darkening world, and one could only try to imagine what grandeur it must have displayed in the youth of the light of the great tree.

Cal had never seen a canopy of green such as this. The plumage of these massive trees began nearly one hundred hands high and rose almost beyond the reach of his sight. The young forests of the northern territory were dwarfed in comparison to this ancient, grey-barked timberland; neither man nor horse needed to bow his head as they rode through the trees. The flame of Wielund's torch flickered and danced in the wake of their riding, and though he trusted Cal's leading, he grew nervous each time it nearly disappeared. He did not question his brave friend, but he did wonder why this groomsman in the strange and beautiful bronzed armor did not carry a torch with him.

League after league of majestic timber disappeared behind the riders as they rode westward in search of something, anything, to report. "Well, one thing is for sure!" Wielund called out as the two of them stopped to water their horses at a small pool deep in the heart of the forest.

"Oh? What is that?" Cal asked.

"That there is enough timber here on the Wreath to light a hundred Havens for a hundred years!" Wielund mused aloud as his eyes scanned the shadowed tree line.

"Well, you might not be *too* far from the truth there, Wielund." Cal smiled at the smithy.

"Have you ever, in all your time in the northern forests, ever seen such *green*?"

Cal froze, his mind unexpectedly racing back to the memory of the green-eyed shadow cats and the blood-thirsty demon bear. While Wielund was wondering in amazement at the green of the imperial oaks and stately birch trees, Cal was overwhelmed with thoughts of the other kinds of green that lived in the forest.

"Cal? Cal ... you all right, brother?" Wielund asked, concern coloring his face. "Cal?"

"What? Oh ... forgive me," Cal said apologetically as he rubbed his stubble. "I was ... just remembering something. A memory from another life, almost, yet it still feels so real, so–"

The unexpected sound of stone against metal cut off his very words, and Cal quickly put his finger to his lips.

Wielund's eyes went wide in anxious surprise, but he heeded the silent warning of his friend. The horses looked up from their drink. The large chestnut began to stomp and snort restlessly, and Farran, the iron grey, stared off into the shadows across the small pond.

"What is it?" Wielund asked in a worried whisper.

"I don't know, I can't quite see it," Cal whispered back. "Do you have your blade?"

"Yes, I do," Wielund answered.

"Come on then, let's have a better look," Cal said, gesturing towards a small outcropping of stone there on the bank of the clear pool.

The two of them crouched low, swords in hand, and moved as quietly as they could manage. Cal's breathing was controlled, for he trusted the instinctual response of Farran. Though the horse seemed to sense that they were not alone, he did not seem to detect any immediate danger. Wielund however, was nervous, and his breathing reflected his anxieties.

"Would you calm yourself, smithy?" Cal whispered in annoyance. "I can't hear anything beyond your panicked wheezes."

Wielund nodded his head apologetically.

"Wait here," Cal ordered. "I want to have a better look."

Wielund nodded once again, and Cal began to climb atop the large, moss-covered stones in hopes of discovering the source of the strange sound from a higher vantage point. The boulder was no taller than the size of a grown man, and Cal quickly reached the top and peered out from behind its protection.

What he saw lit his heart in wonder.

"Wielund!" he called down in an excited whisper. "Come up here, you must see this!"

The smithy reached down and kissed the flint that hung from around his neck, then began to climb the large boulder, torch still in hand, to see what it was that had his friend the groomsman so enraptured. Wielund's eyes finally crested the peak of the moss-covered rock. He strained against the flickering glow of his torch, and what he beheld made his jaw drop in wonder. "Is that what I think it is?" he asked his friend.

"Well, we won't know for sure until we get a closer look now, will we?" Cal said with an excited gleam in his eye.

"You want to go ... in there?" Wielund said nervously.

"Yes, come on! We *are* a scouting party, remember," Cal chided him. "This is the first thing we have found worth reporting, so let's see what exactly it is we are supposed to report!"

"But-" he tried to protest.

"Oh, come *on!*" Cal said with feigned annoyance.

The enthusiastic groomsman jumped down from the rock with little regard to the noise he was making. Wielund held his torch high above his head, and strained against the shadows to survey his friend's movements. When he was satisfied that all seemed safe enough to continue on, and that nothing was lurking in the immediate vicinity, he nodded his reluctant agreement and followed Cal down from the rock to the opposite side of the bank.

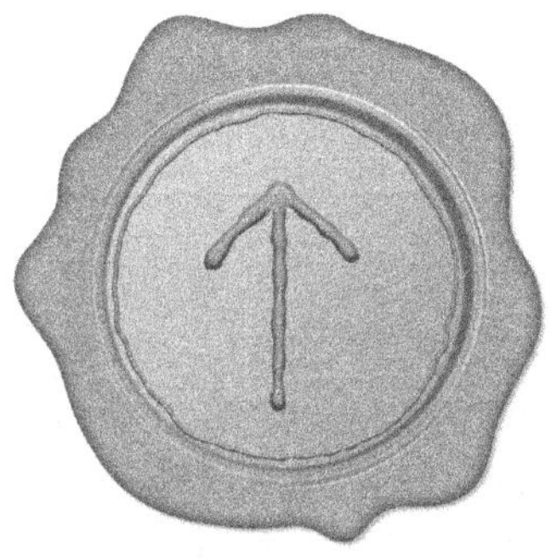

Chapter Four

THE CITY OF HAVEN WAS firmly in the grip of panic and fear. Whispers of war were on the lips of both the feeble and the fearless alike, for the rumors could no longer be contained. It had been nearly three weeks since one of the riders of the Capital guard had come barreling through the borough of Westriver in the light of the pale silver. The message he had delivered with panicked face and foaming horse drove the citizens of Haven into a deeper sense of dread. The impending darkness was no longer the greatest fear of the people, for every ear, whether it wished to or not, had heard the reports from the North.

An enemy was advancing upon the city.

The marshal of the West Gate, Lieutenant Marcum, had assembled the greater part of his company and marched his men northward. The tall, long-haired officer of the green and black was rumored to have reassigned his guardsmen and cavalry without having ever received orders from the Citadel; the people of Westriver couldn't decide whether to label Marcum a hero or to denounce him as a traitor. The strength of the Citadel buckled at the reduction of men here in the heart of the once-bright city. Riots and recklessness had become the normal order of the day, and they feared that without sufficient might, the soul of the city might be lost to utter chaos before the enemy even stormed the gates.

No one could predict how long the last remaining branch of the tree would endure, and it had been weeks since Hollis' woodcutters had sent rations of timber to the panicked people of Haven. The citizens had turned to seizing and consuming whatever they could get their hands on for the chance to fuel their own hearths and fend off the shadows for another day. Now, as never before in the city of Haven, the cold winds of the northern territory invaded the walled city with the foreboding bite of utter and imminent change.

The Priest King had grown paranoid in these darker days, afraid that the lawlessness and irreverence of his citizens would evoke the wrath of the THREE who is SEVEN, quickening the ever-present darkening of the world. He and his chancellor assumed direct command of the few remaining guardsmen of Westriver, compelled to maintain order by employing whatever measures were still available to him. The dungeon holds began to fill with any citizens who dared to question the will or wisdom of the Citadel.

In the cleft of an alleyway nearest to the square of Westriver, a small contingent of guardsmen and hooded Priests escorted a grey-haired man and his son towards the prison keep in the heart of the borough. As the shackled men marched past the alley, a young man with dark hair and kind eyes hid himself from their view. Michael winced as he watched the citizens forced to pay the price of questioning the Citadel, knowing that his own sentencing could very likely be much worse if he were ever to be caught. Since the departure of Lieutenant Marcum and the ensuing chaos, he and Engelmann did not risk a public display of their message as openly as they once had. Still, their faces were known and their beliefs were condemned, and so they were forced to spread the truths of green-eyed evils and enduring hope while they lived in hiding. The remnant of those who still clung to the hope that Engelmann spoke so adamantly of had resorted to gathering in secret, choosing stone cellars and abandoned stables to hold their conferences and plot their preparations so as to not risk the paranoid wrath of the Priest King.

Michael had been busy on an errand of Engelmann's for the better part of the day, spreading encouragement to the remnant and delivering word of their next rendezvous. He had nearly finished his rounds to the small band of outcasts, and in truth he did enjoy the bit of excitement all this sneaking around brought him. His final stop, however, was indeed his favorite part of this errand. Once the arresting party had dragged their hopeless charges down the stone road, Michael quickly made his way towards the home of Margarid.

Margarid was the very first citizen of Haven to entertain the words of Engelmann with any form of sincerity at all, but it was not for that reason alone that her residence was saved for last. Since their very first encounter those weeks ago in the borough's square, the beautiful lady had not for one moment escaped the thoughts of the young groomsman.

Michael rapped his fist three times on the humble door, glancing inconspicuously to either side so as to not invite unwanted attention onto this particular abode. When the door cracked open, the hazel eyes and simple smile of the young woman greeted Michael with an eager welcome.

"Michael!" she excitedly whispered. "I was hoping it would be you."

Michael had begun growing a beard for his trip across the Dark Sea, and when the disappointment of his rejection came, he had become too fond of his dark scruff to shave it off. But here in the light of the smile of the auburn-haired Margarid, his newly-bearded cheeks could not hide the flush that spread across his face.

"You were now, were you?" he replied playfully, feigning surprise.

"Why yes, I was ... is that so hard to believe?" Margarid asked as she coyly rose to the tips of her toes to kiss the young groomsman softly on his cheek.

"I just like to hear you say it to me. It is arguably the best part of my day," Michael said with a foolish looking grin.

"Arguably?!" Margarid blurted out in mock outrage.

"Well, I *was* supposed to tell that Nasrin woman where we are gathering this silver evening," he teased.

She scowled as she took him by the ear and pulled his face down to her level of sight. "You just go ahead and invite that ... that wild rose, and we will see what kind of hope you are going to have to try and muster up then!"

Michael laughed at her anger, enamored by her forthrightness. There was something enchanting in the eyes and the heart of the young redhead who gazed at him. He may have chased the baker's daughter, and tumbled in the hayloft with a tavern maiden a time or two, but this Margarid was different. He had never before felt for a woman what he felt standing here outside of her humble home.

"Alright ... *alright*! You can let me free now, I'll wait to invite her 'til tomorrow!" he said with pleasure, pulling lightly against her hold on his ear.

"Well, we will have to see about tomorrow, then," Margarid said with a wink. She let him go and slid her hand down his face and onto his chest, letting it linger there with the gentle weight of her own attraction. She turned and surveyed the street outside of her home, her face growing more solemn as she brought their quiet conversation to the purpose for which he had come. She paused to listen for any voices of those who might overhear this next and most private part of their exchange. "Is it time?" she whispered conspiratorially.

"Yes, my lady ... it is time."

"Where then? Where does Engelmann," she mouthed his name to be sure no one would hear her say it, "call us to gather?"

Michael leaned in close to her ear. "The old mill, there just on the edge of the borough. He says he has something urgent to share ... something of grave importance."

"Alright then," she said as her hazel eyes betrayed the apprehension that she felt over the danger of these assemblies. "Let us be quick and careful about it."

"Agreed, my lady," he told her. The gaze that was mere moments ago filled with boyish infatuation now held her stare with a nervous tension.

Margarid drew up the hood of her faded, crimson cloak, so as to conceal her hidden intentions from the frightened eyes of this frightened kingdom. "There is a tavern on the edge of the borough, just before the old herdsman's pens. Do you know it?" she asked.

"I do. The Broken Shield, I believe it is called?" he confirmed.

"Yes. I will meet you there, and perhaps then we can walk the rest of the way together." She looked at him and softly whispered her farewell. "Be wary, my groomsman. Keep safe."

With those words, the young woman in the faded, crimson cloak took her leave and began to walk the stone streets of Westriver towards the old tavern on the other side of the borough. Michael watched her walk away, and then, as if nothing had transpired between the two of them, he took off in a slightly different direction.

Their remnant was small, barely a dozen strong. But their hope, or at least their desire for hope, knit them together in ways that they still did not fully understand. The rumors of a gathering enemy in the northern territory had weighed heavy on the heart of their leader, Engelmann the Arborist. His position and power here in Haven had diminished all the more in the twilight of the great tree, for soon his very existence would have no purpose. What need would a people plunged into darkness have for a tree-less Arborist? Still, there were those of the Capital guard who clung to the fading traditions of old, and they dared not so much as meet the gaze of the green-haired old man, let alone question or halt his comings and goings. Their respect for his position and their superstitious fear of his unknown magics kept them at a reverent enough distance.

Engelmann stood near the old mill on the outskirts of Westriver. As he waited for the small remnant to gather, he could not help but stare in wonder at the dying, silver flame. "I wonder what kind of darkness will come on the heels of your departure?" he said aloud to the tree before taking a long, concentrated draw on his green pipe. "Yes ... I wonder, indeed."

The green-haired, old Arborist thought long in the smoky silence of his questions, speculating as to how he might lead this remnant to hold onto the hope they had been given. It was not a desire for illumination that weighed upon his thoughts, for he knew its end was coming. Rather, the heavier burden came from a need to know how best to endure the darkness. In the faint light of the silver flames, Engelmann welcomed the handful of men and women who cautiously made their way along the winding pathway to the gathering place. Greetings were given, arms were embraced, and he could see that in a few of their eyes lived the actual belief that hope would indeed change the outcome of this darkening world.

As Engelmann ushered a young seamstress, Kahri, into the gathering hall, he spotted something peculiar on the road ahead. A figure appeared to be running with great haste towards the mossy-bearded Arborist, cloak whipping in the wake of the reckless pace.

"The damned fool is going to get us all thrown in the prison holds if he keeps on like this!" Engelmann muttered under his breath. "Portus?" Engelmann called softly into the doorway. "Come here a moment." The urgency in the old man's voice was impossible to miss, and the strong tanner crossed the room in a few strides to meet the Arborist by the door.

"Look ahead," Engelmann said, throwing a meaningful look towards the road. "Do you have your blade nearby?"

"Aye, I don't sleep a silver night without it," the tall man replied. He reached to his belt to draw the weapon. "What sort of fool-"

Engelmann steadied Portus' hand. "Easy now, let us not show hostility until absolutely necessary." He turned to eye the tanner. "We do not yet know who it is."

Portus nodded his understanding, but stood with hand on hilt, at the ready if need be.

"Engelmann!" A woman's voice half-shouted through her heavy breathing. "Engelmann, help! You have to help him!"

The Arborist took a long, concentrated pull on his pipe; his amber-colored eyes focused intently on the shrouded face of the one who shouted his name.

Not two-dozen paces from the mill, the hood of the faded crimson cloak fell away and revealed an auburn-haired young woman who ran with as much desperate determination as any racehorse of Abondale could muster.

"Margarid?" Engelmann spoke disapprovingly into the silver night. "Margarid, what troubles you that you would risk our remnant in such a way?"

"It's ... it's Michael! The guardsmen ... they have him!" She gasped, choking out her words. Her voice was a swirl of labored breath and barely restrained tears. "I saw them take him ... they took him in irons!"

"Slow down, my girl, easy now," Engelmann said with a sagely grace. He took her by the arm and ushered her into the meeting hall, motioning for Portus to close the door before they made themselves any more of a spectacle. "Michael, you say? They took Michael?"

Her eyes went wild in unrestrained fear before clouding over in a foggy sorrow. Tears began to trace her soft cheekbones as she caught what breath she could.

"Michael?" Engelmann asked again, prodding her to continue.

She nodded her saddened confirmation.

"But how? Did he get himself into trouble? What happened, girl? Out with it now!" The concern for his young pupil became evident on the leathery face of the old Arborist. He felt the tension of his own intensity, and softened his next word. "Please?"

Portus and the rest of the remnant gathered around the crimson-cloaked Margarid to hear her account of Michael's arrest. She scanned the faces of her gathering friends before focusing her tear-filled eyes on the worried gaze of Engelmann. "We ... we were taking every precaution necessary," she insisted. "I took the main roadway, and he—Michael—he followed me through the back alleyways. Every hundred paces or so I would turn back and make sure he was still behind me." Tears began to fall freely as she recounted what happened.

"Go on, girl," Engelmann encouraged.

"There, just before we reached the tannery, I saw them."

"Saw who?" Portus blurted out.

"The *Chancellor's guards*!" Margarid heaved, looking down at her hands. "A young woman approached Michael, and I do not think he fully understood what was happening. I watched her ask him a question, though I did not hear her words. The next thing I knew, the guardsmen were on him, had seized him, and were leading him towards the prison hold." She looked up from her hands, her eyes reddened by tears as her voice pleaded to her friends. "We have to help him! I know that there are great evils that hunt our city, and I know that darkness is nearly upon us, but what good is hope if we have to hope without him?"

Just then, the bright brass horns of the Citadel rang loud and long upon the cool, evening air. Their blaring, metallic notes cut through the muddy haze of grief there in the old mill, drawing the attention of the gathered few.

"What does that mean?" asked Kahri.

"The sky is still silver-lit," Portus replied. "It cannot be the great tree."

"No," Engelmann replied, his gaze still fixed on the light of the great tree.

"I believe ... it has begun."

"Begun?" the seamstress questioned, a gleam of distress coming into her eyes.

"What does that mean?" Harmier, the merchant, asked.

"It means that whatever green-eyed evil that has been gathering in the North has most likely advanced, forcing our Priest King to finally acknowledge its presence," Engelmann explained.

"Does that mean war?" Portus asked the mossy-bearded Arborist.

"It means, for the moment, that we are being summoned to the Kings' Bridge. I do not doubt that the Citadel will wish to address the situation." Engelmann gave a meaningful look to the tanner, then glanced around the room at the brave company of men and women. "And I suggest that we all heed the call of the trumpets, so that we might find out just what it is that they plan to do about it."

Whispers and rumblings passed back and forth between the gathered remnant as the group quietly weighed the dangers of imprisonment against the possibility of being uninformed and alone if their city fell under the assault of some enemy. The Arborist cleared his throat and addressed them, hushing their conversation with a kind but commanding tone. "To the Kings' Bridge then, but let us make sure to keep our minds about us. Huh? We will join the rest of the city to hear what safety measures and battle plans they have made. But let us remember that our security does not lie in the hands of kings or chancellors, but in the light of the THREE who is SEVEN."

The small remnant nodded in quiet, collective agreement. The agenda of their own gathering would have to wait, for it appeared that the purposes of Engelmann the Hopeful had been usurped by the summons of the Citadel's horns. Baker and tanner, seamstress and shepherd all began to gather their belongings and make their way out the door towards the heart of the city.

"But ... but wait!" Margarid shouted out to those departing. "What about Michael? We can't just leave him there in the irons of the prison hold! He is the one ... remember? He is the one who risked his neck these last dark days for you ... for *us*!"

The small group stopped to listen to her words, looking to Engelmann for how they should respond to this unfortunate crisis in the midst of an even greater one. The Arborist placed a calming hand on the shoulder of the young woman. "My girl, do not fear. For whether it be by our might or cunning, or by the providential hand of the THREE who is SEVEN ... we will not abandon hope, nor will we abandon our friend."

Chapter Five

THE WHOLE OF WESTRIVER GATHERED on the stone highway that ran along the mighty Abonris, just outside of the Kings' Gate. The heralds continued to summon the citizens of Haven with the notes of their trumpets, while the small contingent of guardsmen formed a perimeter around the platform of the Priest King. The rumors of a waiting enemy and the bright, brass call of the trumpets drew the throngs of frightened people. They made their way to hear the report of the Citadel, desperate for news of a defeated adversary, or of the success of the first colony, or at the very least a word on the arrival of the timber carts from the North.

Jhames stood high and pious atop the stone platform, his deep green and silver cloak draped regally off his willowy frame. His features were hardened and his pose was proud, but his posturing could not hide the sallow hue of his face and the gaunt condition of his body. The fiery determination that had once characterized the aged Priest had begun to lessen now in the face of such uncertainty. Though the adornments of his office shone luminous in the faint silver, the light in the Priest King's eyes had dimmed dramatically in these last days. Jhames raised his hand in the three-fingered shape of a *J*. When all fell silent, he addressed the restless crowd of his people. "People of Haven. Today is a dark day for our shining kingdom ... a dark day indeed."

The crowds of people began to whisper murmurs of nervous speculation at such ominous words from their leader. Jhames raised his hand once more to silence the anxious people. "In these dark and uncertain times, we must hold all the more tightly to our traditions and our convictions. Let us not fracture our strength with weak wills and weak minds! Let us not fill our prison holds with the progeny of our *own* rebellion and lawlessness! No! We must strike at the dark by the light of our flints and we most certainly must strike it together!"

The crowd of frightened citizens was silent, greedily drinking up the Priest King's words in hopes of some relief to quell their desperation. "We have received both word and confirmation from the marshal of the Northern Gate and Captain Armas of the Capital guard. It seems that the darkening of the great tree is not the worst of the dangers we face, for the captain reports that an unknown enemy lies in wait just beyond the northern walls of Piney Creek."

Angry and worried whispers escaped the lips of the listening crowd, while a disorienting fog of disbelief clouded their prudence. The men reached for and clung to the flints that hung from their necks while the women prayed worried prayers and kissed their hands fearfully.

"Even now, we have *sent* Lieutenant Marcum and an army of nearly two thousand men to fortify our northern front," Jhames continued to tell his people, weaving his own version of Marcum's actions. "We do not yet know who this enemy is that is encamped in the shadows of the North, but we must not give him aid by eroding our holy strength with lies and lawlessness from within our own walls."

Just then, four armed guardsmen dressed in green and silver appeared atop the barbican of the entry to the Kings' Bridge. They escorted—or rather, dragged—two men who were bound in irons and blindfolded with black linen. The tone of the Priest King turned menacing. "Anyone that is found to be unsupportive of our defense and the way of the flint will be seen as and taken for traitors ... for the disease of chaos and lawlessness *will not be tolerated* here in these proud and beautiful walls, and treachery—as established by King Kaestor himself—is punishable by death."

The citizens looked on in horror as the two old men were freed of their blindfolds, then fitted with nooses. The cry of a heartbroken woman shattered the shocked silence of the on-looking crowd. "No!" she wailed uncontrollably. "He is no criminal! Please, mercy Your Brightness, *mercy*!"

The voices of a brave few began to ring out in agreement with her desperate pleading. Before their disproval could escalate, the guardsman pounded their halberds three times against the ground in an angry display of might as Jhames raised his hand once again.

"People of Haven!" Jhames shouted against the outcries of the citizens. "We cannot fight the enemy on two fronts." His self-righteous anger rippled in passionate waves as his words echoed over the crowd. He paused and looked up behind him to the corporal in charge of the execution before he spoke again, his words somewhat cooler now than they were mere moments before. "I will not risk the collapse of order while our guardsmen and cavalry bleed in the North. Let these men be an example of the lengths our fiery resolve will go to *defend* this bright city of Haven."

Jhames turned to signal the corporal and nodded his approval, then faced the crowd of citizens. "By order of the Citadel of Haven, under the law of treason established by King Kaestor, father of King Cascarie and grandsire of King Illium the light seeker; I hereby sentence you to die for your trespasses. May the THREE who is SEVEN have mercy on your treacherous souls."

The corporal signaled to his men and, one at a time, each of the prisoners fell from the barbican and were caught with a bone-breaking snap by the ropes that circled their necks.

A few tears came up from those who knew and loved these men, but the rest of the gathered citizens watched in silent shock as two of their own hung, lifeless, off the edge of the Kings' Bridge. Whether by forethought or by privilege of office, a palsied voice spoke up from amongst the silent crowd. Ispen, the oldest remaining Arborist, stood to his feet and addressed the Priest King.

"Your Brightness," he said formally, his aged, green-haired head bowed low in a grand display of humility. "If it is indeed true as you have spoken, that there is a gathering enemy to the north, what would the Citadel have our brave citizens do to aid the defense efforts?"

The silence was pregnant with the anticipation of something—anything —that might lift the hearts of Haven's people. Jhames let the tension linger before he answered the Arborist's question. "Pray, dear Ispen," Jhames said sincerely. "Pray that the wrath and anger of the THREE who is SEVEN will be assuaged before our city is taken. Pray that the laziness of our people has not cut us off from His bright favor." The Priest King looked south towards Bright Harbor, catching the faint light of Maris in his eyes. "And pray, Arborist, that the ships will return with the fuel for our city's sustained glory."

Engelmann caught the eyes of Margarid from across the crowded street; her cheeks were stained with the desperate, horrified tears that flowed from the understanding that Michael could have easily been one of those executed. The words of the Owele echoed in his mind all over again; *Endure.*

Endure, indeed. Engelmann prayed. *I never suspected it would come to this. Have mercy on us, and protect my friends, please ... if it is Your will. Send Your light, and send it swiftly.*

The crowds began to disperse in solemn defeat. Their curiosity as well as their animosity had been drained from their sullen bodies, and they filed down the stone streets with a visibly broken spirit. Engelmann waited as they cleared, then finally turned his gaze away from the lone silver branch of the great tree. He scanned the departing crowd for sign of the auburn-haired Margarid, but she was nowhere to be found.

"We will endure, my girl, you will see, if you but keep hope alive in your heart and foolishness at bay," he whispered to the place where she had stood just moments before.

On the west side of the mighty Abonris, built along the main thoroughfare, stood the first and the largest of the prison holds. It was not a tall building, no more than forty hands high at its peak, but it stretched for nearly two hundred paces. It was fashioned out of grey, chiseled stone, and pocked along its walls were thin grates that allowed traces of light in for the ill-fated residents. The prison hold descended deep into the great, stone earth that held back the cold, blue waters of the river. Its cells and dungeons went another four floors below ground, and at the base of its deepest chamber, a tunnel ran underneath the great river into the heart of the Citadel itself.

This damp, dank passageway, known as the Menashe, had once served as a path by which to escort the vilest of the kingdom's villains. Once they entered *the pathway of the forgotten*, neither their names nor their deeds were allowed to be spoken in the presence of the King. The passage was constructed during the reign of King Kaestor, for he had used it often in the wake of his daughter Talfryn's death. Many an enemy of the state, whether guilty or otherwise, had walked the Menashe to their doom.

Engelmann walked a few hundred paces north along the main thoroughfare towards the prison hold, and he was not surprised to see a crimson-cloaked figured already waiting near its entrance.

"What are we going to do for him, Engelmann?" she spoke through her worried tears. "You heard what the Priest King said! You ... you saw what he did to those men! I *know* those men and they are not enemies of the Citadel! They were just frightened and in need-"

"I know, my girl. I may be old, but these eyes of mine could still take in the injustice of the day," Engelmann said affectionately. "I cannot presume to know the full intentions of the THREE who is SEVEN, nor why He would call us to endure in such a manner as we are now." He scratched his mossy beard, and put a hand on her slender shoulder. "But I trust His heart, I trust it above all else ... and I trust that His light, His *new light* is indeed coming, and that all the injustices and all the evils that besiege our hearts will be made right in its arrival."

"Do you truly believe that? Still?" Her eyes pleaded for confidence as she asked the old Arborist.

"I do, lady Margarid ... I do," he said kindly and honestly. "If there ever was a time to hold to those beliefs, would it not be now, when things seem to be at their worst? Otherwise, what good is all the hoping and the trusting that has come before?"

"And what of Michael? What if they throw him from the barbican of the Kings' Bridge before this coming light makes everything right? What good is the light then if he is *dead*?"

"My dear Margarid," Engelmann said softly. "We are not given the specifics of our future, nor the particulars of its timeline; we are merely given a dream to hope for and a heart to hope with. Despair robs us of the energy to dream clearly, and worry ... well, worry, is nothing but unfounded despair, pretending to embody prudence!"

She wiped the tears from her eyes, her gaze questioning the old teacher, asking him silently for an explanation to his ramblings.

"Do not spend all your energy imagining pain that has not even happened yet. What strength will you have left to hope with?" the Arborist continued. "Save your worries and quell your fears, child. For the story—our story—is not yet fully told, and I would rather you put your efforts towards a brighter cause."

"Well, then, what *can* we do?" she said as she continued to wipe the tears from her eyes.

He thought about it for a moment before he spoke. "The laws of hospitality are not exempt from the prison holds, and while there is still a flame on the great tree, I still have some measure of respectability in the eyes of the guardsmen." He smiled his wide, toothy smile at her. "Perhaps we might get him a message. I am sure he will need a cloak to keep him warm in that cold place ... perhaps a crimson one?"

Her eyes lit again with a faint light of hope, for she saw this as something —albeit a small thing—that she could do at this moment for the groomsman that had already done so much for her. She nodded her head and forced a smile. "Yes, I could sew a message inside the lining for him."

Engelmann smiled at the determined eyes of the auburn-haired young woman. A sense of grandfatherly pride washed over the old Arborist as he watched one of his pupils defy her own fears. It warmed his heart to see that the roots of hope that had taken hold in this young lady's heart were slowly transforming her resolve. "Very well, then. Let us go see about finding you some parchment and some thread."

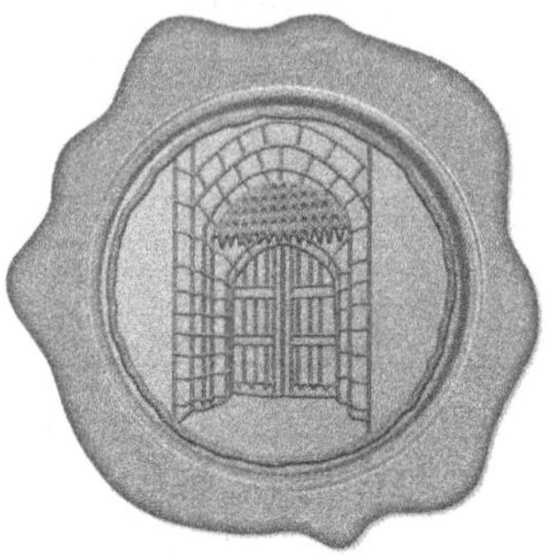

Chapter Six

CAPTAIN ARMAS STOOD HIGH ATOP the Northern Wall, his spyglass trained on the green torches that glowed in a sickly mass of un-light. They remained there, just beyond the reaches of the last traces of radiance from the great tree. For weeks now this Raven Army had waited, camped outside the gates in mocking eagerness, at the ready to hear the bells of war. The green flames flickered their devilry in a taunting accusation of the future to come, while all that the residents of Piney Creek could do was watch, wait, and drown their nightmares in the last remaining barrels of Shameus' amber brew.

"Captain." Lieutenant Marcum interrupted Armas' reverie.

The tall, broad-shouldered captain lowered his spyglass and turned, his green and silver cloak blowing gently in the wind. He brushed his hand across his weary eyes, wiping away the blur of his concentrated observation. It had been weeks since he had arrived at the northern borough, and his once clean-shaven face, though still confident, had grown the salt and peppered beginnings of a beard. Here in the wake of the cold winds and the uncertainty of the impending battle, this captain of the

Citadel was beginning to look more like a true man of the North.

"Captain. They are ready for your inspection, sir."

"Very good, then," Armas commended him. "How goes the training of the militia? Do their arrows fly any straighter yet?"

"A few of them do," he said, rubbing at his tired eyes with his tired hands. "It's a wonder how they didn't starve altogether up here in the colder lands! If it wasn't for the aim of the tavern keep's daughter, I would have said to just give them rocks to throw."

Armas let out a rare, half-audible laugh. "Aye, Keily has a true aim. No one would argue that."

"Well, even if someone tried to, she would probably have him shot between the lips before he could finish his thought!" Marcum added.

"I'm certainly not going to be the one to give her extra target practice," Armas said as he put his hand on the lieutenant's shoulder. "Come then, let's go see about their progress today, shall we? I am sure they will want to hear from their captain."

Armas and Marcum made their way down from the stone battlements and onto the dusty floor of the small borough's square. Armas glanced at the sturdy lieutenant beside him with a thankful expression. Marcum was more than an officer with a company of swords and spears; he was a loyal friend and a prudent leader, and Armas was glad to not have to defend the people of Haven alone.

It was nearly twenty days ago now that Armas greeted Marcum and his five hundred heavy horses and cavalrymen. The warhorses and the knights they carried arrived with a palpable force into Piney Creek, bringing both relief and hope to the small regiment that was already there. Four days later, Armas watched with an even greater hope in his heart as the green and silver banners of fifteen hundred guardsmen marched into the northern borough in succinct rhythm. His message to his lieutenant had been successful, and the troops had been sent to fortify the Northern Gate and prepare for whatever war was to come.

Their army, now two and a half thousand strong, camped throughout the borough, waiting day after day for the tide of battle to rise around them. The militia trained as best they could, ready to play whatever part they might in the defense of their kingdom and countrymen. It was the white-haired corporal, Johnrey, who took command of their instruction and drilling, doing his best to make soldiers out of shopkeepers and farmers. As Armas and his lieutenant watched the resolute people of Piney Creek nock their arrows and loose them into the targets, he felt that there was indeed some hope for the defense of the city.

The officers completed their observation of the militia and made their way back to their command post near the center of the borough. As they approached, Armas took in a rather confusing and altogether surprising sight. "What in the name of the THREE who is SEVEN is going on now?" he mumbled to Marcum.

The horns of the Capital guard rang a brightly-noted pronunciation, announcing the arrival of an unlooked for convoy from the Citadel itself. The marshal of the Northern Gate flung open the canvas door of his tented quarters, his look of both surprise and annoyance evident on his face.

"Is that … is that who I think it is, Captain?" the marshal said as he saluted his commander.

Armas and the lieutenant both crossed their chests in salute to their comrade. "It would seem so. Perhaps the Chancellor plans to see for himself what holds our city besieged."

"Captain Armas," the long-haired lieutenant said with an uneasy tone to his words. "When I received your orders, I did not wait for confirmation from the Citadel to approve my movement." He watched the cavalcade of riders surrounding the Chancellor's carriage. "I pray I did not do harm in acting with such … swiftness."

Armas looked at his old friend with gratitude in his eyes. "You have done well, Marcum. If the Chancellor comes here to punish you for following my orders, I am quite confident that one gaze from out atop the wall will cure his shortsighted ignorance."

"Aye," Marcum nodded as the riders brought their mounts to a stop just ahead of them. "That it will."

"Captain Armas," the young corporal on the lead horse said with a salute. "I present Chaiphus, Chancellor to the Priest King and protector of the flint, into your care."

"As you were, corporal," Armas said with a returned salute. "The marshal here will show your men to our encampment so that you may water your horses. I will see to the Chancellor myself."

"Very well, sir," the corporal said with another formal salute, before riding off to follow the lead of the marshal.

"Captain Armas?" came the nasally, old voice of the Chancellor. His personal attendants opened the carriage doors and helped him out onto the cold, dusty square. "His Brightness has sent me to see first hand the exaggerations of your reports. And to remind you, since you seem to have forgotten, that there is no *real* enemy, no *real* threat to Haven, in the lands of Aiénor. Your demands for action led us to believe that an attack was imminent, *but* it appears that our walls have held strong enough, doesn't it? Of course they have. No one would dare to defy the might of our bright city."

The Chancellor wasted no time with polite introductions, and he approached the captain and lieutenant with a pious, unfiltered arrogance. He stepped closer to Armas, surveying the unkempt disregard for the uniform of his office with barely veiled disgust. "Has the northern air turned your senses, *Captain*? Or just aged your countenance?"

Armas did not retreat from the scrutiny of lords and kings, though his loyalty to his men and his cause would never give him leave to wholly disrespect them either. He smiled a pleasant enough smile and gestured to the wall. "Welcome to Piney Creek, Chancellor Chaiphus. Please, come see the enemy for yourself."

Chaiphus eyed the captain for a moment before stepping back and nodding curtly. "Very well, then. That's precisely why I am here." He began to head towards the gate, and then almost as if it were an afterthought, he turned back to Marcum. "Do not forget where your allegiance lies, *Lieutenant*. For though the captain here is your ranking commander ... *I* am his," he declared coolly. "It would serve you well to remember that carefully in the future."

Marcum nodded and watched as the Chancellor strode off deliberately towards the North Wall.

GAROOM! The ground beneath their feet shook, and the resolve of everyone present quaked in response. *GAROOM, GAROOM!*

"What was that?" Chaiphus demanded, his face paling even here in the amber light of the watch fires and guardsmen's braziers.

Armas stared at the men before him, willing them to remain calm. His fear over the tremors had long-since faded from his outward expressions, though in truth it still unsettled his heart.

"Captain! What kind of devilry shakes the ground itself like this?" Chaiphus demanded.

Armas' steeled expression melted just slightly with his response. "I do not know, though I do fear we are not long 'til we find out."

The guardsmen standing nearby looked back and forth, exchanging glances and listening desperately for ghosts upon the cold wind. Their decorum and courage had begun to fade in the light of the unknown evils waiting past the gate.

"Lieutenant," Armas addressed them. "Send a second contingent of archers to take a watch on the wall, there atop the battlements. You, guardsmen, see that the Chancellor's belongings are taken care of." He pointed just beyond the two barracks that housed the guardsmen stationed here in the North.

"Perhaps I should accompany my belongings to the barracks. I have many correspondences that need my attention before I tour your defenses," Chaiphus reasoned with a discomforted expression.

"Nonsense," Armas responded. "We will prepare the best room that the tavern has to offer! My Lord Chancellor will not be housed in the barracks like a common guardsman. But first, sir, you must come to the wall, and see why both urgency and necessity have driven us here." The captain extended his hand towards the stairs in front of them

GAROOM! GAROOM!

The Chancellor eyed Armas but did not move towards the wall. "Tell me *what that is!*"

Armas turned and began walking confidently up the steps. "It is much easier to show you, Lord Chancellor," he called back.

"Do you even *know* what it is?" Marcum spoke quietly to Armas as he followed him up the steps.

"I have my suspicions ... but I cannot say for certain," Armas replied.

"Tell me your suspicions then, at least, for I have never before felt terror such as this. I have ridden down hordes of violent outliers, and I have stood my ground in the face of rioting citizens, but never once did my heart abandon its courage until I came to aid you here on the wall," Marcum said to his friend. "So I must *insist*, Captain, that you tell me what in the damnable dark is out there."

Armas looked at the lieutenant and took a deep, calculated breath. "I spoke with Hollis, chieftain of the woodcutters, not long before the colony set sail. He told me—no—he *begged* me to heed his warning."

"What warning?" Marcum pressed.

"That whatever this green-eyed evil was that hunted his men with raven-fletched arrows and moved only in the shadows ... that it was not natural."

"Raven-fletched arrows?" Marcum spoke with an all-too-familiar understanding.

"Aye," Armas confirmed. "The same."

"I assumed those belonged to the outlier hordes," Marcum reasoned.

"Is that all this is?" Chaiphus blurted out. "Just another outlying horde with impoverished anger and crude defenses? Is that why you risked the abandonment of our Citadel by the troops sworn to protect it? Is that why you-"

"Take a look over that wall, Lord Chancellor, and you tell me if that looks like a band of outliers," Armas said, cutting short Chaiphus' outrage.

Chaiphus just stood there atop the battlements of the North Gate, staring with eyes wide and mouth agape at the countless torches and braziers that burned their sickly green flames just beyond the reach of the light of the dying tree.

"Who is this, Captain?" Chaiphus swallowed hard in confusion.

"Who? I cannot say *who* it is at all." Armas rubbed his tired eyes with his thumb and forefingers. "It is not *who* that is really of much importance now, is it? Rather it is *what* that is most pressing."

"Do not mince words with me, Armas," the Chancellor growled.

Marcum's face lit with understanding of what it was that Armas was trying to convey. "*What,* then? *What* in the damnable darkness is it that shakes the very ground beneath our boots?"

Armas, unflinching, looked his lieutenant directly in his tired eyes, holding the silent, nervous gaze for a long moment before he turned his attention to the frightened stare of the pious lord.

"Dragons," the captain spoke aloud, his eyes locked with the Chancellor's.

"Do not play me for the fool, Captain!" Chaiphus shouted angrily. His rage, though, was not accompanied by surprise at the mention of the fabled beasts, for this was not the first time that the ears of the Citadel had heard the ridiculous notion.

"I suspect that whoever it is that lies in wait out there ... commands the earth-shaking power of dragons," Armas went on.

Marcum's eyes went wide in the shock of the moment. If it had been any other man who had said these words, or if it had been any other place than this one here in the cold twilight of Piney Creek, he would have arrested him on the spot for lunacy and blasphemy. But Marcum had felt the fear course through his stalwart heart at the rumbling of the quaking earth, and he knew that Armas' suspicions could not be far from the truth of the matter.

"Does the Citadel know?" Marcum asked the Chancellor.

"Does the Citadel know what?" he said indignantly. "I *am* the Citadel, I am the right hand to the Priest King, and neither his Brightness nor myself are ever taken by surprise!"

"Hollis tried to warn us, and you wanted to throw him in irons for it," Armas replied.

"What proof? What evidence do you have, *Captain,* to support your outlandish—no, your blasphemous—claims?" Chaiphus spun towards the North in a whirl of pious anger "I do not know *who* nor *what* that is out there," he said as he pointed his fat, old fingers beyond the wall. "But conjuring up tales of *dragons* shows me the irrational state of your weakened mind, and I ... I should have you thrown into the prison holds for this treacherous fear-mongering!"

"So ... no," Armas said to his lieutenant, disregarding the judgment passed from the Chancellor. "The Citadel does not know because they choose to bury their heads in the sand. Even though they have been warned—even though they come to observe the enemy themselves—they *refuse* to give credence to the word of the woodcutters, and even to the word of their captain." He turned to Chaiphus with a disappointed gaze. "And by the time they realize the gravity of their mistake, there will be nothing more that can be done."

Marcum stood there with a frustrated scowl, then ran his hand through his long, dark hair. "How can this be possible?" he said in an almost prayer-like fashion.

"It is *not* possible!" Chaiphus argued, though the conviction of his own words seemed to waver as he stared at the glowing green fires on the far side of the wall. "It *cannot* be possible!"

"Some evils grow bolder in the dark, waiting for their chance to strike. I believe this enemy intends to strike at the light dwellers with an ancient hatred." Armas looked southward towards the last remaining burning branch of the great tree. "It has been His light that has kept them at bay, relegated to the shadows of this world. And now that the light is all but gone, they sit and wait, like serpents waiting for the right moment to strike and to kill."

"Are you saying that this is all because of the *tree*?" Marcum asked as he exhaustedly ran his hands through his hair.

"I have heard quite enough of this blasphemy for one day," the unnerved Chancellor announced. "You will cease this conversation at once!"

"My Lord Chancellor, I must respectfully disagree with you!" Armas said, doing his best to keep his composure. "You can accuse me of fear-mongering or blasphemy or treachery all you like, but I think you forget the truth of the matter. I have not shared my fears and beliefs with my men. I have not spread them through the borough and I have not given anyone cause to panic *or* to abandon their post." Armas took a deep breath so as to steady the pounding of his heart. "Not even my lieutenant has been privy to my assessment of the situation until just this moment. I have maintained order and I have not let fear take over our defense or our resolve. We are ready to fight this enemy ... 'til the death if we must." He stood tall and looked Chaiphus right in the eye. "Is it more treacherous to speak truth in the face of accusation or to evade truth for the sake of comfort and willful ignorance? You may name me what you like, Chancellor, but my allegiance will always be to the defense of Haven. Where is yours?"

Marcum looked at his ranking commander, a bit nervous for him in the wake of his forthrightness.

Chaiphus glared at the insolent captain, and the moment turned long and tense—a battle of wills there atop the Northern Wall.

"We cannot know for certain yet if it is the tree that holds back our enemy," Armas said as he broke the tension, "but I would suspect that when the last branch falls," he looked back to his friend, "this war begins."

"Then we must be ready ... or as ready as one can be," Marcum replied, his words directed at the Chancellor.

"Come," Armas said. "Come, Chancellor, and see for yourself what it is that we defend against." Armas led him up even further along the stone stairs onto the highest battlements of the Northern Wall. He handed the Chancellor his spyglass, and what Chaiphus beheld made his blood run colder than the icy winds that whipped through the air.

"There must be-" Chaiphus began to count the sickly green torches, but Armas cut him off before he could finish.

"Sixty. There are sixty of those battalion torches." Armas finished for him. "One for each company of theirs, or at least that is the way it seems to me."

"For days now, Lord Chancellor, we have counted their number," Marcum replied.

"And for days now ... we have watched it grow," Armas said.

"Captain Armas," Chaiphus said as he tore the spyglass away from his aged eye, swallowing hard at the bile that had begun to rise in his throat. "Perhaps we could spare a few more men."

GAROOM! The crashing sound came again as two of the largest green orbs rose and fell in the distance. Marcum looked at his captain, and then nervously behind him to the dying tree. "We are going to need more than men, I fear."

"A miracle is more like it," Armas said in a moment of transparency. The three of them stared, fixated at the green horizon. Then, an unexpected and unwelcome sound met their ears. The faint, earthen call of the woodcutter's horn echoed off the wall, carried by the chill of the cold, northern winds.

"Captain!" shouted the marshal as he ran toward the stone stairway. "What was that?" he asked from the floor below. "Was that-"

"Call the men. *Now*," Armas interrupted with a quiet but direct order.

The marshal gave a rushed salute, then signaled the assembly with five syncopated bursts of his horn. Men began to pour into the square below. Officers formed companies of spearmen, cavalry, and archers alike. The gathered army of Haven assembled to face their commander atop the barbican of the North Gate.

Chaiphus and Marcum stood next to Armas, unsure just what this captain of theirs could say in a moment like this one. "Guardsmen of the Citadel, defenders of Haven! Our great and shining city is besieged by this enemy that you have all seen and heard and felt these last days. Nothing in my bones leads me to believe that it is peace or parley that they are after." He spoke with a dignified boldness to his men, his words weighted with a paradoxical combination of certainty and dread here in the midst of the looming unknown. The guardsmen stood resolute and unflinching, the banners of their city waving as their captain spoke. "The horns of the woodcutters have sounded their alarm upon this cold, north wind, and whatever it was they found out there in these besieged outlands," he paused, his mind wandering among all the horrific possibilities that his imagination conjured for him. "We must prepare for the worst, before it rains in upon us." He gulped. "A dark storm is brewing, men, let us make sure that we are not taken unawares by it."

"What are your orders, Captain?" Marcum asked.

"Yes, tell us what you intend to do?" Chaiphus interrupted.

"We will need every able-bodied man and woman who can shoot a bow or wield a blade to prepare themselves to join in our defense."

"Townsfolk?" Chaiphus blurted out in disbelief. "What good will untrained commoners and peasants—"

Armas cut him off before he could say another word. "Corporal Johnrey has been drilling a militia in the stable yard for days. Mind that you do not take the green and silver uniform as the sole sign of bravery; these *townsfolk* will fight just as fiercely alongside us if it means saving their homes and their families." The captain addressed his men once again. "Go now. Make yourselves ready. Only the THREE who is SEVEN knows how much time there is before first blood is spilled, and you had best pray that you are rested and prepared enough to see to it that it is not your own."

Chapter Seven

HOLLIS AND HIS MEN KNEW what it was that they must do if they ever hoped to see the city of their birth spared from the forces that had come to destroy it. The black fog had remained in between the cutter camp and the North Road to Haven, and it had become quite clear that there was only one thing left to do.

Hollis was going to fight.

He had sent scouts for days now, but most of them had not returned. The few that did had nothing to report, save the approximate whereabouts of the fog-shrouded enemy. So Hollis had positioned his men within striking distance of this army of the un-light, and he had prepared them, charging their hearts to fight courageously for the sake of their once-bright city.

Brádách had seen to the sharpening of axes, imploring all of his comrades to hone the bite of their blades until they came to a merciless edge. Silvus, a warrior of the forests, had taken command of Yasen's riders. He was a competent rider and obedient to a fault, and he loved Hollis like an attention-starved child—deliberately and as loudly as possible. The cutter camp held no more than one hundred and fifty able-bodied woodcutters, a handful of healers, and a rather offended Priest. Hollis assembled all of his men daily to prepare both their hearts and their minds for the task that had fallen to them.

Today, their task had come.

Or at least that is what Hollis told himself.

The men sat around smoldering watch fires fueled with scrub brushes and dried dung, listening to their great chieftain give them their last orders. "When the amber fire fades to silver, we move," Hollis said gravely as he looked his faithful comrades in the eye. The furs of his white lion emboldened him with a resolute courage to face whatever evil waited for them in the heart of that black fog. "We will strike this army of the raven-fletched arrows from two positions. Silvus and his riders will charge in from the east, drawing their attention away from our position as we come in from the west." Silvus nodded his understanding to his chief, then eyed the two score of riders who would make the desperate assault with him and pounded his chest in a show of valor.

"As for the rest of you, you will follow me to the western flank. Once Silvus has drawn the enemy out and gained their full attention, then we will strike swift and hard." Hollis ran his hand through his long, greying beard, surveying the men who had served with him. Some had been in his company for decades now, some were older than him in years, and some were not much more than blunt-bladed greenhorns. "Whatever aid we can provide, whatever help or distraction or victory we can offer Captain Armas and his men over there on the other side of the wall ... well, we shall offer it with reckless abandon, lads."

"There will be a fierce battle, of that you can be certain boys," Brádách said to his brothers. "But you have been prepared. Your axes are sharp and your arms are strong. Whatever that monster is out there, my guess is that it will bleed and break just like any scrub oak or young pine."

The woodcutters kissed their flints and whispered among each other, all while keeping an eye on their chief.

"Aye, we cannot hold back," Silvus said in agreement. "Not if we hope to live, that is."

"Aye," Hollis said in turn, though his eyes did not reflect much hope of that at all.

"Do you think they know, Chief? Do you think the Citadel knows yet that they are besieged?" Brádách asked in earnest.

Hollis thought about it before he spoke. "I trust Armas more than I do the Citadel, and though he wasn't ready to hear the warnings of this old, mad woodcutter ... something tells me that they didn't go completely unheeded. I can't say what the Citadel does or doesn't know. But I'd wager that Armas knows all right. He knows, and is ready behind that gate with all the forces of Haven to defend our city."

The woodcutters grunted in agreement.

"Remember lads, we do not know this enemy—this *Raven Army*. We know neither what they are made of, nor what dark magic it is that drives them, but we have seen the effects of their evil. We have buried our brothers who tasted their arrows, and we have seen the un-light that consumed the very life out of the forest." Hollis reached into his tunic where the flint of his faith had once hung. Now, fastened on a small thong of dark leather, rested the dragon's fang. "And even now I wear the reminder of what great monster it is that we are up against." He fingered the deadly black fang in his rough hands.

"Hollis?" came a thin voice from the edge of the firelight. "This cannot be the will of the THREE who is SEVEN ... to risk our lives alone against such a foe?" The Priest walked into the center of the gathered men. His once proud, green robe hung tattered about him, stained and soiled from the last days of pursuing this unknown enemy.

"Whether it is His will or not, we will soon find out," Hollis said gruffly.

"And just how do *you*," the Priest exaggerated the word with an accusatory tone, "a woodcutter, presume to understand His will?"

"I presume, *Priest*, that deeds are required of men in moments like this one. And any deed that is meant to protect and preserve life ... how can that not be true to the heart of our God?" Hollis said as he looked out towards his besieged home. "We shall see if the outcome gives us clarity on the will of the great THREE who is SEVEN; but then again, that all depends on whether or not any of us are alive enough to have the chance to ponder the outcome at all." Hollis spoke matter-of-factly before taking a long draught of his warm, spiced mead.

"Fool! You don't even know-"

"Here's what I *do* know," Hollis interrupted as he wiped the steaming drops from his beard. "I *do* know that pious words and flintish prayers will not substitute in the end for sacrifice and courage."

"Blasphemy!" the Priest shouted in outrage.

"Aye, it may be. But tell me this, Priest, where has all your talk of the flint —of duty and resolve and reverence—gotten us? Huh?" Hollis motioned his arms in a grand display. "The forests are dead, the great tree is nearly gone, the world is darker now than ever before, and evil hunts your Citadel with a fury and a might of monsters more ancient than fear itself!" Hollis' men raised their eyes and met the stare of their chieftain as they listened to him speak. "To hell with it all, Priest! It may very well be that the THREE who is SEVEN has given us the gift of strong arms and sharp axes so that we might bring victory for our people—to *your* people—on this darkened day!"

"Chief," Brádách interrupted him. "It's the tree. The melding of fires has begun."

"Very well, men," Hollis said resolutely. "It is time."

The men began to speak in unison, cued by their lifetimes of habit and service to the Citadel. As their chieftain began the prayer, they recited along with him the words that they had spoken every morning before venturing into the forestlands.

"Oh master of flame and bringer of light,
Make our hearts true and our blades bite.
Fuel our work and worth with your holy might ..."

But the woodcutters trailed off before finishing the final lines, sensing that Hollis would not speak the rest of the words with them. The silence of the moment hung awkwardly there in the smoky tension of the camp.

Brádách broke the quiet. His voice was a bit shaky, but his pride came through true enough as he finished the prayer of the woodcutters with words of his own. "So the world might hope to ... to see a new day!"

"May it be so, Brádách," Hollis said with a proud smile.

"May it be so!" his men shouted in response.

"Riders! Find your mounts! For this silver night we ride for all of Haven!" Silvus shouted to his comrades with a contagious vigor.

Chests were pounded in response as strong, powerful steeds were mounted, ready for whatever green-eyed evil lay concealed beneath the black fog of the Raven Army. Hollis and the rest of the company of woodcutters made the last of their battle preparations. They secured their furs overtop their leather-studded breastplates and fastened simple leather bracers to their forearms. These men, as brave and as mighty as they were, had only ever done true battle with the trees and the beasts of the North. What few skirmishes they had found themselves in were largely unorganized and limited to a few outlier hoards. But here, in the faint firelight, outfitted in simple leather armor and fur clad helms, the small remaining host of Hollis' woodcutters looked more fierce and more deadly than any of Haven's finest companies of guardsmen.

Hollis, dressed in the fur of the white lion, took up the great axe, Víδarr. He held the fabled weapon over his head and charged his men with passion and pride in his voice. "You, woodcutters! You, mighty men of the North! Tonight we give these conjurors of dragons, this Raven Army, a true taste of what every oak and pine and birch and fir has feared for seventy years!" The old chieftain looked up at his old, double-bladed friend and then shouted at the top of his lungs. "*Sharpened steel!*"

A muted cheer went up from the lips of the woodcutters, and they raised their axes in unified purpose. Hollis gave Silvus and his riders the signal they had been waiting for. The ground beneath the camp woke to life with the sound of forty horses pounding the earth as they rode off to the east.

Hollis and the hundred or so able-bodied men who were left began the deliberate trek to the western flank of this Raven Army. The ground beneath them hummed with energy. Hollis could feel the movement of action even now, all this way on the other side of the battle lines, and he knew that Silvus and his men must have engaged the enemy. He felt a cold chill course through his veins as he raised his spyglass to his eye. There, just off in the distance, he could see the faint flickering of lights.

"The time is almost upon us, lads," he whispered to those within earshot. "Hold to your courage, now."

His men exchanged silent glances with each other, and Hollis surveyed as best as he could. Brádách, whose eyes he trusted more than anyone's, had not made the journey with them. Though he protested greatly, his maimed foot would have been the death of him out here upon the field of battle with this Raven Army. And so it was that he had stayed back at the last encampment, along with the Priest and the healers, to offer any aid they might to anyone who might make it back alive.

They marched ever closer to the enemy, while Hollis listened for the sound of battle on the wind. When the attention of the enemy seemed to have focused upon Silvus and his riders in the east, Hollis put down his monocle and raised up Viðarr.

"We strike, now," he said to his men, his face steeled with utter determination. "Give them your worst, and be quick about it! Let's turn the whole lot of green-eyed devils into a field of stumps!"

Hollis and the brave few woodcutters ran swiftly and silently towards the sickly green torches that flickered dimly amidst the black fog. The men had no fear in their eyes, for they had already resigned their bodies to the red earth of Aiénor. Axes were held high and teeth were gritted tight as the men charged into the fog. It was here that the woodcutters, the holy soldiers of the distant Priest King, drew the first blood on the field of battle.

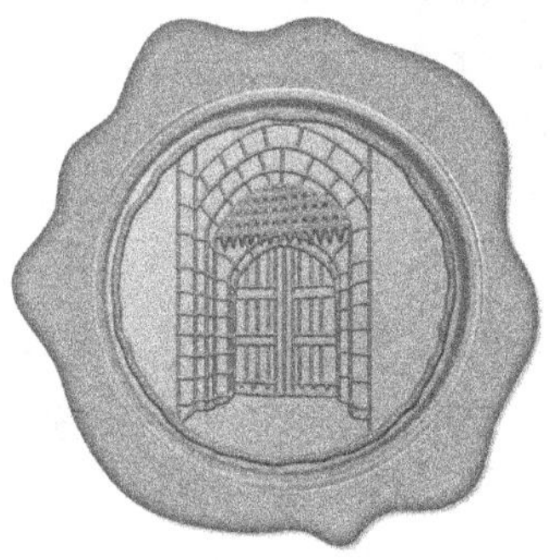

Chapter Eight

KEILY WAS STARTLED AWAKE FROM a restless sleep by the sound of a guttural, soul-chilling noise. Its low, nauseating reverberation hung thick in the foggy air of the northern borough, and on its deep, dark tone came the terror of the unknown. Her eyes shot open, and she quickly reached for the hunting bow and quiver that rested next to her humble, straw-filled mattress. The loud blast finally ceased, and silence crept back in for the briefest of moments, as if whoever it was or whatever it was that was responsible for the horrifying sound needed to catch its breath before it could fill the frosty air with its toxic terror once again.

Keily had fallen asleep still dressed in the same dun-colored pants and tunic and blue bodice that she had worn for the last several days. Her wild, long, curly hair had been bound and tied tightly to her head, and she had replaced her feminine tavern shoes for a pair of her father's high-calved hunting boots. She hurriedly leapt from the bed and laced the thongs of her father's boots. She rushed from the back room of the tavern in a storm of curiosity and fear, eager to see what it was that made this soul-chilling sound. Even now, dressed in the standard of practicality, the tavern-keeper's daughter exuded a wild, dangerous beauty; dangerous not in a seductive or alluring sense, but rather in fearlessly courageous femininity.

She crashed against the wooden door of the Gnarly Knob, peering warily out onto the street. As she did, the silver-lit air erupted in a shrill, violent conflict of notes. The horns of the guardsmen sounded in the bright, brass tones of their office, clashing in the most unnerving way with the foreign, guttural vibrations emanating from the shadows beyond the wall. Keily held her ears, her face grimaced in pain as she was forcibly bound to hearing the torturous sound, for there was no escaping it. The dark and sinister nature of this otherworldly signal seemed to tax her very breath while her courage bent beneath the cruelty of so foul a blast.

"Where is Armas?" she shouted to the dumbfounded citizens who held their ears and watched the commotion of the guardsmen on the dusty streets of Piney Creek. "Where is Captain Armas?"

Companies of men-at-arms rushed in pained uniformity down the streets towards the Northern Gate, making their way to ready themselves for battle. Keily glanced back into the empty tavern and took a deep steadying breath, then slung her bow and quiver across her back and chased after the marching guardsmen. She ran down the busy streets towards the small square, into a hive of frenzied activity. The silver air lit up with sparks of steel as the weapons of war ground against the sharpening stones of the smithy. Guardsmen and officers alike cinched and fastened silver-colored chest pieces to their bodies in preparation for whatever bloody business was coming for them this day.

The war horns of the enemy punctuated the dire mood of these brave guardsmen with taunting brutality. The men steeled their faces, pushing through their suffocating fears while biting back the bile that robbed them of their voices. They knew even as they readied for battle that their chances of surviving for another darkening day lessened with each moment that passed by.

The atmosphere fell breathlessly silent again, as the horns of the enemy unexpectedly and abruptly muted. Soldiers and citizens everywhere looked with terrified anticipation towards the wall, fearing whatever it was that would follow next. Keily spotted Captain Armas atop the barbican, and she took off in a deliberate sprint towards him.

Rolph, a friend of her father and fellow member of the militia, grabbed her arm as she hurried by him. "And just where do you think you are heading, lass?"

She looked at him, surprised, not sure of the meaning of his words or why he would presume to restrain her from her destination.

"It might be best to not involve yourself with the captain's plans," he said through a concerned scowl. "I fear that the wall is no place for a woman."

The air erupted once again with the ghastly noise from beyond the wall. This time, the groaning felt louder, closer, and even more menacing. Rolph grabbed his ears, trying to soften the assault as best as he could. It was not just the men that felt the maddening weight of the enemy's horns; the beasts of burden and the farmer's livestock grew more anxious and unruly with each taunting blast. One of the oxen broke free from his owner's grasp and tore off down the earthen streets, sending supplies and soldiers scattering in the wake of its desperate terror.

Keily looked back to her father's old friend, and then again up to Armas atop the wall. As she tried to make her way to the captain, she felt her arm pulled back again.

"Keily, no lass, I can't ... *you* can't!" he stammered. "I mean, your father would never forgive me."

"Rolph!" she retorted, her voice unwavering now. "My father is *dead*. Where would you rather have me? Huh? Serving a dead man's ale to a city of dead men?"

"I fear the worst is about to break in upon us!" he shouted against the violent cacophony of sound. "Please, for your father's sake, stay far away!"

She looked at him, and a mix of pity and disgust colored her face. Pity for the concern he showed for her, because of his love for her father, and disgust for his inability to recognize her need to fight back against the ones that had stolen him from them both. "That is precisely why I must find Armas!" she shouted against the noise.

"Do you plan to leave this place, then?" Rolph shouted back, somewhat hopeful that his words had convinced this fiery young woman to find safety for herself.

"No, Rolph. I plan to join him!" she replied, and then turned and pulled her arm free of his grasp. "Do not ask me to flee from a chance at vengeance for my father." She left him there, running through the chaotic buzz of activity on the normally sleepy streets of Piney Creek. Keily spied the captain atop the wall and wove her way in and out of the busyness of the frantic defenders, not pausing to make eye contact or heed the shouts of the sentries.

She swiftly climbed the outcropping of stone steps until she arrived at the highest bulwark of the battlement. Archers stood at the ready all along the northern defense. Hundreds of men with scores of razor sharp arrows watched the distant, green horizon for signs of movement. Their faces were set like stone, hidden behind the thin veil of their steel helms. Their silver armor reflected the watch fires and their green tunics were heavy with the cold moisture of the northern fog.

The harsh noises in the air went quiet again, and men everywhere strained to listen in the pregnant pause for whatever was to come next.

"Armas!" Keily shouted out, a bit louder than she intended. Her cry caught the captain's attention, and he nodded to her, welcoming the momentary distraction of the courageous barmaid. She snaked her way through the archers and guardsmen until she reached his command post there on the barbican. As she reached him, she abandoned all care for the order and decorum that his rank demanded and deserved, for he had become more than just a captain of Haven; he had become her friend. She grasped him and hugged him tightly, drawing momentary strength from his touch and his presence.

Not a moment after she reached him, the brutal rape of their senses ensued once again as the air protested in the wake of the violent and ugly sound that they had been forced to endure since waking. She broke her embrace in a startled jolt, for though she was not afraid to fight or to bleed or even to die in the heat of battle, she feared the unknown evils that shook the ground and insulted the wind with so vile a sound.

"Are you alright, Keily?" Armas asked her with an open and genuine concern.

She met his gaze with her own, seeing in his eyes a regard that both flattered and unsettled her, even amidst the intensity of the danger they were facing. Sensing the depth of his care for her, she turned away and looked towards the shadows. "What does it mean Armas? What do they want?"

"It means that war is upon us, girl," a haughty voice answered from behind her. "And you better make yourself ready if you know what's best for you."

She turned, her face colored with the hues of offense towards the one who would presume to refer to her as a mere "girl". Armas lowered his gaze in exhaustion and mild amusement, not ready to manage a second war here atop the wall.

"Captain," the Chancellor addressed him with a disapproving shock to his tone, deliberately looking past the woman in the blue bodice. "Perhaps you might want to spend your concern on the defenses of our city, instead of on the worries of *maidens.*" Chaiphus was visibly shaken by the idea of the war to come, but in a well-practiced act of Priestly piety, he turned his fear into indignant judgment.

Armas looked straight ahead, giving neither rebuttal nor argument to the right hand of the Priest King, though he would certainly not give him the satisfaction of an apology either.

"The ... the enemy is all about us, abusing our senses, mocking the very city we serve, and I *demand* to know what you are going to do about it!" Chaiphus sputtered out madly.

"What am I going to do about it?" Armas said. "I am not going to do anything about their taunts or their mockeries, Lord Chaiphus. For taunts and mockeries are merely the foolish skirmishes of diversion, meant to distract, to disarm, and to dishearten. No, I will prepare my guardsmen and ready our defenses," he turned and met the Chancellor's fearful gaze with his own quiet resolve. "And I will wait until this battle has come within range of our archers."

"The mounts are ready, and the riders wait for your command!" Lieutenant Marcum called as he ran up the flight of stone stairs onto the barbican. "What are your orders, sir?"

"Orders?" Chaiphus said in flabbergasted mockery. "Ha!"

Armas looked at Marcum and nodded his approval. "Thank you, Lieutenant."

"Tell me, Lieutenant," the Chancellor said probingly, "what would *you* tell your men to do in a moment like this?"

Marcum looked back towards Armas, unsure as to what the Chancellor was asking. "My lord, I would wait for my captain's command."

The horns of the enemy roared to life again, stealing the fire from the words of the Chancellor and replacing it with fear. "You would be waiting a long time, it would seem. For instead of commanding the Citadel's army, this captain of yours is cavorting with town girls!" He spat as his panic-stricken voice yelled against the drone of the war horns.

"My lord!" Marcum shouted against the clamor of noise. "With all due respect, this *girl* here is Keily, and she is one of our militia. She is probably one of the best archers I have ever seen. If the captain is *cavorting* with her, it is probably for good reason!"

Chaiphus was stunned by the lieutenant's response, for he had anticipated that allies could be found in the bone-chilled wake of fear-tossed allegiances. "I ... I thought ... I saw him-"

"Lord Chancellor," Armas said calmly. "It is time that you go back to the Citadel and report your observances to our Priest King. This war is not long upon us, and I cannot afford any more time to be distracted by your second guesses. I will have the marshal ready your carriage, and if you wish to display any semblance of reason, you will leave this place before you cannot."

Chaiphus looked for a moment as if an unexpected wave of relief had just washed over him, but he quickly masked it with a veil of outrage. "Speak to me like that again, Armas, and I will take you *and* your girl here back with me to the prison holds myself!"

"I am not his *girl*, and you would be a fool to dispatch either of us from our task of defense!" Keily seethed. "My father was one of the first taken by the shadows, and I will give my life, if need be, to see that he is properly avenged." She spoke with coiled rage as she pointed to the green, un-lit horizon with one of her own goose-feathered arrows. "Whatever hell it is that haunts us out there, it has not counted on the fury of this *girl* in here."

Marcum studied the blue-bodiced woman and noticed the fearlessness inside her fiery eyes. He looked back to his captain, understanding the weight and motivation of her wounded vengeance. This pretty face might be more deadly than ten of his armored and trained spearmen.

Chaiphus studied the three of them, weighing his fear against his pride. Finally he spoke. "His Brightness must hear about this at *once*! Have the marshal ready my carriage. I haven't the stomach for insubordination on a day like this!" The Chancellor shook his finger in Armas' face. "You forget the piety and respect that are woven into the epaulettes upon your shoulders, Captain. You will pay for that forgetfulness, you can mark my words about that!"

"We will prepare your carriage right away, Lord Chancellor," Armas replied, nodding at Marcum. The lieutenant took his cue and ushered the reddened, wild-eyed Chancellor down the stairs and off to the stable yard.

"I am sorry, I did not mean to get you in trouble," Keily said quietly to her friend.

"You did not. His anger at me is just the closest thing to a victory he can manage on a day like this," Armas said with grace in his eyes.

Just then the ground shook, quaking more violently than before, and they quickly turned their attention to the enemy beyond the wall. The two largest pairs of the sickly green orbs flickered in unison and then fell black against the outlands.

"What was that?" Marcum called as he ran back up the stairs.

"I am afraid to guess," Armas replied.

The moment that the green light extinguished, the sky above them was instantly assaulted with a billowing force of air as a rush of wind crashed against the resolve of Haven's defenders, knocking many to their knees or on their backs. Keily gasped, then screamed in terror. Marcum and Armas fell to the deck of the stone battlement, covering the woman with their own bodies so as to protect her from whatever storm had just erupted upon them.

The gale ceased as suddenly as it had come, and a shockwave shot through the northern borough as residents and guardsmen alike tried to assess what had just happened. It felt as though the ground had been slammed with some sort of violent display of rage. As the tremors subsided in the wake of the blast, not a single guardsman even dared to breathe. Whatever monster this was that prowled on the wind and shook the world, it might hear their frightened breaths and bring its fearsome tempest once again.

Then, unlooked for and without warning, the night erupted in a torrent of sickly green fire, accompanied by a bowel-churning sound, more terrifying than any of them could have imagined. The roar was both heard and felt; trained soldiers began to whimper and pray, kissing their flints in the aftermath of the display of such fury.

WHOOSH! Came the faint sound of moving air. *WHOOSH, WHOOSH, WHOOSH*! It came again and again, in volley after volley. Something was being launched, hurled towards the wall, and they could hear them coming ever closer.

"Take cover!" Armas shouted to his men both atop the wall and down in the square.

The entire defense of Haven watched as a terrifying spectacle occurred in the skies before them. A stream of green fire lit up the darkness, blinding them for a moment with the intensity of its light. As they recovered their senses, they watched as the airborne missiles that had been hurled from the enemy camp flew through the green blaze and momentarily eclipsed the fire like a hundred little moons, until they themselves were set alight with its fury.

"Take cover, all of you! *Do it now*!" Armas shouted again to his men.

As they waited for the arrival of the strange and fearsome assault, the stream of green fire suddenly ceased. All that could be heard were humming noises as the projectiles, whatever they were, made their way through the cold air. The moment—though it truly was barely a fraction of a second—stretched out before them all, ripe with pain and pregnant with terror. Both the guardsmen and citizens alike awaited the impact of hell upon their once bright and shining city.

When the collision finally occurred, it did not bring with it catastrophic explosions of green fire, nor piercing raven-fletched arrows as some might have expected. It did not cause merciless destruction of the battlements nor did it kill or wound the men.

What came flying through the darkened air was far more horrific, and produced the most soul-chilling effect imaginable.

The wall awoke with the strange sounds of wet thuds and of sickly cracking, not at all the noises Armas had braced himself to hear. Though still, within moments of the impact, the screams and cries he had anticipated filled the silence of the faint silver night just as he had expected them to. Armas stood to his tired and shaky feet; his hands were wet with the nervous sweat of dread. "What in the damnable ... "

"Armas?" Keily whispered nauseously. "Armas? Oh no ... oh no ... *Armas!*" she breathed, her voice growing more broken and sorrowful with each word.

"What is it, Keily? Are you hurt?" Armas asked her with deep concern. But when he looked down at the blue-bodiced woman, he knew where her pain and panic had come from.

Littered from one end of the battlement to the other, Armas saw the broken and burning bodies of more than a hundred northmen. Their horses had been hurled atop the wall, scattered alongside the lifeless woodcutters, bloodied and aflame. The carcasses of the loyal animals lay defiled next to the corpses of their riders. The horrified captain of the guard nearly retched in disgust as he moved to examine the bodies. His mouth went dry, and his stomach turned at the very thought of what had just happened to these kinsmen of his.

"*No*! No, uncle ... not you too!" The strong, fiery-eyed barmaid began to weep. There, not a dozen paces from where she had taken cover, Armas caught sight of the reddish head of her beloved uncle, Hollis, chieftain of the woodcutters.

Her sobs were deep and violent, for not only had this shadowed army taken her foolhardy father, but it had also robbed the life of the bravest man she had ever known. "NO! This cannot be ... this cannot be," she cried, unable to pull her eyes away from the bloody mess of his once strong body that stared lifelessly back at her.

"Marshal!" Armas shouted shakily. The winter-wearied man came as fast as his unsteady legs could carry him. When he came within sight of the chieftain's corpse, he froze where he stood. "Not Hollis." He swore under his breath.

"Who are all these men, Captain?" Marcum asked.

"The last of the woodcutters. This looks to be about every man they had left," Armas said with a stoic gaze.

"Who ... who ordered them to engage ... how did they ... why?" Marcum asked, not able to form a complete thought, for the shock and horror of the moment was almost too much for words.

Armas just stared at the bloody face of his friend. The questions of his lieutenant passed unobstructed though his mind, raising no will with which to respond to them, nor answers to give. He rubbed the dark stubble that clung to his tired face and wiped away the wet tears that had stubbornly formed in his tired eyes. Finally, after what seemed like an eternity, he broke the silence of the gathered guardsmen. "Marshal, see to it that they are given a proper woodcutter's burial." Armas ripped his eyes away from the mangled face of his dead friend. "We owe them that much."

"But sir?" the marshal began to protest. "What if they mean to continue their attack?"

"This was nothing more than an act to breed fear amongst our ranks," Armas said to the marshal. "Until the tree finally falls, my guess is that fear is their only objective."

"This is a waste," Marcum grunted as he swallowed back his anger over the dead men and horses that littered the cold, stone floor around him.

"No," Armas replied. "Hollis is not a wasteful man. Though this loss is indeed grievous, we will not shame his sacrifice." They just stared, all of them, at the still-burning bodies of their fallen kinsman; their minds were whirling with a frenzy of both outrage and fear. "Marshal," Armas ordered again with a nod of his head, breaking the quiet of the somber moment.

"Aye, sir," the marshal sadly replied. "Sir, if I may ask, what was that? What kind of devil lights the sky with ..." he nervously searched his thoughts for the right words, "with a fire like that?"

Marcum looked to Armas as he answered the marshal, already knowing full well the cursed answer to that question.

"Dragons," Armas replied. "Hollis tried to warn all of us months ago, and none of us—not even me—listened to him. I promise, old friend ... I will heed your warning this time around."

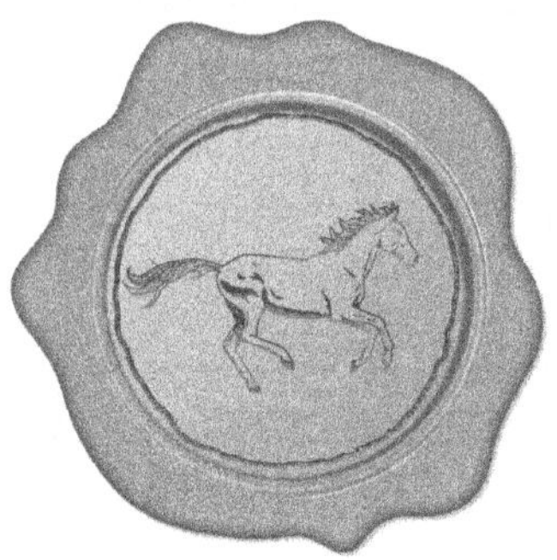

Chapter Nine

CAL AND WIELUND CLIMBED DOWN the rocky outcropping, clinging to the moist, moss-covered stone, steadying themselves so as to not slip and fall into the waters of the pool below. They made their way closer to the shadowed structure that loomed there before them, straining their eyes against the darkness to see what it was that they were approaching.

"Wait here," Cal whispered to his nervous friend. "I want to have a better look."

Wielund nodded his agreement, grateful to remain there upon the boulders until the moment was safe enough for him to pass. "Alright then ... but Cal?"

Cal looked back, a wry grin on his bearded face. "I'll be careful enough. I've got Gwarwyn with me," he said with a wink. The groomsman hopped down from the knee-high outcropping and began to make his way through the tall willow grass towards the overgrown clearing on the edge of the tree line. "What in the name of the THREE who is SEVEN is this doing here, Deryn?" he whispered to his hidden Sprite friend.

"I am just as curious to know as you are," Deryn said as he peeked out from behind the lapels of Cal's cloak.

Standing on the opposite side of the forest pond, Cal stared in absolute wonder at the ancient, stone structure that stood before him.

"What is it, Cal?" Wielund shouted his whisper from the relative safety of the water's edge.

"Why don't you come see for yourself," Cal urged.

Wielund stole a nervous glance back to the horses standing quietly on the other side of the water. He took a deep breath and then chose to trust the groomsman, though every bone in his body would rather have been back in the safety of his forge. He reluctantly turned towards Cal and held his torch high over his head so as to take in as much of these foreign surroundings as he could. When he reached his friend, he stopped and stared in equal amazement.

"A tower?" Wielund asked him. "Here in the middle of this ... this wilderness? I don't like it, Cal. Do you see anything else?"

Cal looked through the thicket of trees and could not see much else besides the falling leaves and swaying branches. Though the forest faded into a clearing that must have been a hundred paces in either direction of the tower, this old relic of aged stone and heavy vines seemed so out of place here in this part of the Wreath. There was a gravity about this place that drew Cal, something beyond his ability to explain. Though there was no Owele or Poet to send him onward, there was a distinct sense that this tower was not merely an accidental discovery on this great quest of his.

Cal shook his head at Wielund and was about to answer his question when a sound stopped them cold.

Cal looked at his friend and once again raised his fingers to his lips so as to keep his nervous curiosity at bay. The two of them listened, but all they could hear was the jagged, heavy sound of their own breathing. They scanned the banks of the forest pool, and squinted in the shadows surrounding this out-of-place tower, but they could find no sign of man or beast.

"What do you think it is?" Wielund whispered.

"I can't say for certain ... it sounded like-" Cal tried to answer, but the sound came again, light and muffled on the thick, forest air.

"It sounds as if it is coming from the tower," Cal whispered. "Someone is up there, I'd wager."

"Then I say that whatever or whoever it is, we let it be," Wielund urged.

Cal reached down and unsheathed Gwarwyn, his ears still trained in the direction of the tower, hoping to catch the sound once again. "Come *on*, we will be safe enough."

The young men gathered what courage they could muster and slowly made their way towards the stone tower, stepping quietly and cautiously on the carpet of tiny twigs and fallen leaves. They approached the forgotten bastion, and as the two of them reached its ivy-covered entryway they heard a different and more distinctive sound: the hushed weeping of a woman.

Cal's eyes went wide in sudden panic, remembering all too well the last time he came upon the unexpected cries of a woman in distress. He swallowed hard as he tilted his head all the way back to take in the looming tower that stood before him. His usually bright face and confident demeanor went an ashen grey as his mind revisited his encounter with the bridge witch, there in the outlands of Haven.

"Are you alright, Cal?" Wielund asked him nervously. "We don't have to go in if you don't feel it is safe?"

What I wouldn't do to have Moa here with me right now, Cal thought to himself, wishing for her protective discernment. He wondered if she would have allowed him to approach this strange tower in this strange land with the all-too-familiar sound of a strange woman weeping inside. The sobs continued to escape the thick walls of the keep. Though Cal felt anxious dread at the possibilities of unknown evils that could be the cause of such sad and sorrowful cries, he knew in his heart that he could not turn and leave her, whoever she was, alone.

"Are you with me, Deryn?" Cal half-whispered.

"Huh?" Wielund said, a puzzled expression on his face.

Cal took a deep breath and steeled himself for whatever he might find here in these forgotten walls. He looked to his friend and placed his hands on the entryway. "Keep your wits about you, smithy. There *are* things in this world worth being afraid of. Let us pray that whoever cries in this tower," he looked up through the dark doorway in front of him, "is ... well ... not one of those things."

Wielund nodded in anxious agreement, and then plunged his flickering torch into the darkness of the tower, following the lead of the brave groomsman. The walls inside of the grey, stone structure had been covered by green mold, and where once there might have hung large, iron candelabras, now only rust-eaten lengths of chain dangled in purposeless abandonment. The stone floor was littered with cracked chests of rotten wood and the smashed, splintered remains of mead barrels. The air inside was nearly suffocating with the rancid moisture that both clung to and corrupted this once strong place.

The sound of the woman echoed from high above their heads, and Cal quickly found the dilapidated form of a wooden staircase that wrapped around the mold-covered walls.

"Do you think it is safe?" Wielund asked him.

"There is nothing safe about any of this, my friend," Cal said. His usually curious and playful mood had been darkened at the realization that this sound upon the wind was indeed a woman. Cal placed his right boot on the first step, carefully gaging its strength before he trusted the old rotting stairs to carry his full weight. When he deemed them worthy enough, he nodded to Wielund. "Wait here. When I reach the top, then quickly follow behind me. I barely trust these old steps to hold my own weight, let alone the weight of the both of us."

"Alright then," Wielund said, nodding in agreement.

Cal began his climb up the worrisome stairs. The jagged sobs of the woman above him came to a sudden silence as Cal's boot crashed through a rotten plank. Cal grabbed and clung to the step in front of him, catching himself just before he fell all the way through to the stone floor.

"Are you alright?" Wielund whispered.

"Yeah, that was almost disastrous. I guess we both better mind our steps, huh?" Cal pulled his boot loose before finding safer purchase on the step below. "Do you hear that? The crying, it stopped."

Wielund looked up, his eyes following the stairs while his ears strained in concentration. "Be careful."

With each step, the weakened wood creaked and groaned, bowing under his weight and threatening to give way. Cal clung to the rusted, iron rail that held resolutely to the moldy, stone walls of the tower, trusting the aging planks even less now after their near-collapse. The stairs rounded and rose for four stories, and the darkness grew heavier and deeper with each step that Cal took. Though he had no torch, he was somehow able to see enough to make out his footing for the treacherous climb to the top of the tower.

When Cal reached the last of the steps, the purpose of this most peculiar tower came to his understanding. Rust-eaten iron bars littered the upper room. He could make out what looked to be a handful of prison cells, and the walls were lined with iron fastenings, some still holding their forgotten chains in place.

Cal nervously scanned the abandoned tower prison, looking for signs of the weeping woman. His hand gripped firmly around the leather-wrapped hilt of his sword, Gwarwyn, ready as he could be in case things went foul. "Hello? My lady ... are you alright?" He spoke as calmly and cautiously as his frightened, racing heart would allow. "My friend and I ... we heard your tears."

"Who are you, that you can see in the dark without a torch?" Her tone was wary, with a bite to its edge. "What kind of devilry and dark magic brings you to me?"

Cal shook his head in confusion. "What brought us to you was the sound of your cries. No magic, no devilry."

A moment passed in silence as the woman considered his claim. "I do not suspect that my tears are the sole force that ordered your steps," she finally said from her huddled position in the corner of the iron cell.

The hair on Cal's neck stood up on end. This moment was eerily similar to moments past. Weeping women, unexplainable foreknowledge, and what was sure to be a painful escape. "My lady, if you are imprisoned unjustly, or trapped, or-"

"I deserve my imprisonment," she interrupted him. "My tears are not for my sentence, for I have already resigned my fate to it. I cry ... I cry because of the darkness."

"The darkness?" Cal asked her.

"Aye, my torch has flickered its last flame ... and I am terribly afraid of the dark," she lamented, her head still buried in her hands. "But you ... you have no torch, and yet you *see*? Are you in league with the sorceress?"

"Sorceress?" Cal said, now quite unsure of the situation. "No, my lady. I am but a groomsman from Haven."

"Then how is it that you see?" she shot back, mistrusting his words. "I may have lived in this darkness for far too long, but even I can sense the pricklings of power that accompany you, *groomsman*." She rose to her feet and came out from the corner of her rotting, iron cell. He watched her with a wary fascination as she brushed her hair from her face and wrapped her slender hands around the rusted bars that held her prisoner. For the first time, there in the darkness of the tower, she met his gaze with her own. The outsets of her violet eyes were alive in a wash of color, yet at their centers, yellow pupils punctuated her hypnotic gaze. Without even trying, Cal was caught up in a storm of both beauty and fear, lost in the tempest of her stare.

A moment passed as she carefully considered him. He could not form a response to her, so entranced was he with the violet eyes that would not release him. Finally she spoke again, startling him with both her words and the conclusion she had come to. "The one who travels with you, then ... it must be him. Is he the one who gives you sight here in this darkness?" Her words were timid, trembling. "If not the sorceress ... then it must be him."

Cal thought deeply for a moment, and though he did not fully trust this violet-eyed prisoner, something in him did not wholly fear her either. He held his blade in one hand and with the other he pulled back his cloak and revealed his secret to her. The lining of his cloak glowed in subtle, azure radiance as a fierce, tiny face appeared from inside his inner pocket. Deryn cautiously emerged from his hiding place; his blue wings beat against the stale air and lit the whole chamber in a faint wash of light.

The woman retreated back into her cell, stunned at the sight she beheld. Her eyes flickered curiously, reflecting the sapphire glow.

Cal watched her reaction in careful estimation, still trying to determine if they could trust her. He hoped that Deryn would discern her true intentions, or at least know whether or not they should help her.

"Cal! Cal, are you alright?" Wielund shouted as he rounded the rickety stairs of the tower. "What is going on up there? I see light. What kind of-" Wielund stopped mid-thought. His words were frozen upon his tongue, for his eyes now beheld the tiny, blue-winged Sprite.

Cal met Deryn's gaze, and the Sprite nodded with a humble yet bemused smile, giving Cal the permission he did not wholly need. "It's all right, Wielund, it's-" Cal tried to say.

"What in the damnable dark is that?" Wielund said in wide-eyed amazement.

"I believe the proper question is, 'who is that?'" the small, blue warrior retorted in feigned annoyance. "For I am Deryn, sentinel of the house of Iolanthe who is queen of the-"

"Sprites," the violet-eyed woman whispered from the back of her prison cell.

Wielund jolted and turned his head, remembering in a wave of lucidity what it was that brought them to this tower in the first place. "The weeping woman," Wielund whispered.

Deryn and Cal followed suit, and the three of them stared at the golden-haired woman in the far corner of the tower cell.

"Yes, my lady," Deryn said, flying slightly closer to her. "A Sprite, indeed."

"You are one of them?" she said in utter amazement, rushing to the iron bars that held her captive. "The fruit of the trees? There are still your kind in this darkening world?" The woman knelt to her knees in a show of worshipful reverence; tears streamed once again from her pearl-colored face.

"Cal," Wielund gulped as he took in the magical, rather unfathomable sights of both Deryn the Sprite and this beautiful woman locked in a cell of rotting iron. "Cal, what is happening here, my friend? What in the name of the THREE who is SEVEN is *happening*?"

Deryn eyed the young smithy, calculating the intention of his heart before choosing to speak. The blue-winged sentinel flew closer now, meeting the gaze of Wielund with his own bright, blue eyes. "Do not be afraid, Wielund." He spoke with a soft confidence. "For it is in the name of the THREE who is SEVEN, our Great Father, that I am here."

Wielund did not understand the full measure or meaning of the Sprite's words, but his worried mind felt instantly at peace at the hearing of them. He nodded his agreement, then looked for Cal's approval. Cal smiled widely, knowing full well that Wielund's reaction to the Sprite must have been similar to his own on that fateful day there under the Hilgari. He nodded back to the smithy and turned his gaze back to the woman and her cell. As he considered her imprisonment, his smile quickly disappeared. For as his Sprite friend came closer to the iron bars of the rotting prison cell, his blue light began to reveal more and more details of this forgotten place. Cal's face registered the complete shock he felt catching in his chest as he noticed the crude carvings that were chiseled into the surrounding walls of the prison hold. He turned his head franticly, scanning the whole of the room as he spun in amazed horror at the words that littered the walls of this forgotten place.

Wielund did not understand what could have so quickly changed the playful smile of the groomsman to this face of dread. "What it is, Cal?" he said as he turned to see what his friend had become so concerned with.

Cal squeezed through an opening between the fractured cells so as to get as close as he might to the words his attention had become fixed upon. Deryn quickly and instinctively flew ahead of him, his muted brilliance lighting the way for them both to see. Cal found the ancient writing that had been scratched here inside this forgotten cell, and his fingers traced their time-worn etchings.

"What is it, Cal? What does it say?" Wielund asked worriedly.

"Seek the light," the violet-eyed woman said without emotion.

"You know these words?" Cal shot back, excitement overcoming his fears. "Do you know what they mean, or who it was that wrote them?"

"Of course I do. All of my people know who it was that wrote them," she replied. "I have come here since I was but a little child. My father and his father would speak of the prisoners of Enguerrand ... the tree men, they called them." She walked to the wall of her unbroken cell, letting her fingers find the carved symbol there where she had known it would be. "Come and see for yourselves," she called out to the three of them.

Deryn flew with great haste back through the bars and into her cell, lighting the wall near her with his illuminated presence.

"What is it, Deryn, what do you see?" Cal asked as he squeezed his way back through the iron bars, stopping at the locked door to the cell of the violet-eyed woman. His eyes went wide in disbelief. He stared, looking straight ahead with his jaw agape in child-like wonder.

"Is that ... ?" Wielund asked. "That ... that's the sigil of the Priest King! That's ... how ... how can that be?" He too was now caught up in the unbelievable excitement of the discovery.

"No, my friend. That is not the sigil of the Priest King," Cal said in slow, deliberate words. "Look here ... do you see it? There is *no flint* upon this tree."

"I don't understand then, why would someone carve the sigil and leave it incomplete?" Wielund asked, confused by the very notion of it all.

"It's not incomplete. This is not Jhames' sigil, Wielund. I do believe this is the marker of King Illium the light seeker himself," Cal replied.

"What? That can't ... it can't possibly be his sigil! Illium set sail nearly seventy years ago, how could he ..." Wielund's words began to trail off as the realization of the moment settled in his mind.

"My father told me that the tree men had sailed here long ago from the east, in search of a great magic, a 'true light', as they called it. But when the sorceress could not sway their intentions, she imprisoned the seven of them here in Enguerrand." The violet-eyed woman offered her story to the three who listened with enraptured discovery.

"*The* King Illium? Here?" Wielund exclaimed. "Did you ever see him?"

"I do not know any of the tree men's names, nor their faces. They were gone from this wretched tower long before I took my first breath of this darkened world," she told him, bemused at the silliness of his presumption. "But this place, and their stories, have always both fascinated and terrified me."

"What happened to them then, the tree men?" Cal asked her.

"No one knows, or at least none of my people know," she told him sadly, her slender fingers tracing the etched words and sigils.

"Your people?" Cal asked her. "Where are your people, and why have they not come for you? Why have they not brought you fire to see by? Do they not know what frightens you?"

She studied him there, this groomsman who could see in the darkness without aid of flame, this friend of Sprites ... and her heart trusted him. There, within the iron prison of Enguerrand, the weeping woman with the violet eyes found hope in the Bright Fame before her.

"My name is Astyræ, daughter of Aius the fallen. My people are the last of Dardanos, the brave few who did not succumb to the power and un-light of the sorceress."

"Is that why you are in here, my lady?" Cal asked, his mind still reeling with all the possibilities of this incredible discovery. "The sorceress?"

She thought about it for a brief moment, then sighed before answering. "Well, not exactly. It was not her hands that bound me in chains, nor her power that forced my heart to get so lost. But her malevolence, her insatiable greed, I still name at the root of it all."

She stared back at him with those intoxicating eyes, and the wonders of king and kingdom blurred into the shadows of his mind. *Getting lost is not as hard as I always hoped it would be,* Cal thought.

Deryn interrupted the moment as he came and rested upon Cal's shoulder. "She is beautiful, and I do believe that she is good and worthy of our rescue. But mind that you do not find yourself too captivated, my young friend. Don't be made prisoner to her beauty," he whispered into his ear.

Cal half-smiled in embarrassed amusement, breaking his gaze and averting his eyes to the floor.

"So this tower ... this um ... Enguerrand?" Wielund said, breaking the awkward quietness. "Is this your people's tower? Or does it belong to the sorceress?"

"Ha!" Astyræ laughed a disgruntled blurt of a laugh. "Nogcwren has no need of prison towers these dark days. There are very few left in this part of the world that have not taken her offer and are not now subject to her vile will."

"Nogcwren!" Cal said with a quiet realization.

"So you *do* know her?" Astyræ asked rather angrily. "Has she poisoned your mind too?"

"What? No! No, I have never ... I've only heard her name from the Sprite Queen herself," Cal answered, fumbling over his words. "I only know *of* her, and that knowledge is limited at best."

Astyræ stood there at the back of her prison cell, debating in her own heart whether or not this groomsman with the kind face and the winsome presence was safe indeed.

"Honest," Cal pleaded.

She let out a surrendering sigh and came forward, holding on to the rusted bars once again. Her soft complexion and golden hair made her seem so out-of-place behind the corrupted black of this dying fortress.

"I will free you ... if you like?" Cal asked her a bit timidly.

"Free me?" Astyræ said playfully. "How do you dare to know if I deserve to be behind these rotting bars? How do you know that I won't be a danger to you if you free me of this prison?"

He held her gaze for a moment, and then cautiously placed his calloused hands over top of her slender fingers. "I cannot say for certain that you are *not* dangerous; perhaps you are. But I have looked into your violet eyes, and I see the goodness of your heart there."

"Did you not see the yellow there as well, groomsman? Did you not see the guilt of my treachery, the crime for which I have been imprisoned?" she retorted, a bit angered at his assumptions of her.

"I did not, lady Astyræ. Though I do not doubt that it is indeed there ... I did not see it," Cal said with mercy on his words and confidence in his voice. He took Gwarwyn and placed the tip of the sword in the keyhole of the rusted, iron lock, and with one swift move he put the whole of his weight onto the fabled blade of the dragon slayer and sprung the lock free.

Chapter Ten

"WHAT?" JHAMES ROARED AS HE pounded his white-knuckled fist upon the writing table. The high, stone walls of the Priest King's chamber reverberated with the angry echoes of exasperated outrage. "What makes you think, Arborist, that I would give special attention to one of the Citadel's prisoners, one of our bright city's *traitors*, mind you, just because he happens to be one of your pupils?" The words seethed out of Jhames' lips in a mix of perplexed shock and satisfied amusement.

"Your Brightness," Engelmann said with as much wisdom and restraint as he could muster, "if our city is surrounded by this ... this enemy, as you have yourself admitted, then would it not make the wisest sense to put our most able-bodied men in a position to defend what you have worked so hard to establish? Instead, you and the Chancellor foolishly lock them in the prison holds over such petty offenses."

"You tell me," the Priest King said, "what business you have in the running of this city? What business do you have worrying about the affairs of king and kingdom, when your own charge is failing right in front of us all?"

Engelmann ran his leathery, dark hand through his mossy beard, thinking hard on both the words and the intent of this frightened leader of the city. "Of running cities and ruling kingdoms, I know very little. But of the hearts of men, all men, even those who riot in your well-kept streets and rot in your iron-barred prison ... I do have wisdom to offer. Perhaps," the old Arborist said, waving his long, gnarled finger, "if you spent less time worrying about what is or is not my business, and more time actually listening to advisors who could help you, you would have a chance to save this great city of ours."

"*You* are but a dying gaggle of scrub pines, the lot of you! Nothing more than tumbleweeds," Jhames cursed. "I name you and your incompetent brothers responsible for the demise of the great tree. Perhaps if you had spent less time with *pupils* and more time tending to your true charge ..." Jhames stood up from the table, letting his sentence hang limp in the frustration of the moment. His face had grown weary with the lines of sleepless nights, and his long white hair desperately clung to the dying remains of formality and poise.

He walked towards the large, glass window, looking out over the great garden that had once been the crowning jewel of the hallowed granite face of Mount Aureole. Here, on this day, with but a single branch remaining, the identity of this once bright and proud people was most inevitably coming to a dark ending. "When that last branch fails us, *Arborist*, when our city is plunged into the madness of night and subjected to the vile foes that wait to destroy us, where will your wisdom be then? Useless!"

"That is precisely why you must win the hearts and loyalty of your citizens now, Your Brightness!" Engelmann exclaimed. "Fear will not hold sway over the panicked rages of the riotous crowd, and it will not defend against the enemy that preys upon us all. Only hope has the strength enough to do that."

Jhames just stared at the old, green-haired Arborist. The lamplight flickered in the wisps of the windy drafts that found their way in through the large, leaded window frame.

"You can talk of hope all the way to your grave, Arborist. You can see just how much good it will do you. But make no mistake, when that last branch fails, so will your privilege to speak so freely and foolishly to me." The Priest

King's eyes narrowed as he spoke. Though his words were cold and forceful, his expression betrayed a wounded pride and an uncertain fear that he no longer had the energy to hide.

"It would seem to me that my *privilege* has long since failed here within the walls of this Citadel, for what use are words of compassion or wisdom on the ears of those too foolish to hear them?" Engelmann shot back.

Offended rage boiled and bubbled beneath the surface of the Priest King's decorum. His face contorted into a wild-eyed snarl for the briefest of moments before he shook himself and let out an incensed breath. Without so much as a word, he nodded to his chamber guards to escort the insolent, old Arborist out of his presence.

Engelmann watched the men approach him, but neither of them dared to place a hand on this once-revered enigma of a person. He looked them over, then smiled a sad smile, raising his leathery hands to show that he did not plan to resist his removal. "Do not worry, my boys. I know full well when my *privilege* has run its final course." Though he lamented the folly of Jhames, his eyes were filled with a kindness still, and he did not wish to wage war on the very souls that he hoped to save.

"Take this to heart, Your Brightness," Engelmann said as he was gracefully escorted towards the tall, wooden doors. "The darkness that is coming— that is, in truth, already here—it will not give heed nor thought for privilege or office, crown or king. As the light of the great tree leaves this city, so does any confidence in man-made defenses and fear-won loyalties." He leaned back into the room, pointedly gazing at the Priest King. "You are not safe behind these walls."

Engelmann left the office chamber by his own strength, fueled by a burning fury in the deepest parts of his chest. His anger was not merely focused on the ineptitude of this city's stewards, nor on the failure to release his young friend and pupil; no, his anger was directed at the arrogance of prideful men in powerful positions whose mulish ears refused the simple wisdom of humble voices. The doors of the annex closed heavily behind him as Engelmann stepped out into the chilly air of the faint amber morning. The winds of this world seemed to take on a more and more unpredictable nature with each felled branch of the tree, and the once temperate climate of Haven had taken on a bit of a northern bite of cold here in these dimly lit days. The Arborist began to make his way towards his home there in the great hall, but stopped short when he heard the bright, brass sounds of the Capital guard's trumpets waking the heavy, silent air with hurried notes.

The horns rang again and again in quick and deliberate succession. "This announcement must be urgent, indeed, I wonder if..." Engelmann's words fell short as he saw one of the mounted guardsmen, riding with maddened haste straight towards the entrance to the Priest King's office. The green and silver of the rider's tunic had been soiled with spots of rusted red and tattered with swaths of burnt black.

"What has happened, son?" Engelmann shouted to the rider as he shakily did his best to dismount the lathered beast. "What in the name of the THREE who is SEVEN has happened?"

The young man, who could not have been any older than Michael, looked dutifully at the old Arborist; it was clear in his eyes that he still held a deep respect for the mysterious keeper of the tree.

"They ... they are ... *dead,* sir. I mean, master Arborist," the rider stammered awkwardly.

"Do not trouble yourself with formalities at a time like this," Engelmann said. "Tell me now, what has happened? Who is dead?"

"The ... the woodcutters, sir," the rider reported.

"The woodcutters?" Engelmann coaxed, puzzled at the rider's response. "Which woodcutters?"

"All of them, sir," the young man replied as he swallowed back his fear. A deep anxiety seemed to overtake his features as he allowed the memory to surface in his thoughts.

"All of them," Engelmann half-spoke, half-whispered in stunned amazement.

"Yes sir, all of them," the rider said. His eyes lowered and his words caught in his throat as he recounted the tale. "Something ... something unnatural, something huge and dark ... it flung their bodies and the carcasses of their horses over the North Wall and into the borough." The rider looked up at the Arborist. "Only ... only the bodies were on *fire,* lit and burning in a blaze of some evil, green flame."

"Green fire?" Engelmann said.

"Yes, master Arborist," the rider said. "They set much of the battlements ablaze and the people ... the people of Piney Creek ... I have never seen so many frightened people in all my days."

"What about the defenses? Tell me quick, now, son, what does Captain Armas plan to do?" Engelmann asked.

"That is just it, master Arborist. He ordered me to ride hard all the way back to the Citadel and deliver this message to the Priest King himself." He spoke hastily as he held up the soiled piece of parchment with the sigil of the captain of the guard sealed into the black wax.

Engelmann thought about it for a moment, wondering to himself just how Jhames would receive the news. He could not bring himself to muster much expectation for a wise and effective response to this aggression.

"Have they attacked yet?" the Arborist asked him. "Have they fired an arrow, or have siege engines been deployed? Have they tried to scale the walls?"

"No ... no, sir. Other than the burning bodies of the woodcutters, there has not been a shot fired, nor a parley offered," he replied.

"But, green fire? Green fire ..." the Arborist muttered, staring at the young man with such intensity that it seemed as if he stared right through him and focused on something in the dimness behind him.

"Yes," the rider finally said, after turning nervously to see what it was that the Arborist could possibly be staring at. "I do think that whatever rumors and tales we have heard from the northern forests, they only tell half the story of what truly is coming for us." The admission spilled from his lips like a pent up flood. "The monsters in the darkness are surely greater even than we fear."

Engelmann assessed the young man once more, seeing the certainty of the end in his eyes. The old Arborist looked back towards the failing tree, there atop the holy mount with its singular branch still remaining, still illuminating the world with the same amber flame that had burned unceasingly for the entirety of his existence. As he watched the subtle dance of the lone flame, he could feel something from deep inside of his wispy frame give way, like a fatal crack upon winter's first ice. The very same power that ran through the rooted veins of the hallowed tree had always echoed its strength within each of the Arborists, and yet in that moment,

Engelmann felt something that he had never felt in all of his days. *Release.* And then he knew, without hesitation, that the end was indeed upon them all.

"Go, son. Go and deliver your message of this green fire, and do it quickly," Engelmann said with tears in his eyes. "Tell them what you have seen, what you have witnessed. Show them your certainty, my boy. Speak the truth with the earnestness that you have shown here. The floodgates that have restrained the wrath of our enemy are about to burst upon all of Haven, and I fear that you are quite right ... the waters are even now rising swifter and more dangerously than any have yet to imagine."

The rider saluted the old Arborist and then turned to run towards the annex entrance. He had only gone a few paces when he stopped and turned to ask one last question. "If it is true, and war is about to break upon us all, do we even stand a chance? I have never seen magic like that before; the fire consumed the courage and will of brave men, seasoned guardsmen. It was as if its very flames were somehow *fueled* by our waning resolve."

"Well then, we must pray that the heart of Haven is not as easily consumed as its guardsmen if we hope to endure the crashing tides of war," Engelmann told him.

The young rider nodded his head, but the look on his face made it plain that he held no such hope for the heart of Haven. He turned back to carry out his duty and deliver the message from his captain.

"Son," Engelmann called him again.

The rider stopped and looked back.

"Haven is not merely these walls, nor that sigil on your breast. It's not even that ... that dying tree there atop Mount Aureole," Engelmann said as he wiped a deep-blue teardrop from his leaf-green eyes. "This whole damned city of ours could be razed to the ground, and yet the spirit of Haven would not be wholly quelled."

"Then why defend it, Arborist?" the rider asked. "Why fight and bleed and die?"

"*We* are Haven, my boy. And the very essence of what our city of light was born to be is ingrained in our nature. If we find the courage, we will do what we were always meant to do," Engelmann said as his bark-covered lip curled into a knowing smile. "We will shine, defiantly and proudly—or perhaps in the end only relentlessly and imperceptibly—but nevertheless, we will shine."

The rider looked to his soiled boots and took a deep, steadying breath before nodding his understanding. "That is what we will defend then ... the chance to challenge the darkness."

Engelmann watched the guardsman disappear into the large, iron doors of the Chancellor's annex. He steeled himself with a deep breath, knowing now just what it was that he would indeed have to do.

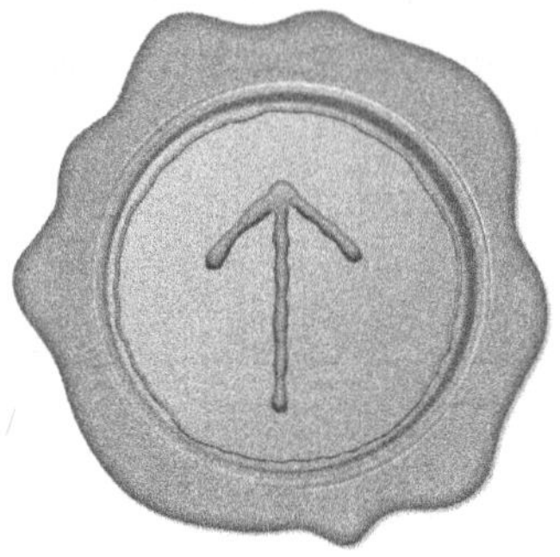

Chapter Eleven

THE OLD ARBORIST PURPOSEFULLY WOUND his way through the intricate roadways of the Capital. With great haste he moved past the libraries and residences, each step taking him higher and higher up the Capital mount, past bronzed statues and ornate fountains until he reached the great garden of the burning tree at the very end of the road.

"Did you feel it too?" Engelmann called to the lone figure standing there, staring fixated on the last branch of the sacred tree. "Did you feel that-"

"Tremor in the roots of my soul?" Elmer said before his elder brother could finish his words.

"Yes," Engelmann confirmed quietly.

"I felt it, Engelmann. I felt it in such a way as one would feel hot soup in one's belly, radiating its savory warmth ... only, this feeling ... this kind of feeling was in reverse." Elmer tried to explain. "Something just ... let go, I think. Something has gone cold."

"Yes .... yes, that is about the best way I could have tried to explain it," Engelmann said reassuringly to the young, green Arborist. A calming grin parted his mossy, bearded lips, appearing in contrast to the gravity of the moment. "Like the opposite of soup."

"Do you know what it means?" Elmer asked.

"I think it means that the end is near. That the power and the light of the great tree is leaving Aiénor, and perhaps, with it, our connection to its mysterious strength."

"What will become of us, of our kind? What good is an Arborist without a tree to tend to?" Elmer said, shaking his leafy-haired head.

Engelmann sat down on a rock there in the garden and drew out his slender, green pipe from within the folds of his ancient robe. He flicked his fingers and lit the bowl, drawing the fragrant smoke in deep and exhaling his worried burley breath.

"Engelmann?" Elmer prodded, unsure just how deep in thought his elder brother was. "What does it *mean* for us? What place in this world will we have when our life's work has passed into the shadows of night?"

"Ah!" Engelmann exclaimed. "There it is, my dear brother."

"There what is?" Elmer asked, clearly missing the meaning of this revelatory outburst.

"The real question," Engelmann replied. "For what was, or rather, what really *is* our life's work? Huh? This great burning tree existed long before our kind was brought to the bright shores of Aiénor, and if truth be told, it has always lived and thrived without the help of our kind."

"What are you saying, brother?" Elmer scoffed, slightly offended at the implication being tossed about here in this so holy of places.

"I am saying precisely what you fear I am saying," Engelmann blurted out amidst a plume of sweet-smelling smoke. "Tell me, have you ever cared for the amber flames, or stoked the silver fire? Have you, or I, or *any* of our brothers for that matter, by any magic we might possess or by any authority we hold, have we changed or altered the course of power that flows through these sacred roots? Huh?"

Engelmann starred at his young brother, pipe in mouth and mossy eyebrows raised in playful expectation for whatever answer was to be given.

"Well," Elmer said tentatively as he stole a glance back over his shoulder to the lone, burning branch, "well, no, I suppose not."

"And have any of us, by prayers or practice, rite or ritual ... have we ever for one moment succeeded in altering the course of this great tree's failure?" Engelmann pressed on.

Elmer's eyes had taken on a pleading quality to the look of them, as if he were asking Engelmann to stop taking his heart to the eventual conclusion that he already knew it would find. It was clear that he both feared this line of thought and knew that truth lived somewhere amidst the world-crushing words. "*No*," he answered gravely.

"Ha! Precisely!" Engelmann agreed, standing from his seat upon the rock. "This great tree has truly *never* been subject to the plotting of old, green-haired fools, nor to the worries of flint-wielding Priests! So then, tell me, brother, what have we really been charged with caring for?"

Elmer stood there humbly in the great garden of the burning tree, dumbfounded at the irreverent possibilities that Engelmann's questions gave birth to in his mind.

"The prophecy has always told us that this illuminated gift would not last forever, that the tree would indeed one day fail by the very hand of the One who gave it to Aiénor to begin with," Engelmann kindly told his younger brother. "Our role was never to prolong its failing, nor to sway the intention of the THREE who is SEVEN. No. Our task has always been to point the hearts of man towards the Maker of light. To inspire them to seek His light from a source that does not fail, rather than just to live in the mortal influence of His burning branches."

Elmer peered at Engelmann, shocked at this revelation from his elder brother. "You are saying there is no purpose to our service to the tree, then? Is that what you are saying? And why are you just now deciding to let me in on this ... this ... *notion*? There has not been one moment in all these years that I have not believed my duty was to the tree!"

"Calm your leafy beard, Elmer. We all have believed that at one time, I think. But time has a way of shifting our self-perceptions, does it not? Perhaps it is a paradox of sorts that we find ourselves in—our assignment started out so clear, and yet now it seems that maybe we were destined to fail all along. Or ... perhaps our great intentions and our established authority were always meant for an assignment that we can only now truly understand in the passing of the former."

Elmer's eyes fell towards the manicured carpet of lush, green grasses, for the weight of realization weighed heavy there in the amber-colored air.

"So you see, Elmer, our power and magic will now have a greater purpose and a more costly urgency than our kind has ever known before," Engelmann continued. "For we will plant the seedlings of hope in the soil of the hearts of these frightened people, or at least we will try. And we will tend to the saplings of their fragile, green faith as they endure these dark and deadly times."

"I feel ... I feel so foolish, Engelmann," Elmer said, his face wrinkled in a disappointed scowl.

"Well, we are all a little foolish, brother, so pay you no mind to those accusations." He chuckled as the fog that clung so stubbornly to the mind of his friend began to lift from his solemn mood. "What will be more foolish in the end, huh? For an Arborist to believe his task was merely to tend to the tree, and then to discover it was something else entirely? Or for a whole world of men to abandon hope that a new light will ever come, simply because they have already learned to make their homes amongst the darkness?"

Elmer's eyes locked with Engelmann's, and a calm sense of acceptance overtook his young face. "You are right. It was the *new* light that has been promised all along. We cannot let them forget that."

"And that is precisely why we must remind them while the light still holds some attraction to them, brother."

"How much longer do you feel it will last?" Elmer asked him.

"Not much, my friend, not much longer at all," the elder brother said in a sad, singsong sort of lilt. The two Arborists stood there in the quiet of the moment, heavy with the tension of all the possibilities, hoping for courage enough to sway their own hearts—let alone all of Haven's—towards the foretold hope.

"What do you suggest we do first?" Elmer asked him.

Engelmann thought about it for a moment as the smoke from his pipe accentuated his scheming thoughts. Finally, a wry smile broke out across his leathery face. "While there is still light enough to leverage our office, I say we find a way to get arrested."

"Arrested?" Elmer replied, flabbergasted at the notion. "What good is it going to do for Haven if all those who point to the coming dawn find ourselves locked behind irons and hidden deep within a prison hold?"

"A siege is already set against our city. When the light of our great tree finally fails us— as you and I both know that it will here very soon—I do not trust our defenses, however brave our guardsmen are, nor do I have any confidence in the wisdom or strategy of that damned fool of a Priest King."

"I still do not understand, brother," Elmer said, earnestly doing his best to make sense of it all. "What good will be done there in the prison holds?"

"Our greatest strength will come from man's ability to hope ... or at least that is what I have been told." Engelmann's eyes glazed over, as if he were reliving the vision of storm and words all over again. "And perhaps my final audience for this message waits for me there behind those stone walls on the other side of the river Abonris. Besides, Michael is in there and I ... well, I will not leave him to despair alone."

Elmer's eyes lit up with understanding as he nodded his green-bearded head in agreement. "What would you have me do, brother? Would you have me arrested with you?"

Engelmann thought on it for the briefest of moments. "Perhaps not—I have another assignment for you. But first, come with me. I have something I must show you."

The two Arborists entered through the iron gate of the mother willow, descending the winding stairs with great haste. They both knew that time was all the more now of the essence, and squandering it was not a luxury either of them wished to indulge.

Engelmann spoke hurriedly over his shoulder as he led his younger brother past the line of wooden busts, in between the rows of book-laden shelves, and through the spindled root columns. "If all else fails, and my inklings are indeed right, when the city falls ... you must find a way *out*. You must gather what remnant remains and find a way out of the city."

"What? Where would we go? There is nothing beyond the city but darkness!" Elmer argued.

"The darkness is coming *here*. But darkness can be overcome. It is the foul corruption of darkness, the *un-light* of our enemy that we must flee from," Engelmann continued, undeterred by Elmer's reasonings.

"But what if the gates are shut? What if the evil that assails us is already upon us?" Elmer asked worriedly.

"Then you must bring them here," Engelmann replied.

"Here? Here, into the great hall? Our home?" Elmer could not begin to fathom a public contamination of these hallowed chambers. "But this place is sacred!"

"It may very well be the sacredness of this great hall of ours that will provide an escape after all other paths have been closed," Engelmann said as he stopped and stood before a large portion of the jagged, granite wall.

"I am not quite sure what it is that you mean by those words," Elmer replied, a bit exasperated and slightly out of breath from trying to keep up with his excited elder brother. "Why have you brought me here, to the depths of our hall? More riddles? Our time is short, Engelmann."

Engelmann ceased his stride and turned to face the younger Arborist. "Then let me be clear. While there is still strength in these rooted columns, we may yet call upon it. If the time is right, if we deem the sacrifice worthy ... we might ask the THREE who is SEVEN to make a way through this holy mountain, and trust that He *will hear* the intention of our words for the sake of His remnant." Engelmann spoke with a fervent intensity as he held tightly to the robed shoulders of his friend.

Elmer looked past the mossy-bearded old Arborist and locked his gaze upon the enormous, glowing roots of the burning tree. "Why? Why would He do that for us, and yet not answer the prayers of the Priest King, or the Chancellor, or the whole maddened, desperate city of ours? Why would He desecrate this ancient and hallowed hall if *I* ask Him to, but not bring about His light for *them*?"

"We can hope, my friend," Engelmann said with a softer smile, "that He is in fact answering *both* kinds of prayers, only not in the way that any of us would have suspected. But we can be sure that the remnant must survive, that it *will* endure. We can be sure, because we have been told." Engelmann leaned closely to Elmer, a passionate fervor sparking in his eyes. "You must ask Him for this desecration, my younger brother. For it is your duty ... and it may be that by this sacrilegious act, *He* will honor the heart of the sacrifice."

Elmer thought about it for a moment. The gravity of this notion, that the God of Aiénor would indeed heed *his* words, was a bit undoing to the young Arborist.

"But which way should we go? I mean, if I actually manage to bring the remnant here, and if I should know *how* to ask Him, and if He should indeed grant me my request, how then will I know where it would lead us? I mean, where would I take them?" Elmer's words spilled from his green-bearded mouth in rapid succession, his fledgling heart tripping over his tongue.

"North," Engelmann said without hesitation. He strode deliberately to the granite rock and placed but a single finger against the wall. Then, he closed his eyes and breathed deeply, whispering a silent prayer. Elmer watched with rapt attention while the mystical words formed their soundless shapes upon the lips of his elder brother. As the Arborist pressed his long, bark-covered finger to the rock, it began to glow underneath his touch. His hand moved slowly along the rock, leaving a trail of light as a large arrow was revealed, or rather was drawn, onto the hallowed, black mountainside. "You will take them north ... here ... if the THREE who is SEVEN wills it." Engelmann spoke with words ancient and deep in timbre, words that were not meant to be questioned or clarified.

"North, then," Elmer said in muted astonishment, for the magic held within this old spruce of an Arborist was indeed greater than he had ever known it to be.

Engelmann closed his eyes and in a whispered breath of a prayer he spoke the ancient prophecy over this northward marking. *"Though the tree may fail you, and though fear may assail you, I will place My light in the hearts of those who hope."* He opened his eyes and looked at his brother. With a true sense of finality he said, "May it be so."

The moment the words left his lips, the illuminated arrow faded to an almost imperceptible marking upon the black granite backdrop of the great hall. The two of them stared at it in silence for a moment, marking the experience deeply into the foreground of their memories, lest the onslaught that was to come tried to make them forget it.

"See to it that provisions enough might be had for the journey ahead, my friend, and tell no one - neither Priest King nor councilmen. The survival of Haven might very well be tangled up in these last deeds of our strength."

Elmer nodded his head in understanding, and Engelmann smiled a reassuring smile. "Very well, then," the old Arborist said as he turned and strode deliberately back towards the iron stairs.

"Wait!" Elmer shouted out. "Are you leaving now? To get thrown into the prison holds, I mean?"

"Soon enough, but first I need to see the lady Margarid and tell her of what I told you," Engelmann said without so much as looking back to see his younger brother.

97

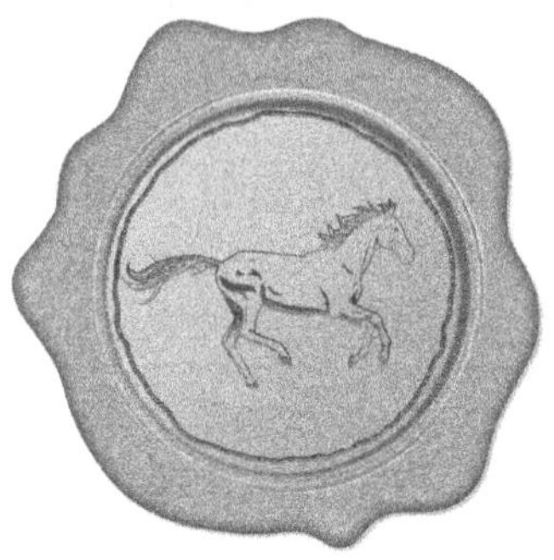

Chapter Twelve

THE TOWER WOKE WITH THE creaking, grinding sound of the ancient hinges as they screeched in protest to this unexpected rescue. Cal held the tarnished blade of a diminished warrior, though to all there in that prison hold, Gwarwyn sparkled anew with the light of a hidden and powerful strength.

"Did you see that, Deryn?" Cal whispered excitedly. "The branches of its hilt, they sprouted more violet leaves!"

"They what?" Wielund asked disbelievingly. "Again? But-" His words caught short in his mouth as he, too, saw the new blooms there upon the hilt of the relic.

"So it has, Bright Fame." Deryn's words were reverent, laced with pride. "So it has, indeed."

Astyræ's eyes glittered in a wash of torchlight as the light of the sword faded before them, flecks of amber afloat on a violet sea. She was less afraid here, so near to the flame that the young smithy held. "Thank you. Though I am not certain that I have earned my freedom, I am grateful for your kindness," Astyræ said to them all.

"My lady Astyræ," Deryn said as he bowed his head in a gesture of respectful friendship. "You are now free, and freedom will always afford you the choice to prove yourself worthy of the liberty."

She considered his words with a sincere smile, her red lips upturned in a warmth of wonder. "You speak with wisdom, good Sprite, and I would expect nothing less. I always believed that your kind still existed, though I never dared enough to hope that I would be honored with the presence of another offspring of the violet trees."

"Another?" Deryn said, eyes narrowing slightly in curiosity.

Astyræ lowered her gaze as a sudden and unexpected wash of sadness befell her beautiful face. "Perhaps things would have turned out differently for all of us, if ... if we would have dared enough to hope for the Sprites to come again," she lamented aloud.

"Now then," Cal said kindly as he came to her, "don't you begin to punish yourself for such things. All of Aiénor has forgotten that Sprites ever existed at all. They are nothing but fairy tales to my people; that is, when we have the heart to even tell them."

"My people never forgot," she said, meeting his gaze. Astyræ's mouth went dry with fear as a cold gust of wind blew through the ancient prison tower, howling ominously through the tension of the moment. She opened her mouth to speak again, and then stopped before the words could form on her lips.

"Go on, then," Cal urged.

Deryn's gaze was locked upon the violet-eyed woman, for something deep within his little Sprite chest prickled with a kinship to a deeper magic, and he did not wholly trust the silence of her story.

"Are you saying that you have *known* another Sprite? That you and your people have met one?" Cal asked.

"That is impossible, my friend," Deryn said matter-of-factly. "The Jacarandas were destroyed long before this young woman took her first breath ... and the only Sprites who survived the rape of the trees of beauty live in Islwyn alone."

She looked sadly into the glowing, azure eyes of the tiny Sprite guardian. "He is right."

"Then ..." Cal stumbled over his words, not understanding what she was not saying. "I ... I mean, how does ... how would you have-"

"I would rather not say!" she bristled, cutting him off before he could form the question. "I barely know you, and though I am truly grateful for your aid, I am not sure I am ready to bare my ill-fated soul just yet!"

"Oh, of course!" Cal said earnestly. "I am sorry, my lady."

His polite words disarmed her, and she let out an exhausted sigh before she spoke again. "It is just ... another story for another time, groomsman," she said apologetically.

Cal nodded to her, but his eyes caught hers again and exposed his disappointment.

"Not all mysteries need be revealed at introduction," Deryn said, soothing the woundedness of the moment. "For friendships are but a lifetime of discovery, if we grant them the permission to be so."

"Thank you, dear Sprite," Astyræ said. She looked back to Cal, seeking his understanding.

"Of course," Cal said with a warm smile. He gestured towards the stairs. "Come on then, let us be done with this dreadful tower."

"But wait!" Wielund chimed in. "We can't just leave here with nothing to report, can we? What of the scouting mission?"

Astyræ's multi-colored eyes narrowed in curiosity at Wielund's comment. "Scouting mission?" she asked him playfully. "Just what *are* the three of you hoping to discover here in the dark wilderness of the Wreath? Huh? And for that matter, where do you come from? There cannot be anyone left wandering—let alone *scouting*—on this side of Aiénor who has not felt the wrath of Nogcwren and her army of Nocturnals."

Wielund looked to Cal, unsure of what he should share with this woman who had been taken captive for reasons that were still unknown to them.

"We ... we came searching for a new light from across the Dark Sea," Cal said cautiously.

Her eyes widened with understanding as to why they had been so fascinated with the etchings on the prison walls. "You seek the same magic as the tree men?" she asked excitedly, her gaze shifting between each of them.

"No! Well, our ... our governor just sent us to ... uh, to *scout* this wilderness," Wielund stammered, a bit caught off guard by her question. "Look, all I know is about metal! I forge axes to fell timber and swords to defend our city. I don't know about missing kings or sorceresses, and I certainly don't know about magic-" he paused mid-sentence, his eyes catching the blue-winged Sprite who appeared at that moment to be the very embodiment of magic itself.

"Yes, my lady," Cal said confidently, ignoring Wielund's ramblings. "The same magic indeed."

Wielund turned his head in confusion at the groomsman's words. "Cal? Wait—what are you saying? Are you saying the colony is searching for Illium?"

"No, I am most certainly *not* saying that," Cal said with an amused smile. "Seig and Tahd—and even the Priest King himself—are not looking for Illium any more than they are looking for the true fulfillment of the prophecy of old. No, they seek nothing more than timber enough to light the world in the only way that they know how."

"Then ... then what do you mean, groomsman?" Wielund said still bewildered. "You speak of magic, you search for Illium, and you befriend fairies!"

"*Fairies*!" Deryn protested angrily. "Do not presume to confuse me or my people for some dainty little pixies!" He drew his tiny blue blade and held its deadly point at the throat of the smithy.

Wielund, unaware of his offense, looked nervously to Cal and Astyræ for some form of help.

Cal laughed, shaking his head at the absurdity of the moment before coming to his friend's rescue. "Deryn, he did not mean any harm. I will have very few friends left in this world if you keep drawing your blade on them."

"There are grander things at work in the world, smithy, than timber and governors. There are older and more dangerous things than mere blades and bows," Deryn scolded as he sheathed his tiny sword. "My people have suffered and bled for the betterment of your kind, and we do not deserve to be lumped into the likes of the make-believe."

"Forgive me then, master Sprite," Wielund said apologetically as he rubbed the sore, red spot on his neck. "All of this is just a bit much for me to take in. When I was asked to sail with the colony, I thought I would be bending blades and forging shoes for the horses, not scouting the wilderness or freeing prisoners or meeting fair- I mean ... I mean ... Sprites."

Deryn just stared at him, hovering as he listened to the awkward apology. His azure eyes cooled in light of the smithy's ignorance.

"Come on, you two," Cal said, breaking the tension of the offense. "Let us be done with this place, alright?"

"I agree." Wielund's voice cracked as he replied. "I'll go first."

Wielund began the slow and treacherous journey back down the rickety, rotting stairs. Cal looked around the room once more, reveling in the possibilities that this discovery could lead to. He could still barely believe that Illium's men—and maybe even Illium himself—had been held in this tower and had carved these very words that surrounded them.

"Cal, is it? Is that what they call you?" Astyræ said timidly.

"Calarmindon, Bright Fame!" Deryn interjected, bowing towards Cal in a display of honor.

She raised her eyebrows in surprise at the formality of the Sprite. "Oh, well I am sorry, master Sprite," she replied. "Such a noble title for a young groomsman! There must then be something more to him than I am yet aware of." She glanced back to Cal again, and the playfulness of her words caused a warmth to spread across his bearded face.

"You may call me Cal, lady Astyræ," he said with a charming grin.

"Very well then." She returned his smile and then looked towards the littered stone floor. "Cal, I would like to show you something else."

"Oh?" Cal said.

"There is yet another word that I have found written upon the forgotten walls of this damned place. I think ... I think I must show it to you." Astyræ walked back inside her prison cell with a sense of significance that the others did not miss. There, on the small sill of the narrow window, she smoothed her hand over something hidden, brushing away the dust of the old tower before she motioned for Cal to come and see it for himself.

Cal and Deryn looked at each other and, without a word, agreed to follow Astyræ's lead. They came through the open door of the iron prison, and as they made their way to where she stood, Cal let his rough fingers run along this newly discovered marvel, tracing the etched lines of Illium's sigil once again.

"What have you found, my lady?" Cal asked her.

Astyræ pointed with her slender hand, welcoming him to see with his own eyes.

"*Shaimira?*" Cal said aloud as his features lit up with wonder. "Do you know what this is? Do you know what this means?"

She shook her head slowly, and a look of disappointment washed over her face. "I ... I was hoping that *you* might, Cal. Neither my father nor his father before him even knew that this marking existed, but in the week of days that I have spent in this iron prison I have pondered it almost without ceasing."

Deryn flew in closer, landing lightly upon the crumbling masonry. As he did, the blue glow of his brilliant wings illuminated a most curious marking. There, slightly removed and just above the "i" of the mysterious word, where its eye should have been, a crude yet deliberate point had been made instead.

"Is that what I think it is?" Cal asked his friend. He ran his finger along the sharp tip of the carved point, and as he did some of the stone began to crack and rub away, revealing something rather intriguing to all who might see it.

Carved upon the stone, above the word, *Shaimira*, was an arrow.

The three of them stood in silence for a moment as they considered this newly discovered marking. Finally the groomsman spoke. "Which way is this window pointing?"

"North," Astyræ and Deryn said in surprised unison.

"Do you ... do you know what it means then?" Astyræ asked him again, slightly more hopeful now that he had discovered this new and hidden marking.

"I don't know what *Shaimira* means, my lady. But something tells me that the tree men are pointing the way for us to find out," Cal told her.

"Us?" she asked him, her face clouded in an unreadable curiosity.

"I-" Cal tried to say, but the sound of the smithy stole the words from his lips.

"Alright!" Wielund shouted from the bottom of the prison tower. "I made it down safe enough. Who is coming next?"

She held his gaze for a moment, her mind caught up in the mystery of the discovery and the potential invitation to seek its resolution.

"You go first, Astyræ," Cal offered. "I am sure by now that you have seen your fill of these rotting walls."

Her attention returned to the prison tower, and then to the thick darkness that shrouded the stairs below. Fear colored her beautiful face as she spoke. "But how will I see? I have no torch, and no magic of the tree men like you." Her voice grew panicked and strained at the thought of traversing the stairs alone in the darkness. "Will ... will you come with me? Please? I can't do it alone."

Cal's heart was a mix of confusion and compassion. *This woman is a contradiction of fright and fearlessness, wonder and angst. How can both be housed behind the same violet eyes and beneath the same crimson lips?*

"I will go with you, lady Astyræ," Deryn volunteered. "For it is not my presence alone that gives sight to the torchless one, and he is not so afraid of the darkened places as you. Come. I will light the way to your freedom from this place."

Astyræ nodded in grateful agreement. "Thank you, master Sprite," she said meekly.

The azure light of his wings set the rotted, winding stairs of the prison tower awash in a glow of protection, both for the safety of her steps and for the unrest in her heart. Cal watched as his companion escorted this mysterious woman down the treacherous steps to the ground floor of the forgotten bastion.

"*Shaimira,*" he whispered into the empty iron chamber. "Is this where you are leading me? Is this what you want?" Cal waited and listened, hoping for the familiar yet terrifying screech of an Owele to break the inky silence of his thoughts, desperate for direction. But all that he heard was the stillness of his heart, and the creaks and groans of the protesting stairs.

"Cal!" he heard Wielund shouting again. "Alright then, come on now, groomsman!"

He looked around once more, breathed deep in the moment, and then began his descent. "I am coming!" he shouted to his friends below.

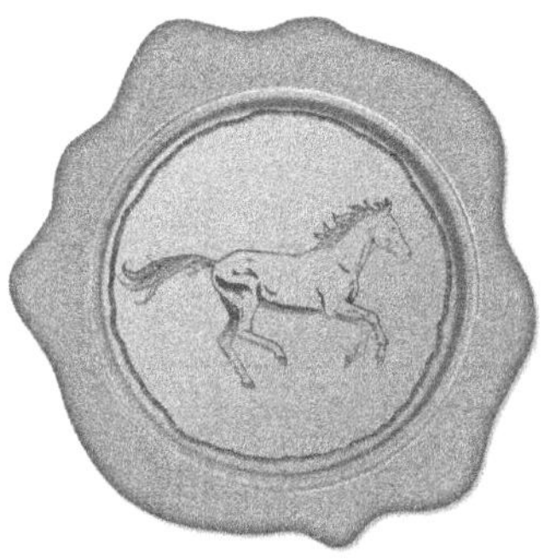

Chapter Thirteen

"WELL?" WIELUND ASKED THEM ONCE they had all reached the bottom of the tower. "What are we going to do now?"

"What do you mean?" Cal asked.

"Are we going to take her back to the stronghold? Back to Governor Seig? Or are we now supposed to go chasing after the tree men?" Wielund looked confused, not sure just what Cal expected him to be a part of.

"Wielund!" Cal said with a good-hearted laugh. "She is not ours to *take* anywhere that she doesn't wish to go. Why would we free her from one prison only to chain her to one of our will?"

"That is not what I meant," the smithy apologized. "I only meant about the darkness, and ..." his voice trailed off, as he was unsure whether he should speak his concern aloud.

"And there is the matter of why I was in a prison hold to begin with," Astyræ finished his nervous thought for him.

Wielund nodded his head in embarrassed agreement. "Well ... well, yes."

"Ah ... I see. Well, you are no prisoner of ours, my lady, regardless of why you found yourself chained in irons," Cal said diplomatically, his response punctuated with a pointed look at Wielund.

Astyræ smiled with a grace that reminded Cal of the barmaid of Piney Creek, and for a brief moment he felt a pang of homesickness there in his empty stomach.

"Do not trouble yourself too much, Wielund," Astyræ said playfully. "I am only slightly dangerous."

"Dangerous or not, are you able to find your way back home?" Cal asked her. "You said you came from a place called Dardanos. Do your people still live there?"

"Nothing *lives* there any more, groomsman," she said ominously.

"Then who was it that put you in that tower?" Cal pressed. "Who taught you of the tree men? Can you at least tell us where you are from? Where is this Dardanos?" His voice hinted of confusion and a bit of mistrust.

"You ask so many questions, don't you groomsman?" she bristled with the prickliness of self-defense. "And I am not so sure I am ready to trust you with all of their answers just yet."

"Fair enough, my lady," Cal said apologetically. "Fair enough."

She looked into his eyes and calculated in a single stare the measure of his goodness. Again she trusted him, for his kindness and his courage compelled her. "I am from south of here," she said finally as she gestured towards the city of her home. The band of rescuers turned their heads, following the direction of her pointed finger, but they could not see much at all through the darkened thickness of the forest. "In the cleft of the Itzal Valley; Dardanos is ... *was* ... my home," she told them, sadness coloring her words.

"Are they all dead?" Wielund asked.

"But ... but I thought you said ..." Cal began, but trailed off when Astyræ's gaze looked away from him sharply, her attention now focused on something in the thick of the shadows. Behind them, Cal heard Farran snort heavily, agitated by something there in the forest. The large chestnut joined in the restless protest, stamping the ground and straining at her hitching.

"Their eyes ... " Astyræ muttered absent-mindedly

"What in the damnable dark?" Wielund said.

"Cal?" Deryn whispered in his ear. "There is a dark evil that has emerged here. We must leave now."

"The Sprite speaks the truth," Astyræ whispered, her eyes still locked on the forest.

"Do you see the green lights?" Wielund said as he peered closer. 'Tiny little specks of green … there must be hundreds of little glowing lights."

"Cal?" Astyræ whimpered.

Deryn's wings grew brighter, summoning the whole of his small albeit fearsome power for what he knew could become a deadly fight. "Cal, we must leave now," he demanded.

Cal nodded his understanding and reached for Astyræ's hand, pulling the frightened young woman closer towards him and the horses.

"What in the name of the THREE who is SEVEN are those lights?" Wielund exclaimed. The smithy then turned to see the terrified look on Astyræ's face. Her soft, pale coloring had turned a sickly, ashen color there in the light of his torch, and a sense of dread had overtaken her features.

"They are not lights," Astyræ said quietly. "They are eyes."

The four of them began to retreat back to the bank of the forest pool. Slowly and deliberately they moved towards their mounts while the hundreds of pairs of tiny green eyes stared back at them, menacing and unblinking.

Cal unsheathed Gwarwyn, preparing himself for whatever new monsters these were that lived here in this cathedral of ancient trees. The rusted blade of the dragon slayer caught the light of Wielund's torch, and as it did the violet gems and silver leaves that had begun to reappear on the hilt of the fabled sword woke to life. The sword reflected the torch's fire into the trees ahead of them, and in an instant a cacophony of sickening caws and rustling branches erupted from amidst the enormous pines.

"Ravens!" Cal shouted to his friends.

"*Her* ravens," Astyræ whispered in a hopelessly frightened voice.

Cal held his sword high, ready to do his worst, the blade alive with the light of both the torch's reflection and the unknown power within. Suddenly, a violent mass of swirling aggravation shot toward the darkened sky, cutting through limbs and branches as the host of green-eyed birds fled in an explosion of angry protests and dark feathers. Cal met the frightened eyes of Astyræ, searching her panicked face for some sort of understanding.

"They did not attack, why did they not attack us?" he asked her, confused by the turn of events.

"I do not know, Cal," she said after a deep, self-steadying breath.

"Well, I for one do not want to wait around for them to regain their courage," Wielund said as he put his foot atop the stones that guarded the bank of the pool.

"The smithy is right," Astyræ said. "You must go ... go before her nocturnal servants return in force."

Cal looked out into the massive wilderness that lay before them. The only visible lights were Wielund's torch and Deryn's wings. Concern colored his face, though not for his own safety. "But what of you, my lady? Will you go back to your people? And if so, how will you see enough to find your way?"

"I do not think they will have me back, groomsman," she replied.

"Well then, she should come with us," Wielund said, obviously in a hurry to be back behind the safety of the colony's stronghold. "I am sure the governor will have many questions he would like to ask her."

Cal studied her face, asking questions without uttering a single word. He did not wholly like this idea, but something instinctual did not want to leave this beautiful, violet-eyed woman to fend for herself in the green-eyed darkness all alone.

"Alright then," she said as she nodded to them.

"Cal, I fear we *must* leave now, and with great haste," Deryn said as he flew back to them, sword ablaze in a wash of protective blue.

The three of them, Cal, Wielund, and Astyræ, climbed over the rocky outcropping and back down again to the other side of the pool. By the time they had reached their horses, the nerves of the large chestnut had become agitated beyond Wielund's ability to manage. Her eyes were wild, her nostrils flared, and a foam of sweat appeared at the edge of her saddle.

"There is no way she is going to let me ride her!" Wielund pleaded. "She has gone mad!"

"She is not mad, smithy," Cal said, a bit annoyed at the Ignorance of his friend. He grabbed the chestnut's reigns and tried to sooth her fears. "She is just frightened."

Farran's ears shot straight to attention, and Cal sensed the alert nervousness of the well-muscled courser. The large chestnut neighed and snorted as she pulled at her ties, blatantly frightened and ready to run as fast as her legs would carry her. The dark sky above them began to grow somehow darker, thick with the weight of a black heaviness. As their eyes strained to focus on the strange cloud, they heard the sounds of wings upon the wind. Suddenly, they saw a mass of black bodies and tiny green eyes moving with ravenous intent towards the horses.

The chestnut reared back and snapped the rope that secured her to the tree before her, ready to flee. Cal reached quickly and grabbed at the flailing rope as he struggled and strained against the nervous strength of the terrified chestnut. "Easy girl!" he shouted through the commotion of the moment. "Easy now!"

I am going to need you to listen, to trust me if we are all going to make it out of here in one unbroken piece. Cal spoke the words only in his mind and in just the briefest of moments, but he knew that somehow the horse could feel his thoughts. The mare ceased her rearing all at once, eyeing Cal with a wary gaze, her breath coming in deep heaves of panic and exhaustion.

"Cal!" Deryn shouted to him. "*Now*! We must ride now!"

Cal looked back behind him. The green-eyed birds circled above the massive canopy of pine and oaks, collecting themselves for what he knew would be a violent attack. He had to get them to safety, but there was no way that the smithy would be able to ride the frightened horse.

The birds stared greedily at them with their sickly green eyes as they taunted them with the sound of murderous caws.

"Why are they circling us?" Wielund screamed against the noise.

"Fear!" Astyræ shouted back. "It is always fear that makes the easiest of prey!"

"Astyræ, Wielund! Come now!" Cal said as he gestured for them to mount his own horse, Farran. Cal looked the grey courser in the eyes as a trust-filled understanding, a confident knowing, passed between the two of them. "Quickly!" Cal shouted as the soul-chilling caws of the ravens droned in the dark air of the wilderness. Wielund leapt into the saddle in a hurried, fearful heap, while Cal took the golden-haired Astyræ by the waist and helped her atop his large, swift horse, there behind the wild-eyed smithy.

"Ride!" Cal shouted to them. "Ride now!"

"Cal! I don't know the way back!" Wielund shouted.

"Trust Farran. He knows it well enough," Cal said as he released the iron grey courser and clicked his mouth, signaling his command to run. Farran snorted his response, then took off with great speed back towards the road they had first come by. Just then the cyclone of ravens broke their dizzying pattern and began climbing once again, higher and higher into the black sky above them until even their fierce, green eyes were out of sight.

Cal held tightly to the lead of the large, frightened chestnut. "Come on now, girl! I am going to need you to trust me, we don't have much time!"

The horse's eyes were wide in horror. Cal's mind flooded with the memories of a time long past, and there in the midst of this ravenous assault, with the wild fury of the horse's fearful snorting beside him, the groomsman began to sing. His voice cut through the ugly clamor of the chaos around him like a silver-colored current of cold, rushing water. No words were sung, rather his voice carried the haunting sounds and notes that came from somewhere beyond his own strength.

Deryn, his friend and guardian, had taken a position directly behind the singing groomsman. His tiny, blue sword was drawn in defiant bravery, willing to defend this seeker of the light—with his life, if he must. When Cal's song found the maddened horse's ears, peace began to wash away her maniacal fear. The large beast breathed heavy in the aftermath of such a frenzy, but her eyes had calmed enough for the groomsman to know that she would indeed now listen to his words.

"We must ride now, girl. It is not safe here anymore and if you trust me enough to carry me back, I will reward your confidence well," Cal whispered. He felt the horse agree to the terms, and he moved to the side to mount the saddle of his only means of escape. As he did, the sight he caught from the corner of his eye made his heart sink in defeat. The mass of birds was crashing once again through the canopy of the mighty forest, and this time it did not seem as if they intended to merely instill fear.

"Cal!" Deryn said with a nervous gulp.

The hurling flock of ravens was mere paces from where he stood. Their sickened, angry voices defiled the ears of their prey, cawing in chaotic chorus that there was no time to flee and nowhere to run. All that Cal could do now was to draw his blade alongside his blue-winged protector and hope.

"Deryn!" Cal shouted. "What do we do?" The green-eyed ravens were nearly upon them, and the storm emanating from the multitude of wings raged against their determined faces. The taunting caws of the carrion fowl mocked their perilous outnumbering, and Cal and Deryn braced themselves for a wave of sharp talons and biting beaks.

Suddenly, unexpected and unannounced, the piercing screech of an Owele radiated from somewhere high in the ancient branches of the mighty forest. The sound of the holy bird of prey silenced the murderous mouths of the vile ravens with immediate authority. In an instant, the raven formation broke, and the wave of their assault spiraled out into a chaotic, angered squall of black-feathered protests.

"The Oweles are here with us?" Cal asked in a breathless whisper.

Deryn looked back to his friend, his glow of blue awash with the hues of relief. "Yes, it would seem so, and I, for one, owe them a debt of gratitude."

"Were you worried?" Cal asked him, his chest still rising hard and his hands still shaking with the tremors of adrenaline that pulsed through his veins.

Deryn thought on the question for a moment as an empty silence filled the darkness around them. Finally, he let heart find his tongue again. "Not for me, Bright Fame. Not for me," he said.

"For me, then?" Cal asked playfully, his confidence returning. "You were worried for me, weren't you?"

"For Aiénor," Deryn said gravely. "I was worried for Aiénor, Cal. If you were to have perished, or been carried off on the wings of that ... that abomination ... who then, Calarmindon Bright Fame, would have been left to seek the light before the darkness consumes us all?"

Cal looked back to the tower that loomed oddly out of place here in this ancient, overgrown forest. He thought of Illium the light seeker, the long-forgotten markings, and the beautiful prisoner with the violet eyes. He rubbed his face and pinched the bridge of his nose as a deep awareness of his purpose here on the Wreath filled his thoughts.

"Thank you, Deryn," Cal said with kindness in his dark eyes. "Thank you for your blade, and thank you for your heart. I do not know where I would be without either of them."

Deryn bowed formally. "It is both my assignment and my honor."

"Come on then, let us go see about finding Farran, and hope he still has a rider or two upon his back," Cal said with a wink and wry smile.

Cal mounted the large chestnut without any protest, for she had given him her trust. As they took off in a burst of speed after Wielund and Astyræ, the mare set leaves and dirt clods to flight in the wake of her powerful hooves. Cal rode hard, but the journey was not wearisome for him. It was as if he was made to ride, and as he did, he felt the expressed pleasure of the THREE who is SEVEN with every surefooted stride that this horse took. He did not come across anyone or any light until he reached a small clearing near the edge of the forest. There, sitting with worried eyes and weary expressions, his friends were resting their tired legs and waiting for him.

"Oh!" Wielund exclaimed as he reached down inside his shirt to fish out the flint that hung around his neck. "Thank the THREE who is SEVEN you are alive! I thought you were a goner for certain, and here ... here you are, not even a scratch on you!"

Astyræ gave Cal a smile that would have made him stand against a thousand ravens a thousand times a day for the gift of her happiness as such. She stood, brushing absently at the leaves and twigs that clung to her dress, and moved towards him. "What about the Sprite? Is he ... is he alright?"

"I am indeed, lady Astyræ," Deryn replied, peeking out from inside Cal's cloak. "And I am most grateful for your concern."

"What did they want with you?" Wielund blurted out. The intensity of this day was beyond his capacity to comprehend. "What were they after? I have never seen ravens—nor any beast for that matter—with eyes like that. Something in me says that their presence here cannot be good at all."

"They are *her* ravens," Astyræ said without hesitation.

"Are they after you?" Cal asked her.

"I cannot say one way or the other," Astyræ answered him, but her expression betrayed a knowledge, a saddened story, that she had clearly not yet shared with them.

Cal looked at her and shook his head disapprovingly at her guardedness. "Then what *can* you say, my lady?" His curt words were a mixture of concern and annoyance all at the same time.

Astyræ flinched at his tone of voice and stepped back from him, averting her gaze to the Sprite. Deryn returned her stare, letting out a rather large sigh for such a small figure.

"If you tell me your story, it might just be that I could *help* you," Cal offered.

She scowled and spun around, turning her back to him and giving her attention to Farran, who stood close behind. "I doubt that the Raven Queen is after me, groomsman. She already has *possession* of what she wanted from my family." She gently stroked the mane of the silver courser as she answered. Though her hands were kind and soft, her words were cold and hardened with a pointed hatred and a deep regret.

"What did she take from you?" Cal asked as he put a hand on her shoulder.

"What she touches ... what she takes, will never be good again. Once she has had her way, there is nothing left but darkness." She rested her head lightly on Farran, blinking away tears. "No matter how good they might have once been before." Her whispered sadness hung heavy in the air as the band of explorers quietly weighed her words.

"Did she take some*one*?" Cal said as he finally realized what it was that she was trying not to say.

She turned back to him, her hand on Farran's neck, with an unreadable expression on her face. "*Him*. She took him from me, she took him from all of us. Now he is just as possessed as one of her damned ravens." Her eyes locked on something in the distance as her heart felt the weight of her pain. "Then again ... it was my fault, after all."

"I ... I don't know-" Cal started to press her further, but the heavy hand of his tiny, winged friend stayed his words.

Astyræ wiped a single tear from her soft, pearl cheek and straightened the bodice of her dress, collecting her emotions before they took her over.

"A-*hem*," Wielund interjected as he made a show of clearing his throat. "I don't mean to be crass, but can the two of you continue whatever this is after we are safely behind the walls of the colony? It seems to me that this story is going to take much longer than I feel safe about, and besides, who knows what other frightful creatures are roaming about in this darkness while we stand here just talking?"

"He is right. The Wreath is full of her nocturnal slaves, both men and beasts alike. And I can say for certain that the presence of yourselves and your tree men has not gone unnoticed," Astyræ said, seeming grateful for the change in subject.

"You mean our colony?" Wielund asked. "But-"

"We need to warn the woodcutters," Cal said. "I need to tell Yasen."

"You do *not*!" Wielund said in a condescending tone of voice. "What you need to do is to tell the captain or the governor! Don't you go interrupting the woodcutters with matters meant for the guardsmen. Our city needs this timber, and the woodcutters are the only ones that are going to get it for them."

Cal stared, dumbfounded, at the smithy. Even with all the mysteries and magic that they had encountered this day, he could not seem to understand or grasp the gravity of the moment. "Very well then," Cal agreed, shaking off his frustration with his companions. "Astyræ, will you ride back with us? I can't leave you out here alone with this ... this sorceress and her green-eyed evils lurking about." He looked at her with a sincere softness. "And I would very much like to help you, whether you believe me quite yet or not."

She thought about it for a moment, looking into the thick darkness of the wilderness before them, and then back again to her rescuers. "Very well," Astyræ said as an energy came back into her eyes. "I will go to the stronghold of the tree men, as long as I get to ride with you, groomsman. That smithy friend of yours is absolutely uncouth in the saddle."

Cal let out a goodhearted laugh, one long overdue here in the shadows of the Wreath. "Done and done, my lady! You will ride with me, and I will keep you safe along the journey."

The lot of them rode off through the wilderness, urgency compelling them as they retraced their steps back towards the colony on the shores of the Western Wreath. With all of the excitement and dangers, the new possibilities and strange curiosities, none thought to wonder about the screech of the Owele that had rescued Cal and Deryn from the ravenous horde. But there, perched high in the cathedrals of soldier pines, the violet eyes of a watcher looked on with great anticipation.

Chapter Fourteen

ENGELMANN MADE HIS WAY AS fast as his old, spruce legs would take him. There was a fire burning in his chest now, and it propelled him with great swiftness down the winding, stone streets of the inner Capital, past the courtyard of the Citadel, all the way to the portcullis of the Kings' Gate. The gate warden was still a tree-fearing man, and he did not for one moment question the passage of the mysteriously powerful Arborist upon the Kings' Bridge. And so it was with relatively great ease that Engelmann the hopeful stepped once again onto the humble streets of Westriver.

It was not too difficult to find the lady Margarid. Since the day of Michael's arrest and imprisonment, she had spent much of her time outside the walls of the prison hold, waiting, watching, and praying for his release. Portus had often come with her. Though he was not nearly as brazen in his attempts to convince the guardsmen of Michael's release as she was, he still did not wish for her to wait alone.

"Michael! Michael, can you hear me?" Margarid would shout at the top of her lungs. "Michael, we are here! Michael-"

"You have to be quiet, you have to stop that now," Portus said in a stern whisper as he interrupted her incessant shouting. "They are going to throw you over the barbican if you are not careful!"

"But we cannot just leave him in there alone to wonder if he is forgotten!" she said defiantly as she met the eyes of the large merchant.

"What good is shouting your greetings in the street if the ears of those prison walls have long since fallen deaf?" Portus argued sympathetically. "He cannot hear you, Margarid, and clearly no one else cares to listen either."

"He will hear me ... he will hear me, and he will take heart. I know it sounds mad," she said as her hazel eyes now misted over in the wake of such strained, exhausted emotions. "But I do not care, nor do I plan to stop, Portus."

"How is riling up the already agitated guardsmen going to free him any sooner? What if they mistreat him in there because of your insistence out here?" Portus asked softly, for though he was a strong, tall mountain of a man, his heart was soft and his compassion was great.

"I cannot say, and yet, I cannot bring myself to stop, either," Margarid replied.

The two of them stared in wounded silence at each other, both of them feeling the void of Michael's absence. "What would Engelmann do, I wonder?" Portus asked her.

"I am not so certain. I haven't seen him, nor heard anything from him since Michael was taken," she said.

"Would *he* keep shouting to the prison walls? Or would he just bide his time and wait for an opportunity to free Michael to present itself?" Portus pressed her again.

"Well ... *neither*, I should say. Neither of those ideas makes for a very good plan at all!" Engelmann interrupted their conversation, startling them with the surprise of his presence.

"Engelmann!" Margarid shouted gleefully as she spun around and wrapped her arms around his wispy frame, burying her auburn-colored head in the thickness of his robe.

"There now, my girl," he said sweetly. "It would seem that today has turned out to be a rather fortunate day, after all. For I have something that needs telling, and now I have two sets of ears that might be willing to listen."

"Tell me you have a plan?" she pleaded.

"Have you spoken with the Citadel? What word have you heard from the northern borough? What of the enemy? What of the siege?" Portus let his questions rain down in rapid, breathless succession.

Engelmann nodded to his merchant friend. "I do, and I have. But for the moment let me address the fears of the lady Margarid before I go into the business of wars and rumors of wars."

Portus nodded in submissive agreement. "Alright then."

"I do have a plan. It will require your strength and your trust, and it will beg of you to protect the hopeful and lead them out of the city. When the evil that ravenously besieges us finally comes to roost here within these walls of ours, the only place safe enough for the remnant will be beyond the Northern Gate."

The two of them stared at Engelmann in shocked silence for a moment, for neither had expected this sort of a plan.

"*Out* of the city? Surely you cannot be serious," Portus finally said, mustering the courage to question the one whom they had always turned to for answers. "What death awaits us out there in the darkness?"

Margarid laid a calming hand on Portus' shoulder. She locked eyes with Engelmann, willing to hear the Arborist and his plan. "If it will help Michael, I will leave the city. What would you have us do?" she asked him.

"You must trust Elmer, my younger brother. He has been given a path to follow, and he is willing to aid our remnant to endure this coming tide," Engelmann told her.

"But why him? What do you mean?" Margarid implored him. "Where will *you* be in all of this?"

"Well, my girl, that is where this plan of mine will come into play." The tenderness in his leaf-green eyes conveyed his understanding of her confusion. As she looked at him, she realized that such gentleness given could only mean that she would not want to wholly embrace what was about to be asked of her.

"I am not going to like this plan, am I?" she asked.

"Whether you are affectionate towards it or not is of little consolation to my confidence in your ability to see it on to completion," the old Arborist encouraged.

"Enough with all the riddles and dancing back and forth!" Portus blurted out. "The tree will be dead and dark before we finally get to hear this plan of yours!"

Engelmann smiled a kind yet slightly mischievous smile at the both of them. "When the tree fails, and indeed it will fail very soon, you must gather the remnant and find Elmer ... and do not tarry along the way."

The mossy-bearded Arborist, without warning or further explanation, walked away from his befuddled friends and strode towards the main gate of the prison hold with deliberate haste. In his heart he was sad for the confusion that was sure to assault his young pupils, but he hoped that this next move of his would indeed be the first act of rescue for his friends.

"Engelmann?" Margarid whispered after him. She took one step to follow after him and then instinctively stayed herself. "Engelmann?"

"Citizens of Haven!" Engelmann shouted at the top of his lungs, merely a dozen paces from the guarded gates of the prison. "Citizens of Haven, hear my voice, hear my words!"

Merchants and maidens alike began to stop along the stone street, halting their business and busyness to hear the brave and reckless words of the old Arborist. Guardsmen atop the prison hold began to stiffen and bristle, pointing and motioning towards the shouting on the street.

"There is a dark and deadly enemy camped outside our very walls!" he continued shouting. "Even now the tears of our fellow citizens are silenced by the suffocating evil that rains a fearsome green fire upon our northern brothers! *Death is coming for us*, and our city and its walls will not be able to keep it at bay!"

"What is he doing? Is he mad? Arborist or not, the old fool is going to get himself arrested," Portus whispered in Margarid's ear.

Margarid looked wildly at Portus, knowing that his words were true. Again she moved to go to Engelmann, and again she stopped herself. "Arrested ..." she thought aloud.

"When the great tree fails us and the green lit evil breaks our lines and invades our walls, where then will you place your trust? Where then will you place your hope?" Engelmann continued on, shouting his ominous words without even a hint of reservation.

The gathering crowd began to grow both frightened and angry at his words. "When the tree fails us? Isn't that your responsibility, Arborist?" someone shouted at him. The people began to press in towards him, hurling insults and enraged questions as they fueled one another's anger.

"You have failed, and now you just want to blame the Citadel for your shortcomings!"

The portcullis opened and four tired-looking guardsmen with halberds in hand began their deliberate march toward the ranting Arborist. As the gathering mob around him intensified their offense, the wary guardsmen hastened their pace.

"Will you trust in the *wisdom* of your Priest King, then? Will you hide in bullied silence and follow in his cowardice? Will you wait and hope that the colony sends back the timber of the Wreath? Ha! What good will a Priest King and his coerced fidelity do us when our light has failed and evil has overtaken the city? What good will timber do us if our homes and our freedoms have been reduced to a pile of rock and rubble?"

The crowd gasped in horror at the very thought of what this Arborist dared to proclaim.

"Lies!" came the enraged voice of a Priest. "Blasphemy!"

"Shut your mouth, Arborist!" one of the guardsmen snarled as he tried to push his way between the angry citizens and this brazen fool of a caretaker.

"How do you know these things?" an old woman demanded.

"Open your eyes, woman! The answers are right in front of your blinded face!" Engelmann's retort was pointed enough to enrage the woman, pushing her for the moment past the point of her own fear. She seethed at him silently before she leaned in and spat at him.

"Your fear-mongering doesn't scare me, Arborist!"

"Perhaps it should, my child," he replied with an intensity that settled the woman down.

"Engelmann, shut up!" Portus shouted at him. "What are you *doing*? They are going to-"

"Arrest him!" the sergeant-at-arms ordered his men.

Engelmann turned his gaze and met the disbelieving, hazel eyes of Margarid. "We must hope together! We must not trust in a Priest King or in the dark evil that approaches. We must hope that the promised light will still come for us! The Citadel has no hope! They cower and they compromise and their confidence is foolhardily placed in the strength of their own might."

The guardsmen reached towards Engelmann a bit timidly at first, for he was still an Arborist after all. But as his shouting continued, they grabbed the arms of the traitor and began to drag him towards the gate of the prison hold. Engelmann gave little resistance, but rather chose to put the force of his strength into his final words.

"But *you*, citizens of Haven, you must endure! You must endure,. and you must seek the light!"

"Engelmann, *no*!" Portus shouted. "We have to help him! We have to do something!" he implored his auburn-haired friend.

Margarid took in the scene playing out before her. As she watched the guards drag her teacher away, the disbelieving look in her eyes shifted to one of fresh understanding.

"What about his plan? He never told us his plan!" Portus continued.

"No ... he showed us instead," Margarid said matter-of-factly. "He didn't tell us because we would have stopped him."

Portus stared back at her, clearly not understanding her meaning.

"He wants to be arrested. He is going inside for Michael," she said.

"What?" Portus exclaimed. "Well, that is great for Michael, but what about us? What about the rest of us out here? What in the damnable dark are we supposed to do now?"

The iron bars of the prison's portcullis slammed closed with a deafening boom, and the onlookers stood and stared in drop-jawed amazement at the arrest of Engelmann the Arborist.

"He just told us, Portus. We are to prepare the remnant to escape the city," Margarid replied.

"I don't believe that Engelmann is in his right mind ... he just wants us to run right into the spears of that green-eyed enemy?" Portus argued. "That sounds like a spectacular plan, Mar." The large tanner shook his head in sarcastic displeasure.

"Engelmann said that Elmer will know what to do ... perhaps we should trust him," she retorted. "Of course ... we have to find him first."

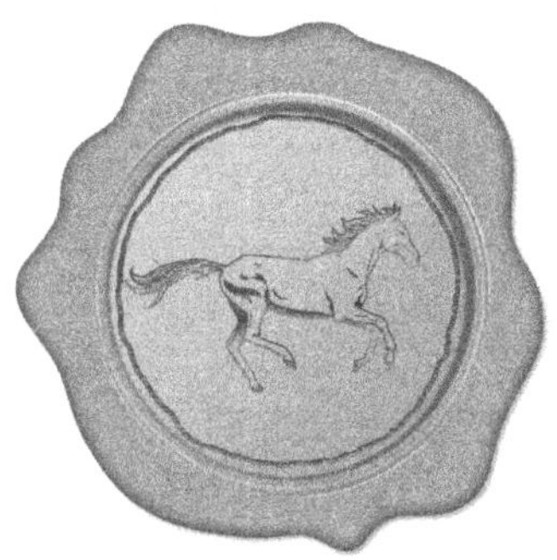

Chapter Fifteen

THE CLOSER CAL CAME TO the edge of the colony's stronghold, the more nervous and unsure he felt about bringing Astyræ into its tense environment. Something inside his heart mistrusted the militant civility of the guardsmen and their governor. Just before they got to the edge of the forest, Cal stopped his small company and took the moment to consider his misgivings.

"What is it now? Why in the damnable dark are we stopped here?" Wielund asked, a bit annoyed to be so close to safety and yet not permitted to enter it.

"I ... I just have this feeling, Wielund," Cal said earnestly. "A feeling that says I need to find Yasen first before I bring her into the stronghold."

"Cal-" Wielund tried to interject.

"Just ... just trust me, smithy," Cal retorted, cutting off his protest before he could even give breath to the words.

Astyræ shifted behind Cal in the saddle. "Well, while you figure out your feelings, groomsman, would you mind if I stretched my legs a bit?" She dismounted Farran, not waiting for his answer, and walked towards the edge of the trees, peering into the darkness towards this colony of the tree men. She swallowed hard, for both curiosity and trepidation threatened to choke her breath all in the same moment.

"Astyræ!" Cal said with warning in his voice. "Don't be foolish. You don't know these men."

She turned and looked at him coyly. "And they do not know me." A glint of yellow flashed in her violet eyes, and Cal felt all the more unsettled. His genuine concern must have shown on his face, for her features softened. "I understand, groomsman," she told him earnestly. "The tree men were friends of my grandfather once, and I am sure ..." her voice trailed off as she heard the booming crash of felled trees colliding with the hardened soil of the Wreath. Astyræ turn her gaze towards the torch light of the colony, and then after a silent moment she found Cal again. "I am sure I will be alright."

"Your grandfather?" Cal prodded, hopeful that he might learn her story.

She nodded silently at him, but offered nothing more.

Deryn hovered next to Cal, taking in the exchange. "If finding the North Wolf is what your heart tells you is prudent, then do not ignore its words, my friend. I'll watch over these two." He drew his blue sword halfway from its scabbard in a convincing display of sincerity.

Cal allowed himself a grin at his trusted friend. "That you will, Deryn!" He dug his heels into Farran and departed the group before any of them had a chance for further protest.

The sounds of the biting rhythm of the woodcutter's axes littered the dark, midday air, while dozens of watch fires cast an amber glow along the western line of the colony's reach. Cal rode alone into the midst of the holy soldiers of the Citadel, observing the hewing and heaving of the Wreaths' timber.

"Hail, master groomsman!" Goran shouted out in mocking heraldry.

"And hail to you, mighty woodcutter," Cal replied with an amused shake of his head.

"Have you returned from your scouting alone?" Goran asked a bit suspiciously, carefully inspecting the attitude and behavior of his young friend. "I pray that nothing ill has befallen that smithy of ours."

"No, nothing ill yet. Though if that chestnut were to have her way, we all might as well get used to the heat of the forge and the heart of the anvil," Cal told him playfully, hoping to defuse the obvious suspicions.

"Ha, ha!" Goran bellowed. "That would be a sad day for those horses of yours indeed, for they might have to get used to wearing wooden shoes then! Huh!"

Cal scanned the line of the fur-clad woodcutters until he spotted their chieftain and his friend. "Thank the THREE who is SEVEN that there is nothing wrong with the smithy other than a few bruises and a sore backside!" With a smile and a laugh, he said goodbye to Goran and rode off to speak with Yasen. Cal approached his friend who was busy laying waste to an enormous, red-barked cedar. "Yasen!" he called softly as he gracefully dismounted the silver horse.

The chief of these woodcutters here on the Western Wreath turned his attention from the task at hand. His dark beard and long, untamed hair were accented in the flickering light of the watch fire nearby, giving him a wild and dangerous quality that was quite fitting for the time and the place. "So, the great scout has returned in one piece from the mighty forests of this mysterious land, now has he?" The North Wolf spoke in playful deference, but his features showed a hint of relief at the safe arrival of his friend, the groomsman.

"Indeed I have, and ... well, I am in need of your wisdom for a moment," Cal said quietly, and the serious tone of his words was not lost on the woodcutter.

The levity that had not mere moments before colored the lone, unpatched eye of this mighty axe man seemed to vanish at the call for private counsel. "Very well, then," Yasen agreed. "Are we talking here, or should I fetch a horse?"

Cal thought about it for a moment and decided it would best if the two of them rode back to Wielund and Astyræ. "No, I think it might be best if you come with me."

Yasen narrowed his gaze, doing his best to listen in between the non-spoken words. "Have you seen Seig yet? Tahd? Do they know that you have come back?"

"No, you are the first I have seen. Well, that is unless you want to count Goran over there," Cal laughed.

"Aye, well then," Yasen said as he wiped his double-bladed axe with a red cloth. "Let's go see what kind of wisdom it is that you are after then, brother."

The two friends mounted their horses and rode back out towards the edge of the watch fires that burned there on the westernmost border of the mighty forest. They did not speak as they rode, for the horses' pace was swift, and Yasen could see that his young friend seemed to not want to make his presence known until he had made it safely back into the cover of the forest. When they had reached the tree line, Cal and Yasen brought their horses to a halt and quickly dismounted. "What is it, brother?" Yasen asked him, clasping his shoulder with a firm hand. "What did you find out there?"

"Trees, mostly," Cal said matter-of-factly. "Leagues upon leagues of them, probably enough to fuel the whole walled city for a decade of time."

"Well, that is plain enough, but you didn't ask me to follow you here just to show me trees, did you now?" Yasen asked.

"No. No, we found an old prison tower," Cal said, then paused for the briefest of moments so as to allow the gravity of his words to come and settle upon the conversation. "A prison tower ... complete with a prisoner," Cal finally revealed.

"Oh?" Yasen said with a depth of intrigue as the implications of the discovery rolled in like a thick fog.

"And ... well, I, ahhh ... I let her free, too," Cal blurted. "And ... I brought her here." Yasen just stood there for a moment as he took in the meaning of these last few words. He looked much like an older brother, merely observing the young, flushed groomsman who stood at his side. "I don't know why exactly, but I do not feel like I should bring her to the stronghold ... and yet I cannot just leave her out here to the dark unknown either, Yasen," Cal continued.

"There is much unspoken still, my friend, of that I am certain. And yet, I can see plain enough for the moment," Yasen said kindly, his eyes lit with the light of understanding. "I think your caution is on the side of wisdom, though I will need you to tell me a bit more about this *prisoner* of yours."

The two of them walked into the trees, beyond the reach of the watch fires. Cal told Yasen of the old tower and of the mysterious woman from Dardanos it once held prisoner. He spoke of the green-eyed raven assault that had almost taken his life, but he chose to not yet tell his friend of Illium and the hidden markings.

"They have green eyes you say? The ravens?" Yasen asked curiously as his mind flooded with the images of the demon bear that had claimed both his horse, Philip, and his eye.

"Aye, the very same," Cal replied. "Astyræ said that they are *her* ravens—the sorceress I mean—and that there are very few who still inhabit the Wreath who are not also servants of this Raven Queen."

"Is that why this pretty prisoner of yours was locked in the tower?" Yasen asked. "Because she does not serve the sorceress?"

Cal thought about it for a moment before he responded. "I do not know why it was that she was imprisoned, but I know that there is no love in her eyes for the likes of Nogcwren."

Yasen and Cal stopped when they came within sight of the large chestnut horse and the two shadowed figures standing nearby. Yasen could see plain enough the glowing magic of her two-toned eyes, resplendent there in the dark cover of the trees. "What in the damnable dark kind of magic is she?" he asked as a nervous sweat began to form upon his brow.

"She ... well ..." Cal had thought long how he would try to explain her magic to his friend, but his words were interrupted before he could even begin.

"How do you know that *she* isn't the sorceress herself?" Yasen huffed with suspicion.

"Yasen?" A worried and confused look washed over the groomsman. "She is not-" Cal tried to settle the chieftain with a steadying hand, but Yasen brushed it away.

"You may be brave, Cal, and you may be a part of some sort of story that I don't fully understand, but beware, brother, that you don't become a fool, or a pawn, or ... or worse."

"I am no sorceress," Astyræ said slowly as she walked towards them. Her eyes flamed with passionate outrage at the accusation, and their violet and yellow hues burned bright in the darkness.

"Cal!" Yasen said as he grabbed the shoulders of his friend and spun him around, forcing Cal to look him in his eye. "We have both seen that kind of yellow before, on the isle! That witch ..."

"Astyræ is not a witch," Cal said firmly, doing his best to bring calm to the storm of unease that had blown in upon the tree line. "But there is some kind of magic in her."

"But the yellow!" Yasen demanded, pointing at her face.

Cal stepped between Yasen and Astyræ with deliberate confidence. "I trust the violet, Yasen, more than I fear the yellow. Regardless, she and her life are still of great value to the THREE who is SEVEN, and you know just as well as any that I could not leave her to rot away in the dark of any tower," Cal said.

Yasen stared at his friend, breathing deeply through his nose so as to calm his concern. There was something about the groomsman's voice and posture, here in this very moment, that reminded Yasen of that night back at the Gnarly Knob, when Cal had first revealed the armor of the Poets and had dared to tell Yasen a piece of his story. He was less a groomsman and more a hero in those moments, and here again his brash confidence was enough to convince the seasoned woodcutter.

"Aye, I do know that," Yasen replied with a smile and a brotherly, albeit gruff, pat on the shoulders. "I'm just protective of you is all."

Cal nodded, then reached towards Astyræ and beckoned her to come closer.

"My lady," Yasen greeted her. "I apologize for my rudeness. My name is-"

"I know who you are, woodcutter," Astyræ interrupted him with a smile. "For good-heartedness often needs no introduction; it wins over trust by its posture alone."

"Well then," Yasen said with a bit of surprise and hint of a laugh to his words. "I see now all the more reason why Cal would not have left you to the irons of a prison."

"Besides, no Sprite would befriend the ill-hearted, and I trust *his* judgment implicitly," she said with a playful smile and a deep humility. The blue-winged sentinel hovered near Astyræ's shoulder, still watching over his charge. He beamed under the radiance of such a compliment and his azure wings woke the dark forest with a gentle glow.

"I have many questions to ask you, my lady," Yasen said politely, "but now is not the hour. Although I wish you a safe place to make your rest this dark night, I do not trust the stronghold of my fellow countrymen to offer you such a sanctuary."

"Well then, where should we put her?" Wielund blurted out.

"She is not ours to *put* anyplace," Cal retorted, a bit annoyed at the lack of hospitality in his friend's tone.

Astyræ smiled appreciatively at the groomsman, then looked away; overcome by his kindness. She was not quite sure what to do with the way in which he so wished to protect her. "Do not worry over me, Calarmindon Bright Fame. I have met enough of the fearful and the ferocious alike, and somehow I have still lived to tell about it. But you and your friend the woodcutter are probably right, and I will heed your warning and stay away from your colony for now. Though ... may I ask that you help me find a safe enough place?" She glanced back at him with her last words, and her face betrayed her fear.

"My lady, there is a small cave not fifty paces in that direction," Yasen said as he pointed north. "Perhaps you might make your rest in the safety of its stone walls until the morning?"

Cal looked at her, his expression communicating his concern without the need for words.

"I'll be alright until morning, groomsman. Perhaps a torch and a bit of something to eat will make my rest all the more ... restful?"

"I do not wish to find you crying over the darkness again when I return, my lady," he said quietly.

She thought for a moment before answering. "If I know you plan to return ... then I won't find the darkness nearly as terrifying as it once was."

Her candid answer warmed his heart, and he knew she meant her words. "Alright then," Cal said in reply. He reached into his pack and dug out his water skin, a few links of dried sausage, and half a loaf of bread. "Stay here until the woodcutters leave the tree line at day's end, then make your way to the cave and wait for me there until morning."

"You are too kind, groomsman," she said with a sweet smile. "I am grateful for such care given on my behalf."

Cal still wore his concern upon his face, and though he knew she would be much safer here, he did not wholly like the idea of leaving this mysteriously beautiful woman all alone. "Perhaps ..." he started as he looked pleadingly into the eyes of his winged guardian. "I mean, would you,

Deryn ... would you stay with her, at least until morning?"

Deryn understood the meaning of his friend's request, and so it was with great reluctance that he flew towards the soft, pearl face of the Wreather woman and kindly spoke. "I cannot stay, my lady. And though you ..." his voice trailed off as he searched his Sprite heart for the right words. "Though I very much wish I could protect you, dear sister, here in the darkness, I have been charged by Iolanthe herself to watch over the groomsman."

"It is quite alright, dear Sprite," she said, slightly embarrassed. "You have already—all of you— shown more than enough hospitality to me."

"Do not mistake our hospitality for complete selflessness, lady Astyræ." Yasen told her. "You could be of great help to us as well, for there is much we do not know about this strange and foreign land, and I would rather you share its secrets freely ... that is, before one of my brothers gives you cause to wish our colony ill will."

"Ill will?" Wielund blurted out. "If it wasn't for Cal and me she would be still crying her eyes out behind those iron walls."

"Wielund!" Cal said, a bit angrily.

"You are right, smithy," she said kindly. "And I do owe my thanks to you three for my liberation."

"You owe us nothing," Cal insisted. "Your secrets are yours to keep for as long as you wish, and not one of us will bother to press them from you." He gave Wielund and Yasen a convincing glare as he spoke the words.

"All the same," she said softly, turning her enchanting eyes back to him. "When you come for me tomorrow, I will tell you what you wish to know."

"Will you tell me who you are? And how your eyes can carry both colors in them?" he asked her.

"I will, Calarmindon Bright Fame. I will tell you my story," she said as she nodded her head reluctantly.

Cal's breath caught a little at the promise. "I will be honored to hear it."

"Very well then," Yasen agreed. "And let us agree that no one here will speak a word of her to any of Selg's men until we have had the proper time to think on all that this might mean."

"Alright then," Wielund submitted sheepishly.

Deryn flew to this mysterious woman who carried in her eyes the traits and traces of both the familiar and the unknown. "Lady Astyræ, though I cannot say whether or not the darkness will be kind to you, I do feel in my bones that our stories are indeed woven together. So take heart this long night, and pray for dawn."

Cal smiled at the scene unfolding before him, and at the protective heart of Deryn. "I will find you come morning, my lady."

Her gaze moved from the blue-winged Sprite to the eyes of the groomsman, and a soft, kind smile spread across her lips.

DING. DING. DING. The sound of the iron bell called the men of the colony back to the stronghold, signaling the end of the work day.

"Come on now, scouting partner," Cal said playfully to Wielund. "The bell is ringing, and we still have a long day left, you and me."

"A *long day*?" Wielund whined.

"Aye, horses to groom and shoes to make," Cal replied as they turned to mount their horses and make their leave.

Yasen stood there for moment, silently staring at this mysterious Wreather woman. His face was wrinkled in contemplative concern and his lone, uncovered eye betrayed his sense of worry.

"What troubles you so, mighty woodcutter?" she asked him sincerely.

Yasen took a deep breath, searching his mind for the words to make sense of and articulate his foggy dread. "It is hard to say exactly, though I cannot help but feel as if something *dark* closes in upon us all."

"Of course you feel it. It is this place, woodcutter," Astyræ said, devoid of emotion. "It is this very land that we stand upon—all of it, from trees to towers, soil and salt—it all serves in subjection to her nocturnal will."

"And *you*?" Yasen asked pointedly. "Are you also a slave?"

She looked to her slender, pearl-colored hands and she picked at her fingernail in nervous contemplation. "Not wholly. And although I am afraid of the darkness, I do not ... I *will not* serve its master."

Yasen stared at her for a long moment. "I owe my life to that groomsman," he finally said, surprising her with the emotion in his voice. "I would not take kindly to anyone who would seek to manipulate his heart for their own gain."

She considered her reply carefully. "He is lucky then. For a true friend is a rare find in these darkened days, and I can see how much you wish to protect his heart," she said, meeting his stare with her own. "I promise you that although I have only known him a short while ... I feel compelled to protect it as well."

"Very well, then," Yasen told her. He turned and mounted his large, black Friesian, whose long mane and lean legs made the woodcutter appear as more a king of the forest than a servant of the axe. "Please do not wander far from safety. You may know this land better than I, but we both know there may well be treacheries still afoot in its shadows." He rode off towards the high palisade walls of the colony's stronghold, leaving her standing in the cover of the trees, watching and waiting for her moment to run to the safety of the cavern.

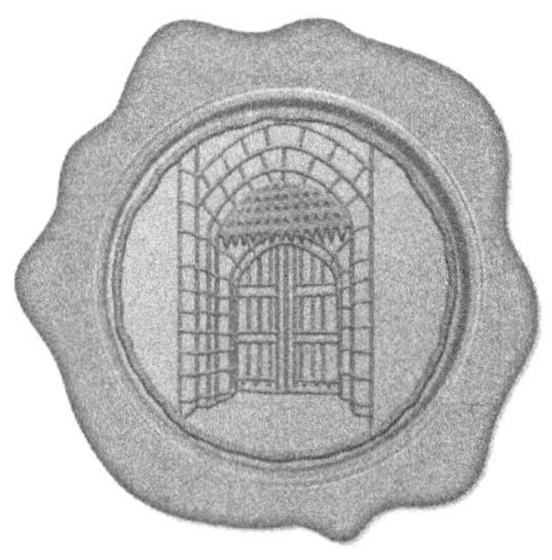

Chapter Sixteen

STEAM ROLLED AND SWIRLED, DANCING upon the heavy cold air as it rose from the two wooden flagons of hot mulled wine. The tense, fearful mood of the guardsmen positioned along the Northern Wall was not abated much by the scent of the drink, though perhaps it gave them a momentary reason to think of something other than their impending deaths. Many of the men had engaged in minor skirmishes throughout their military careers, but none had ever engaged in war. Their experiences were tame and nearly juvenile compared to the coming battle with this great, looming enemy that lay in siege just beyond the dying reaches of the amber light. Every soldier knew that this green-eyed army with its earth-shaking monsters and its mysterious un-light was something to truly fear.

Armas walked the battlements with a deliberate stride, doing his best to look each one of his men in the eye. There was no sense in pretending that he did not feel the suffocating weight of the impending assault just as much as any of them, but with each steeled glance and each silent nod of his helm he conveyed to his men that although he too was afraid, he was still *here*.

And more than that, he silently but deliberately showed them that he was proud of them for being here too.

"There you are," Armas said with a kind, concerned smile to the curly-haired barmaid turned watchman.

Keily peeled her eyes away from the green-lit shadows that she had so intently been observing for the last handful of hours. She turned to see her friend, Captain Armas, standing there with two flagons of something steaming hot and sweet-smelling. A sad smile crept across her tired face as she spoke to him. "Is that for me? Did you walk past all of these men of yours to bring this to *me*?"

"Yes, my lady, I did indeed. Here ... I can't vouch for its taste, but it is warm enough to revive those bones of yours." Armas smiled as he handed her the piping hot flagon of mulled wine.

"Thank you, Captain," she said gratefully as her slender fingers wrapped themselves greedily around the warm flagon.

"That makes two men of yours now, huh?" Armas said gently as he sipped his mulled wine. "Your father and your uncle ... I am sorry. I know you must miss them." The moment was quiet between them; the weight of loss hung heavily there in the cold, darkened air of the morning. She looked at him and nodded almost imperceptibly, acknowledging his kindness. "Are you ... are you alright, Keily?" he said with great compassion in his tired eyes

"Three," she said matter-of-factly.

"Three?" Armas asked.

"Aye ... three," she said sweetly. "Two of my men have fallen to whatever damned hell that is out there, but *three*, three of my men have dared to bravely defy the threats of darkness."

"I suppose they have," Armas said slowly, with a pang of gratitude quickening his heart.

"And I will do likewise, Captain," she said stoically. "We all have our losses and our reasons to fight. If I'm going to face that damned green fire again, and whatever those monsters are ... I'm going to look them square in the face when they come for me."

"Well," Armas wiped the spiced froth from his greying stubble, "I do not know if the direction our eyes are pointed will do us any good when they finally attack ... but I understand the sentiment," he said pointedly, looking out at the hazy green mist below.

Keily took a sip of the steaming drink and felt the warmth instantly return to her cold face. "Thank you for looking after me, Armas. Yasen would be grateful."

Armas exhaled a disappointed whisper as a look of understanding passed over his features. "Three."

They let the silence hang between them for a moment, for neither could think of anything appropriate to say. Finally Keily spoke. "I don't understand," she said. "Why not just attack us? Why all this waiting? With fire like that ... that evil abomination of a flame ... why wouldn't they dispatch their fury and be done with us already?"

"So quick to wish for death?" Armas said to her quietly. "There may still be reasons enough to hope for life."

She shook her head, unsure what to make of it all. "I'm merely stating the facts, Captain. They can light our woodcutters afire, and hurl their lifeless, bleeding bodies at our walls and our citizens, but not a single line of their formation has moved a step towards our defenses. What are they *waiting for*?"

"Lieutenant Marcum believes that perhaps they are wanting to draw us out onto the field of battle in the outlands, just beyond the wall," Armas told her. "And many of my men are ready to do such brash deeds. Some of the citizens here believe that this enemy is merely waiting us out, hoping our resources will fail and we will then be too weak to defend the city."

"What about you? What do you think their reason is for holding back their attack?" she asked him.

Armas looked out into the shadow-covered lands, now pocked with the sickly green flames of the besieging enemy. "I do not think that they are able to," he told her.

"Not able to?" she asked.

"Something has to be keeping them at bay—but they are ready. I can feel it in my bones. Mark my words, my lady, when they are no longer restrained, they will descend with ravenous fury upon us all."

"Are you afraid, Captain?" Keily asked him while the steam of her drink wisped around her worried face.

"I am ... I am most certainly afraid," Armas took a long draught of his hot, mulled wine, letting the transparent honestly linger there in the foggy morning air. "Come then ... it is time you got some rest. I must insist."

"Don't trouble yourself with worry over me, Captain. You have plenty of others to worry about, and I still have some fight in me yet," she said with a hint of her old playfulness.

"Oh, I do not doubt that the fight is still there, my lady, though I would feel better knowing that you are indeed rested enough to know how to use it when the time comes," he said with a tired smile.

Keily stared at this captain of the Capital guard. His kindness towards her was somehow unexpected. Although she was certainly used to the attentions of men who flirted or groped their way in search of something for themselves, Armas was different. His concern seemed *genuine.*

"Have you heard any word of the colony?" she asked him, her thoughts drifting now to Yasen.

"I have not, nor has the Citadel. Not to my knowledge, anyway. No word of timber, or of your North Wolf, my lady," he teased.

Keily's face flushed as her thoughts betrayed her innocent question. She nodded to him, a bit embarrassed, and then began to take her leave from the lookout post there atop the battlements. Armas watched her walk away, amazed at the vast amounts of both beauty and bravery that lived inside this tavern-maiden of Piney Creek. With each sip he took of his steaming drink, he could not help but feel a pang of jealousy for his friend on the Wreath.

Keily stopped, suddenly, and turned around to ask him another question. "If you are afraid, Armas, why do you stay here to fight? Why not run? Or, at least, why not drown your fears in the casks of ale as many have been known to do?"

"I resist while strength remains, and maybe ..." he turned to look southward, back towards the last remaining branch of the once-great burning tree, nodding his head almost imperceptibly as he spoke, "maybe I still hope, my lady. Hope that by some defiant act of blade and bow we might live to see each other in the dawn of a new day, of a new light."

Keily turned to look at the tree, but only for the briefest of moments. She smiled at him then, a sad sort of smile, and continued on her way.

"What now, Engelmann?" Armas whispered into the faint amber light.

"What now?" he released his exhausted breath. Without a warning, Armas felt the ground beneath his boots begin to vibrate and tremble. At first it was barely perceptible, not much more than a small rumble, like the movement of a dozen heavy horses on the coming road. "What in the damnable dark is that?" he said aloud, his eyes tracing the movement of guardsmen and citizens there behind the relative safety of the North Wall. Not many people seemed to notice the rising quake, not until the horses began to snort in agitated protest. Then, all of a sudden, it seemed that their desperate voices alone woke the fearful borough from its drugged weariness.

The vibration steadily grew, becoming angrily swollen like the rolling tide of a storm-tossed sea. The mighty walls of Haven began to shake as man and beast alike filled the once-silent streets with the worried noises of unexpected panic.

"Lieutenant!" Armas shouted down the line of the battlements. Marcum had grabbed his spyglass and was already surveying the enemy line from his position atop the wall. "What do you see?"

"Nothing, sir!" Marcum shouted, straining to be heard over the chaotic noises of his frightened men.

"What then? What is this?" Armas shouted back.

The quake became so violent that even the green-lit fires of the enemy encamped in the shadow lands began to waver and falter. Dust began to pour out from the cracks of the stone walls, and men and women everywhere tried and failed to steady themselves, grasping for purchase 'til the violence of the tremor passed.

"Armas! Armas, what is it?" The bewildered voice of the barmaid cut through the gathered confusion below.

"I don't know!" shouted the captain.

Just then a sound split the sky, like a chorus of a hundred lightening bolts ripping apart the unsuspecting morning in violent unison. Screams of women and children everywhere echoed in response, and in one single instant the whole of Aiénor was changed forever. The amber light of the great tree imploded, sending a shockwave of silver brilliance out from its center. The light from the tree flew outwards, exploding in a furious hurry, riding upon a tempest of gale force winds from the center of Haven to the ends of the world. Torches and watch fires everywhere, regardless of nature and hue, were extinguished in the mighty gust of light and wind.

And then, as swiftly and suddenly as the moment had occurred, it was gone. The last branch had fallen, and Aiénor was plunged into blackness.

Armas stared blindly in utter disbelief. His jaw hung agape, his breath came in short bursts, and the sweat upon his brow trickled down his face as his mind raced to comprehend what this terrible moment would truly mean for him and for his once-bright city.

"Captain!" Marcum shouted, though in truth his voice was the only one making any noise here in the hanging black of the lightless world. "Captain, look! The green-lit fires ... they are gone! Vanished!"

Armas wheeled around, searching the inky darkness for a hint of the green light. Blackness was everywhere; it seemed that no one was immune to its hold. Brazier or siege fires alike ... all light had bent its knee to the dying tree.

"Quickly now, light the torches!" Armas shouted to his men. "Use your flints, lads, and get these watch fires lit *immediately*! Lieutenant! Are you sure those green fires are gone?"

"Look for yourself!" Marcum replied, his voice sharp with the adrenaline that coursed through his veins.

Armas reached for his spyglass and placed its brass and leather to his eye, scanning for sign of the enemy beyond the walls of the city. All he could see was blackness, an ominous and horrifying darkness that boded nothing but doom. As he searched, he could hear the tearful cries erupting throughout the streets and homes of Piney Creek, voices and hearts united in a terrified lament. Off in the distance, the gilded horns of the Citadel sang their sad song for all to hear. Hearing the dreadful sound of those trumpets, he could scarcely wrap his mind around the truth that the citizens of Haven would never again hear this mournful song. The final branch ... the final lament ... the final death.

And now, evil was coming.

GAROOM! The sound of a great, crashing weight upon the darkened earth rattled the blackness. Armas' eyes slipped closed. The time had come. There was no sign of the sickly, green fires, and what was once a distant shadow land out there beyond the influence of the great tree had now become an invading country of settled darkness.

GAROOM! It fell once again, shaking both man and masonry.

"To the wall!" Marcum shouted to the guardsmen below. "Archers to the ready!"

Armas scanned the distant outlands once again, but although he felt the giant reverberations of what he knew to be a dragon, he could still see nothing out there.

A moment passed, but only a moment.

"*ROARRRRAHH*!" A chorus-like sound of deep and terrible monsters erupted in the pregnant hiatus of sound and sight. The malevolent roar grew and swelled in soul-chilling volume, and at the peak of its crescendo came two violent streams of green fire that climbed high into the sky, revealing by their evil glow the vast army that waited at the very gates of Haven, ready and hungry for war.

"God help us," Armas whispered. "Two dragons?"

He could barely make out their massive, darkened forms as the streams of fire spewed forth, illuminating the darkness about them. Then, as the light dimmed again in the aftermath of their flames, he could see nothing but the glowing orbs of their eyes. The two beasts lowered their great, horned heads as their menacing green eyes shifted towards the Raven Army positioned in front of the massive, scaled bodies. They let out another roar, and in a burst of green fire, they washed their ranks with a sea of deadly blaze.

Armas jumped back in frightened confusion, unsure why the dragons would do such a thing to their own army. But as the burst of green fire passed over the invading soldiers and faded, he saw the horror of the truth. Ranks upon ranks of the Raven Army stood unconsumed and unaffected by the dragons' flame. The intent of the flames was not to burn the men ... it was to ignite the torches extinguished by the death of the great tree. The enemy now stood in menacing rows of fierce, evil warriors decorated in both the ravens' feathers and dragons' green fire.

Marcum looked in panicked shock back to his captain, and Armas did his best to swallow away the ominous truth that threatened to rob his belly of his morning meal.

"Ready the cavalry, and get me a rider!" Armas ordered to his lieutenant.

"And get every bow to the wall! Now!"

And then, he heard it. The same guttural, otherworldly reverberation that had assaulted the air when the corpses of the woodcutters were flung in a fiery heap of chaos ... now began again. Armas and the army of Haven felt the tightening of their chests and the blurring of their eyes as the ghastly sound rose and fell in bellowed tones of terror.

Armas knew exactly what it meant for Haven. The soul-chilling sound was a signal for war.

"Captain," gasped the rider who was trying to catch his breath after rushing to the wall. "What are my orders, sir?"

"Alert the Citadel." Armas looked back to the green-lit army as the sound of clanging iron and marching boots woke to life. "They are on the move." Armas let out a settling breath and then looked the rider in the eyes. "Tell them that war has found us, and that whatever evil now drives it, dragons are at its vanguard. *Ride*, guardsman, and pray to the THREE who is SEVEN for some miracle to break in upon us, for some new light to keep these monsters at bay."

The rider saluted his captain, his right arm crossing his chest, and without another moment of hesitation he sprinted down the steps, mounted his courser, and spurred the steed to a flurry of haste.

Armas knew now what he must do, what his men and blades and bows would dare try and accomplish for this once-bright city. He placed his gloved hand against his tired yet resolute face, releasing the tension in his spine as he cracked his neck before addressing his soldiers.

"Guardsmen of Haven! Men and women of Piney Creek!" His words were interrupted with the deafening roar of the green-eyed monsters. Men and maidens, guardsmen and greenhorns alike all began to cower under the oppressive fear that unleashed its suffocating taunts from beyond the gates. Armas tried to stand strong against the fiery threats; he willed his head not to lower and begged his fortitude not to falter—at least, not to falter on the outside. "Hear me now, my friends, while there are yet moments to be heard! War has come to us, and evil besieges us with ravenous intent. Vile monsters taunt and torture our minds, feeding on what courage we still have left!"

GAROOM! The pounding of giant, taloned-feet on the distant ground shook the air out the moment yet again.

"But if we run ... if we try to escape its hunger ... it will not relent, it will not cease its hunting. This borough and your homes are not the prize of our enemy. Dragons and legions are not assembled for such small intents and purposes!" He shouted with what bravery he could muster in the face of such peril, and did his best to keep his strong voice from wavering. "I fear ... no, I *know* that this Raven Army will not stop until all of Haven is under the rule of whomever sent it."

GAROOM! The thunderous quake came once again.

"We can run and it will find us still. Or we can *fight!* We can take whatever sharpened edge we might find, whatever courage we might muster—no matter how frail and wilted it seems—and we can stand. Even if victory is not our fortune, perhaps we may still stand for the briefest of moments." The world grew quiet for a moment, as if the enemy were giving the army of Haven a chance to consider Armas' words. He seized the silence once more. "And maybe," he shouted as he found the strong, tear-laden eyes of the beautiful barmaid, "we might deal this enemy a fatal blow and live to see the light of a new day." With his gaze, he entrusted his words to her heart.

Silence hung there in the terrified moment, as citizens and soldiers alike did their best to take heart in the wake of these desperate words.

"May it be so!" shouted an old man out of the crowd of gathered people.

Armas' eyes lit up with the faint and slightly savage light of determination. He crossed his arm, his clinched fist reaching the braided cords of his office in a humble salute to this ill-prepared people. "We, by the THREE who is SEVEN," he said in practiced formality.

"We, by the THREE who is SEVEN," the people called in reply, kissing hands and flints, and looking with resolved intent towards the green fire that awaited them.

Chapter Seventeen

THE STRONGHOLD WAS RUMBLING WITH the tired sounds of tired men, and the smoky air was filled with the fragrances of roasted boar, baked salt-breads, and piping hot mulled wine. The woodcutters both left and returned to the stronghold each day as a single company of brothers, so they had waited hungrily for their chieftain to ride up to the colony's gate before they would permit themselves the luxury of rest and hot bread.

"Well, it is about time, North Wolf," exclaimed Rolf, a slightly older woodcutter with a long, black beard. "Goran over here was looking at me a bit too intently if you know what I mean! I have never been more afraid of a growling stomach in all my life."

"Nah!" Goran said in mock disgust. "There is not enough muscle on those scrawny arms to fell a sapling, let alone satisfy the hunger that I have worked up today."

A good-hearted laugh washed over the exhausted men, and Yasen was indeed grateful for such a company of brothers to battle this darkness alongside. "Alright then, comrades, let us go rest our blades and fill our bellies, huh?"

"Aye!" his men shouted. The woodcutters did not walk in uniformed formation or with any noticeable trace of practiced discipline, but the bond of brotherhood and the harsh life of the axe had brought with it an almost impenetrable respect, and neither hunger nor hurry would disrupt their company.

The banners of the Citadel and the canvas of the barracks whipped and popped, for a cold wind had blown in from the east, and the flames of the watch fires and braziers danced violently in its chilly wake. The exhaustion of the men stood in stark contrast to the flurry of windblown activity sprinkled throughout the encampment. Yasen's men walked proudly into the center of the pine fortress, having accomplished much for their mission and their city. Here at the heart of the colony there was an open square of assembly; this was the place where the meals were shared, prayers were prayed, and the orders of the governor were given.

The men filled flagons with steaming drink and passed loaves of the salted bread. As they dipped the rolls into the red juices of the roasted meat and ate their fill, the mood of the colony exhaled the tense uncertainty of the day. Laughter began to bubble and stories were told, and as the spirits in the mulled wine warmed the bellies of the woodcutters and guardsmen alike, their spirits too began to lift in the wake of this easterly wind.

Tahd stood to his feet in an effort to gain the attention of the hungry crowd. "Men of the first colony, a job well done today, indeed. It would seem that his Brightness had a grand and glorious vision after all when he sent us here to the Wreath ... and I am proud of your relentlessness." The captain raised his flagon to his face and took a long draught before pounding the wooden vessel twice on the table in honor of a hard day's work.

"Our governor has some important words to share with you, so mind that you listen while you eat! Huh?" said the silver-haired captain.

Seig rose from his chair at the head of the table. When he stood erect, it was easy to see why this tall, charismatic man commanded such attention. His dark, closely cropped beard punctuated his sharp features, and his voice boomed with an authority that could not merely derive its power from his office. The tables fell silent under the weight of the governor's authority. Though the woodcutters did not hold much love or respect for the man himself, they believed in their cause enough to listen when he spoke. That, and they mistrusted his use of power enough to be wary of whatever he might say.

All eyes were turned to Seig, and all attention was directed at the governor. Were it not for the heightened sense of alertness the men had acquired due to living on the Wreath, they may not have even noticed what happened next. Out here, this far from Haven, the world was already dark enough; all that was left of the great tree was a small, distant flame of amber or silver, a mere twinkling in the blackened sky. But at the very moment that Seig rose to address his men, the distant flame across the Dark Sea vanished.

Not many even detected it at first; the diminishment of light was nearly imperceptible. Seig, who just moments before had smiled with the bravado of complete confidence, froze momentarily at the dimming. Nervousness colored his tight-jawed features as he searched for the words that he could not quite seem to find. Slowly, whispers could be heard amongst the men as some began to perceive that the great tree had finally failed.

Woodcutters and guardsmen alike began to turn and squint in the direction of the tree, trying to make out if what their more observant brothers were telling them was true. As all attention somberly shifted from the square of the colony to the darkened shores of their distant home, their fears were confirmed with violent assurance. A gale of cold winds came rushing across the black waters of the Dark Sea, and as it hit the colony, every watch fire and brazier was extinguished in a single, chilling gust.

The realization of what had just happened settled fully upon the whole of the colony. They sat in silence, unable to see even their hands in front of their faces. Finally, Yasen found his way to a nearby brazier and managed to light a flame again, casting an eerie, flickering, amber gleam upon the gathered company. The firelight slowly woke the frozen wills of the stunned colony, and the watchmen began to light torches once again.

The silence of the moment was finally broken by the shaky voice of the young Priest.

"The tree has failed," he said. "Let us pray in earnest, for our assignment here is now all the more paramount." The men of the colony took up their flints, and the teary-eyed Priest said the words. "The hope of our past is gone, for the world as we have known it has left us here in darkness. But give us strength anew, and may we place our hope in the gift of resolve. Save us by the work of our hands."

The colony agreed in unison. "May it be so."

Seig looked out among his men as the words of the Priest still echoed in his thoughts, and the nerves that had not moments before robbed him of his confidence were pushed aside in favor of action. "Three days' time," Seig proclaimed with confidence. "Three days' time will be all that we will need before the captain here can sail back to Haven with a ship full of fresh timber and new light for our countrymen."

Yasen looked to his men grimly. They were tired and weary from the weeks of hard days there in the forest of the Wreath, and he knew what this proclamation would mean for their calloused hands and fatigued backs.

"Our Priest King sent us with this mission: to seek and to find a new light, and to return it back to our shining city," Seig continued as he stared into the eyes of each and every one of his men. "We have sought, we have found, and by the will of the THREE who is SEVEN, we will return this first harvest to our people, for it would seem that our great city needs us all the more this dark day."

"Three days' time?" Goran whispered to his chieftain. "I would wager that the hold of that ship is barely half full."

"*Glory*. Glory is ours for the taking, men," Seig continued, sensing the uncertainty that often accompanies exhaustion. "And glory we shall have, both for ourselves and for our city."

"Here! Here!" shouted the guardsmen.

The woodcutters did their best to muster excitement enough to appease their governor and rally their exhausted spirits, for they felt all the more the weight of their responsibility here on the Wreath. They had dedicated their whole way of living to the will of the Priests and the way of the flint, and they knew, like all the others knew, that Haven needed both their time and their timber.

"Glory is not what I seek, North Wolf," Rolf leaned to Yasen and whispered. "It ... this ... this has never been about glory. It has been about doing something worth doing."

"Aye," whispered Goran in agreement. "What will glory get you? Naught but a bright boat at the bottom of the Dark Sea."

Yasen listened silently as he sipped his steaming flagon, not giving much acknowledgement to the quiet commentary that continued amongst the ranks of the woodcutting brothers. Though he may agree with his comrades, he would not openly say so just yet. The risk of mutiny in this necessary albeit fragile partnership of guardsmen and woodcutters grew greater each day, and this swelling tension brought him an added sense of caution. When his thoughts were collected enough for the moment, he gave his men a silencing stare that put an end to their worried speculations and criticisms.

Sitting silently at the edge of the gathered men, Cal finally caught Yasen's eye. The chieftain read something deeper, something heavier than mere worry or reproach, there on the face of the groomsman. Cal sighed a defeated, sorrowful sigh and then looked out towards the palisade gate to the west as if he were reading his destiny written upon the cold, dark sky.

"Eat up, men of the first colony, and may your rest this night come quickly and deeply!" Seig bellowed on. "For tomorrow we wage war against the darkness with a greater ferocity than ever before, and by the THREE who is SEVEN ... we will fight relentlessly!"

The men ate and drank under the weight of the morrow, and not many words were spoken among them. Finally, they made their way to their beds to find an uneasy rest. The night patrol took their position atop the watchtower, and three riders, led by the knight Pyrrhus, mounted their horses and waited for the gate warden to open the defenses.

"Sleep well, lads" Pyrrhus said with an arrogant snarl. "And don't you worry your sleeping heads ... this dark wilderness fears the *fire knight,* so I am told! Ha!" The heavy timber gate opened up before them, and Pyrrhus kicked his horse with a dramatic flair. He and his riders disappeared with torches in hand out beyond the safety of the stronghold, gone to patrol the nearby area and to protect the timber they had claimed. As the gate shut behind them and the men of the first colony prepared to make their rest, Cal lay awake, staring at the thatched roof of his bedchambers.

"We didn't find it. We failed ... we failed to find the light in time," Cal whispered his frustrations to the small, winged guardian perched in the rough-hewn rafters above him. "I didn't find it." His voice carried an uncharacteristic darkness to its tone.

"Well," the wise Sprite said thoughtfully as he read the meaning of his friend's words, "then I suppose it is a good thing we are still here to seek it."

"Is it?" said Cal. "Or is this just the end?" He wiped a weary, disappointed tear from his stubbled face. "I failed Deryn, I ... how was a groomsman from Westriver foolish enough to believe he could find what *kings* never could?"

Deryn did not respond, and the pregnant silence grew between them.

"Well?" Cal said impatiently. "Haven't you anything to say? Some wise words of inspiration to compel me onward?" his voice cracked with frustration.

The Sprite waited for a long moment before he answered. "And what do you think those wise words would be?"

"Isn't that what you are here for? Is that not why Iolanthe sent you?" Cal's wounds bled out amongst his words.

"I *chose* to come with you, but not to be your clairvoyant, or your diviner of fortunes. No, I am your guardian, and your companion. So perhaps I might protect that mind of yours by simply reminding you of what you already know, Bright Fame." Deryn's words held both gentle rebuke and genuine kindness, with no hint of offense at the belligerence of the young groomsman.

Cal peered at the Sprite with an expression that transformed itself from frustration into determination. "I know that I was called here to seek the light. The Poets, the Oweles, the Sprites ... you *all* believed that I was meant to find it."

"And with all that you have seen, and felt, and experienced ... do you still believe that you are meant to find it?"

"I do. With all my heart, I do," Cal affirmed.

"Then nothing has truly changed, has it?" Deryn replied.

"How can you say that? Everything has changed, Deryn. You saw the tree die, just as all of Haven did!"

The azure-winged guardian flitted down from the rafters and hovered not more than a handbreadth from the reddened eyes of his charge. "Not failure, not darkness, not even death can change the heart of this calling, for it is of magic that is from a place beyond the shadowed shores of Aiénor."

"But-" Cal tried to reason.

"We did not come to save a tree or a city. We did not come to keep a dying light aflame, we came to seek and to find something much brighter indeed. For deep magic calls us towards deeper magic still, my friend," the Sprite said.

Cal was silent there in the faint azure glow. He dried his tears and then sat up to the edge of his bed. "This is not how I expected things to happen, Deryn. I wanted to be a hero for Michael, for Engelmann ... for Tolk and Klieo and all of them. Now it feels like I failed everyone."

"The *tree* has failed, as we knew that it would. But this calling, this story ... is not finished." Deryn said as he sat upon the groomsman's shoulder. "Do not forget the markings, and do not yet forget the woman."

The two sat in silence again as Cal pondered the words of his guardian.

"Deryn?" Cal asked, "the marking on the wall said to go north, but what do you think *Shaimira* means?"

Deryn flitted up and hovered in front of Cal's face. "The word is old, the tongue is from long before the heart of my people was hidden in the depths of the mountain. It means *guardian,* but though I know what the word means ... I do not know what or where *Shaimira* is."

"Guardian?" Cal said through a heavy yawn. "I wonder ..." He tried to continue the conversation, but the weight of the day and the exhaustion of emotion robbed his curiosity of its vigor as sleep overtook him.

"I wonder as well, my friend," Deryn whispered as he flitted up into the rafters. "Though perhaps rest might birth fresh illuminations in the morning. Sleep well, groomsman."

Only a few hours had passed before their sleep was interrupted with the sounding horns of the night patrol. The blasts of Pyrrhus' signal woke the whole of the colony, and Cal let his dreams of Shaimira fall into a pile of unfinished rubble. He wiped away the fog of sleep and clumsily rose to dress himself so he might see what the signal was calling for. "Wait here," he said to Deryn as he buckled his belt and sheathed his ancient sword. "I'm going to see what all the commotion is about."

The center square of the colony's stronghold was awake with the curiosity of woodcutters and guardsmen alike. Cal caught the eye of Yasen and could plainly see the worry etched across his features.

"What is it? What is going on out here?" Wielund said groggily as he walked towards Cal and rubbed the sleep from his eyes.

"I am not sure, but something in me is very unsettled," Cal replied as he stared intently at the gate.

"Perhaps you drank too much wine. My stomach has been all out of sorts since supper," Wielund said, oblivious to the tension of the moment.

Just then, the heavy gates opened up and in rode Pyrrhus and his two riders. At the center of their mounted triangle, arms bound in a length of rope, was a golden-haired woman in a dark blue dress.

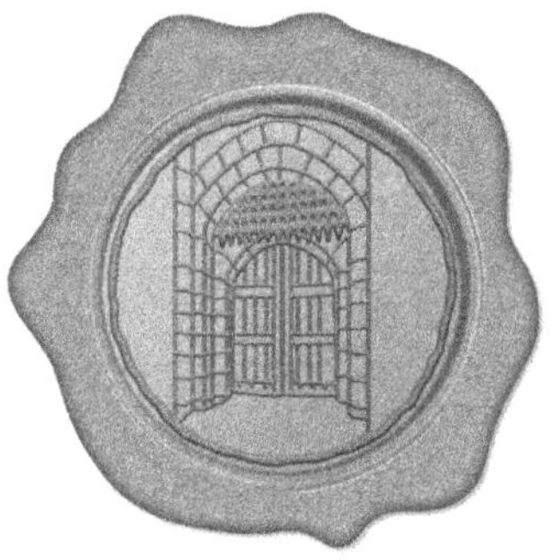

Chapter Eighteen

BAROOM! THE WAR HORNS OF the enemy sounded, over and over, as the army continued to mobilize. Their deep, sickly tones mocked the waning resolve of the few thousand guardsmen who stood in the green tunics and silver mail of the Citadel they served. The battlements atop the Northern Wall were filled with wave after wave of hurried archers, and the cobblestone streets in the borough below were alive and pulsing in rhythm to the clomping hooves of the mounted cavalry. Torches were lit and passed among soldiers and citizens alike; the substantial expense of the timber could not be considered when the alternative was existence in complete darkness. Armas rushed down the stairs of the battlements, taking account of the defenses he had to command. Whatever reinforcements the Citadel may decide to send to the wall, they would clearly not get here in time.

He pushed his way through the chaos of the moment, his men parting before him like black waters against the keel of a stubborn ship. Keily reached out and grabbed ahold of his arm. "It was the tree, wasn't it?" she asked him. "It was the tree that did not allow them past the wall ... the tree held their strength at bay?"

"It would seem so," Armas replied distractedly. His mind was racing down a dozen different paths as he looked for something, anything that he might employ to thwart the inevitable advance of this Raven Army.

"And now that it is gone, Armas? Now what? Our light is gone, how can we keep back this army of darkness?" she said in frustrated anger. "There is nothing that will stop them."

WHOOSH, came the sound of rushing wind.

WHOOSH, WHOOSH, WHOOSH. It came again, now in a succinct rhythm. The men in the courtyard froze instantly in silent fear, eyes searching the blackened sky as the sound of wings upon the cold air stole the moment.

"They are coming ... the dragons are coming!" Keily whispered.

"What did you say? A moment before?" Armas asked.

"The dragons are coming?" she replied

"No ... no, about the light being gone!" he said excitedly. "That might just be our salvation, my lady." Armas took her by the shoulders, a weary smile now coloring his tired face. "Thank you ... thank you."

"Lieutenant!" Armas shouted over her shoulder up to his second in command. "Man the wall, the archers are yours to command. I will ride with the cavalry, and we will run down whatever you cannot manage to shoot."

"Aye, yes sir," Lieutenant Marcum said with a salute.

"Keily." He fixed his gaze back on her again, his words coming fast and with great urgency. "I want you to burn the borough down."

"*What?*" she said in confusion. "I thought that we were trying to defend the borough, not aid in its destruction!"

"Anything that will catch fire, I need you to gather it. We are going to throw it over the walls in massive heaps. I know that it is not the same as the tree, but fire makes light, and perhaps ... perhaps we can make one big enough and bright enough to stay the dragons so we can cut down their numbers," he told her.

She nodded in understanding, knowing now what she must do.

"Go now and be quick about it. Anything that will burn, pile it outside the wall, here and over there," he said pointing to either side of the North Gate. "Whatever light we can make, we'd best make it now. Gather whomever you can to help you, Keily. There is not a moment to lose!"

Keily took off as fast as her legs would carry her, dashing straight towards the Gnarly Knob in hopes of rallying some help. She barreled through the large, iron-braced door of the tavern and gasped her plea to the gathered citizens who were taking refuge against the coming attack. "Help me, please! Grab the tables, the chairs ... anything that will burn! The captain needs our help! The enemy is coming!"

The frightened women and older men stared blankly at the barmaid, not moving to help her, frozen in their own fear. She leaned over, her hands on her knees, her breath coming in heaves; all the weariness of the last few weeks and the heart-breaking death of the great tree finally caught up to her. Her face crumpled with the heavy truth. "The enemy is coming."

"What good are we going to do against such an army, huh?" An old man growled beneath a trembling voice. "We are nothing more than tired skin and weary bones!"

"Aye! He's right you know!" The whispered words of a nursing mother agreed. "What does the captain expect us to do? *Fight*?"

The worried grumbles of suffocated courage threatened to steal what breath she had just managed to catch. Keily rose to her full height, defiantly straightening both her face and her resolve before she spoke. "It's not strength that's going to win this war," she said as an angry tear streaked her face. "It's not younger backs or sharper blades!"

"What do you want then, girl?" said the old man. "You can't tell me that the captain hopes to fend off the dragons with tables and chairs!"

"I want you to move! I want you to pick yourself up off this floor and *choose* to live, choose to do something other than cower here waiting to die!" She felt her strength return in force as she addressed the lot of them. "These tables, like this ... these makeshift shelters won't save you from what is coming. But carry them to the wall with me and set them on fire, and these table just might save you after all."

She grabbed two wooden stools, slung them over her shoulders and kicked the tavern door wide open, stepping out once again into the cold, ominous dark, determined to start a fire even if she had to do it herself.

Sharp blasts of the guardsmen's horns began to signal the company positioned all along the North Gate. Marcum, with his spyglass to his eye, tried hurriedly to calculate the size and strength of the marching Raven

Army. The legions of enemy forces seemed nearly innumerable. Each battalion was marked by a unique standard and a flaming, green torch that was accented by raven feathers and dragon teeth. The army was clad in unpolished steel, muted chainmail, black tunics, and capes. Their shields were each crafted in the shape of a deep black chevron, their only embellishment a messily painted white raven in the center. None of the Raven Army rode atop a mount, though they moved with the deliberate speed and deftness of hungry ants. The helms of their warlords were adorned in black-feathered plumes, and it was these generals that trumpeted the sickening tones of those godforsaken horns.

Marcum surveyed the army with a growing sense of dread. They looked human enough, though their skin looked ashen and their eyes were aglow with that very same putrid green as the eyes of the dragons. "Armas!" Marcum called as he looked down from the battlements to relay the information to his captain. "It looks as if there are six battalions, roughly a thousand of whatever those damned men are per battalion." Marcum tried to keep his voice steady, but his tone betrayed the dread he felt.

"Six thousand?" Armas shouted back up to his lieutenant. "That is nearly double our strength—*if* you count the farmers and shopkeepers." Armas looked back towards the borough and whispered, "Come on, Keily."

The enemy forces were still not within bowshot. Marcum had calculated a point in his mind. When they came to it, he would unleash a rain of pointed vengeance upon this encroaching abomination.

"Tell your bowmen to aim true, to fire sure. We are going to need their accuracy!" Armas shouted.

WHOOSH. WHOOSH. WHOOSH. The sound of pounding dragons' wings suddenly filled the air and captivated the attention of the forces of Haven. The pair of ink-colored winged serpents climbed and clawed their way high into the black sky, disappearing into the darkness and then reappearing in the green-lit dim as they hovered back and forth over their advancing army. Armas and his riders fastened and secured their armor, taking up shields and swords, tightening saddles and steeling themselves for carnage.

The men and women of Piney Creek had found their last measures of courage, and were aiding Keily's efforts to start a fire. They worked feverishly to gather anything that might possibly burn, and one after the other they passed tables and frames, sideboards and footstools from person to person until all was tossed into two massive piles just outside the Northern Wall. One of the archers let loose a torch into the pile of kindling and soon a blaze was burning and growing, the flames climbing nearly halfway up the walls of the city.

"Keep the timber coming!" Keily shouted. "We have to keep this fire burning!"

Two short, bright bursts of Marcum's trumpet signaled to all the archers that the enemy was now within bowshot of the North Wall. The guardsmen pulled tight their bows, charged and ready with the steel-tipped points of ruinous offering. The sound of the drawn bows sang in a desperate, tension-filled chorus along the defense line as they waited for their lieutenant's third and commanding blast.

Armas nodded to the gate warden from atop his armored mount. His men moved into formation behind him as the clank and strain of the heavy iron portcullis began to lift in front of them.

Marcum's trumpet rang its third and final tone; its bright, brass note was long and deliberate, and with its sounding came the volleyed twangs of five hundred longbows. "Again! Make ready!" Marcum shouted his orders. Two blasts and then a third quickly followed, and again the rain of arrows flew out from the wall towards the encroaching army.

The fires on the outside of the wall burned hot and high. The light that shone from their blaze lit up the blackness that surrounded the outer edge of the once bright walls of Haven. The Raven Army continued to advance, despite the barrage of arrows that fell upon them, but even now the enemy was still too far for Armas and his cavalry to risk a charge. They held their formation a safe distance behind the wall, holding their wild-eyed horses back as they waited for their captain to signal the order to strike and prayed that the dragons would not target them.

Two blasts and then a third, and more arrows were loosed. This time, before they could reach their mark, they were consumed in a blaze of green as a duet of fiery roars came from out of the mouths of the twin dragons. "Again!" Marcum shouted. And again, two blasts and then a third and a wash of green fury consumed the arrows mid-flight, all while the army marched closer and closer to the North Gate of Haven. Marcum's heart beat quickly in his chest as he faced the doom of the moment; the dragons had crippled his ability to inflict much damage, if any, before Armas and his cavalry could charge the approaching hoard. He looked down the line at his archers' frustration and gave them a new order. "Fire at will and *not* together; those damned monsters can't burn them all up if we stagger. But mind you watch for the captain and his riders ... your arrows are meant for the Raven invaders!"

The guardsmen fit their bows, and with silent prayers and deep breaths they began to fire at will. Some aimed for the legions of ashen-faced, green-eyed soldiers and others tried their luck aiming for the twin flying serpents. The enemy soldiers, though motivated and compelled by some dark and sinister evil, fell much the same way that men would fall in battle. It seemed that the weapons of the guardsmen inflicted the expected damage upon the army of the un-light. Although they fell like men would fall, they had no sense of fear or dread. They did not flinch or break under the rain of loosed arrows, but marched emotionlessly towards the walls of Haven.

The arrows, however, were no match for the dragons' scales, and the twin monsters swarmed and flew in between the archers and the marching army below, much like a winged shield.

"Riders!" Armas shouted to his men as he wheeled his well-muscled steed around to face them. "This is for Haven, and for all those who have not the blade or the bravery to stand today." He slowly reached for and unsheathed his bright, silver blade. The mark of the tree and flint etched in its pommel caught the firelight, and for a moment it looked to Armas as if amber burned once again on its lifeless branches. A bead of nervous sweat rolled down his face and his eyes blurred for just a breath of time. Then he blinked away the fog and raised his blade high for his men to see it.

One thousand heavy horsemen followed suit, drawing their own weapons and lifting them to the darkened sky. The thick, quiet tension behind the wall was interrupted with the ringing song of a thousand singing, silver blades.

"May the THREE who is SEVEN protect us this dark, deadly day. May His strength guide our blades and fortify our hearts, and may we live to see a brighter dawn!" Armas called.

"WE, BY THE THREE WHO IS SEVEN!" shouted the cavalrymen, and with blades in hand they crossed their arms and saluted their captain.

"Keep your shields up, and stagger the lines. They may have dragons, but there are only two of the damned beasts, and I would rather meet them out here in these outlands than within the city walls," Armas told them.

He surveyed his men. Fear was present, but courage and duty prevailed, and as he scanned the faces of these brave guardsmen his eye was caught by the blue-colored bodice and brightly determined face of Keily the tavern maiden as she still carried on with the orders he had given her, leading old men and frightened women to drag and carry whatever they could find that would burn towards the wall.

She felt his stare and met his gaze. No words passed her lips, but respect and worry were screaming in unison from her eyes. Armas smiled a sweet, albeit sad, smile, doing his best to reassure her that this was not against his will, but was for her and her people. He nodded his gratitude and then wheeled his horse around to face the open gate and the impending doom.

Arrows flew and the green-eyed men fell, though not a scream or cry of pain could be heard there on the field of battle. The twin dragons soared in and out of the rain of arrows, consuming what they might with their green fire, and biding their time to unleash their fury upon the city.

Armas let loose a long blast from his horn and the North Gate of Haven exploded in a storm of pounding hooves and snorting steeds. The cavalrymen, with green and silver shields raised high, charged in lined formation towards the marching Raven hoard.

Chapter Nineteen

"HAVE NO FEAR, MIGHTY MEN of Haven!" Pyrrhus shouted triumphantly as he dismounted his large horse and grabbed the pearl-skinned arm of the golden-haired woman. "It looks as if the only things that stalk us out here in this dark wilderness are *pretty little monsters.*"

The crowd of woodcutters and guardsmen let out a nervous laughter, for they were both relieved and confused to find this woman bound in cords.

"She will make for an interesting prisoner, indeed!" Pyrrhus said with a greedy stare.

"Prisoner?" Cal shouted out from across the square as he made his way closer to the fire knight. "Since when is it the task or assignment of our colony to make or take prisoners, pretty or otherwise?"

"Oh, groomsman!" Pyrrhus laughed a patronizing laugh. "Why don't you stick to minding those ponies and mules of yours, and let the guardsmen worry about the ins and outs of *our* assignment."

"What is going on here?" Tahd said coldly and with great authority as he approached the scene and the spectacle unfolding before him.

"She is a Wreather, not a prisoner!" Cal argued on, ignoring the presence of the captain. "She knows this place better than any of us, and we would be fools to make an enemy out of her!"

"Of course she does," Pyrrhus agreed maliciously. "And I for one have ways of getting her to tell me all about this place!"

Cal drew his sword Gwarwyn, and his face went hard in a furious rage. "Let her go Pyrrhus, she is not some beast for you to bully around."

"What do you care, groomsman? Do you *know* this woman?" the knight asked suspiciously.

"I know that she has done nothing wrong, and that she will *not* be treated unfairly. So let her be ... *now*," Cal spoke in tones of barely-bridled outrage as he edged Gwarwyn closer to the fire knight.

"Enough!" Tahd shouted into the growing tempest. "Neither of you shall make any judgment on the affairs of this holy colony."

"You think that old, rusted relic of yours frightens me, groomsman?" Pyrrhus went on, disregarding the words of his captain. "You *are* going to talk to me, aren't you, *pretty* girl," he said, reaching out to stroke her soft cheek with the back of his hand.

Astyræ swallowed hard. She did fear this cruel and arrogant knight, and yet at the very same moment she was fascinated by the presence of this army of men from Haven. "Why am I in cords? What harm have I caused you tree men?"

SMACK! Came the sound of flesh on flesh as Pyrrhus struck the violet-eyed woman across her beautiful face. "Do not presume to question me, woman," the knight said in disgust.

In an instant, Cal lifted his blade and jabbed its sharpened point into the gullet of the fire knight. "Touch her again and I'll-"

"*Relent now*!" Tahd shouted, his temper boiling over at the lack of respect. "Put down your sword, groomsman! He is still an officer in my company, and I will have no one—however justified they may presume themselves to be—draw a blade on one of my men!"

Yasen moved closer to the volatile skirmish, fearing the worst for his friend. He reached out and placed a hand on Cal's shoulder. "Easy, brother," he whispered. "This is not the way to fight for her ... not like this, not now. Stand down."

"Aye! Talk some sense into this fool of a groomsman, *woodcutter*." Pyrrhus spat, defiant regardless of the point that threatened to pierce his neck.

Tahd made a signal, and half a dozen of his armed guardsmen approached cautiously, hands on the hilts of their sheathed blades, ready to bring order at the command of their captain.

Cal searched Astyræ's twice colored eyes, his chest heaving from his barely restrained anger. "It is alright groomsman," she said kindly. "I am not worth any bloodshed."

"Sheath your blade *now*, groomsman!" Tahd commanded in a shout of frustrated anger.

"Come on, brother," Yasen urged again. "This is not your battle to win right now."

"She is not theirs to ... to just do with as they will," Cal retorted, defiance rising in his voice.

"But neither is she yours to make into such a spectacle," Yasen replied matter-of-factly.

A confused look wrinkled Cal's face. The injustice of it all and the sharp words of his pleading friend did not seem to make much sense. He took in all of the assembled company that had gathered around him, surveying both the curious and the indignant, and it was in that moment that Yasen's words began to sink in.

Cal pulled back his sword, revealing a trickle of crimson that was slowly running down the neck of the bullish fire knight. Pyrrhus reached up for his neck and wiped at the blood, then examined his red-stained fingers with a snarl of disgust.

"A Wreather, are you?" Pyrrhus looked at Astyræ much the same way a serpent would eye a barn mouse. "You *are* still a woman though, yes?" He reached out his right hand to territorially grab a piece of her backside in a crude display of power.

"C a l ,   n o !"   A s t y r æ   b l u r t e d   o u t   i n   a   d e s p e r a t e   p l e a .

But it was already too late. Cal, in a fit of righteous anger, raised his ancient blade and in one swift, deadly motion, severed the arm of the arrogant knight. Pyrrhus screamed in shocked disbelief, holding up a bloody stump where his arm should have been, watching in horror as a river of crimson flowed out from his elbow.

"My arm!" screamed Pyrrhus. "The little bastard cut off my arm!"

Cal stood there in shock as the world around him rushed in chaotic movement. His senses were dulled while the scene unfolded in a spray of blood. Men tried desperately to stop the bleeding and calm the enraged knight, and then a rush of hands and hurried breath overtook Cal as Tahd's guardsmen ran in to seize him.

In the midst of the madness, not many took notice of Yasen as he hurriedly grabbed the still-bound Astyræ and led her off toward the heavy timber gates. He took a dagger out from his leather belt and cut away the cords of rope that held her slender hands prisoner. "You haven't much time, my lady," he whispered intently to her. "Cal has foolishly bought you a chance to run. Please, be quick about it ... and get as far away as you might."

"But what will happen to him?" she begged. "What will they do with him?"

"I cannot say, though I will use whatever sway I have to steady their wrath; this I promise you," Yasen told her, eager now for her to flee before anyone remembered her.

"I am sorry, woodcutter!" she said through worried, tearstained eyes. "I ... I didn't mean to-"

"How did they find you, woman?" Yasen interrupted. "You were supposed to be safe enough in that cave."

"It was the tree ... that tree, I had to see it! Something in me, something drew me out ... and then when its fire died, I felt a lament and loss that I cannot quite explain."

"This part of the world has been dark long enough ... why do you choose to mourn now?" he grumbled more to himself than to her as he swiftly walked with her towards the gate.

"I do not know ... only, that I do mourn its passing, woodcutter," she said.

"Go then. Back to the cave with you, and *stay hidden* this time, if you know what's good for you, lass," Yasen barked in worried whispers.

"But the darkness, Yasen," she whispered, and he could hear the terror in her voice.

He led her to a small opening between the heavy gates and handed her his dagger. "You will have to endure your fear, or I am afraid that you might find new ones here inside these bloodied walls." Yasen looked over his shoulder as four guardsmen dragged his friend towards the prison hold on the east side of the outpost. "*Go!*" he whispered back to her. "Go now and be quick about it."

"Tell him thank you ... and that I am sorry," she said as she steeled herself to face the dark unknown. "Thank *you*, also." And with a sad smile she disappeared into the black wilderness of the Western Wreath.

Yasen walked back into the thick of the commotion, eyeing the black dirt of the earthen floor that was slick with an oily, red sheen.

"Where is the Wreather woman?" Tahd asked him.

Yasen hardened his face, and with his lone eye he narrowed his gaze and met the stare of the short, silver-haired captain. "Isn't that the concern of your men, Captain? My men and I ... we are here for the timber, we are here for the light—not for prisoners."

"There was much we could have learned from her," Tahd countered. "You know that, and you let her get away."

"I didn't *let* her do anything," Yasen retorted. "Next time it might be wiser to try conversation instead of just resorting to cords and shackles." He let out a frustrated sigh and ran his hand through his dark beard. "What do you intend to do with him?"

Before Tahd could answer, the sound of a violent scream and the smell of burning flesh filled the dark, smoky, night air, and the assault of the senses punctuated the tension of the moment. "That all depends on if my knight lives or not," Tahd ominously answered. "Sergeant!" he shouted.

"Yes, Captain?" the broad-chested guardsman replied.

"Take Pyrrhus' night patrol. Get back on your horses and see about finding and keeping that Wreather woman this time," Tahd ordered.

"Yes, sir. Right away, sir," the sergeant replied.

"Well," Seig said in mock surprise as he strode angrily towards the two of them. "It would seem that we are not alone here in this wilderness after all. The woman ... have you found her yet?" he asked the captain.

"The night patrol has just left to search for her," Tahd answered.

"What did the fool Pyrrhus say about her, huh?" Seig continued. "Was she alone? Was she armed? Did he find a settlement or a village?"

"I ... he ... I am not sure," Tahd stammered out his reply. "That damned groomsman lopped off his arm before he could report much of anything." It was in that moment that a great realization came to the captain as he replayed the incident in his mind. "That groomsman of yours?" he said to the chieftain of the woodcutters. "How did the Wreather woman know his *name*?"

Seig narrowed his dark gaze at the one-eyed woodcutter, inspecting him with unveiled suspicion. "Was this not the same groomsman we sent out to scout the wilderness?" the governor asked.

"Yes," Tahd said angrily. "Yes, he was. Perhaps we should pay your groomsman a visit? Eh, woodcutter?"

"You do understand that this colony and our whole effort here to harvest timber enough for our city does and will continue to require a skilled groomsman," Yasen said boldly to the governor, his voice barely able to conceal the protective edge. "You would be best served to be prudent in your dealings with the few men we have here that are able and willing to aid our cause."

"Careful, woodcutter," Seig cautioned with disdain. "You presume to talk too freely. I am not one of your fur-clad axe men, nor will I lower myself to take council from the likes of your kind."

"My *kind*?" Yasen said in angry amusement. "It is by the strength of my kind, my brothers, my fur-clad axe men, that this colony of yours will have any hope of the *glory* you so seek."

"Your disrespect will cost you, woodcutter!" Tahd barked in wounded offense.

"Pyrrhus is a fool. It is men like him, *your* men, Captain, that we can do without—but a groomsman, we cannot," Yasen continued.

"That's enough," Seig seethed quietly. "If you and your axe men are so keen on saving this city of ours, then you had best see about the timber and leave the matters of the colony to me." Seig looked to his captain. "It is time we hear a scouting report, Captain. Come, let's see what this *groomsman* has to say."

"Yes, Governor," Tahd agreed.

"Three days, woodcutter," Seig threatened him. "Groomsman or not, the hold of that ship will be filled with timber, of that you had best be certain."

"Certain?" Yasen asked sarcastically. "The same way you were certain that we could outrun that storm?"

Seig just stared, and contempt for his dependency on this man seethed out from his gaze. "Three days," he said and then turned, his black cape catching the wind as he strode off angrily towards the prison hold.

Yasen stood there in the center of the square, worried both for his friend and for that violet and yellow-eyed woman. "What would you do, Hollis?" he asked under his breath, but his ruminations were interrupted by a familiar voice.

"Is she going to be alright, North Wolf?" Goran asked with concern. "The woman, I mean?"

"I know who you meant, brother," Yasen replied. "Not if Tahd's men find her first, she won't."

"Who is she, then, that Cal would dare defy the whole company to keep her safe?" Goran mulled aloud. "I mean, sure ... she is pretty enough, but she must be somebody more than a pretty face to risk the governor's wrath like that. Ha!" Goran blurted out in self-amusement. "Either that or he's just a damned fool. Though my guess says it is probably a bit of both."

Yasen let out a breathy grunt of a laugh before he spoke. "I need you to find her for me. Well ... for Cal."

Goran stared and nodded at his chieftain. "Me? Well, aye, I guess it can't be you, can it?

Yasen shook his head and exhaled a deep, weary breath. "Something tells me that you are right, my old friend, that there is more to her than her pretty smile, and my gut tells me that Cal has an inkling as to what that something is."

"Do you know where she is?" Goran asked.

"There is a cave on the edge of the forest line, a few hundred paces into the trees. Hopefully she is still there. Tell her that you are a friend to Cal, and that he sent you to keep her safe," Yasen told him.

"And who is going to keep *him* safe, huh?" Goran asked with a pained glance at the prison hold.

Yasen thought about it for a moment. "I'll do my best for that boy, I owe him as much," he said with forced playfulness. "Besides, I would hate to see the governor get his hands dirty trying to shoe one of Cal's horses."

"Now that would be a sight, wouldn't it?" Goran bellowed out a laugh.

"Poor horses!"

The two woodcutters locked arms and Yasen whispered a goodbye. "Thank you for this. I'll see you on the tree line come morning."

"Mind you bring me a loaf of bread and a skin of mead, huh?" Goran said with a wink.

"Aye, maybe two skins," Yasen agreed.

The two brothers parted ways, one towards the timber gates and the other towards the prison hold. As Yasen passed the stables, his eye was caught by the faintest, azure glow peeking out from underneath the exposed rafters.

"Deryn," he whispered.

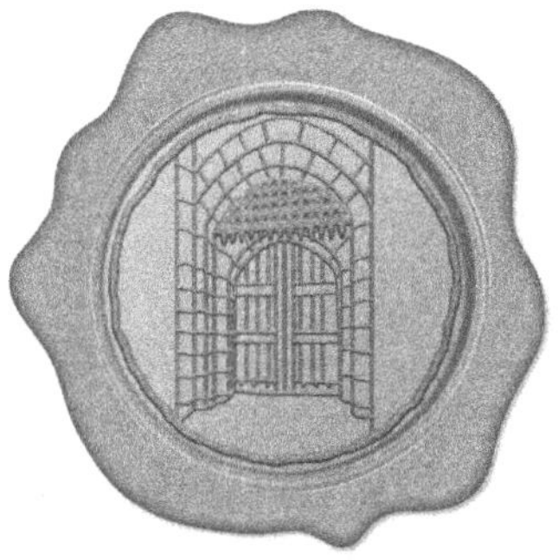

Chapter Twenty

"RIDERS BELOW!" MARCUM SHOUTED TO his archers there atop the battlements. "Mind your aim, men, and save your pointed darts for the enemy alone!" The air popped and whirred with the sounds of loosed bows and deadly arrows. The guardsmen watched and waited, kissing flints and breathing desperate prayers as their captain rode into the storm.

The twin dragons, which had been circling above the army as a flying shield and a deadly omen, unexpectedly broke away and dove straight for the rocky, treeless ground below them. In the light of the green-lit torches, their black scales appeared distorted, reflecting a poisonous byzantium underneath its inky sheen. Their massive bodies rolled in mirrored movement, collapsing their enormous wings against their serpentine frames. The ground rose fast to meet them, and then in an instant the air was assaulted again as two pairs of black, reptilian wings caught the wind. The dragons leveled their bodies for a focused assault.

"Ride hard! Do not give way to fear, brothers! Ride hard!" Armas shouted, doing his best to bolster his own wavering resolve.

The dragons glided a mere ten hands above the terrain in a sickly silence that whispered of imminent death and a fiery fury. Arrows bounced and pinged off of their hardened backs, and the cavalrymen pointed their silver blades with desperate hope.

"Hold the lines, move forward together!" Armas shouted to the uneven stripe of his thousand riders.

The company of men was not half a league from the twin monsters, and at the pace of their flight the collision would be much too soon for any riders to reach the Raven Army before the beasts could wheel around and attack again from behind. The lines held, and the heavy horses snorted and heaved with wild passion as the dragons closed the space between them with a malevolent glee in their evil green eyes.

"Hold!" Armas shouted again.

Riders of Haven. A duo of sickly, deep, booming voices was heard inside the minds of Armas and his men.

"Do not listen to this devilry!" Armas shouted to his men as his chest panged with a new sort of fear at the thought of *speaking* dragons.

Men of the dead tree, the voices continued in a vile and terrifying harmony. *Why must you cling to such folly? Labor for pious superstitions?*

The gap between the dragons and the riders was nearly gone. Armas shakily raised his horn to his lips to signal his men.

Do not die so needlessly, fools, when salvation is yet offered this day. The dragons' voices were mesmerizing. Their deep, growling malice threatened to paralyze whatever hints of bravery the men of Haven dared to hold to.

The blast of the captain's trumpet woke the foggy minds of his men. "BREAK! BREAK NOW!" he shouted down the lines. Armas let out a relieved breath as the riders heard him and complied, breaking their formation and cutting hard to the right and to the left, barely missing the yellowed fangs and black, pointed talons of the twin dragons.

Armas signaled once again to his men, and the main strength of his cavalry rode as hard and as dellberately as they could towards the marching host of the Raven Army. He and five score of his fiercest riders wheeled about to face the dragons, hoping to provide distraction enough for ruin to be brought upon the advancing horde.

"Spread yourselves, and secure your shields! Parley may not be their intention this time around," Armas shouted.

The dragons slowed their advance and began to climb into the sky, twisting and turning together in mirrored symmetry. Before anyone could give much thought to what they might be doing, the dragons descended again to the ground and seized two enormous boulders that had long ago made their home here in the fields beyond the walls. Their monstrous talons gripped the rocks effortlessly and pulled them free from the earth below. The dragons pounded their massive wings against the black air as they rose again in a slow, deliberate arc towards the walled city.

"What are they doing, Captain?" one the riders asked nervously as his chest heaved in and out.

"They are displaying their power," Armas said with despair.

The movement of the dragons was so symmetrical and deliberate that it appeared almost choreographed. When they had reached a precise point of their ascent, they swung the massive stones with immeasurable power towards the North Wall. As they let the boulders go, they set the ancient pieces of mountain ablaze in a wash of their sickly, green fire. The flaming boulders hurled straight for the North Gate of Haven.

"Take cover!" Marcum shouted to his men.

But the men were not swift enough, and the impact sent both archers and archway crumbling into fiery rubble. Every rider with Armas, now nearly a league away, felt the reverberation of the destruction.

The dragons ascended again, hardly visible in the darkness, rising, twisting and billowing vile smoke. Their green eyes pierced through the dim, foggy air just enough to give away their position, and Armas could see that they were now shifting directions in order to unleash their wrath upon the riders.

"We must charge them," Armas said. "We must keep them from the rest of the cavalry. CHARGE!"

The hundred heavy horsemen spurred their mounts and took up their long spears, preparing to engage the beasts that were supposed to only exist in the stories of old. As they rode hard towards the monsters, they knew full well that this ride, on this dark day, might very well be their last.

Bend your knees, and put down your blades! The dual voices of the dragons roared inside the minds of the men of Haven. *Why scrape and toil over twigs and timber when the gift of sight is yet offered to all? Surely you would at least turn your ears to the terms of the Queen before you die in a causeless offering of burnt, foolish flesh?* The dragons seemed to sing their last words in the bone-chilling blend of their venomous voices.

"Do not listen to their lies!" Armas shouted as the sounds of armor clashing began to come to life behind him. "Our brothers have reached the legions! Buy them time!"

The main strength of the cavalry crashed on two fronts into the vanguard of the marching Raven Army. The black-plumed warlords blew their soul-chilling horns and the ashen faced, green-eyed men let loose their raven-fletched arrows into the company of Haven's riders.

Screams and grunts, clashes and clanks woke the darkness in a cacophony of battle. The first wave of riders were cut down in a sudden collapse of strength as nearly two hundred of their horses were felled by the black arrows of the dark bowmen. Those that survived the falls from their horses were thrown into a sea of madness, trying desperately to cut themselves free from the black tide that surrounded them. The riders that were still mounted continued to kick and slash their way through the initial ranks of the enemy horde, trampling hundreds under the weight of the horses' heavy hooves, but the endless sea of muted steel and black-helmed enemies seemed to grow.

Armas and his men rode hard, the silver points of their heavy spears reflecting in the firelight before them. The dragons flew now in mirrored terror once again. The ground passed swiftly and silently beneath their leathery wings as they glided toward an inevitable collision.

Her offer is a gift to your weary bones, but our wrath be will be no such gift to the weak-minded men who choose it, the dragons implored.

"We by the THREE who is SEVEN!" Armas shouted in defiance, his men nervously echoing his words.

FOOLS! The dragons' voices erupted in an angered crescendo. *Shiny, stupid fools!*

ROARRAAHH! Green fire poured out of their fanged mouths in terrible unison. The riders broke hard, willing their horses to cut right and left to avoid the fiery blaze, but the heat of the vile, green fire was too much, too fast, and nearly a dozen of Armas' men were consumed in a wash of screams and scorches. The riders that did manage to escape the dragons' fury wheeled their horses fast around. They hurled their spears with desperate force, hoping to catch a chink in the inky, scaled armor that protected the terrible monsters. Their aim was sure, but to their dismay neither blade nor spear was able to penetrate the scales of the winged terrors.

The dragons roared in angered protest, then laughed in a maniacal duet of dark and haunting rage. *Spears? What use are spears and blades and bows against the son and daughter of Aerebus? ROARRAHH!* The sky went bright in sickly illumination at their green, violent upheaval of fire. *Bend your knees or we will break them from your bodies!*

"Break the line! Ride fast and split the twins!" Armas shouted to his diminishing company as the dragons arched in mirrored movements higher into the dark sky. "Erik!" he ordered one of his corporals. "Go west, and I will go east ... ride! Now!"

Armas spurred his mount, and half of his men followed suit, riding hard to the east in hopes of distracting the two beasts long enough for the remaining archers and cavalry to do their worst upon the marching Raven Army.

Erik paused just a moment longer than he knew was prudent and watched as his captain rode. "You heard the captain. To the west, now!" The smaller company took off in valiant haste, while the dragons maneuvered themselves into a swift and terrible decent. "Here they come!" the corporal shouted.

The dragons did not take the bait. Instead of splitting their strength and attacking the riders on two fronts, they set their evil, green eyes directly upon Erik's riders. *All hail the mighty corporal!* came the mocking voices of the dragons. Though he knew now that this charge was indeed futile, Erik did not falter in his resolve.

Armas halted his men where they were and wheeled around to watch the scene unfold. "Damn it all!" he shouted.

The noise of bows being loosed could be heard on two fronts now. The arrows of Haven sounded crisp and long, whirring against the air as they flew though the black, morning sky in search of vengeance. From the north came the arrows of the Raven Army; the sound was forced and short and finished with the unmistakable sound of spilled blood and punctured flesh as the riders fell off their mounts.

The twin beasts caught and held the current of wind propelling their massive, leathery wings. *Enough of your running now ... our amusement has dimmed. This is your final mercy, men of the dead tree. Bend your knees and take her promise!*

Erik looked back behind him while he desperately rode. The eyes of his fellow riders and their horses were bulging wide in sheer terror as they did their best to escape the doom that closed in upon them. His throat went completely dry, and his voice cracked under the strain of his emotions as he bounced in the rhythm of the pounding hooves and the rocky terrain.

"We, by the THREE who is-" his hoarse voice was stolen from him as the two dragons slammed their taloned feet into the company of men with incensed rage, crushing spine and steed as they leveled the group of riders to the ground. The monsters worked in tandem, slashing with their arms and biting with their yellow fangs, severing limb and head and horse. When the carnage was dealt to their satisfaction, they stepped back in mirrored unison before lighting the bloodied, mangled heap in a wash of green fire.

"No!" Armas whispered from across the field of battle. The few riders with him brought their mounts closer to the captain, their faces stunned at the merciless butchering of their brother guardsmen.

"What hope have we with horse and blade when dragons rule the air and scorch the ground?" A young, red-haired cavalryman spoke up with somber practicality, the fight drained from his eyes.

"Maybe we should accept their mercy and meet this woman who commands dragons to do her parley," another suggested to the remaining riders.

Armas knew they were probably right, that accepting this Raven Queen's offer was the only way to save their lives, and yet he could not bring himself to trust that any promises offered by these fearsome creatures would be a true mercy to anyone.

"Captain?" The red-haired rider spoke up. "Captain, what say you? Do we bend the knee and accept the mercy, or go on dying in a heap of burnt blood and broken bone?"

Armas looked across the outlying field, his eyes staring unbelievably at the slaughter before him. The longbows of his archers continued to rain down upon the still-marching mass of a Raven horde, and the remaining few hundred of his heavy horsemen were still slashing and fighting their way with flagging strength into the enemy ranks.

The twin dragons perched arrogantly atop the heap of horses and guardsmen, green fire billowing out from around their monstrous forms in a cloud of vile flame.

"There is no mercy this day, men," Armas replied. "And I fear the morrow will fail us as well. No. We must find a way to fight for those who cannot fight for themselves. And if it means that we who were once bright citizens of a shining city are now nothing more than the outliers and exiles we have all once scorned ... well then ... *may it be so.*"

Armas kicked his horse and rode hard and deliberately to the center of the outlying field. The dragons, nearly a league away, fixed their venomous, green-eyed gaze upon the lone rider there in the middle of the battle. Their massive feet shook the ground as they positioned their ink-scaled bodies to charge this brazen fool.

Captain of the dead tree, why must you order so much death and so much bloodshed? The dragons bellowed inside Armas' mind, and their haunting voices seemed to get louder as he approached them. *Do you come now to finally put aside your pride and bow to the Raven Queen?*

The cries of falling men, the snorts of warring steeds, and the clank and thud of biting blades still roiled on to the north as Armas' company fought and defended themselves against the black tide. He surveyed the field, his bowels churning at the carnage. The main strength of his host had been diminished to less than two hundred of the thousand cavalrymen he had led onto this bloody, black field of war.

"This is a dark day for you, once-bright fields and forests. I name you *Melania,* for your soil is watered black with the blood of men and ravens, tainted and burnt by the fire of dragons," Armas whispered to the wind.

GAROOM. GAROOM. The dragons' feet pounded upon the black earth, awaiting an answer from the captain.

Armas raised his horn to his lips and with defeat in his eyes and desperation in his lungs, he sounded the retreat. The sad notes cut through the chaos of the battle and the men clad in the soiled garments of green and silver raised their bloodied heads in shock. As they parried blow after blow of the sharpened steel, they beheld their captain, alone, with his horn to his lips.

The signal sounded again, and the few men who still lived wheeled their horses around and shouted to their fellow riders, "RETREAT!" Within seconds the lines broke and the heavy horses rode hard and weary towards their captain. The raven-fletched bolts of the crossbows whirred and whizzed through the air, doing their worst to further diminish the strength of the retreating cavalry of Haven.

Armas remained stalwart atop his steed, watching and waiting for his company to meet him there so that they might face the impending doom together. Though he may have wished to evade his own demise, he would not ride to his safety and watch the massacre of the men who had fought so bravely alongside him all this time. He signaled to his smaller company that still waited to the east, and in reluctant obedience the remaining thirty departed the field and rode towards the North Gate.

ROARRAH! came the violent, raging voices of the twin dragons as the dark sky woke in another wash of their evil green fury. The ground to the south was rumbling with the retreating sound of pounding hooves, while the sky to the east began to fill with the massive forms of the winged monsters.

"Come on, men!" Armas said behind gritted teeth. "Come on now."

WHOOSH. WHOOSH. WHOOSH.

The leathery wings of the invading monsters beat the air in an ominous cadence of coming ruin as the remaining riders approached their captain. The space around Armas was suddenly filled with the blood-soaked and breathless forms of his weary horsemen; exhaustion and confusion were written plainly upon their faces.

"Retreat, Captain?" came the heaving voice of a white-bearded officer.

"Johnrey, we have fought while we could, and now we must fall back and turn our blades to the task of rescue," Armas explained.

"But Captain, there is still yet fight in our tired bones and bite in our broken blades," Johnrey argued.

"Then we must use that fight with a new purpose now, for the citizens that our brothers have died defending will surely perish if we stay here upon this black field of war," he replied. "Ride for the gate, and prepare both yourselves and our people for exile. The city will fall," Armas said with ominous certainty. "Our city will fall to this Raven Army of the un-light."

Johnrey was not pleased with this kind of talking, but knew his captain to be a brave and wise man, and he felt the reverberations of nearly four thousand black boots marching in union behind him. With protest in his heart but respect upon his face, he agreed to the orders. "Aye, Captain, we will save our people."

"Ride then!" Armas ordered. "Ride hard and ride now!"

The captain spurred his horse and his company followed suit. One hundred and fifty brave horsemen of Haven rode with desperation for the gate that lay between the two massive watch fires.

"RIDE!" Armas called again.

As the ground rolled out before them, twin pairs of dragons' eyes appeared between their position and the city wall. The men did not adjust their trajectory, for they knew a collision with the beasts was unavoidable.

"Watch for their fire!" the captain yelled to his men.

The two dragons glided effortlessly as their black, leathery wings silently spanned the dim sky. Their gaze was hungry and their yellow fangs were stained red with the blood of horse and hero. They rushed over the ground in a stealthy blur, coming to deliver their final assault.

Arrows flew at the dragons from the lingering archers from atop the ramparts of wall that was still intact, but they flew in vain. Shields were raised and spears were pointed as the cavalry rode hard towards the city, bracing themselves for the impact.

Know you this day that it was your pride that brought forth your doom ... foolish men of the dead tree.

The voices seemed even angrier, more full of hate and vengeance and contempt.

Perish then, if you must, for the reign of the Raven Queen shall know no border.

Armas pointed his sword at the beasts and stared the closer of the two right in the eye. The dragon caught his look, and a sickly, self-satisfied grin distorted his features for just a moment.

ROARRAHHH!

The mouths of the dragons opened in mirrored fury, and the green, all-consuming fire erupted from within their venomous bowels. Like a rogue wave upon the unsuspecting shoreline, their anger was relentlessly and finally unleashed upon the last remaining cavalrymen of the Citadel.

Chapter Twenty-One

"THIS REALLY IS A PIECE of horse dung, isn't it?" a young guardsmen said to his fellow man-at-arms. "It's not balanced at all ... in fact, it feels like there is a sack of rocks tied to the pointed end of this useless blade!"

"I say that we take it to the smithy and have him melt it down into a pretty pair of prison irons!" the other guardsmen mused. "I for one wouldn't be caught dead with this gaudy old relic."

Cal sat locked inside the iron-barred hold on the eastern wall of the colony outpost, listening to the taunts and jests of the guardsmen. Though they mocked Gwarwyn, he paid them little mind, for his thoughts were focused on replaying the events that had landed him here. The injustice of the moment had triggered something deep and primal inside his heart, and his actions against Pyrrhus had felt true and sure. When he had swung his blade and defended the lady, the consequence of such an action had not mattered in the slightest. But now ... now, here behind the bars of this crude prison hold, his heart was filled with shame and guilt.

What if she didn't get away? What if ... what if I just made things worse for her? Please protect her. His thoughts turned to prayers as he sat powerlessly in the cell.

Just then the lock clicked and clanked as the latch released its iron hold on the prison door, and Cal looked up from his defeated posture to see the governor himself standing in the doorway.

"You made quite a scene today, *groomsman*," Seig seethed. "You nearly killed one of my best knights, and in case you have not noticed ... I do not have very many knights to spare."

Cal sat silently, afraid that if he were to speak he might evoke an even greater wrath than he was already due.

"Tell me, groomsman," Seig paused for effect, running his tongue over his teeth in disgust. "The Wreather woman, how is it that she knew what name to call you by? How is it that a scout, such as yourself, would fail to report the discovery of a *native Wreather*?"

"I ... I was afraid-"

"How is it, *groomsman,* that you would risk the safety and the strength of this colony and its holy assignment for the selfish secret of a *woman*?" Seig shouted his questions, punctuating them with a pounding fist on the timber wall.

Cal stood to his feet to face his accuser. "No sir, I risked no such thing. I feared ... I feared for the well being of that woman, because I hoped to win her trust and learn more about this wilderness. But it was the cruelty of that knight of yours that I could not let go unopposed."

"And who has given you the authority to oppose anything, groomsman?" Seig snarled, his eyes bulging with untempered fury.

"What authority could be needed to defend life, to protect the innocent?" Cal said indignantly.

"*My authority*!" he bellowed. "Mine! When your *defense* of it weakens my ability to carry out the very will of his Brightness himself, then you shall have no such authority!" Seig stopped his shouting for a moment and looked Cal up and down. "I do not think I can trust your judgment to ... to run rogue within my walls for another moment," Seig decided.

Cal shook his head and let out a frustrated sigh, both for the single-mindedness of this man towering before him and for his own rashness that had landed him inside this prison hold.

"I can no longer trust you to keep the primacy of our mission in the forefront of your mind," Seig rendered his judgment.

"Governor," Cal pleaded. "You saw what Pyrrhus was going to do to her. How can any servant of the Citadel be expected to allow such actions?"

"You assaulted and maimed one of my men, one of the Citadel's men, and you risked the peace of this outpost for your own selfish agenda," he continued without so much as acknowledging Cal's words. "When our ship sets sail in three days time, you, *groomsman,* will be aboard it, and it will return with the groomsman I should have chosen to begin with."

"Governor, no, please! Who will see to the horses in the meantime?" Cal's voice became desperate. "Please, sir, I will accept a fair punishment, but do not shame me so!"

"You have already done the shaming, groomsman," Seig said as he eyed Cal with furious disappointment. "I am simply seeing to it that your shame is no longer able to spread through my colony, and you should be grateful that your dignity is all I am stripping from you, instead of your own arm or your own life." Seig looked around the small holding cell and a satisfied smirk crept across his bearded face. "Take a good look around you. This is the last of the Wreath that you will ever see." And with that, the door was slammed shut and locked behind him.

Cal collapsed in defeat on the cold, stone floor of the cell. "What have I done?" he cried out loud, shaking his head in utter disbelief. "Please, forgive me," he prayed. "Please ... I was only trying to help her." Cal's heart sank as the sound of the governor's voice faded with each and every angry step he took towards his quarters on the eastern wall of the stronghold. "What have I done?" he cried over and over again in the dark solitude of his cell.

"I saw what you did," a gruff voice whispered. "There is no need to ask forgiveness for your actions, brother. The bastard had it coming if you ask me."

Cal's eyes were wet with the tears of hopelessness as he looked up to see Yasen peering in from the other side of the small, barred window.

"But they are going to send me back to Haven," Cal explained. "How am I supposed to seek the *light*? How am I supposed to follow the call of the THREE who is SEVEN and honor the will of the Poets ... and how am I ... I don't know." Cal knelt, pinned to the floor of his cell, feeling a weight of defeat that he had never known before. "How am I going to do any of it locked in here, let alone exiled back to where I started? I *cannot* go back!"

"Do you not think that our Great Father foreknew the deeds that would culminate in this moment?" A tiny yet powerfully bright voice added itself to the conversation. "And yet, Bright Fame, still it was your hands that held the torch, it was your heart He called forth, and it is you to whom He has given the beautiful and terrible gift of the dawn's blade."

"And He is probably regretting those decisions at this very moment," Cal responded dejectedly.

"And that," Deryn said as he left the hidden confines of Yasen's wolf fur and flew into the tiny prison hold. "That is where you are most certainly mistaken, my friend. For there is not a trace of regret in the heart of our Great Father, though many of His children have caused pain with their folly. He alone knows the paths of His purposes, and it very well may be that yours runs wholly through the walls of this very prison."

Cal's eyes welled again with the tears of desperation, but his heart knew that what the Sprite spoke was indeed true.

"I am sorry," Cal said to the both of them. "I don't know what came over me out there."

"Oh trust me ... I do," Yasen said with a knowing smirk. "Beauty like hers is worth a thousand nights in a thousand prison holds, and to defend it from the likes of that bullish ass of a knight ... well, all the more reason you have nothing to regret."

"But what about her? Astyræ?" Cal asked him. "Is she alright? Did she-"

"She is alright for the moment," Yasen interrupted him. "As far as I know she is safe enough. I sent Goran to look after her."

Cal exhaled for what seemed like the first time since he was dragged away from the square, and relief washed over him in the most holy of ways.

"Yasen, Deryn," Cal said as he regained his composure. "I cannot go back to Haven! I cannot go back on the ship ... not when I am so close, not when Shaimira is still out there."

"Shaimira?" Yasen said, a bit confused. "I thought her name was Astyræ?"

"No brother ... Shaimira is not a woman," Cal told him as he searched the face of his Sprite guardian for approval. Deryn nodded his agreement, and Cal began to whisper of all the things he had found in the tower of

Enguerrand. He spoke of Illium and the tree men, of the markings and the hidden word and the northward arrow.

"I am just a woodcutter, one with only one eye at that," Yasen said in response to the tale. "But even I can see that there is indeed a greater magic at work in this world. Perhaps this light, Illium's light, is really there to be found." He ran his hand over his tired face and rubbed the tension from his eye, but for those who would care to look, there was something indeed awake in him. "It may still all be nothing more than old Poet lore, but perhaps ... perhaps it may be something more than just flints and fire knights, huh?"

"Help me, Yasen," Cal appealed, sensing the spark that was igniting in the heart of the mighty North Wolf. "Reason with the governor. Make him reconsider, will you?"

"I doubt that man has ever reconsidered anything," Yasen replied with a sullen expression. "But I will see to it that you are not aboard that ship when it sails for Haven."

Understanding fell upon Cal in such a way that its gravity robbed the hopeful moment of any possible joy. "Are you saying-"

"Aye. Quiet now! Not another word about it," Yasen interrupted him, afraid of the listening ears of the nearby guardsmen. "Perhaps your Sprite friend here is right. This prison might be the very gift of rest you'll need to prepare yourself for your journey north."

Cal nodded his understanding, and there was a mix of hope and sorrow and a healthy measure of trepidation in his dark eyes. "Things won't be much the same anymore, will they?"

"The same?" Deryn asked. "I don't think that was ever the intention of our Great Father, was it?" Deryn replied. "For if it was, the great tree would still burn its immortal flames, and I would still be locked away in the bowels of the Hilgari, and you ... well, you would not be here now, would you?"

"But there is so much that is now unknown," Cal said. "This wilderness is not familiar to me yet, and at least ... at least I could count on these timber walls to provide some sort of safety and respite from the search," Cal said anxiously. "But now ..."

"Only scared men long for what they have always known," Deryn postulated aloud.

"Maybe you're right then, I suppose," Cal replied with amusement.

"I should hope I am, my friend," Deryn said warmly as he came to rest upon Cal's shoulder. "But do not be afraid, Calarmindon Bright Fame, you are still and will always be in good company."

Cal chuckled to himself, finding the presence of laughter in the midst of such uncertainty oddly appropriate, though completely unexpected.

"It is the best that I can offer you, brother," Yasen said. "Rest while you can, and then, when the time comes, find that violet-eyed woman of yours, and make your way north." Yasen looked to his left and then again to his right, worried still that the intention of his plans would become known to the guardsmen. "Find this *Shaimira* ... it very well might be the only guardian of real hope for us all."

Cal rose to his feet to clasp hands with his friend through the vertical, iron bars that held him captive. "I am sorry for all of this. It was never my intention to cause such a mess for you, or Pyrrhus even ... or for me." A weight came over his face; not one of sorrow, but rather of great responsibility. "I am thankful for your help, regardless. You are a true and brave friend, Yasen, and even if you only have one eye left ... I am glad that it still watches out for me."

"Aye, I'll watch out for you alright!" Yasen said. "Though I don't know which of the bears we have met is the more frightening of the two; the green-eyed demon one of the northern territory, or this pompous governor of ours." He laughed a satisfied laugh. "Ah ... they are probably equally as terrible. Rest well, brother, but stay ready ... I'll come for you soon."

The excitement of the evening had finally died down as the night patrol had returned to the colony's stronghold unsuccessfully. The guardsmen, eager to please their governor, had resolved to redouble their efforts after a flagon or two of hot, mulled wine and a bit of sleep to warm the body and sharpen the eyes.

Rest, however, did not come easy for Astyræ. At the urgent bidding of the woodcutter she had fled with reckless haste into the darkness of the Wreath. With nothing but a small, meager torch, she ran towards the narrow cave just beyond the line of trees. Every creaking branch, every caw of bird and every howl of wilderwolf sent a chill of fear reverberating through her body, for she knew that she was indeed being hunted.

It did not take her long to find her dark sanctuary there, hidden in the midst of the massive trees. Her breath came in desperate gasps, and the exhaled wisps of exhausted fear billowed in the cold as she entered the cave. She mustered her resolve, focusing her violet eyes to peer through the darkness by the failing light of the last burning embers of her torch. She looked at the stone formations by the flickering torchlight, and she noticed an outcropping of rock that stood not too far within the bowels of this hiding place. She hurried in, glancing behind her again and again with dread that her pursuers would indeed find her and drag her back to the tree men's outpost. She crouched low behind the jutted rock, hidden so as to keep from sight of the cave's entrance and yet still keep an eye and an ear on any who may enter.

She glanced up from her hiding place and saw the light of the torch illuminating the interior of the cave, and knew that if anyone should be nearby, they would see the glow and, in fact, find her. So it was with a single sob and a deliberate burst of force that she flung the torch to the ground and buried the last bit of her remaining light under the dirt of the earthen floor. The deep blackness engulfed her then, and the waves of overwhelming emotion crashed fearful and silent upon her dirt-smudged cheeks. Her heart raced and her body shook as she waited for her fate to come and find her inside the cavern.

Hours passed as she sat, crouched in the black darkness, staring at the mouth of the hidden cave. Her mind was nervous, wide-awake and ready to flee or fight at the first sign of trouble.

Crack. Crunch. Heavy footsteps sounded upon fallen twigs and dead leaves. Astyræ's breath caught in her chest, and she raised the dagger of the woodcutter, ready to make her stand if necessary.

Crunch. The sound came again, and the beating of her heart began to pound wildly in her ears. She swallowed hard, willing away her fear and praying that it was an animal, or Cal, or anyone but those tree men.

"My lady?" came a deep, whispered voice. "My lady, are you there, are you safe?"

She remained quiet, as still as she could will herself to be, for she did not recognize this voice and feared the worst had come for her. She closed her eyes, willing him to leave the cave.

"My lady, I am a friend of the groomsman ... and Yasen told me that I would find you here." Goran stood and listened to his whispered words bouncing and echoing off the stone cave walls, but no sound save the trickling of water could be heard. He stepped into the cave then, shining his torch around as he searched for the missing woman. "Ah ... blast it all!" he cursed to himself. "What kind of trouble did you get yourself into now, lass?" The large woodcutter spoke into the darkness as he pulled on his beard, surveying the rock by torchlight, hoping that he had found the right cave after all.

Just as Goran was about to give up, a small whisper stopped him. "Woodcutter ... wait, please," Astyræ begged.

Goran spun around, thrusting his torch further into the dark, stone hold of the forest cave. The flickering light caught the violet and yellow eyes of the hidden woman as she leaned out from behind her hiding place. The sight of her gave the mountain of a woodcutter a glorious fright. "My lady?" Goran asked timidly. "Who, or should I say, *what* are you?"

Chapter Twenty-Two

"ENGELMANN?" CHAIPHUS CURIOUSLY ASKED THE lieutenant as he ran his fingers over his embellished flint in an absent-minded ritual. Satisfaction at hearing this news was dripping from his words.

"Yes, my Chancellor," the lieutenant responded. "The old Arborist began ranting and shouting his treasonous propaganda there on the streets of Westriver, right in front of the prison hold."

"Why was I not informed of this earlier?" Chaiphus demanded sternly, the fleeting glee of Engelmann's arrest fading into the background of power and decorum. "Do you not suppose that the arrest of one of our city's Arborists might have warranted a speedier report?"

"Yes ... yes, my Chancellor," the lieutenant said, feeling the weight of the scolding. "When the great tree fell, I ... well, I thought your office might have more important things to consider than the roster of traitors and rabble-rousers that inhabit the prison holds."

"Yes, well, indeed my attention has been in great demand as of late. Regardless, lieutenant, the next time the master warden welcomes such a guest to his subterranean abode, I do expect to be informed immediately," the Chancellor insisted. "Now, be off with you."

"Yes, my lord," he agreed, and with a bowed head and cross-armed salute, the old lieutenant turned on his heels and left the high-walled chambers of the Chancellor's office.

"Well, perhaps there is a bit of light here in this damnable darkness after all," Chaiphus mused aloud as he poured the steaming hot tea into his silver chalice. "At least my ears will be given respite from all that badgering they have taken as of late from that fool of an Arborist."

The large, ironbound doors swung open in practiced unison as two green-cloaked guardsmen stood at attention, ushering the Priest King himself into the office of the Chancellor. Chaiphus stood. The smells of strong tea, dried citrus, and baked raisin croquets warmed the cool air of the morning with a hospitality that seemed rather out of place in the midst of the current chaos.

"Your Brightness," he said with a well-practiced bow. "Would you join me as I break my fast this pleasant morning?" Chaiphus nodded to his arch-backed scribe. Without so much as single word, the old man left to retrieve a second chalice.

Jhames eyed his old friend quizzically; the curiosity was unable to remain fully hidden beneath the pious posture of the white-bearded Priest King. "Tell me, Chaiphus, what it is that has so brightened your spirit on this dark morning?" Jhames asked.

"Engelmann," Chaiphus said with a wry smile.

"Engelmann?" Jhames questioned as the two of them sat down to Chaiphus' table. "He has only given you great measures of grief as of late, questioning my rule and subversively leading the naïve hearts of our citizens to chase after wind-whispered myths and frivolous old fantasies." He took the newly offered chalice of tea and blew a cooling breath over its surface. "What in the name of the THREE who is SEVEN could he have possibly done to produce such an air of levity?" Jhames continued.

Chaiphus smiled. He sipped his tea and pinched one of the crispy, sweet croquets between his thumb and forefinger, eying the doughy morsel with deliberate hesitation before he took a deeply satisfactory bite. "It would seem, Your Brightness, that Engelmann the hopeful has now become

Engelmann the arrested."

"Oh?" Jhames said with a lift of his heavy, white eyebrows.

"Indeed," Chaiphus gloated. "The green-haired fool is across the river in the care of the master warden as we speak."

"Did you authorize this, Chaiphus?" the Priest King said with a surge of disproval. I thought we had agreed-"

"No, the old Arborist brought it upon himself. The sergeant-at-arms had no choice but to lock him up, for he took his rants too far this time. Too far, indeed."

"And the people?" Jhames asked, a bit concerned that their energies would now be spent quelling yet another uprising of the frightened and irresolute citizens. "Have his people rioted? For I have not heard news of pardon demands or bloody skirmishes reported from any of our officers."

"Neither have I, Your Brightness," Chaiphus said as he savored the last bite of his pastry. "Neither have I."

The chamber doors of the office of the Chancellor burst open with a loud bang. They turned in startled unison to see the frightened and weary face of the bedraggled rider who entered through them, and his visage quickly stole the momentary joy of the dark morning without even so much as a word. The Priest King and the Chancellor exchanged worried, knowing glances before rising to hear the message this guardsman had traveled long to bring.

"Your Brightness," the rider said with lowered eyes. "My Lord Chancellor," he greeted with a nod of his head. "Captain Armas sent me to inform you that the North Gate is under attack."

"Does the captain know the ... *nature of* our new enemy?" Chaiphus prodded.

The rider took a deep breath, bracing himself for the fallout that might very well come upon the answer of his question. He looked the Chancellor in the eye and then turned his gaze towards the white-haired Priest King. "Dragons," he said stoically. "Their legions advance under the winged protection of twin monsters, and even now I fear that the defenses have broken and the wall is ... lost."

Clang. The sound of silver on stone reverberated through the chamber as the chalice fell from the Priest King's hands and clattered to the floor. His eyes slipped closed as he took in the news. "Our once-bright city," he lamented aloud.

"What will you have of me?" the rider spoke resolutely. "What word if any, would you have me send?"

Chaiphus took a moment to think in the tension of the silence. The weight of the attack and possible breach threatened to rob his very chambers of the necessary breath to will words to be spoken.

"Ride to the barracks of the Capital Guard." Jhames spoke more confidently than Chaiphus expected, his lament now turning to outrage. "Deliver this message to the commanding officer." Jhames turned his gaze from the weary guardsman to the hunched scribe sitting at the ready. "Take this down," he ordered.

The scribe nodded his obedience and retrieved a small piece of parchment from the writing table. His quill moved quickly across the page as he wrote the desperate words of the Priest King.

"Assemble the remaining guard of Haven with banners unfurled and blades terrible, for an enemy has breached the North Wall, and we will ride out to meet them," Jhames said, his words devoid of emotion.

"But Your Brightness!" the rider objected. "They must be nearly ten thousand strong! The whole of our strength is already on the wall; those who remain here in the city barely number seven hundred."

"I do not intend to march the leagues of our kingdom to be willfully slaughtered, *rider*," Jhames said to the young guardsman, annoyed at the insubordinate questioning. "We will ride to conference, to parley with the enemy ... and I will not do so with my tail tucked between my legs like a wounded dog. I will ride, and our people will ride, as though we are not afraid to strike back at the night!"

"But what if they will not parley? What if our remaining strength is consumed in the green evil of the dragons' fire?" he asked.

"Tree or no tree, we are still the *center of the world*, and that, by its very nature, demands audience!" Jhames fumed, clenching his spindly fingers into an angry fist. "The strength of our kingdom has NEVER been subject to magic trees or holy fire! Rather it was built—and has remained—because of our determination and our resolve to shine!" Jhames turned his attention from the young rider back to Chaiphus. "This is what our Priest fathers before us once spoke of, the great darkening of the world. The task now falls to us, my old friend, to remind our city and our enemies that *we can make our own light."*

Chaiphus nodded in nervous agreement while the scribe dripped the melted wax upon the newly commissioned orders. Chaiphus walked to the desk and raised the brass sigil of the Priest King, speaking as he pressed the seal into the molten green. "May it be so."

Jhames took the rolled parchment from the hands of the Chancellor and turned to give it to the rider. "Ride now, for soon we will meet our enemy together."

"Yes, your Brightness," the rider replied in defeat, understanding the intentions of the orders and yet mistrusting their effectiveness in the face of the dragons. He saluted the Priest King and the Chancellor with all the respect he could muster, then turned to take his leave.

"Rider?" Chaiphus said with a condescending tone, stopping the man mid-step.

"Yes, my Chancellor?" he replied.

"What is your name, son?" he continued.

"Benhiram, my lords," the rider said.

"Remember this day, *Benhiram*, who it is that you serve, lest your treasonous allegiance to fear rob you of both king and country," Chaiphus scolded.

Benhiram nodded his obedience and then left the chambers in great haste.

Jhames watched as the heavy, elaborately carved doors closed behind the frightened and weary rider. "Send for Ispen and Aspen, Chancellor. Perhaps there is some hidden strength still left in their gnarled old trunks."

Outside the walls of the Chancellor's office, there under the rotunda of the Citadel, Benhiram whispered a silent prayer for his brothers at the North Gate. "Protect them please ... and if there is still a way for victory," he said as he exhaled an exhausted breath, "make it clear somehow, and lead us down its true ways."

A faint thunder could be felt beneath soles of his boots, and Benhiram looked up toward the northern borough of Piney Creek. There in the far and distant blackness of the great darkness that had shrouded the entire kingdom, he saw the bursts of green light that faintly illuminated the black sky in a terrible unison with the rumbling ground tremors.

"Oh victory ... please," he said aloud.

"Look out!" came a frantic shout from behind him. "This fool of a beast has lost her senses!"

He turned too late to move out of the way of the oncoming brewers cart, and he went sprawling to the stone street in an aggravated heap.

"My pardon to you, son!" yelled a green-haired Arborist. "I don't know what in the damnable dark has gotten into the old nag, but she is spooked right out of her good sense! We are about a very important task now, please, forgive us!"

Benhiram got to his feet, dusted off his tunic and rubbed the throbbing spot on his lower back. He watched as the Arborists rode off down the stone street, trying to control the reckless mule that seemed to lose her mind each time the ground shook beneath her.

"I don't blame her," he called after them. "Important task? Why don't you look north and see where the real importance lies!"

But the Arborists was already well removed from ear shot, so Benhiram mounted his weary horse and rode off with parchment in hand to deliver the words and wishes of the Priest King.

Chapter Twenty-Three

"HEY!" MICHAEL SHOUTED THROUGH THE iron bars at the frantic guardsmen running urgently out in the main courtyard of the prison hold. "You there!" But despite his calls, not a single guardsman slowed to pay any mind to the prisoners.

"It is no use," he said to the men in the hold. "They have been at it all morning like this, running here and there, loading down mule carts and whispering their orders. Whatever it is that has their attention has robbed them of the good sense—not to mention the common courtesy—to feed their prisoners."

"Aye, all their commotion has got me a bit on edge, to tell it plain," said a long bearded brewer who went by the name of Timorets. "I've been inside these damn blasted walls, behind these damn blasted bars for three weeks now and I've never seen any of the green-coats like this."

"Three weeks is all, huh?" said Celrod, a round-bellied schoolmaster. His small eyes and full cheeks made his face appear as if he were always smiling, even when he was most angry. "Well, you are the expert now, aren't you?" he said sarcastically.

"Don't you worry, Michael," Timorets said while staring daggers through Celrod. "If they forget to feed us, we can just eat the schoolmaster here; there is plenty of him to go around."

But Michael was not concerned with the banter between the two inmates. The fearful and hurried state of the guards made him worry for Margarid. She was still out there, somewhere, without him in the madness of the darkened city.

"It would seem to me, my dear friends, that what we have feared most is perhaps happening ... *now*," Engelmann said matter-of-factly.

"Oh yeah, Arborist?" Celrod asked. "And just what is it that we have most feared? If you ask me, I do not know what else there is to fear now that the tree has failed us and darkness has taken up its permanent residence over our city."

Engelmann smiled a knowing smile at the large man, much the same way a grizzled and battle-wise old knight would smile at his naïve squire. "It is not darkness that poses the real threat to us, nor is it the absence of light ... no, it is not even the death of our stalwart bastion of brilliance. What we should fear—and what I suppose these anxious guardsmen are indeed preparing for—is not the darkness itself ... but rather what lives within it ... what moves in the wake of its ravenous wings."

The words of the green-haired sage left the cell silent as their meaning took form in the minds of the prisoners.

"Just what are you saying, Arborist?" Timorets asked nervously.

The bright blast of the guardsmen's trumpets filled the air and cut through the inmates' conversation. The men moved to gather near the window of the prison hold, straining to hear what might be said in the courtyard and hoping that the Arborist's assumptions were indeed nothing more than the senile superstitions of an old man.

The master warden brought the whole of his company to order with a raised hand and a grim expression. He was neither tall nor short, not particularly threatening or commanding by appearance alone. However, since the death of the great tree, his dark skin and hairless head caused him to nearly disappear in the blackness; lending him an air of intimidation by the fires of his torchlight that he could not have manufactured on his own.

"We have received our orders, and we have made our preparations," the master warden bellowed to his small company of guardsmen. "We will be the last to join the parade of the Priest King, but make no mistake, men; our position will not provide for your safety." The dark man scanned the faces of his tired men. "So say your farewells, kiss your flints and speak your words. The vanguard approaches as we speak."

"And what of the inmates?" Engelmann shouted with authority through the iron bars that looked out onto the courtyard where the guardsmen gathered. "What if you do not return? Will you just leave us here to starve, helpless in these iron graves?"

The eyes of the master warden reflected angrily in the flickering fire of the torches, and he turned to meet the gaze of the defrocked and imprisoned Arborist.

"While you and your men are off, hopeful to parley with the residents of darkness, what will become of these men who have made their homes in the city of light?" Engelmann continued.

"While we may hope to parley with the enemy, we will not entertain the badgering of mossy-bearded traitors," the master warden rebuked.

"Badgering or not, my dear jailer, the question still remains ... and these men are still in your charge," Engelmann pressed. The air around him seemed to invisibly pop and thunder, a storm of indignant offense brooding in the atmosphere around him. "Do not foolishly dismiss the possibility that these very men you are leaving trapped behind your iron bars will be all that is left to defend our city."

"The Priest King himself ordered that *every* able guardsman is to march with him to meet our enemy face to face." The gaze of the master warden softened almost imperceptibly as he turned his attention towards Engelmann's iron cell. "I cannot disobey the will of the Priest King to care for you traitors."

"Do NOT damn these men to iron graves just because you willingly walk to yours," Engelmann roiled.

The master warden stomped angrily towards Engelmann, his impatience with the whole matter pushing him beyond the limits of decorum. "What would *you* have me do then, Arborist?" he growled as he made his way across the courtyard. "Huh? And why should I listen to you? You could not even save the one thing you were meant to care for, so what makes you presume you can lecture me about how I should care for mine?"

Engelmann stood, silently resolute. His mind was a storm of words and yet he refused to give into the brooding tempest, for he knew the exchange of thunderclaps with this small-minded man would not yield the results he was hoping for.

Michael and the rest of the prisoners watched nervously as the standoff continued. "You demanded this conference, *Arborist*! Now tell me what it is that you think I should do that will make any difference to the length or quality of *anyone's* lives? Or do you not truly see, fool, that we are *all already doomed*?" The master warden's voice scraped and stretched his vocal limits. "Tell me now!"

The master warden's guardsmen shuffled nervously in the courtyard as the words of their leader rattled the empty darkness.

"Not all things that are lost are inevitably doomed, and not all treasons are truly treacherous," Engelmann spoke quietly. "And for that matter, all oppositions are not spoken from the lips of enemies alone." The Arborist paused to let his words sink in. "Perhaps ... perhaps the voice of life might come from one who rightly dares to not so easily abandon it, regardless of its perceived length or quality."

The dark-skinned man just stared, the flickering light of his torch dancing in his frightened, wide eyes.

"Release the prisoners," Engelmann confidently demanded.

The horns of the Capital vanguard woke the heavy atmosphere with bright, brass tones, breaking the standoff and rousing the urgency of the guardsmen. "It is not my place to riddle with irrelevant old sages. It is my duty to serve the will of the Citadel." The master warden turned to his men and gave the order. "Do not turn your ears to this fool of a traitor, for he is merely trying to save his own skin. Raise the portcullis and fall into formation! We march with the Priest King, and we will meet our enemy in the way that all enemies are meant to be met." He turned back to the mossy-bearded prisoner in an effort to emphasize his next words. "Blade to blade and face to face."

The tired and terrified company of guardsmen began their march as the iron gate of the prison hold was raised with ominous intention. The remaining strength of the Capital guard was moving in slow, practiced steps along the stone streets of Westriver towards Kings' Gate, and as the last of his men passed through the raised iron bars of the prison hold, the master warden spoke for the last time.

"What I *value* is obedience, and the lives of my men. I do not have the time nor the energy to care otherwise. If you want to sort through the rubble and determine for yourself which of these traitors are truly treasonous ... well then, so be it. The Priest King waits for his guard, and I will not keep them from him."

Just then came the soul-chilling reverberation of a distant crash, as if something massive and heavy had unexpectedly collided with the ground.

"What in the name of the THREE who is SEVEN was that?" Timorets asked.

Michael looked to read the brown-barked face of his friend and teacher, but all he could find was some sort of worried understanding.

"That, brewer, is our doom coming to pay us a visit," Celrod said mockingly. "I, for one, am grateful it had the courtesy to knock before just barging into our cozy cell."

"I do believe that the schoolmaster is not too far from the truth, my friends," Engelmann said, his gaze not for a moment wavering from its northward stare.

"What does that mean, Arborist?" Timorets demanded. "*What* doom? What is coming for-?"

"Shhh ... quiet your worries for a moment," Engelmann interrupted. "I must listen."

"Quiet my worries?" Timorets said in utter disbelief. "You speak of evil riding on the wings of the darkness, and the master warden screams of our doom, and the teacher here babbles on about something coming for us, and the guardsmen have all left us here to rot! My worries are quite un-quietable!"

BOOM. The distant rumbling sounded yet again. The faces of the three men seemed to drain of color as dust and sand began to fall from the cracks of the stone ceiling overhead.

"Engelmann?" Michael asked, but no answer followed. The old Arborist stood there, stone-like and unmoved, and the green of his eyes faded to a milky white.

"What is he doing?" Celrod asked, his jovial demeanor now replaced with a sickened worry.

Michael looked at his two cellmates, unsure how to answer. "Engelmann?" His words were laced with uncertainty. "Engelmann, are you alright?"

"Wake up, you old fool!" Timorets said, his fear now overwhelming his senses. "Come on now ... you're giving the scholar here quite a fright." He reached out to shake the shoulder of the entranced Arborist, but when his hand touched Engelmann, a current of some deep magic grabbed hold of the brewer and threw him against the stone wall with a breath-stealing thud.

"Brewer!" Celrod exclaimed as the large man knelt down to help his friend.

Timorets' face was ashen and his dark eyes were wide with terror. The distant boom repeated its ominous rumbling. "They ... they ... *they are coming*," the brewer said in a shaking, frightened stutter.

"Who is coming?" Celrod begged.

"They ... they ... they are coming for us ... they are coming for us!" Timorets continued.

"Dammit you old drunk, who is coming?" Celrod demanded as his large face began to moisten with a cold sweat.

BOOM! The distant sound grew louder and the rumbling reverberation shook the walls of the prison hold with even greater force.

"Engelmann!" Michael screamed at the absent Arborist. "Engelmann, wake up! Wake up, please!" The distant memory of Cal there atop the west wall, his mind and body held in the unrelenting grip of whatever magic assailed him, flooded the thoughts of the imprisoned groomsman.

Timorets grabbed the lapels of the round-bodied teacher. A tear escaped his wide, terrified eyes and rolled down his bearded cheek. "They are coming!" he whispered in a panicked scream.

"Michael, can't you wake him? Can't you do something?" Celrod shouted to the groomsman.

"They are coming. They are coming," Timorets continued on. His whispers rose in ominous intensity, and their terrified cadence quickened the hearts of his cellmates with the pulsing tension of utter fright.

"Engelmann! What is happening?"

BOOM! This time, the force of the sound shook the entire ground beneath the prison hold, and prisoners nearby began to scream out in panic from their own iron cells.

BOOM! It came again, quicker and closer and deeper.

"They are coming! They are coming for us!" Timorets continued.

"Brewer! Get ahold of yourself!" Celrod demanded as he shook his bearded friend. "What did you see? Who is coming for us?"

"Over there!" came a voice from across the courtyard. "What in the damnable dark?"

A pounding wind gusted through the courtyard in short, violent bursts.

Celrod looked to Michael, his eyes wide like a frightened dog. "What is it? What do they see?"

Michael ran to the iron wall. Gripping the bars with his calloused hands, he lifted himself up to see above the stone battlements in hopes of spotting whatever it was that the other prisoners had seen.

"They ... they ..." Timorets tried to speak, but his panicked voice could not seem to maintain control of his words.

"What is it, Michael?" Celrod shouted as he held the frightened brewer tight, willing sanity to return to Timorets.

"They are here," Timorets said, his voice suddenly flat and unwavering.

Celrod's eyes went wide as a cold shudder washed over him and the skin on the back of his large neck rippled with goose-pimpled flesh. "Michael?" His voice wavered in the wake of his fear. "Michael, for the love of the THREE who is SEVEN, what do you see lad?"

WHOOSH! WHOOSH! The same torrents of angered wind sounded again, closer. Michael lowered himself from the iron bars he had been clinging to, there at the top of his cell. His face was sickly white with disbelief. The young groomsman turned to look at his mossy-bearded mentor, whose sagely wisdom and unshakable courage had once persuaded him to hope when all others despaired. Now, though, the champion of hope stood stone-like and bewitched, nothing more than a statue.

"Engelmann, please!" his voice whispered his plea.

Celrod searched the groomsman's face as he knelt beside the brewer. Their silent conversation was held for mere moments before the sounds of a violent crash and bloody screams woke them from their reverie. The ground shook in rhythmic succession as stones and turrets began to collide and crash onto the sacred ground of the holy city.

"Down!" The brewer shouted from his corner as he watched a fiery projectile hurtling towards the courtyard before them. "Everyone find cover!"

The collision sent fodder and fire splintering in a thousand destructive directions.

"What is happening?" Celrod demanded as he shouted above the chaotic noise.

"Dragons!" Michael finally said to the round teacher. "Two of them as far as I can see."

Celrod's face went slack in utter disbelief. "Dragons? But there have not been dragons in Aiénor for *centuries*!"

"I know ... and yet ... their flames light up the city," Michael said with shocked acceptance. "Engelmann was right."

ROARRR! The soul-chilling screams of the twin dragons sounded on the wind as the mighty serpents soared in mirrored unison, assaulting the walled city of Haven with a barrage of missile-like boulders.

"We have to get out of here!" Timorets blurted to his fellow prisoners. The fever that had possessed his senses just moments before had now cleared from his eyes. "It is no longer safe here in the city."

"Where are the guardsmen?" Celrod fumed. "Where are those damned green coats when you need them?"

ROARRR! The violent screams of the monsters threatened to drown their conversation in wave after furious wave of annihilation. Off in the distance, Michael and his fellow prisoners could see a wash of sickly, green fire pour over the many roofs of Westriver, filling the black sky with a smoke-riddled, deathly glow that was punctuated by the panicked screams of Haven's citizens.

"We will roast alive in here!" Celrod said with a hard swallow. "They left us to roast alive!"

"Come on then," Michael said. "There has to be a way out of here!"

Another wave of crashing stones and falling strongholds filled their ears with the sounds of city collapsing all around them.

"Margarid!" Michael whispered to himself, worry now fueling his resolve to escape. "Grab that rock, grab whatever you can!" he ordered. "We have to break the lock! We have to get out of this iron hell!"

The three men went to work, hurriedly and clumsily using whatever they could get their hands on to smash and pound the locking mechanism, all the while praying that their efforts might spring the hold of their doomed fate.

ROARRR! The twin dragons screamed their maniacal roars once again. The whooshing of their leathery wings seemed closer now, and the fury of their violent wake blew Michael's long, dark hair in an ominous gust of foretelling. He stopped pounding, his hands bloody and aching from the crude, sharp edges of his shattered stone. As he looked to the sky, what he saw robbed the resolute groomsman of any hope of escape he had endeavored to collect.

The two pairs of hungry, green, glowing eyes seemed fixed in a ravenous stare upon the trapped inhabitants of the prison hold. The faint, sickly hues of byzantium scales caught the roaring fires of the besieged city below and reflected their deadly intent.

Completely unlooked for, the voice of Engelmann the hopeful broke through the madness of the moment. "Get down!" he shouted with a thunderous authority. "Away from the gate, now!"

The three inmates, though completely startled by the forgotten voice, did not for a moment hesitate to follow his instruction. They leaped with terrified deftness, sheltering themselves behind the thickest part of the stone walls. Within mere moments of their obedience, the iron gate that had once doomed them to a fiery death exploded in a jumble of mangled bars and splintered stone.

They shielded their faces, recoiling from the blast, cringing away from the heat of the green flames. A small measure of relief washed over them as they watched the twin beasts circle away from the prison yard and back towards the center of the city to inflict more doom upon whatever living residents they could find.

The four of them looked each other over, quickly checking for broken bones and bloody flesh. A collective sigh of relief was given before Engelmann spoke again. "Come on now, my boys. It would seem to me that the THREE who is SEVEN has not written off our lives just yet, at least not with the disregard of our friend, the master warden. So let us return the same courtesy to the forgotten citizens of this wretched place, shall we?"

"Engelmann!" Michael blurted out with a bit more concern to his words than he expected. "What happened to you? Are you-"

"We haven't the time to find answers to all of our unasked questions, my boy," the old Arborist proclaimed, unwilling to let him finish his thought. "At least not when there are dragons afoot. Come now, we have work to do!"

The three men nodded in agreement, choking back their questions beneath the thick clouds of deadly smoke that billowed from the burning roofs around them. They carefully climbed their way out from the heap of fallen stone and mangled iron, but what they saw before them made their hearts sink.

The courtyard was ablaze, washed in the wake of the sickly green fire. The high guard towers stood decapitated, their finished keeps now nothing more than rubble on the ground of the square. The smell of burning straw and painted timber was poisoned with the horrid stench of burning hair and melting flesh, and the stark awareness of the carnage slammed into the swirling thoughts of the three men as they beheld the horror before them.

A dozen of the prison chambers on the north side of the courtyard had been engulfed in flames. The small, freed company of men scanned the wreckage and peered through the smoke-laden carnage in search of survivors, but the only residents they could see upon first glance were blackened and charred, clinging lifelessly to their iron bars.

"Are they all dead?" Timorets whispered tentatively as he leaned into the rubble.

"Help us!" choked a voice from out of the thickness of the smoke. "Help us, please!"

"Over here!" another called. "Help!"

"Come on! Quickly now!" Engelmann ordered. The old Arborist moved with determined agility, leaping over fallen rubble and hurdling broken battlements as he wound his way towards the desperate voices calling for help.

"Do you see them?" Michael shouted to his old friend. "I can't see anything in all this blasted smoke!"

"Help us! Please hurry!" a voice begged again.

There, at the eastern end of the prison hold, two lone figures waved and shouted their cries for help from within a mangled, burning corner chamber. "Over there!" Michael shouted. "I see them! Hurry!"

"Help! Please hurry!" the two men screamed desperately as the growing flames began to lick their hungry way closer and closer towards the cell.

"Quickly now, my boys," Engelmann urged. "They haven't much time left."

Michael reached the fiery prison cell first and went straight to work with a broken piece of stone that he had picked up in the courtyard. As he grabbed the iron lock that held the two prisoners captive, an agonizing pain shot through his left hand. Michael screamed out in excruciating shock, but it was too late. The blistering metal lock had seared an angry impression on the groomsman's hand. Instantly, blisters began to form on the tender side of his palm. With great agony and pain-induced rage, he smashed the piece of rubble against the molten metal until it gave up its resistance and released its lock.

Michael held his left hand in his right, willing his mind to focus on something other than the damage to his skin. The corners of his eyes were wet with tears, both from the intensity of the smoke and from the burning pain. Timorets was next to reach the cell, and he kicked the door open with the sole of his boot so as to not repeat the same flesh-melting mistake as his new friend.

"Come on now ... is it just the two of you?" the brewer asked the two men.

"No," the taller of the two tried to cough out, but the thick smoke and the intense heat were robbing the very breath from his lungs. "No ... our brother," he coughed violently again, his words getting lost amidst the din of the chaos. "He ... is still-"

"Hurry now!" Timorets interrupted. "Let's move before this whole place goes up in flames and takes us all!"

"Hurry lads!" Celrod shouted against the roar of the fire and the crushing sounds of chaos, while Timorets did his best to help the two prisoners from their fiery cell.

BAROOM.

BAROOM.

BAROOM.

The guttural, sickly horns sounded off in the distance. Their otherworldly tones pierced the ears of the newly liberated prisoners of Haven and instantly stole whatever hope they had managed to revive in their weary and terrified hearts.

"What kind of devil makes a signal like that?" Celrod asked the mossy-bearded Arborist.

"The same kind of devil that marches in the shadows of dragon's wings," Engelmann responded. "We have to hurry. We must leave this place ... now."

Timorets led the two weary but grateful prisoners out from the rubble of their prison cell and into the smoke-filled courtyard, where his friends waited to receive them.

"Are you alright?" Michael asked between clenched teeth as he held his badly burnt hand.

The taller of the two men coughed and wheezed against the smoke. "One ... one more."

"One more what?" Michael asked.

"Of ... of *us*!" the man labored.

"Brewer!" Michael shouted. "There is another still in there!"

Timorets hesitated a mere moment, calculating the likelihood of another successful trip into the fire. Then he steeled his face, nodded to Michael, and pulled his sweat-soaked shirt up over his nose and mouth so as to try and filter the suffocating smoke. He wound back through the debris of ruined stone, but before he could make it to the fiery rubble of the prison cell, he heard a whooshing sound overhead. A large support beam alight with the sickly green flames crashed heavily and finally into the remains of the iron door, dooming the third brother to a bitter death.

"No, dammit all!" Timorets shouted in angered rage as he shielded his face from the growing flames. The heat was too intense and the smoke became too thick to even breathe. Another one of the massive support beams plummeted in a heavy blaze only a few paces from where he stood, and Timorets had no choice but to let the fallen prisoner go.

Engelmann was the first to see the brewer emerge out of the smoke, and the defeated shake of his bearded head was all the evidence the Arborist needed to prod the men into action. "Come now, my boys, the prison hold is lost, and I fear this city of ours will not stand much longer. I do not intend for you to go the same way."

BAROOM. The soul-chilling reverberations echoed again. The war horns of the invaders momentarily drowned out the frightened screams of the besieged citizens.

"What do they want?" Celrod asked anxiously.

"Quickly now!" Engelmann demanded. "There is no time to ponder the intentions of such bringers of death when there is still life to preserve." The Arborist looked the weary prisoners over. "We have to leave now!"

"But the portcullis is locked, and the walls are ablaze with whatever hellish fire comes from the bowels of dragons," Celrod reasoned aloud. "And how do you suppose we will survive out there with no blades and no armor, when the streets are overrun?" He turned his gaze to peer beyond the smoky rubble.

"The *Menashe,*" Engelmann whispered with deliberate intent, his eyes lighting with a hopeful glow as the word crossed his lips.

"*Kaestor's doom?*" Celrod recoiled. The large schoolmaster gulped nervously as he spoke. "That is where men go to disappear."

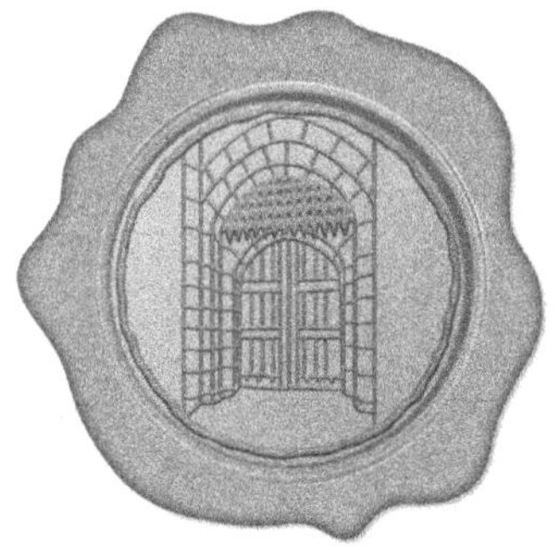

Chapter Twenty-Four

"SHHH! QUIET NOW," JOHNREY WHISPERED as he and a handful of riders and citizens watched from the hidden safety of the tavern's root cellar while legions of the black-cloaked Raven Army march in hardened unison. The menacing eyes of the invaders were devoid of life, and yet they seemed aglow with an evil, green enchantment. It had not taken long for the North Wall to fall and the strength of Haven's defenses to break under the fury of the mighty twin dragons and the overwhelming ranks of their marching forces.

It was Johnrey and a mere two score of his fellow cavalrymen that were able to return to the city and find a temporary reprieve within its walls. As for the remainder of the great company of Armas, they were lost there on the *Melania* field, killed or at the very least wounded and left for dead. Once the walls had been breached under the bombardment of massive stones and green fire, whatever resistance remained had quickly become overwhelmed and scattered.

The remnant of citizens and soldiers hid, huddled in the darkness as they watched the unfolding terror through the foggy windows of the cellar. The click of a latch above them caused the gathered citizens to freeze as the sound jolted their attention to the entrance of the cellar. Hands went to sheathed blades, and the collected breath was held in anxious silence as a pair of boots became visible on the steps. The room stayed quiet as the suffocating fear permeated the air, and the guardsmen and citizens alike stared at the soles of the feet of whoever this was who descended into their hiding place.

"Corporal?" came a whispered voice from atop the stairs.

A step down, and then another. "Is Corporal Johnrey down here?"

The men and women looked up to see a guardsman climbing down to them. A collective sigh of relief could be heard as the group realized that their position was still secure.

"Corporal?" the guardsman whispered as his feet touched the dirt floor. "Where is Johnrey?" His words came hushed and rather out-of-breath.

The white-bearded Johnrey tore his gaze away from the invading army to see one of the younger archers, his green tunic burnt and bloody and his right eye swollen shut. "What is it, son? What word do you bring?"

"Marcum has counted nearly two hundred of our bows and swords remaining, all of us scattered and hiding in cellars and in lofts throughout the borough," the archer explained.

"Two hundred?" Johnrey lamented. "From over two thousand strong ... to this." He shook his head and ran his hands through his snowy beard.

"Is there any word as to the captain?" Keily blurted out in unbridled worry.

All eyes were on the runner, hoping against the fiery odds that somehow Armas had been counted among the living that had survived the last charge, but the young guardsmen just looked to the dirt covered floor and shook his head sadly.

"What does the lieutenant wish us to do?" Johnrey asked, hoping to awaken some kind of confidence in the handful of people who had hidden here in the cellar.

"He has scouts combing the borough as we speak, passing the word to whomever they can find." The archer looked to the old officer. "Marcum says to *stay hidden*, to stay quiet until the raven storm passes-"

"That is ridiculous!" Keily demanded in a whisper. "Why should we cower like rats in the cellar, waiting for a storm to pass? You and I both know that it will do little good at all!"

"What good will it do for us to waste our lives for a battle that is already lost, my lady?" Johnrey said with saddened compassion to the fiery barmaid.

"I know this borough better than any of the guardsmen!" Keily protested. "I have memorized its streets and I know the back alleys like I know the lines on my own face. I can be an asset, I can help!"

"Help to do *what*?" Johnrey asked softly, his eyes pleading the question that none of them could answer. Tension filled the earthen-floored basement as the pull to do something, anything, competed with the prudence of remaining safely hidden.

"Dispatches have been sent to the Citadel," the runner explained. "The invaders march without hesitation towards the Capital, and I pray," he said as he kissed the flint that still hung to his neck, "that the THREE who is SEVEN will give them speed enough to warn the Citadel before it is too late."

"My lady," Johnrey whispered in an effort to calm Keily's unrest, "the Priest King, he will know what to-"

"What good are flints going to do when *dragons* rain fire upon the other boroughs?" she interrupted heatedly. "Tell me that, Johnrey!"

The white-bearded corporal winced at her flippant disrespect, but did not correct her. Instead he nodded to the archer, dismissing him to carry out his orders without further delay. The young guardsman saluted him and then turned to climb the rough-hewn ladder back up into the kitchen of the Gnarly Knob.

The weight of the barmaid's questions hung thick like a suffocating fog that had all but overtaken the root cellar, and no one dared to oppose her. They too had nervously asked themselves the very same questions and reasoned the very same troublesome answers. The group waited in the thickness, listening to the endless, rhythmic sound of marching boots and guttural signal horns, the underlying orchestral music of this nightmarish tragedy. The invading Raven Army advanced through the northern borough destroying both order and peace with a devastating and relentless fury.

Then the enemy war horns sounded once again, only this time, unlike all the other times before, the blasts were not deep-toned and infinitely resonate. The signals that issued forth from the ungodly instruments were sharp, staccato, high-toned bursts, and their melody gave a whole new perspective on terror. In an instant the marching army halted. Their boots fell silent on the dirt and stones as if they were waiting for the arrival of some great general or perhaps a mighty king.

"What is it? What is happening out there?" a young girl asked, frightened and curious. "Why have they stopped?"

"Shhh now, lass," Johnrey begged her. "I don't quite know."

"Why won't they just leave us?" she continued.

Keily came and put her arm around the freckle-cheeked little girl, and as she did the beautiful albeit hardened lines on her face softened ever so slightly with compassion for the little one.

Thunder roiled off in the distance, like the sound of a northern storm racing down from the Hilgari to pummel the already battered people of Piney Creek.

"What is that?" the young girl asked. She looked up to the curly-haired barmaid for guidance. When Keily placed her slender finger to her lips, she reluctantly obeyed and listened, terrified of what new hell would come for them.

Johnrey stood atop a barrel of Shameus' amber ale, peering out through the lone, muddy window, hoping to see whatever it was that he could see happening on the streets of the borough. The thunder grew louder by the moment, though its rumblings did not come and go like northern storms were known to do; this tempest was constant and ever-increasing. The tavern above began to moan and creak as its stone and timber became subservient to the rush of howling wind. The wood floor above them began to shift and shake. Dust unsettled itself from within the cracks and rained upon their frightened heads. The small group collectively held their breaths as the sound of rushing wind grew louder and louder.

"What is that sound?" said the old tailor as he strained to listen to the layers within the rolling thunder.

"Are those screams?" asked Johnrey.

"Some kind of brass ... some kind of signal?" Keily proposed.

Closer and closer came the ruinous gale, its thunder a rumbling cacophony of noise and wind. As the ground began to tremble beneath their feet, the sounds of the storm began to come into focus.

"Ravens!" shouted the little girl. "That is the cawing of the black birds!"

Keily knelt down and took the little girl by her small shoulders. "Where, girl? Where are the black birds?"

"In the storm ... the ravens are in the storm," she whispered.

Keily's eyes went wide. She leapt to her feet and climbed atop one of her father's ale barrels, determined to see this squall that was now swiftly and loudly upon them. What she beheld through the muddy cellar window made the very blood inside her veins run cold with terror. At first it looked like nothing more than a fast moving storm cloud. But as this mass approached the heart of the borough, the invading army's soldiers bowed their heads in an unsettling homage to whoever rode upon the loud, black winds.

Soon it became quite clear to Keily, as she did her best to swallow back her fears, that the thunder was no storm and that the black wind was no cloud; rather, this tempest was a murder of ravens that numbered at least five hundred strong.

The black-winged horde was driven by an unnaturally malevolent force; each of the birds' glowing, green eyes burned with a powerful hatred. It seemed as though the vile creatures were domineered by something much more sinister than their own evil strength. The enemy soldiers kneeled effortlessly in the wake of the storm of ravens, seemingly unaffected by the brutal winds. Not a feather in their black plumes rustled. Not a strand of their long, gangly hair moved. However, the thatched roofs and watch fires in the borough did not fare as well underneath the ravenous force of such evil.

Keily could hardly contain her horror as she beheld what came upon the heels of the storm. The closer it came to the Gnarly Knob, the more she could make out the details of this eerie and terrifying spectacle. The green-eyed birds flocked tightly and dangerously together, flying roughly thirty hands off of the ground. Hundreds of tightly wound leather thongs streamed out from behind the black brood and came to an end in the hands of a well-muscled, ashen-skinned driver.

The driver sat atop a black carriage, whose very shape resembled the flayed, feathered wings of the same murderous birds that drove it onward. The wings of the carriage fanned out until the tips of its iron-scaled feathers met at a peak; forming an ominous covering over a hidden passenger. Its four large wheels looked nothing like wood and iron. Instead, they had an obsidian quality to them, a shiny, onyx-like stone with a craftsmanship that did not show a single tool mark or imperfection; rather, these otherworldly wheels seemed to have been formed by a magic spoken into the black stone.

The dark carriage came to a rest in the center of the borough's square, and the kneeling soldiers of the invading army rose to their feet. Their black-feathered helms made the monstrous men seem like giants, while their unpolished chainmail caught the flicker of the burning city and caused their frames to glow with a muted green reflection.

"Who are they?" Johnrey heard the barmaid whisper.

"Shhh, quiet now," the old officer hushed back. "I do not know."

The world was silent there in the ruined center of Piney Creek, almost as if the very tongue of the place had been cut from its once-jovial mouth, rendering its voice paralyzed by fear and with no means by which to speak it.

The most decorated of the green-eyed soldiers approached the raven-drawn carriage. His glowing green eyes did not waver, nor did he lower his head to hide his gaze. Rather, he seemed devoid of emotion altogether, reverence or otherwise, and it was this detached nature that disturbed Keily most of all.

"As you commanded, my dark queen," the Raven General reported in a vacant voice. "The city of the dead tree has been breached, their warriors have been broken, and even now *Abaddon* and *Angrah* wreak their fiery havoc upon the infidel citizens."

The general stood fully erect at the edge of the carriage. His large, mailed shoulders were adorned in a dark charcoal cape, and his head was crowned with an intricately inlayed helm. Its prominent, beak-like shape and menacing eyeholes nearly covered his entire face save an angular section over his silver-bearded, ashen-colored mouth.

"This is very ... *pleasing* to me, General Aius." A woman's voice spoke out from within the winged safety of the raven-drawn transport. "Very pleasing to me, indeed." Her words cut through the moment with a luxurious edge, like a battle-sharpened blade wrapped in the finest Abondalian silk.

"The way to the dead tree is clear, Raveness, for our legions have gone before you and have prepared these unenlightened souls to receive their new liege," General Aius reported.

"Well done, my nocturnal General," she gloated. "Perhaps it is time we show these pious flint-wielders just what true power *looks* like, and where their reverence is rightfully due."

The Raven Queen stood to her feet to survey the carnage of her army's conquest. Though her back was turned towards the watching remnant in the root cellar, the very sight of her caused the hairs on the back of Keily's neck to prickle in cold fear. Her long, braided hair was as black as the lightless sky; it caught and reflected the siege fires in a luminous shimmer that glowed with sinister origins. She wore an iron bodice, inscribed with intricately chiseled runes of an unfamiliar speech. Its very embellishments seemed somehow fluid, ever changing, shifting in the shadows and laced with dark magic. The skin of her pale arms was covered in deep, inked markings of the ancient sorcerers. The green light of the enemy torches illuminated what little of the motifs could be seen, for they were barely hidden by the cascading layers of raven feathers that crowned her armor, encircling her neck before falling down her shoulders.

The white skin of her back was exposed, a long triangle of vulnerability that began at her shoulders and revealed a small pink imperfection of a scar just below her left shoulder blade. Her gown was a deep byzantium, much akin to the sickly hues of purple that colored the inky, black scales of her two winged serpents, and she carried in her ornately ringed fingers a long, obsidian staff.

"Aius," she said with a sultry command.

"Yes, Queen Nogcwren," the green-eyed general replied as he raised his raven-helmed head to meet her gaze.

"Burn this place. Raze it to the ground," she ordered him as she sniffed the night air like a predator who has caught scent of her prey. "Either these citizens of the *dead tree* will pledge their fealty to me, or they will have no place to remain citizens of. Resistance," she said greedily as she turned around and faced her general, "resistance is no longer an option." The deep, sickly yellow of her eyes smoldered with a self-satisfied supremacy.

"As you command, sorceress," the general obediently responded.

Without so much as another word, the Raven Queen took her seat in the fold of the winged carriage. The driver stood to his feet and raised his ink-marked hands towards the sky, commanding the ravens by the hundreds of thinly braided thongs that issued forth from his fingers. His green eyes were aglow with understanding as he opened his beardless mouth and screeched forth a command in a nightmarish voice to the flock of bridled birds.

The black sky erupted with a tumult of violence as the ravens woke the cold, north air with the pounding of their heinous wings. A thunderous crack of the driver's whip brought the carriage to life, and it barreled with great intention towards the Capital of Haven.

"Who was that?" Keily whispered to the old, white-bearded officer. "What kind of hell makes that kind of woman?"

"I cannot say. Though ... if I am honest," he said as he wiped the sweat from his brow, "I do not wish to find out."

"Do you think Marcum heard?" Keily said. "That they intend to raze the borough?"

Johnrey glanced at the dozen or so faces that looked desperately to him for some kind of guidance. He knew that hiding here would no longer be safe, not if the whole place was to be set aflame. "Gather what you can ... wine skins, salt pork, those dried apples over there. They mean to burn us out, and so we shall leave before the fires are upon us."

"Johnrey?" the little girl asked the old officer. "Where will you take us? Where will we go if we have no home? Will we go to the Capital?"

Johnrey looked to barmaid. His expression pleaded for her help to find the words that might bring this little one comfort.

"No, little Sharon." Keily knelt to meet the gaze of the young girl. "No, Johnrey would not dare take us there. We will have to find a safe place to hide until this storm passes."

"What place is safe?" Sharon asked innocently, but Keily could not seem to find the right kind of answer for her.

Without warning, the dark sky began to glow. The green and orange flames began to lick the sky as home and tannery, barn and butchery succumbed to the fires of the remaining Raven soldiers.

"Burn them all!" the general shouted to his men as he mounted his green-eyed warhorse. "And when the rats flee the flames, see to it that they do not run very far." With that command he wheeled his froth-mouthed steed around and rode hard on the North Road after his Raven Queen.

"Do you have what you are taking with you?" Johnrey urged. "We must move quickly now!"

The sounds of swords and screams cut through the roar of the burning fires as those who had been hiding tried to run from the flames and in turn found the spears of the invaders.

"Alright now, lads," Johnrey spoke to the six other guardsmen there in the cellar with him. "Keep a sharp eye out. We are going to make our way towards the broken gate."

"The North Gate?!" said a silver-haired woman. "Are you mad? Do you know what kind of evils wait for us out beyond the wall? We will be dead before morning!"

"No, my lady, I do not." Johnrey said with frustrated kindness in his eyes. "But I have seen the evils that hunt us here, and I would risk the morning for the chance to live another hour. *We must go now.*"

Two of the guardsmen climbed the steps to either side of the root cellar's entrance, and positioned themselves so that they might open the overhead doors while the remaining guardsmen set up a small perimeter around the handful of frightened citizens that were in their care.

Keily drew back her bow, the sharpened iron point of her arrow trained on the entry way, ready to dispatch any who dare stand in the way of their escape.

"On my mark," said the old officer. "Quiet as a mouse now, lads." Johnrey nodded at the two guardsmen, and they slowly lifted the heavy cellar doors. The other four guardsmen padded quietly to the top of the stairs with brandished blades, eager to see if the way was clear. One of the men nodded that all was indeed safe, so Johnrey, Keily, and the half dozen citizens climbed the old steps into the darkened alleyway behind the Gnarly Knob, thick with the smoky sadness of their burning homes.

"This way," Keily ordered.

"But the North Gate is this way!" the silver-haired woman protested.

"We have to stay clear of the square; that is where most of the fires are being started. Our best chance is to head east, deeper into the borough, before we double back towards the wall," she reasoned.

"Aye," Johnrey agreed. "Let's be on with it then."

Not more than a moment later, when the small remnant had fled the cellar of her father's ruined tavern, Keily turned to see her home catch fire and go up in a torrent of sickly green and bright amber flames.

The barmaid froze for an instant, saying a sad goodbye to the place that she loved while the tears quietly rolled down her smoke-stained cheeks. "Goodbye, Papa," she whispered into the greedy flames. "Goodbye."

"Keily?" Sharon asked as she reached for the woman's hand. "Keily, come on now, we must go."

"Aye, I hear you lass," she said sweetly as she wiped away the tears. "You lead on now."

As Keily moved to take her first step to follow little Sharon into the borough, the wall above her head reverberated with the sound of a raven-fletched arrow piercing the wood, not a handbreadth from her head.

Keily's eyes went wide with fear. "Run, Sharon! Run fast!" Three, four, a half-dozen arrows pierced the wall around her, splintering the wood and waking her from her sorrowful reverie. "*Run now!*"

The two of them raced as fast as they could. They turned left and cut between a row of shops, hoping that their change in direction might buy them a few more moments to put distance between them and the archers who meant to take their lives from them.

"Johnrey!" Keily shouted out as she ran, careless as to who else might hear her panicked voice. "Johnrey, they are upon us!" But the old officer did not answer her, and the walls of the shops began to feel the bite of the arrows once again.

"Quickly now!" she said to Sharon. "In here ... there!" Keily pointed to the large stone structure of an old chapel. "Over the fence!" The barmaid and the little girl burst through the alleyway and into a small, cleared field that was hemmed in by a stone knee wall. "Johnrey!" she shouted again, but all she could hear was the rushing of blood in her ears and the sound of Sharon's little, booted feet scampering upon the cobblestone pathway.

When the two of them had reached the knee wall, Keily quickly reached down and lifted Sharon up and over the stone fence before she, too, vaulted over. "Inside, Sharon, we will have to hide in there. Quickly now!"

Sharon's eyes were wide with fear, but she trusted this brave barmaid and so she nodded her childish agreement and took off towards the humble entry of the old Piney Creek chapel.

Whoosh! The sound of the raven arrows came near again as they fired past.

"Almost there! We are almost there!"

Keily and Sharon ran hard, and though their bodies were exhausted they were not yet ready to surrender their lives to the hands of the invading Raven Army. Keily risked a glance backwards, pausing for a brief moment to see the night sky behind them waking to life in an ominous glow as the fire began to consume the borough. A dozen black shadows appeared in her line of sight, and her breath caught in her chest as she heard the sound of loosed arrows once again.

"Sharon!" Keily shouted to the little girl who had run on ahead of her towards the chapel doors. "Sharon!"

Keily ran even harder, her will pushed her weary body as the rush of wind raced over her curly-haired head. The large wooden door that stood mere paces before the little girl was, in an ill-fated instant, riddled with the deafening thud of sure-fired arrows, fired from the Raven archers that pursued them. For the briefest of moments Keily hoped that maybe, just maybe, Sharon had escaped unharmed, for in the darkness she could not see if the arrows had indeed pierced the child. But Keily's relief was short lived. Sharon spun around, and the light of the siege fires illuminated the sickening sight. The little girl dropped as if the floor had been swept out from underneath her feet, and Keily's heart fell in sync with the small, lifeless body hitting the ground.

"No!" Keily shouted in horror. "Sharon! Sharon, no!" She fell to the ground beside the girl, too brokenhearted to go on.

Unexpectedly and without warning, the large chapel doors burst open and a score of arrows issued out of the once hallowed structure, flying straight over the head the tear-struck barmaid. Keily's eyes went wide as her mind registered just what had happened, and with what little awareness she still held, she flattened her body in an effort to avoid the clash of vengeance above her.

Chapter Twenty-Five

"HURRY NOW!" ELMER BECKONED. "THEY could be here any moment, and I for one would like to forgo any sort of introduction."

"I never in all my days knew a nag to run that fast," Portus said as he helped Margarid, Kahri, and the few others out from the brewer's cart.

"Madness is a mighty powerful motivator," Elmer said with a worried smile. "Come on now, hurry my friends! It is a miracle that my kind still has any privilege or power at all in these dark and deadly days, let alone the kind of clout that can still open portcullises."

"I think a maddened mule was the least of the guardsmen's worries," Kahri offered.

"Perhaps they thought you still had some magic in those grey-barked hands of yours," Margarid said as she watched Kahri and the others duck their heads and enter through the iron willow gate. "You do still have magic, don't you Arborist?" she asked nervously.

Elmer looked over her shoulder and saw, off in the distance, two pairs of sickly green orbs hurtling across the darkened sky towards them. The soul chilling sound of leathery-scaled wings pounding the cool air nearly robbed him of his voice.

"I don't know what kind of magic I still have," Elmer told the auburn-haired woman. "Certainly not the kind that staves off the winged beasts of darkness. But perhaps, I mean quite possibly, what I do have is enough to ..." he touched her soft face with his coarse, grey-bark fingers, "Enough to do something."

Margarid forced a smile. "Me too, Arborist," she said as she ducked her head beneath the iron branches and began her descent down the winding iron staircase.

The leaf-green, jeweled handle glowed underneath the grip of the youngest Arborist of Haven. As he pulled the iron door shut, he whispered ancient words of deep magic for the protection over this small remnant of those who wished to endure.

There were very few eyes privileged enough to behold the glowing hall of the Arborists, to take in the vibrant wonder of so much mystery held within these hallowed walls. Margarid, Portus, Kahri, and the rest were wide-eyed in stunned disbelief. The rooted columns of the great tree still glowed with life, and the very air around them hummed and prickled with a mystical charge to it.

"I never in all my days thought I would live to see what grows beneath the great tree," Portus said, a bit overwhelmed.

"I didn't even know enough to wish for such fantasies," Kahri said, her big, grey eyes watering at the fantastical display.

"Come now," Elmer urged them down the steps.

"These columns ... they ... they glow?" Portus said as he reached a hand out to touch the illuminated roots.

"Do not touch *anything*!" Elmer nearly screamed. Their surprise at such an outburst caught them all a bit off guard. Portus sheepishly withdrew his hand like a wounded child whose bare knuckles had just felt the backhand of his mother's wooden spoon. "Do not be mistaken, my new friends," Elmer lectured the small group. "Amber or not, silver or not," he raised his leafy green beard towards the black granite ceiling, "there is an untamed fire that still courses through these rooted columns, one that is still planted in the bowels of Mount Aureole—and it still demands our reverence."

Elmer lowered his gaze and fixed his eyes on those of his newly captivated audience. "And I do not wholly trust that it has faded beyond the point of peril. It has claimed the lives of holier men than the lot of you, and I do not wish to have your blood on my hands when Engelmann returns."

"Engelmann?" Margarid said as if waking from a dream. "Where is he, where is Engelmann?"

Just then an enormous shockwave shook the chamber. The ground beneath their boots quaked in the aftermath of some sort of cataclysmic collision. Dust and pebbles, rocks and debris began to rain down from the heights of the Arborist's great hall, filling the glowing air with irreverence. Shelves of books and scrolls toppled over all around them, and both Kahri and Margarid grabbed fearfully onto the tall tanner.

"I didn't mean anything by it, I swear." Portus whispered his repentant prayer while he kissed his flint.

The quaking stopped, and the dust-laden air became thick with the kind of fear that is only found in the frightful curiosities of the unknown.

"What was that?" a voice trembled out.

"Hurry, brother!" Elmer whispered to himself, his leaf-green eyes surveying the vaulted canopy of holy granite. "We haven't much time!" Just then, the glowing columns that made up the very structure of this ancient hall began to creak and groan, responding as if some great weight was stretching them beyond the core of their strength.

"What is happening?" Kahri asked. Her hands were held over her mouth in utter shock. "No!"

ROAAAR! The muffled sounds of the twin dragons shook the hall once again with a terrifying reverberation.

Elmer looked up towards the cavernous ceiling of the great hall. Though he could not hear the vile words that were being spoken, he knew their origin without question. His mind went reeling at the dark endings that may be waiting for him and this small remnant of the hopeful.

"Arborist?" Margarid asked. "Arborist!" But Elmer's gaze was fixed above, and his thoughts were too preoccupied with the coming doom to hear the nervous questioning of the frightened few. "Arborist, answer me, please!" she pleaded in between the muffled mockeries of the enemy. Her eyes stung as they filled with tears. Even here in Haven's most hallowed of places, hope itself was suffocating under the ever-present wings of this heavy darkness. "Elmer!" she screamed at last, daring to shake him by his wispy shoulders beneath his brown cloak.

The Arborist blinked his eyes. The bluest of tears rolled down his grey-barked skin as the thick fog of reverie thinned out before him. "I saw it." Elmer spoke as if waking from a dream. "I saw my own doom on the wind of their words. I saw the desecration of our holy mountain, of the gardens that my kind has tended with great pride, and the great tree..." He paused, swallowing hard against the blue tears that gathered and fell from his leafy beard. "This tree, this star at the center of the world, the very one we have served for generations ... there will be nothing left of it ... nothing."

"Then why have you led us here?" Margarid said, her frustration and fear now boiling over. "Did you bring us to this chamber to *die*?"

BOOM! The sound of falling stone reverberated through the hall as a massive boulder exploded into a hundred glittering pieces upon the granite floor. The glowing, rooted columns that supported the ceiling over this great hall began to writhe and moan, moving and stretching against their very will almost as if they were weeping while their brilliance intermittently flickered in distress.

"Why, Elmer?" she yelled as her small fist pounded the trunk-like chest of the holy man. "Why did you—"

"Because Engelmann told me to," he said, interrupting her. "He told me to gather the remnant and bring them here."

"Well, where is he then?" Portus demanded.

"What did he tell you? What was his plan, Elmer?" Margarid demanded.

Elmer looked longingly, rather desperately, towards the staircase, willing Engelmann to glide down the iron steps and help everything make sense. Though Elmer had magic woven throughout the rings of his body, he did not yet possess the confidence or insight that his elder brother so effortlessly displayed. The leafy beard of the Arborist began to turn color as he stared helplessly at the staircase. Almost imperceptibly at first, but then faster and to a greater degree, the youthful leaves that had crowned his innocent face began to die as the terrified group looked on. Then they began to float lifelessly down to the floor in a brown flight as the moment overtook him.

"Elmer, please!" Margarid pleaded. "You may have seen your doom, but you have not seen ours. Please do not curse us to the same fate!"

Elmer reached to his chin to find his once-green beard half-barren, bereft of leaves and crumbling. It was in that moment that he saw his grey, bark-covered finger, almost as if it were the first time. His attention caught upon it for just a moment, and then light flickered once again in the eyes of the youngest Arborist of Haven.

"North," he whispered, as if the very word were foreign upon his lips. Then he spoke the same word again and again with an excited swell of volume to each utterance. "North, north, *north*!"

"Has he gone mad?" Kahri asked as she hid behind Portus.

Elmer wheeled himself around in a flurry of falling leaves as his eyes searched the glittering walls in the deep recesses of the hall. "Come now, come quickly, my friends, for my doom will not be your doom. I think I understand now what I must do."

"Please, Elmer, please, tell me what it is that you must do?" Margarid pleaded, her voice unsure in the midst of all this madness.

The young Arborist took her by the shoulders. The blue tears fell slowly in dew droplets down his grey cheeks. "I must desecrate this mountain while I still have the magic enough to do so. That is, if HE wills it," Elmer told her as the light behind his eyes burned with a fierce certainty.

Margarid looked back to her scared and confused friends, and then again to the Arborist who held her shoulder. "I ... I do not understand? You would aid in the destruction of this place?"

"My child," Elmer said with a sagely tone he had not exhibited before. "You do not need to understand ... you simply need to go *north*." Elmer exhaled an oddly confident breath, and in doing so sent another browned leaf towards the granite floor. "Come now, we must hurry."

With that, the Arborist took off past the rows of shelves and tables. He weaved in and out of the creaking, weeping, rooted columns. Waving his grey, spindly finger out in front of him, he laughed with a madness of final purpose. "North! The remnant shall go north!"

The ground continued to shake beneath their feet, and without warning a scream awoke from within what seemed like the columns themselves. So terrifying, so soul chilling, and so terribly heartbreaking was this sound that the hairs upon every neck stood erect and the tears in every eye fell in an uncontrollable sorrow. The very roots of the great tree were weeping and screaming in an audible lament of their final death.

The light began to pulse in the room, rising and falling from a brilliant, electrified bright to an utter black, then back again.

Portus grabbed the hands of his friends, his mouth parched with fear. "What do we do now?" he asked. The dying illumination in the hall around him throbbed unevenly, like the last few breaths in the failing lungs of a hunted stag.

"North! You will go north!" came the insistent sound of the Arborist's voice.

Margarid looked up at the tall tanner. Their faces were both grimaced in pain as the roots still screamed in agony, yet somehow they understood each other's thoughts. Portus nodded his agreement and signaled for the remnant to follow the maddened Arborist to whatever doom or refuge awaited them.

"Over here, and hurry!" Elmer shouted in between the screams of the dying roots.

Margarid and the others did their best to find their way amidst the eerie, throbbing light, deeper and deeper into the recesses of the once-hallowed hall. After a long, tense moment of searching, they came upon the Arborist. He stood still, tracing his spindly, barked finger along some unseen pattern within the glittering rock of Mount Aureole.

"What are you doing, Elmer?" Margarid asked with a panicked exasperation. "This is the end of the hall! There are no more doorways or iron staircases. Why did you lead us to this ... this lifeless end?" Before the death of the tree, no citizen of Haven would have dared to question the mystical wisdom of the Arborists with such disregard, but here upon the panic-soaked floor of her desperation, the auburn-haired young woman did not give much thought to decorum.

"I—if the THREE who is SEVEN indeed wills it—am leading you north, my dear." Elmer mumbled, quite unoffended, eyes still fixed on the rock wall before him.

"But how? There is no way out," Portus reasoned.

Elmer held his finger out before him, staring at it intently and mumbling the fluid words of some unheard tongue. Finally, the tip of his grey finger glowed a fiery, amber hue akin to the long dead flames of the once great tree.

"Not all impasses are impassable," he said quietly, as if trying to reassure his own wavering resolve. "Not all ends have resigned themselves to death. Though our holiest moments may very well be our un-godliest hour, a fragile faith might move mountains yet."

"I ... I don't under-" Margarid's words were interrupted as she watched the youngest Arborist of Haven take his glowing finger and touch it to the secret pattern written in the granite walls of Mount Aureole.

Like fire to hot pitch, the shape of the northward arrow grew in fiery definition, glowing with the same amber magic that shone from the Arborist's finger.

"What does it mean, Elmer?" Portus asked.

"North, I think," Margarid answered.

"If HE wills it," Elmer said solemnly.

The ground beneath them began to rumble, and the breath of life seemed all but removed from the lungs of the rooted columns. Elmer knew, with as much certainty as one could have about anything in this darkened world, that his time here upon Aiénor was nearly over.

"Will you ask Him? Please?" Margarid begged.

Elmer nodded his answer and closed his leaf green eyes. His lips began to move in a blazing succession of brilliantly unrecognizable words, while blue tears formed cylindrical droplets in the barked corners of his eyes.

The tall, wispy Arborist swayed to and fro, as if he were being moved by an unfelt wind. Then, in a breath-ceasing moment, his grey eyelids burst open in a tumult of blue flames. The very sight of such magic caused the remnant to startle in fear, and Elmer himself seemed rather astonished at his own display. He looked at each of his hands, and then again at his frightened friends gathered there in the darkening recesses of this once great hall.

"Please!" Elmer whispered desperately before he placed his finger upon the glowing amber arrow. He took a deep breath, eyes still burning blue, and with his other hand he clasped the dying roots of the burning tree. As soon as his left hand made contact with the hallowed column, a torrent of amber light shot through the elm-like figure of the keeper of the tree and bore its way deep into the glittering rock of the mountain. The very earth that hung heavy above their heads roared and rumbled in violent protest, and Elmer arched his back in excruciating pain as the holy fire of the tree channeled its way through his body. He opened his mouth to scream in anguish, and as he did a dozen tendrils of amber magic shot forth from his lips and grasped in greedy fury for the granite ceiling of the hall.

The gathered remnant held onto each other in frightened horror as they watched their friend bear the wrath of hopeless prayers answered. Black rocks began to fall from the high ceilings and crash around the Arborist in bullying explosions, but though this searing pain ripped through his body, he did not relinquish his grasp nor waver in his cause. Portus, Kahri, and the rest watched through tear-blurred vision, unable to remove their stunned gazes from the unfolding horrors before them. It was Margarid and Margarid alone who looked back towards the iron staircase, there across the failing glory of the great hall.

"Hurry Michael ... please hurry, my love," she beckoned.

Without warning, the quaking ground stopped its shaking, and the whole of the hall fell instantly black. The smell of burning timber filled the chamber with a fireless smoke, and all who were gathered there beneath the hallowed hill held their breath in fearful anticipation.

The room, black as the darkened sky of Aiénor, began to slowly find illumination. The dying light held within the rooted columns seemed to swell again with life, and slowly but deliberately the room began to burn brighter and brighter.

"Elmer!" Margarid shouted into the deafening silence. "Elmer, are you alright?"

The head of the Arborist hung low. A hundred dead leaves piled around his leather-thonged feet, and as the light in the columns grew brighter, Elmer was able to lift his gaze to meet the eyes of his friends once more. The Arborist opened his mouth to speak, his eyes still aglow in the blue magic, but the voice that came forth was not the voice of their friend. The words that issued forth were deep, and resonant, both beautiful and terrible, though not of the tongue of men. The friends stood in mesmerized stillness as they listened to the cadence of magic and mystery.

Then, almost as if possessed by another spirit, the tone and timbre changed drastically, mirroring the sound of the winged serpents. "Do not dismay in the death of foolish tales, for the Raven Queen has brought your rebirth upon the wings of darkness." The two voices spoke in sickly harmony through the very lips of their Arborist friend, whose eyes were now aglow with a more sinister green. "Fill your sight with the gift of her un-light, and fear no more the limitation of human vision."

"No!" Elmer said in a faint whisper. His eyes blinked away the sickly green, but they did not change back to the blue of the powerful magic. Instead, they turned almost grey, ashen, as if the sap of life was all but drained from them. One final blue tear rolled down his cheek as he spoke one last time. "North, my friends. Seek the light. Seek only His ... *light.*"

His dying words hung for an eternity of moments in the brightly lit, dust-filled air of the hall. Finally, the sound of a great exhale caused the light to fall from the columns, like the last breath of a dying beast. It gathered and grew, collecting itself into a pinpoint of brilliance in the center of the dead Arborist. Then it shot through his outstretched hand and split a channel straight through the glittering, black rock of the holy mountain. As the amber shockwave coursed through the bowels of Mt. Aureole, the whole of Aiénor groaned a sorrowful groan while the light of the THREE who is SEVEN departed completely from the holy mountain.

Blackness threatened to suffocate the small, gathered remnant in its heavy silence until Portus finally called out to the lot of them. "Look!" he said in mystified wonder. "Over there ... the arrow, the one Elmer made appear ... it still glows. The amber magic lights the arrow."

The eyes of the hopeful friends found the glowing arrow. What seemed to have been the darkest of all moments now became illuminated in a new and unexpected way.

"He did it!" Kahri exclaimed. "He made a way North!"

"You did do it, didn't you?" Margarid whispered to the Arborist, though she knew in her heart that he would never hear her words.

Suddenly, the air around the small remnant prickled and glimmered with the faintest violet light. The blackness of the moment lifted, and in the dim yet palpable illumination, they could see that there was indeed a way of escape.

"Come on now," Margarid said. "Gather what is useful ... it is time that we say farewell to Haven." She placed her hand on the smoldering timber face of her Arborist friend. "I, for one, will not waste the sacrifice made to set us free."

"Aye," Portus said as Kahri nodded her agreement.

The seven of them gathered what few cloaks and leather satchels they could find, then passed under the amber arrow into the glittering granite bowels of Mount Aureole.

Chapter Twenty-Six

"DISAPPEARING IS EXACTLY WHAT WE need to do at the moment, my friend," Michael said, recognizing the wisdom in the Arborist's plan.

"Where does it lead?" Timorets asked nervously.

"The Capital, if I am not mistaken," Celrod replied.

"The walls are stronger there, and if Jhames is still within them ..." Michael reasoned.

"Out of the smoke and into the flames if you ask me," Celrod muttered.

"I'll take my chances with the swords of my countrymen over the fangs and fires of dragons any day," Timorets said decidedly to the large schoolmaster.

"We will take the pathway of the forgotten, under the mighty Abonris," Engelmann instructed. "We must *endure* ... and if we hope to have a fighting chance, we must flee this fallen place at once."

The five men, the beaten and bedraggled lot of them, all nodded in fearful understanding of the plans of the Arborist. The rumble of a not-so-distant crash startled their senses and woke them into action as they beheld their once-bright city glowing anew in a wash of green fire.

"Come on! Quickly now!" Engelmann urged.

The company of six began to make their way, though their wounds and weariness made difficult the trek towards the largest keep there at the center of the courtyard. The way was littered with broken battlements and flaming ruins. A charred ox-cart was turned on its side, making a gruesome mess of the once meticulous grounds. And yet, in a small turn of fortune that came at just the right moment, the cart also created a shallow cover by which they might hope to avoid the ravenous eyes of the twin dragons.

WHOOSH! WHOOSH! The pounding gales of wind from the leathery wings of the flying serpents reached their bodies as they took refuge behind the cart.

"Everybody get down, here they come again!" Engelmann whispered.

The company of prisoners waited and watched as the two dragons circled high above the Capital like a pair of carrion birds, claiming their ground and waiting for their long-tracked prey to finally give up its life and die.

"What are they doing now?" said the oldest and tallest of the two rescued brothers. "What are they waiting for?"

"Is it a display of power, I wonder?" Michael asked as he looked the lanky, dark-haired man in his smoke-reddened eyes.

"Haven't they done that already?" the brother replied.

"Come on, lads!" Celrod beckoned as he motioned for the two of them to move towards the keep, following Engelmann's lead.

The question bothered Michael. While he and the remaining prisoners did their best to traverse the massive courtyard of the prison hold, he could not help but worry as to the twin monsters' intentions. As he pondered the movements of the dragons, the moment took another turn for the worse. There, marching down the street in front of the prison hold with banners unfurled and eyes glowing green, the Raven Army approached in the deadly rhythm of invading doom. Michael's hand shot out and grabbed Timorets on the shoulder. With eyes wide, he motioned at the army that was passing a mere forty paces from where they stood. The men signaled each other and they took cover as quietly and completely as they could back behind the ox cart in the middle of the courtyard.

Their breath came in desperate gasps as they willed the marching invaders not to look their way through the iron bars of the prison hold's mangled main gate. Just then the sky spilt once again in a storm of green fire. The sickly horns of the invading army sounded their ominous tones and the very ground of the city shook and rumbled in offended protest.

"Look there!" Timorets mouthed the words to his friends as he pointed eastward toward the glittering, granite hill on Mount Aureole. The company turned in stunned unison, and what their eyes beheld nearly stopped their beating hearts. There, above the sacred hill where once the great burning tree of Haven stood, the twin dragons circled. The massive, lifeless trunk was a stark reminder of what had once been the light of Aiénor, the beacon of hope that had illuminated all the world with its unmade brilliance. Now it stood, hopeless and broken, surrounded by the screeching of the vile beasts who seemed to celebrate its demise.

"NO!" Michael screamed with involuntary protest. "Get away from there you damned devils!"

"*Quiet, groomsman*! Do you want to get us killed?" Celrod whispered in disgust. But it was too late. The sound of his voice had caught the attention of the invading Raven Army. Within moments, a dozen pairs of green, glowing eyes had parted from the marching ranks and turned their direction. By the faint light of the green flames, the six of them saw the soldiers raise black, iron crossbows and point their raven-fletched darts in through the portcullis.

WHOOSH. WHOOSH. The sounds of arrows flying through the iron bars threatened more than the skin of the small company of fleeing prisoners.

"What do we do now?" Timorets asked the Arborist. "They have us pinned down."

Engelmann raised his eyes above the over-turned ox-cart to see whatever it was that he hoped to see, and nearly a dozen black arrows raced passed the top of his head. He fell back down in hurry, and for the first time in all these last months, Michael saw fear in the eyes of his friend and teacher.

"Can we move this cart?" Michael asked, trying to offer a solution.

"Not unless we flip it right side up again," the older brother replied.

"Very well then," Michael said determinedly. "If we can right it, then we can push it all the way over there to the entrance to the keep—and then we can take our chances in the *Menashe*."

The men nodded their agreement, looking to Engelmann for his approval. He smiled a nervous smile at Michael. "To the tunnels."

WHOOSH. WHOOSH. The incessant sound of flying darts spurred them on, and relief revived their spirits as they saw that the arrows did not pierce through the burnt sides of the cart.

"Now, how are we going to move this blasted thing without one of us becoming a raven-fletched pincushion in the meantime?" Celrod asked.

"And what about the beast?" Timorets said as he pointed to the charred flesh of the large ox that lay lifelessly tethered to the cart.

"We will have to cut it loose!" the older brother replied.

"With what?" Celrod countered. "In case you have forgotten, the Citadel's guardsmen are not too keen on keeping sharp blades within reach of their prisoners."

ROARRR! The black winged monsters breathed fire in the sky above them. Their green blaze lit up the reflective wall of the granite mountain in the most terrifying of ways, and the company of prisoners knew that their time was short if they hoped to escape this fallen place.

"Underneath!" The older brother suggested. "If we are going to have to push this thing, let's at least cover our backs from the aim of the archers."

"But the ox?" Timorets exclaimed. "We can't push this cart and drag a dead beast too!"

"He is right, Engelmann," Michael said, scanning the face of his friend and mentor. But Engelmann did not say anything at all. Instead he placed both of his bark-covered hands on the underbelly of the ox cart. His lips began to form foreign words, words that neither Michael nor any of the other men recognized. Before the groomsman could ask what Engelmann was doing, the Arborist's eyes turned white. The prisoners all stared at the sage in fascination.

The words kept pouring from Engelmann's lips, faster and faster, not audible but certainly powerful. Then his eyes went wild in a wash of blue flame. In that moment, a magic somehow transferred from the Arborist to the wood of the cart he was touching, and the very grains of the dead timber began to wake again in its presence. Within moments, the iron bolts that had held the tongue of the wagon fast to the yoke clinked and clanked their way to the ground, almost as if they had been spat out in disgust from the wood frame of the cart.

The men shivered a little in the wake of the magic, unsettled and awed all in the very same moment.

"Alright then," the older brother finally said. "That takes care of that, I should think ... but we still have our work ahead of us. We are going to have to push this thing now. Come on, let's turn it upright."

The men nodded in agreement. They had somehow found their vigor and strength returned to their fear-sapped resolve and within moments they had pivoted the charred shell of the cart up onto its four iron-rimmed wheels.

Engelmann's chest heaved as the old Arborist tried to recover his breath. It seemed to the rest of the group that the magic, though powerful in craft, cost the mossy-bearded sage a great deal of strength. "I'll be alright in a moment, lads. Hurry now, we haven't the time to waste."

All, save Michael and the younger of the two rescued brothers, crawled underneath the blackened ox-cart. Shielding themselves behind the heavy, iron-rimmed wheels, they heaved and strained against its ruined weight while a barrage of ill-intended darts continued mercilessly in their direction.

The younger brother could hardly catch his breath after nearly succumbing to the suffocating strangle of so much smoke. He had just enough strength to walk on his own two feet, and was no help with the cart. Michael's badly burnt hand still raged and throbbed in searing agony, and though he had strength to give, he had not the means to give it. The two of them crouched low and moved along with the cart, willing it with their very spirits to move faster towards the entrance to the *Menashe*.

"Push lads!" Celrod shouted. "Put your backs into it!" But the weighty structure was compromised and the damaged wheels protested. The cart barely budged.

"All together, now!" Celrod shouted again against the sound of arrows being loosed. This time the cart creaked and groaned.

"Come on! Come on!" Timorets chimed in. "She is moving!"

More arrows, more screams from beyond the walls of the prison hold, and more flames burning hotter and brighter—but in the midst of it all, the hopeful creaking of a damaged cart was the loudest of all noises in the ears of the six men.

"Ha ha!" Celrod bellowed in satisfaction. "Fifty paces to go, lads!"

The small company moved slowly, straining their muscles under the awkward weight of their fractured salvation. The entrance to the large keep was right there in front of them, and for the first time since the boulders and the fires rained down upon them, the small band of six dared to believe that they would breathe the breath of a new day.

"AHHH!" came the agonizing scream of the schoolmaster. Celrod dropped to his hands and knees, and as he did the ox-cart groaned to a halt. "They shot me! The green-eyed devils shot me!"

Celrod drug his bleeding body out from under the cart, and Michael examined the wound. Protruding out from his left calf was a single raven-fletched arrow. The large, pale muscle was as easy a target as any, but thankfully the bolt had gone clean through the leg.

"Blast it all!" Celrod shouted through gritted teeth. "How bad is it, groomsman?"

"I think it will be alright," Michael told him. "But I have nothing to cut the barb with ... so, I ... I can't yet remove it."

Celrod grimaced in pain as he spoke to his friends. "Hurry now, before the rest of you feel the bitter beaks of these ravens too."

Engelmann, Timorets, and the older brother pushed with all their might, but without the force of the large schoolmaster, the cart would not budge.

"Can you manage?" Michael said to Celrod. "Can you manage to walk on your own?"

"Aye, groomsman," Celrod winced.

The desperate grunts of the three men echoed in the courtyard as they strained to push the massive cart in the sandy courtyard.

"Hold on here then," Michael told him, placing Celrod's hand on the wagon's edge. Without so much as another word, the wounded groomsman crawled underneath the cart and took up the vacant spot. Michael gritted his teeth and set his jaw, steeling himself for the pain that was sure to come. "Help us, please." He whispered his prayer and then in reckless abandon he threw the full weight of his strong frame against the damaged axle of the ox-cart. Tears streamed down his face as the shock of immense pain shot through his wounded arm, and he screamed in frustrated agony. After what seemed like an eternity of wasted pain, the cart slowly moved forward.

Thirty paces, twenty paces; the men pushed the broken cart against all odds until the distressed wheels finally broke, rendering the cart useless not ten paces from the entrance to the keep. "*ARGH!*" Michael shouted as the impact of the splintered wood bit all the harder into his badly burnt hand.

Arrows continued to fly, and the sounds of the siege set the backdrop for a deadly decision. The six of them knew they would have to run desperately and dangerously towards the open entrance to the keep with no cover.

"I'll go first," the older brother said as he squatted in the cover of broken cart, waiting breathlessly in the wake of the great effort it had taken to move it.

Michael nodded his nervous agreement, while Celrod wiped the sweat from his brow with the back of his sleeve.

"Be safe, Fryon," coughed his younger brother. "Please."

The older brother nodded his understanding and steeled himself for the perils that this journey of just ten paces would hurl at him. Just then, before he could make his move, the startling, otherworldly sounds of the besieging army's horns broke out in echoed unison and stopped him dead in his tracks.

"Wait just a moment, my boy," Engelmann said, putting a hand on his shoulder.

"What in the name of ..." Timorets said in horror.

Celrod picked up his flint from around his neck and kissed it nervously, his eyes fixed eastward, to the top of the sacred mount. "Help us all," he whispered.

Michael looked to his friend and mentor. Tears ran down his smoke and dirt-stained cheeks as he saw the mockery of the Arborist's life unfolding there before him. The leaf-green eyes of the old tree-tender clouded over in great pain as the reality of the moment came into focus.

The twin dragons that had laid waste to the order and beauty of the city —the same monsters who had pillaged and sacked the strength of a once-strong people and brutally devoured the shadowed lives of Haven's citizens —now defiled the very icon of a faith in the THREE who is SEVEN. There, perched atop of the massive trunk of the great tree of Haven, the twin dragons clung to its branchless tower with blood soaked talons. Their leathery, black wings were unfurled in an abominable display of power, and their massive green eyes glowed with the gloating mockery of a victory ill-gained.

"Engelmann?" Michael said, his voice cracking under the weight of confused emotions. But all the Arborist could do was stare, eyes fixed on the unfolding desecration.

The dragons turned in unison. Their gaze moved from surveying their city of conquest and resolved in a settled stare at each other as if to signal the next movement in this unholy drama.

Citizens of Haven, their deep voices boomed inside the minds of every man and woman. *Behold ... your new light has come!*

Without warning, and to the sickening horror of all who watched, a wave of green fire issued forth from behind the fanged dykes of each dragon's massive mouth. The flames poured out in a torrent of deliberate defilement, and though they engulfed each dragon, their fires did not harm nor consume them. The dragons clung to the once holy tree, wings outstretched upward in a charade of the long dead branches. Their forms were alight in the fire of a ravenous evil, and the silhouette broke the hearts of all who had once hoped in the great gift of the THREE who is SEVEN.

The darkness that had shrouded the once bright city now glowed dimly in the green un-light of these winged devils. It illuminated the march of the invaders, the Raven Army advancing towards the Citadel with conquest on their lips and hate in their eyes.

"Quickly now, while the arrows have ceased!" Fryon whispered urgently. "To the keep! There is nothing we can do from within these iron walls, and you know as well as I do that your tears cannot wash away this ..." he looked back at the image of the beasts, writhing in satisfaction atop the once immortal tree in mocking illumination. "They can't wash away this blasphemy, no matter how many join your sorrow."

"He is right," Michael said wiping the tears from his eyes. "Engelmann, can you still lead us out of this place?"

The storm in the eyes of the Arborist broke, and tears of his anguish clung to the moss of his beard like drops of dew after the morning mist. He nodded his head as he spoke. "We must hurry, then." His words held no sense of riddle or hidden wisdom, for he had neither the time nor the stamina; instead, he turned and without caution strode deliberately towards the entrance of the keep.

229

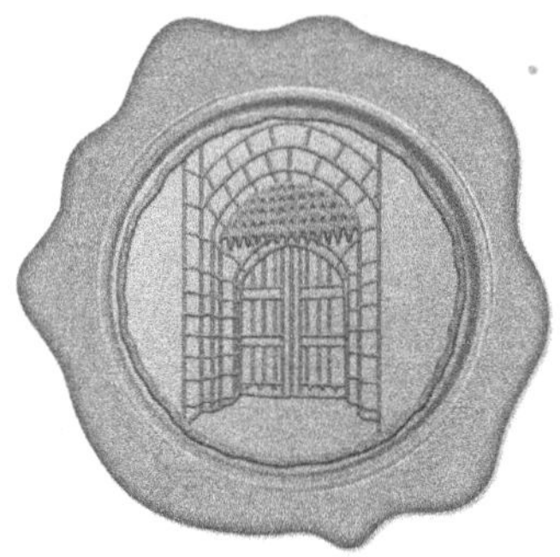

Chapter Twenty-Seven

"GET HER OUT OF THERE!" came the shouted orders from Lieutenant Marcum after a dozen of his archers cut down the Raven scouts. Four guardsmen with blades in hand rushed to the aid of the fallen barmaid. As they reached to lift her to her feet, the sound of her sobbing took the battle-weary soldiers by surprise.

"Sharon! Wait, Sharon ... please, no!" Keily wailed into the smoky blackness. "The little girl! Please don't leave her!"

One of the guardsmen met her wild, tear-filled eyes with his own heartbroken gaze, and he nodded his agreement to her sorrowful plea. The tall man walked the few dozen paces to the child's lifeless body. With little effort he picked her up and carried her broken, small frame back into the stone chapel, entering it to hide with the rest of the gathered guardsmen and frightened citizens.

The atmosphere in the cold, dark room was silent and heavy, for all of Haven had lost much this day. And though their losses were many, the fear of what was still unknown was too much for these homeless citizens of

Piney Creek to even dare to whisper about.

"Are you alright, lass?" Marcum said as he examined the tear-stained face of the barmaid by the muted glow of a small oil lamp.

"*Alright*?" Keily blurted out. "What in this damned *hell* of a world would lead you to believe that I am alright?" she said as she removed the two raven-fletched arrows from the small, pierced body of little Sharon. "Our borough is burning, the tree has failed us, thousands of our brothers are dead, and *little girls* are being hunted like rats in the alleyways by whatever those green-eyed monsters are out there!"

"Aye," Marcum said quietly. "I think we are all being hunted, aren't we?"

The large door burst open, stealing what little breath was left in the lungs of the gathered remnant as they startled at the sound. To their great relief, it was Johnrey and a handful of others that appeared on the other side of the open door, and the group found their fears assuaged for a brief, blessed moment.

As the newcomers found their way inside, Johnrey called out for the barmaid. "Keily?" he grunted amidst the whispered greetings. "Keily? Did they make it? Have you seen them?" The white-haired officer stopped dead in his tracks as he caught sight of her crestfallen and heartbroken face. She knelt on the floor, holding tightly to the blood-soaked body of a little girl who not an hour ago had held his hand in the cellar of the tavern. "Oh, I'm sorry, girl," he whispered his apologies. "Where did you go? What happened?" He put his bloodstained hand on the barmaid's shoulder in an effort to console her grief. "It's not your fault, you know. None of this is."

The door burst open again. With their exhausted senses teetering on the edge of reason, the group could not help but gasp in fright yet again, though it was only a scout from the army of Haven.

"Where is the lieutenant?" the bandaged runner asked.

"What is the word, guardsman?" Marcum asked as he moved closer to the door, hoping that there were others coming to join their ranks.

"They are burning it all, the whole borough, one building at time; we cannot chance staying here much longer," the scout urged.

"But what about the others?" Marcum asked. "You told them to meet here, did you not?"

The still breathless runner just shook his head. "No. No, there are ..." he paused as if replaying some horrific nightmare in the theater of his own thoughts. "There are no others."

The occupants of the room stood in stunned, hopeless silence as the reality of the scout's words settled upon their weary hearts.

"How many does that make then?" Johnrey asked the lieutenant, finally waking the group back to the urgency of their situation.

Marcum surveyed the dimly lit hall of the old Piney Creek chapel. He counted quickly and nervously to himself. "Forty, I think ... I count forty guardsmen, and then two or maybe three dozen citizens, and ..." he paused, a sadness washing over him, "four children."

"That is not a very promising tally," the runner said, a bit too frankly.

"Aye lad, but a great deal more than that died out there in the bloody, black field beyond our broken walls," Johnrey reprimanded with the seasoned kindness of a veteran of war. "And whether it be two of us or two thousand ... I am going to *live*, so as not to make a waste of their valiant deaths."

The runner nodded his apology, and Marcum turned to address the huddled remnant. "The corporal is right!" he whispered with worried authority. "We have to go north, and if the THREE who is SEVEN has any mercy left in His heart for us, perhaps we will find that the whole of the Raven Army has left the field of battle unattended whilst they storm the Citadel."

"But where will we go? I mean, once we have left Haven?" a dark-haired young woman asked the lieutenant.

"Aye!" an old man interjected. "There are no forests for us to hide in! And even if there were, we would have to cut them down in order to see!"

"Perhaps there is still a cutter camp?" Keily blurted out. The weary sadness faded now to the back of her mind, waiting there to be dealt with when the time was right. Instead, she allowed a seemingly ridiculous hope to replace the weight of sorrow. "I know that many of them were lost, but not all, I'll bet. And if they too have survived, well ... they know the cold northern outlands better than any of us."

Marcum thought on this for a long moment, for the very idea of woodcutters remaining in the North had not crossed his mind. When he was satisfied with the soundness of the notion, he spoke again. "Perhaps the barmaid is right. Perhaps there are still more woodcutters who managed to escape the assault upon the city. And they could very well be our best hope of surviving out there in the darkened middle grounds."

"And if not?" Johnrey asked aloud. "What if they are all gone, then what?"

"Then we will head for the foothills of the Hilgari, and we will carve out whatever life we can from its cold, grey bosom," the lieutenant reasoned.

The crack and the crash of collapsing buildings woke them from the postulating and reminded them all too soberly of the imminent danger that hunted them here in this burning borough.

"Men, take what you can carry on your backs only," Marcum ordered. "There will be no time to load carts of any kind, and we cannot risk the noise. We will move into the darkness as quickly and quietly as we can."

"Corporal," Marcum continued on. "Take a dozen guardsmen and see to it that we are not surprised from the rear. And ... barmaid?"

"Yes, lieutenant?" Keily answered him, taken aback that she would be singled out for an assignment.

"I want you and two other scouts to go on ahead of the main group and see to it that our way is clear. You know this borough better than any of my guardsmen, and I for one do not have the luxury of pretense at a moment when our need is so great."

"Aye, I'll do it," she replied.

And with that, the seventy or so that made up the strength of this remnant gathered up whatever food, tools, and provisions that they could carry and prepared their hearts for the long and dangerous exile from the walls of their home.

When all had been gathered and secured, Marcum gave the word for the scouting party to advance. Keily and the two other guardsmen opened the eastward facing door of the old, stone chapel and began to chart the course towards their freedom.

"I think we are far enough east from the borough square that they might not notice us; at least not for some time yet," she said to the two other guardsmen.

"But getting nearly seventy people to move quickly and quietly might not prove to be a simple task," the taller of the two reasoned.

"Aye, they are going to kill us all," the other said in defeat.

"Do not count it over just yet. This is our best chance. We will have to make our way across the open field first, and then we can take shelter on the other side of the stone knee wall," she told them. "Then it's not but a few alleyways before we reach the stone of the North Wall itself."

"Do you have a plan?" Marcum asked the scouting party as he stepped through the humble threshold and out into the heavy, smoke-filled air of the darkened borough.

"Yes sir, we do," the shorter of the scouts replied, glancing at Keily and drawing a sort of courage from her resolute gaze. "The hardest part will be this open field, but ... if we can make it to the knee wall ... well, then we all stand a better chance of sneaking our way out of here."

"And you agree, lass?" the lieutenant asked.

"Aye, I do," she nodded. "We will go ahead, five hundred paces in that direction." She gestured to a shrouded point off in the darkened distance. "When you see our spark, then you will know it is time."

"Very well," Marcum agreed. "We will send the main strength of the convoy as soon as we see your light. Johnrey, you and a dozen men will stay behind to act as our cover. Once the citizens are safe behind the knee wall, you and your company will join us on the other side of the meadow."

"Yes, sir," Johnrey agreed with a salute. "We will guard your backs, just do us a favor and be quick about it, huh?"

Marcum smiled an exhausted smile. "Well then, there is no time to waste. Go, now," he said to Keily and the scouting party. And with that, the three of them bounded off into the smoky dark in search of cover for the last remaining citizens of the North.

"Do you see them?" Johnrey asked. "My eyes seem to get less and less useful the older I get."

"No," Marcum said, his words drawn out and tired. "I do not see much of anything except dancing shadows from the flames of this burning place." The lieutenant held up a spyglass and scanned the shadowed horizon. "Wait!" he said with a renewed excitement. "There they are, I see their spark ... there, right there!" He placed the spyglass in the white-bearded corporal's hand.

"I see them now," Johnrey said in agreement. "Time to be off then, huh?"

Marcum nodded his head and then turned to focus his attention on the remaining party. "Be quick and quiet, and no matter what, keep going forward. There is no home or safety for you here within the walls of Haven; our only hope now is to flee." The gathered group whispered their understanding and with only a dozen bows strung at the ready to defend their movements, Marcum led the host across the chapel yard.

Chapter Twenty-Eight

"HERE THEY COME," THE TALLER scout pointed out in a nearly silent whisper. "Quiet now, lads ... come on ... come on!"

"How much further?" Keily asked, not taking her eye off the horizon even for a moment.

"Maybe two hundred, two hundred and fifty paces?" the scout guessed. "I'd say they are nearly halfway."

Keily whispered her worried prayers as she kissed her clenched fists. "Come on then ... hurry, please."

The tension grew as the taller scout quietly reported on the diminishing distance between them. "Two hundred ... a hundred and a half ... just a hundred paces now, and all is still quiet."

The fleeing remnant half-ran, half-stalked their way across the meadow, crouched low so as to try and make themselves as small as possible. The guardsmen were at the vanguard of the mismatched movement of shadows, scanning the flame-riddled horizon for any sign of danger. The four children kept quiet under the nervous, whispered lullabies of the frightened women who carried them while the men transported the burden of their supplies over their own anxious shoulders.

"Hurry! Hurry!" Keily whispered anxiously.

As the main body of the remnant came within fifty paces of the wall, the sound of fire catching to thatch broke the tension, and the scouting party watched the roof of the old miller's house catch fire and go up in a blaze of hungry flames. The light of the fire washed the meadow in an unwelcome illumination and the group of citizens and guardsmen alike froze in fear, now exposed to all who would look to notice them.

"Run! *Run now*! They will see you!" The three scouts shouted in the loudest whispers they could muster.

Soldiers and citizens alike broke their organized formation and took off in a sprint towards the wall as if it held the last long drink for the thirstiest of all mankind.

THWANG came the sound of a bow loosing its arrow. "Oh no!" Keily whispered. "Run!"

Just as the first people reached the stone knee wall, a single raven-fletched arrow pierced and cut down one of the guardsmen, sending him rolling in a heap of vanquished life.

"Come on, hurry!" Keily urged them as she nocked an arrow to lend cover.

Johnrey and his twelve found their target and quickly dispatched the Raven archer with arrows of their own.

"Steady now, lads!" Johnrey urged his men. "Keep a sharp eye about you … you never know when one of these damned carrion soldiers will show his ugly beak."

As soon as the last of the main host leapt over the rock wall, one of the scouts—the shorter of the two—began to strike his flint, sparking the signal for Johnrey and his men so that they might make their way across the meadow.

"Cover their movements, men," Marcum ordered, and another dozen or so bowstrings were quickly pulled taught and aimed at the burning borough.

Johnrey saw the signal light from the other side of the field. "Alright lads, let's be as quick and as quiet as we can. I'm sure that wasn't the only Raven we will meet today." With those words, Johnrey and his twelve were off and running as fast as their tired legs would carry them.

He and his men were not more than halfway across the chapel field when the unmistakable sound of fire catching tinder woke the silent night sky with its hungry crackle and its all too familiar roar. "The chapel," Marcum whispered. "They are at the chapel."

The final escape lost all cover as the yellow and amber flames of the now burning chapel fully illuminated its surrounding fields. "Hurry, lads!" Johnrey urged again and again. "They are going to see us if you don't get your legs to move any faster!"

The rafters of the old chapel went up quickly in a blaze of hungry flames, and all who watched did so in horror as the once holy place was reduced to nothing more than a casualty of war. The first of the twelve reached the stone wall and in a single bounding leap, he hurdled himself over the knee wall and crouched in its relative protection to catch his breath. Within moments the rest of the men had done the same, until all of the remnant gathered and crouched behind the stacked stone perimeter.

Marcum took account of those who had made it safely across the meadow, and then turned to address Keily and her scouts. "Alright, barmaid ... it is your turn again. Get us out of here."

She nodded her agreement, and in a flash she and the two scouts had bounded across the alleyway and made sure that the back of the old widow's home on the opposite side of the street was not infested with any Ravens.

Sparks flew from her signal, and the lieutenant began to send small groups of the main host across the alleyway a few at a time until the whole party was safe in the shadow of the stacked log house.

"How much farther now, lass?" Marcum asked her.

"Just another couple alleyways to cross, and then ... then we will be right there, staring at the mangled North Gate," Keily replied.

"Alright then, lead on," Marcum ordered.

Yet again, Keily and her scouts crossed the cobblestone back streets of Piney Creek, and likewise Marcum sent the host following in succinct fashion as the whole lot of them ducked and hid behind the ruined and abandoned houses of the northernmost borough of Haven.

"There," Keily whispered to the lieutenant as she handed him the spyglass. "Right there, look ... just between the guard house and the smithy's shop. Do you see it?"

Marcum held the spyglass up to his eye, scanning and searching the muted horizon for whatever it was she was hoping to point out.

"There is a breach in the stone. It must have been from where the dragons assaulted us. If we can get there we might not have to risk the attracting attention at what was once the Northern Gate."

"Very good," Marcum agreed, with hints of both relief and respect crossing his face. "You and your scouts ... make your way."

She nodded and then whispered her orders to the other two men. As they took off in the flickering shadows towards the breach in the North Wall, a small volley of Raven's arrows cut through the black, cold air and robbed the tallest scout of his life.

"Take cover!" Marcum whispered to the gathered remnant. "Stay silent, now."

Keily and the last remaining scout were pinned behind one of the large pieces of broken wall that littered the ground all around them. Marcum signaled Johnrey to make ready. Seven of his archers positioned themselves in front of the hiding host, while the rest of his bowmen moved to the rear so as to cut off any surprise to their already vulnerable flank.

The Raven sentries were quiet, save their labored, gurgling breathing and the clank of their cumbersome armor, which grew louder and all the more distinguishable as they caught the scent of the scouts and moved to eliminate their presence. The host of Haven held their collective breath as they listened to the enemy move closer and closer to the scouting party.

"Easy now," Keily said to her partner as he drew his bowstring and aimed through the open, jagged crack in the middle of the fallen wall that provided their cover. "We don't know how many they are. Let's not tell them how many *we* are just yet." Keily peered out through the crack, risking exposure in hopes of counting the enemy's number by the light of the siege fires. "Four? Maybe six ... it's hard to tell," she whispered back to the scout.

"Let's hope that they don't have any friends nearby," the scout whispered back.

The Raven sentries were nearly upon the fallen scout now. Nerves were frayed, and even in the bite of the cold, north wind the men and women of the fleeing host perspired with fear as the clanking of the invaders moved closer and closer.

One of the Nocturnals bent down to examine the bleeding body of the fallen scout. As he stood back to his feet, he jabbed the point of his blade through the exposed throat of the dying man in a swift, violent motion. Blood spurted out in a spray of shadowed red, and as the life streamed upon the cold, dirty ground, one of the young children gasped her innocent horror. To Keily's dismay, the sickly, glowing, green eyes of the two Raven sentries turned their attention in the direction of the huddled remnant.

An older woman reached her hand up over the mouth of the frightened child so as to stifle any further sound, but the green-eyed invaders needed neither sound nor fire to navigate their way through the darkness, for the nocturnal army of the Raven Queen both saw and obeyed her malevolent un-light.

The head of the sentry snapped back towards the main, cobblestoned square in an unnaturally sharp fashion. His iron-armored hand drew up the twisted, black horn of some ill-found beast to his own ashen lips, ready to signal the prize of his hunt from the very heart of this fallen borough. Just before the sickly sound of the horn pierced the silence, the sharpened point of the barmaid's arrow tore through the ashen gullet of the Raven soldier.

The sentry fell to his knees, then collapsed in a lifeless heap. A gurgling, sickly growl emanated from the lone-standing sentry as he barred his rotted teeth in rage. The sounds of drawn bows loosing their bolts broke the tense silence as the archers of the rear guard defended their remaining countrymen against the band of nocturnal scouts. The sentry charged the host, but in not much more than a moment's time the guardsmen had dispatched him from this world. They waited in frightened anticipation and heightened awareness, knowing it was only a matter of time before more of the invading army would break in upon their small, huddled ranks.

One, two and then three sparks of the scout's flint caught the eye of the lieutenant. He listened and watched carefully, waiting to see if the signal garnered any attention from the enemy.

"A few at a time!" came the whispered plea of Keily from just fifty paces out in front of them. Marcum waited another moment, then signaled back with his own flint, determining that the risk was greater to wait than to run.

He commanded his men to make the treacherous dash across the road towards the broken wall. The guardsmen went first, blades drawn and ready for whatever might assault them, but they did not meet any resistance save for their own uncertainties.

The residents of Piney Creek, women and children alike, were the next to cross the street. Lieutenant Marcum himself chose to lead them out from behind the relative safety of the alleyway, covered by the watchful eyes of Johnrey and a dozen of his bowmen. The rush of heat and the sound of flames exploded overhead as the hungry fire caught the dried wood of the building at their backs. Johnrey knew that he and the remaining archers had not a moment to spare if they hoped to make it beyond the broken wall without being spotted.

"Come now, lads," Johnrey ordered in a whisper. "We have done our duty for our city, and now it is time we fight for our future." With that, the twelve of them ran out from behind the burning building and across the open cobblestone clearing to where the rest of their new family knelt and crept before the breach in the once invincible wall of their once invincible city.

"What now, Lieutenant?" Johnrey asked. "Where would you have us go?"

Marcum did not hesitate in his response. "There is—or at least there was once, long ago—a hospitable land to the east of the hallowed mount." He spoke in a hushed voice as he scanned the faces of all those who gathered and listened. "But that was long before we laid waste to our world with the axe of the woodcutters. I would not risk such a long journey without the cover of the forest."

"So if not east, where then?" Keily asked. "All I have ever heard about these outlands were tales of witches, outliers, and shadow cats—that is, until the groomsman returned not two months ago. He said he went north, tracing the western fens of the Abonris with his road-weary feet. For months he was missing from the company of the woodcutters, and far after we all had thought him dead, he showed up in my ..." Her voice trailed off as she pictured her tavern being consumed by the hungry flames. "He showed up in my tavern, and he looked far too healthy to have been foraging and wandering on his own for that whole time."

"Where did he go, lass?" Johnrey asked, both curiosity and necessity compelling him now.

"I don't know. He would not say," she told them. "Wherever it is, or whatever it is, let us pray that this Raven Army has not found it first."

"North and west, then," Marcum decided.

"North and west," whispered the frightened mass of people in agreement.

And it was with those few and simple last words that the fleeing host rose to their feet and climbed up and over the broken fragments of the once mighty wall of Haven. With tear-streaked faces and quiet courage, they moved out into the black wilderness of the untamed outlands in search of a place they might make home.

Chapter Twenty-Nine

TWO NIGHTS HAD PASSED SINCE Cal had been locked away in the crude, timber prison of the colony's stronghold. Two long and restless nights of internal battles, whereby the quiet condemnation of hindsight wrestled arm in arm with the stubborn hubris of his rash confidence.

The small, square chamber held not many distractions for his wandering mind, and so it was that Cal waited anxiously, nervously hopeful that the decree of the governor would not become his doom, and that Yasen would find the means to set him free. The noises and sounds of the colony filled his ears, and he strained against the timber walls for even the faintest sound of Astyræ's voice, or for word of her capture. To his great relief, none was heard.

On this third morning of his imprisonment, the whole of the colony had been roused from their heavy slumber with the unnecessarily bright brass of the governor's trumpets. "What do you think it means?" Cal said groggily to his Sprite companion.

"It means your days here on the Wreath are over, groomsman!" an old guardsman growled. "The governor has filled the hold of the ship with fresh timber for our great city, and he has saved *just* enough room to squeeze your scrawny backside aboard." His tone was rude and mocking, and as he spoke he tossed a torn loaf of bread and an overripe orange into the timber cell.

"That may be ... but why all the fanfare?" Cal said as he gnawed at the half-stale loaf of black bread.

"Glory begets glory," the old guardsman replied, "and the governor has his heart set on a right smart portion of it!"

"Glory ill-gained is not glory worth relishing, my friend," Cal said to the old jailer.

"Your friend? Ha! I should say not. And just who do you think you are, *groomsman,* to judge the gains of any man, ill or otherwise? Eh?" said the old guardsman.

Cal chewed on the hardened bread, wondering with each bite what weight his words would ever have again on the minds of the men who saw him take the arm of Pyrrhus with his sword. He wanted to explain, but the shame of his deeds brought doubt to his mind and he thought better of it, resigning to keep his words to himself, at least for now.

"Men of the first colony!" Cal heard the booming voice of Governor Seig through his timber prison walls. "Today is a glorious day, indeed! Today we set sail once again. When first we took to the water, the holds of our ships held nothing more than the mere inklings of possibilities and the desperate dreams of our desperate people. But now!" the tall, dark-haired governor said proudly as he stood atop the platform in the square of the stronghold. "Now we set sail with *evidence,* proof that the vision our great Priest King was given has indeed come true. This very day we shall return to our city with timber, with the new light we were sent here to find!"

The men of the first colony, guardsmen and woodcutters alike, roared in triumphal agreement. Although great tension had grown between the two factions of Haven's servants, their course was still one and the same ... and, likewise, their victory.

The flames of the watch fires flickered and danced in the cool, sea breeze, casting an orange glow over the men of the first colony. Tahd scanned the dirty, tired faces of the guardsmen. The last few days had taken a great toll on the morale of his men, and the strain that rose between him and Yasen caused all the more worry about his loss of control. Worse, he had begun to feel a gnawing fear that an overthrow of power may very well occur in the event of another disheartening incident. This made the short, silver-haired captain of the colony guard quite eager for the *Determination* to return from her timber run with a fresh company of guardsmen to replenish his dwindling ranks.

Wielund had a hard time celebrating the words of Seig, for his thoughts were occupied with sadness over his imprisoned friend. "I told him to just leave her be," he grumbled under his breath. "You're too curious, groomsman! What good has curiosity ever done for those who have gone poking their unwelcome noses in its business?"

Seig's voice bellowed out again, disrupting Wielund's musings. "Captain Tahd will return to our bright and shining city with the hold of great riches from the Wreath! He will bring word of our advancement upon this ... this wilderness, and he will return to the colony with fresh supplies, strong backs, and sharpened blades so that we might continue our quest and gain even greater glory!"

The men cheered and applauded his words, thumping the handles of their axes on the rough-cut tables that littered the square. Tahd walked to the center of the platform. Taking his cue from the governor, he addressed the gathered crowd in his own way. "Men of the first colony, I have been given the great honor this day to deliver this wealth of timber that we have harvested here! We shall not keep the impoverished people of Haven waiting any longer, so I will see to it that we set sail before midday has come upon us. In light of what our great governor has charged us with, let us be busy about our preparations and ask for Godspeed upon our voyage."

The captain nodded to the Priest, who stood pious and self-important in his green, dirt-stained cloak. He raised his flint to his lips before he spoke, and the whole of the gathered men followed in suit.

"Oh great and mighty giver of light
Who rewards each sharpened axe and fell swing made.
Give us now your blessed ear and bring your blessed favor here,
For we have fought and labored hard against the wild,
Biting back the dark with our blessed spark.

Grant us winds of speed and strength of might as we strive and toil against the night."

"May it be so," came the collective response as the men of the first colony as they once again kissed their flints in agreement with the words of the Priest. The gathered men then went about their business, some atop the watchtowers, others making final preparations for the *Determination*. The woodcutters marched with their axes in hand towards the tree line, invigorated in their mission to subdue the wilderness of the Wreath for the glory of the Priest King and the light of the THREE who is SEVEN.

"Do not make a scene ... walk as if you are on your way to the forge." Wielund startled violently as a familiar voice whispered in his ear. A steadying hand settled on his shoulder. "I said, do *not* make a scene," Yasen said with a tinge of amusement. "I do not want to draw any unwanted attention to our conversation."

Wielund nodded his understanding and turned his head to meet the eyes of the mighty woodcutter. They fell into step with each other as Wielund did his best to calm his frightened nerves, and Yasen held his great axe up in front of him while they walked. The black leather that wrapped its handle was braided in intricate patterns, and the two well-experienced blades still shone as if they had been forged the day before, reflecting the yellows and oranges of the watch fires.

"I need you to make me a key," Yasen said softly while he pointed out a phantom flaw in his axe.

"A key?" Wielund asked, confused as to how a key had anything to do with this exquisite work of craftsmanship that he was being shown. Furthermore, Wielund was a bit nervous around the one-eyed chieftain of the woodcutters, for his orders were to come from Captain Tahd, and he did not wish to find himself in the middle of a battle of wills between the two unfriendly leaders.

Yasen caught the young man's eye with his own. "Yes, smithy ... *a key.*"

"But ... but I don't understand-" he tried to explain, but Yasen cut him off.

"A key that will open the lock of the prison hold," Yasen whispered forcefully, glancing around the yard to make sure that he and the smithy were out of any prying earshot. "Cal will not be going on that ship back to Haven, and I would prefer to help him out of his imprisonment without having to shed any more blood or waste any more lives."

"But where will he go? I mean, if I manage to craft a key that works, it's not as if he will be able to stay here in the colony any longer, is it?" Wielund asked, trying to wrap his worried mind around the plan of the woodcutter. "And what if I am caught? What if Tahd or Seig or some other nosy guardsman sees me forging a key out of iron—what then?"

"Aye, you are right about Cal," Yasen admitted. "He will not remain here with us; his story will continue to unfold from beyond this assignment of ours and these walls that we have built. Although ..." a tender, knowing smile crept across the woodcutter's scared face, "I suspect this will not be the last that we see of our friend."

Wielund looked nervously to his right and to his left, clearly uncomfortable with the risk that such a task would require.

Yasen took Wielund by the shoulder, hoping to convey the urgency of the moment. "We owe him this kindness, Wielund," Yasen pressed. "Do not so quickly forget the man who pulled you from the cold, black grasp of the Dark Sea."

"Aye, he did do that, didn't he?" the smithy conceded.

"You must work swiftly. Do not let anyone see what it is that you are up to; the wilderness of the Wreath has corrupted the sense right out of these *brothers* of ours. I would hate to lose you as well to the rash stupidity of our great governor."

Wielund nodded in nervous agreement. "Alright then. I will forge one, if only to repay the debt of rescue."

"Now be quick about it, smithy," Yasen said, loudly and with great authority. "I will find you within the hour, and I expect my axe to be sharp enough to fell the whole Wreath itself." He shoved his axe into Wielund's unsuspecting hand, then turned and walked towards the stable yard.

With that, Wielund stood stunned and motionless just outside the walls of his forge, holding the mighty axe of the North Wolf. He exhaled a long, shaky breath, steeling himself for the dangerous deeds he knew that he must do. "Alright, Cal, alright," he said to the dark morning mist, and then turned to walk inside and stoke the forge fires to life. He blew fresh wind into the coals from his massive leather bellows, and the amber and gold colored sparks flew up from the hearth in a whirlwind of productivity. He walked over to his workbench and looked about for some scrap, some piece of iron that could be melted down to forge his friend's freedom.

He reached for a broken horseshoe and laughed an ironic laugh as he held it in his hand. "Ha! How fitting."

"No, I don't think that it is fitting at all," said the thin voice of the captain of the colony guard.

Wielund froze where he stood. His eyes went wide in shocked surprise and his mouth went as dry as the desert lands east of Haven as the taloned fingers of fear crept their stranglehold over his resolve.

"I beg your pardon, my lord?" Wielund gulped in a cracking voice.

"The shoe, smithy," Tahd chuckled. "It isn't fitting at all, otherwise it might still be firmly in place on the hoof of whatever unlucky beast threw this mangled piece of iron in the first place."

Wielund just stared nervously, his right eyebrow beginning to twitch under the strain of stunned shock. "My lord?" he said again, his voice laden with confusion.

"The *shoe*," Tahd said, annoyed over the misunderstanding of his jest. "The one in your hand!"

Wielund reached to wipe the frightened sweat from his brow, and smeared a line of blackened char across his freckled forehead.

"Never you mind," Tahd growled in frustration. "I didn't come to your forge to exchange laughter, I came to ask you a few questions about your friend, the groomsman."

"The groomsman, my lord?" Wielund squeaked.

"Yes, the groomsman. The very groomsman who took you on a scouting assignment not three days ago; the very groomsman who also happened to sever the arm of my best knight from his body," Tahd said with obvious exasperation in his voice. "The *only* groomsman here in service to the colony."

"Oh ... yes, yes I know him," Wielund answered. "Though I have not seen him since the ... um, the incident. Is he alright?"

Tahd eyed the young smithy suspiciously, trying to calculate the meaning of his nervousness. "Is he alright?" Tahd asked incredulously. "If by alright you mean locked in the prison hold and about to be exiled from our colony, then I suppose you could say he is rather splendid at the moment."

Wielund looked sheepishly to the straw and dirt that covered the floor of his humble forge; his dirty thumb fingered the rough edge of the broken horseshoe. "I ... I am sorry, my lord-"

"When you and the groomsman scouted the Wreath, where exactly did you find the golden-haired woman that he so foolishly defended?" the captain interrupted.

Wielund raised his head, but his gaze never really seemed to meet Tahd's own. "In a tower, my lord."

"A tower?" Tahd asked, stepping closer.

"Yes, a tower. It was old and made of crumbling stone ... nearly a half a day's ride from the timber gates," Wielund volunteered.

Tahd reached out and plucked the broken, iron shoe from Wielund's hand. "Which direction might that be, smithy? Then I will let you be about your work."

"West? West, I believe, my lord," Wielund said hastily.

Tahd smiled a vengeful smile. "I will find that woman, and she will tell me all about the secrets of this wilderness, and there will be no more foolish groomsman to interfere this time," he said as he handed the horseshoe back to the smithy. "That is all. You can be about your work then," he ordered. "I believe that woodcutter Chief is waiting for you."

Wielund's face went white with panic and he swallowed hard against his rising fears, knowing that the captain's words were ripe with the fragrant fruit of a double meaning. "Yes ... yes, of course. He asked for my help in waking the edge of his axe is all."

"I'll bet he did," Tahd said as he turned his back on the shaken smithy and walked out into the torch-lit square.

Wielund quickly reached for the flint that hung from his neck and kissed it three and then seven times, all the while whispering desperate prayers. "Never again, I promise you! Keep me safe and I swear I'll never risk my assignment again."

Before his nerves could get the better of him, Wielund began. He placed the broken, iron shoe in a small crucible and then positioned the two instruments of his craft in the white-hot coals of his forge. He pumped the bellows, breathing scorching life to the flames. Soon, the once broken and soiled piece of iron glowed a bright amber color before it melted down into a molten pool of infinite possibilities. Wielund, whose forearms were protected by his high-wristed leather gloves, took his tongs and clasped the crucible in their metal grip, then slowly removed the liquid iron from the forge's flames.

Atop his anvil sat a small mold, and with the deftness of well-practiced movements, the smithy poured the molten remains of the melted horseshoe into the very form that would soon give a rebirth to the metal. The liquid amber sizzled and popped as it cooled into a small, cylindrical rod, whose flattened head was given three square teeth.

Wielund quickly exchanged the heavy, two-handed tongs for a much smaller pair of grippers and a pointed hammer. He went to work pounding the glowing, rounded base, forming it with each precise blow into something more than just a tool of practicality. Rather, he fashioned his debt to the groomsman who had once fished his floundering body from the black waters of the Dark Sea. The iron key no longer glowed a fiery amber color, for the cooling metal had been doused in a water pail and the cloudy grey markings returned to the newly fashioned tool. Wielund held the still-warm key in his hand, applying pressure and examining his handiwork. "Let us hope you are keen enough to release the lock that holds my friend captive, but not so keen that your origin of craft traces back to me when this is all over."

The smithy pocketed the key and reached for the mighty axe of the North Wolf. He knew that Yasen would be back looking for both at any moment, and if nothing else he would be sure that his story would indeed hold up in the event that all of this plotting crumbled to pieces. Sparks littered the air of the small forge as the stone wheel spun faster and faster against the cutting edges of the double-bladed timber axe. "Gentle there, smithy," Yasen said playfully. "I still have a Wreath that needs taming, and I intend for this axe here to last long enough to bring the wild timber to order. If you keep up that intensity, I'll be needing you to forge me a new one altogether!"

Wielund's feet stopped pumping and the sprays of sparks instantly ceased as the nervous smithy wiped the sweat from his dripping brow. "I ... I am sorry, my lord," Wielund apologized.

"Firstly," Yasen said with a playfully correcting tone of voice, "I am no lord, and secondly, I was only mostly serious." His scarred face smiled as he reached for his mighty blade, intent on examining its edges.

"Yes, of course," Wielund continued.

"This will do," the chieftain spoke as he ran his thumb over its newly sharpened bite. "I trust that this was not your only accomplishment this morning," he said without making eye contact.

"Aye," Wielund agreed. "I have what you asked for, but do not ever ask something like this of me again." Wielund reached inside his pants pocket and produced a three-toothed, black, iron key.

Yasen barely glanced at the small key; his eye was fixed solely on its maker. "Lost your courage already?" he said warily.

"I came here to bend iron and sharpen edges, my lord- I mean, *Yasen*." Wielund fumbled over his words, shaking his head in frustrated fear as he spoke. "That is all ... and well, my debt is paid and I don't rightly intend to be shipped back in shame."

"Aye, your debt is paid enough. Though if you merely intend to do your work and stay out of trouble, I trust that you can keep your lips from the ears of Tahd's men." Yasen's gaze was not threatening, but it was certainly convincing.

Wielund nodded his sheepish agreement. "I wish to stay out of the way is all," he said with a petulant tone to his voice. "He is my friend, but ... but it is not my battle to fight nor my wrong to right."

"You know just as well as I do that *he* does not deserve this exile." The chieftain held his mighty axe out before him, letting the scrutiny of his unpatched eye examine the full edge of the blade as he spoke. "He is a brother to us both. He liberated me from the green-eyed jaws of death once before, and he rescued you from the cold, black mouth of the hungry sea. So do not labor needlessly over the *rightness* of this deed, for both of our debts have been paid and perhaps an even greater good has been done."

Wielund felt ashamed at the fear he held, for he knew he owed this small debt to his friend. "Just ... just see to it that he is free and that I am not found to be the source of his liberation."

"Aye," Yasen said to the young man. "Thank you, then, for the fresh edge. The governor and his Brightness the Priest King himself ... in fact, all of Haven will be grateful to you for your selfless service to their cause." A hint of disappointment colored the voice of the wizened woodcutter.

"Very well, then," Wielund replied, obviously eager for this conversation to be over.

Yasen nodded his dark-haired head and left to make his way towards the prison hold, carrying the tool of liberation in his cloak pocket.

"Yasen?" Wielund called after him.

Yasen turned his head ever so slightly back to catch the smithy's eye.

"My debt is paid now, isn't it?" Sadness traced the tone of his worried voice. "Then please see to it that it is paid *in full*."

Yasen simply nodded his head in reply, bridling the urge to react in frustration to the cowardice of the smithy.

The square was alive with hurried preparations and hopeful expectations. Ox carts loaded down with barrels of fresh water, salt packed boar, and smoked venison rolled through the east gate carrying provisions needed for the *Determination*'s voyage home.

"The governor is looking for you, brother," the large-bellied Gvidus said conspiratorially. "Though I doubt it has much to do with the felling of trees this fine morning."

"Aye, I suppose you are right about that," Yasen grunted out an exhausted laugh. "Did you bring what I asked for?"

"That I did, though I hope the lad understands the magnitude of this sacrifice." Gvidus handed over the small, still-warm loaf of black bread as he spoke with a cautiously reproachful tone to his chieftain.

"Aye, I think we all understand the magnitude," Yasen chided playfully. "For the sake of all our ox-carts, I am sure you missing out on a loaf or two won't be such a bad thing! Huh?"

"Easy there, North Wolf," the round woodcutter said defensively.

"Thank you, Gvidus," he said, shaking his head in mock apology. "You can have mine come supper."

"Ah, never you mind. Besides, I would hate for the lad to make his journey on an empty stomach." The large woodcutter winked as Yasen took the newly made key from his pocket and pushed it inside the bottom of the black bread.

"Well then," Yasen raised his brow as he passed the bread back to Gvidus. "See to it that he has something to fill his belly before the leagues of salted sea rob him of his strength."

"Aye, Chieftain," Gvidus said as he lumbered off towards the timber prison. "Oh, and I almost forgot." He stopped, turning to meet the eye of his leader. "The oxen, they have been acting rather sluggish today, and I figured that with all the commotion about the captain's departure, and being that we have no groomsman to aid me and my aching hands ... I might be a bit slow making my way to the forest line today."

"Well, see to it that you are out on the tree line before Tahd has any time to notice the error of his ways in all of this," Yasen said, his words were still colored with frustration at the captain.

"Aye, I'll do my best," the large woodcutter agreed and then continued on towards the prison hold.

Yasen ran his thumb over the newly sharpened axe blade while he surveyed the noise and commotion of the stronghold. The guardsmen were busy hauling supplies for the journey home down to the shoreline, the watch fires danced their amber tango with the salty sea air, and his woodcutters were already well on their way to the mighty forests of this wilderness land, ready to do battle against this suffocating darkness.

"Protect him, for if any of us here remain true of heart and directed in purpose, it is him." Yasen whispered his anxious prayer into the morning air of the stronghold. "And perhaps I, too, believe that our fates are tangled in the threads of his seeking." He reached into his shirt and grabbed the flint that hung around his neck. Holding it between his thumb and forefinger, he paused, contemplating his ever-repeated actions before finally placing the small, shiny stone to his lips. "May it be so," he finished.

"About our morning prayers, are we?" The commanding voice of the governor himself sounded from behind the chieftain of the woodcutters, and his unexpected words startled the one-eyed man. "I took you as more of a man of action, Yasen, whose devotion was exercised with blade upon bark. Yet I find you here, overlooking *my* colony, forsaking the acts of worship that are meant for your kind ... for what?" Seig chided. "Solace? Sanctuary? Or are you merely sulking about the fact that you will have to saddle your own horses and hitch your own oxen for a few more weeks?"

"No, Governor, certainly not," Yasen replied with steel to his voice and sarcasm on his lips. "I was merely reveling in the competency of our leadership here in this colony of Haven."

"You *dare* insult the anointed governor of this holy outpost?" Seig's voice lost all hint of humor, and the tall, dark-haired man grabbed the shoulder of the North Wolf, demanding him to meet his gaze.

"Tinted oil and official titles do not make any man holy, Governor," Yasen growled as he raised the biting edges of his mighty axe up between the bodies of the two men. "Let there be no confusion amongst the two of us: I serve the Citadel, and the people of our once shining city; I do not serve you or your silver-haired fox of a captain!"

"I should have you thrown into the prison hold along with that damned fool of a groomsman," Seig barked back.

"I should remind you which of us commands the greater number of blades here in this colony, Governor," Yasen said evenly and deliberately, his eye fixed on Seig's raging, nervous expression.

"It certainly is not you, *woodcutter*!" Seig spat. "Every back and every blade in this wilderness is under my authority, by order of the Priest King himself."

"Well then," Yasen said, sucking his teeth, "for your sake I hope that the merit of that order still remains here on these distant shores of this darkened wilderness. Now, if there is nothing else, I must be about my *devotion*, for my axe is freshly sharpened and ready to break its fast."

Yasen pushed past the stunned governor and walked without turning back towards the large timber gates of the colony's stronghold. Seig seethed as he watched this brazen woodcutter mount his massive, black Friesian. In the same moment that he signaled the Friesian forward, he grabbed the reigns of a large chestnut and silver-grey courser, leading them in tow out into the darkness beyond the wall.

"Captain!" Seig shouted into the busy courtyard, his fists balled and his jaw clenched in wounded anger. "Captain!"

Chapter Thirty

GVIDUS LUMBERED THROUGH THE STRONGHOLD'S courtyard, moving past the granary and the storehouses until he reached the small, two-celled prison hold there on the east wall of the colony. In light of all the activity within the stronghold, every able-bodied man was set to work either on felling more trees or transporting supplies to the shoreline in preparation for the *Determination*'s first voyage back to Haven. With so much excitement and still so much work to be done, Seig required that every man aid in the preparations to launch. There were no men to spare, not even to guard the renegade groomsman on this busy morning.

"Are you ready to break your fast yet, lad?" Gvidus whispered into the iron-barred window of the timber jail.

Cal had not slept much the previous night, for his mind was anxious and his heart heavy. Yasen had told him three days before that he would not be banished back to Haven—but that was three days ago, and he had not heard a word or a whisper since.

"I do not think I have the stomach for food on a day like this," Cal said to the man outside the locked cell door.

"Oh, but this is a fresh loaf of black bread—a rare commodity here among the ever-hungry, hard-working likes of men in this colony of ours," Gvidus reasoned. "It would be an insult to every hunger pang and growling belly to refuse."

"Oh how the governor must despise me indeed, sending me fresh bread before sending me away," Cal replied, his words heavy in the suffocating fog of his self-pity.

"Oh, I am sure that he does," Gvidus said with a chuckle. "But it was not the governor who sent *this* loaf of bread, brother."

"If not him, then ..."

Light flickered in Cal's eyes as the possibility of what might be happening occurred to him.

"Here, take it, eat it before it grows cool and loses its ability to warm your belly this cold, dark morning." Gvidus stepped in front of the iron window, revealing his round, smiling face. "Besides, I fear a storm is coming this day, and you'll need something to fuel your bones for this *journey* of yours." The large woodcutter reached through the timber slats and passed the loaf of black bread to his younger woodcutter brother.

Cal clasped his arm in a sign of gratitude and took the bread with his other hand. "Thank you, Gvidus."

"No time for that now, lad," Gvidus said. "Mind you chew carefully though, for there are no guards out here to rescue you if you bite your tongue or chip your tooth." The large, bushy eyebrows of this fattened woodcutter accentuated the true meaning of his words, and Cal was able to read clearly his meaning. "Now, eat up, for the seas will not be kind to the hungry. As for me, I still have to fill these water barrels and drive these lazy oxen out to the tree line before our mighty woodcutters die of thirst."

Cal stood there, holding the now cooled loaf of black bread in his eager hands, smiling a warm, grateful smile to the woodcutter.

"On the other side then, lad!" Gvidus said as he lumbered his way back across the courtyard to a barrel-filled ox-cart waiting by the well.

Cal turned his back to the iron window and wasted no time in breaking the salt-crusted bread into two jagged halves. "What is it, Cal? What did your woodcutter brothers send you?" The voice of the blue-winged Sprite whispered into the dimness of the cell as he flitted down from his hideaway in the rafters.

The groomsman excitedly whirled around to examine the large, iron lock that held the latches of the prison door firmly secure. As he did, hope lit alive in the tired eyes of the young prisoner. "Our salvation, my friend," Cal whispered, holding the skeleton key for his Sprite guardian to see.

Deryn flew towards the hand that held the key, and he too could sense the palatable taste of relief that this small piece of iron carried within its small frame. "All is not lost, for our Great Father has indeed provided a way for us."

"Indeed, my little blue warrior," Cal said with a laugh. "Now come on, let's be done with this damn wooden box and see if we might fetch ourselves a long draught of water from the well," Cal winked.

The hopeful smile that had painted the azure face of the small Sprite faded to a more serious expression. "This key will certainly open the door to this prison cell, swinging wide the gate for our momentary freedom," he said as he flew towards the iron lock that held them captive. "But I sense that it also opens another door, the door to our exile; and once opened, I trust you realize that it might very well never be undone."

"This colony was never the point, Deryn," Cal argued, his brow furrowed with perplexed confusion. "You know this."

"No, not the walls of timber, or the office of honor," Deryn spoke. "But you must see that the way things are ... that they may never be the same again." The small Sprite flew up to meet the gaze of his ward. "Lines will be drawn, and loyalties will be tested; true intentions will bare their ugly fangs in name of survival and righteousness. And you, my friend, will become an *enemy* of the very city for whom you have sought out a greater light."

"That very well may be," Cal replied. "But my home was never truly within the walls of our once bright city, nor was it here on these wild shores of this wild land. So if it takes exile to find my true home ... well, then I pray that you will be an exile with me."

Deryn smiled a curious smile as he surveyed the stubbled face of this young groomsman, and his bright, azure eyes betrayed deeper thoughts.

"What in the damnable dark are you smiling about?" Cal said playfully.

"There is something ancient about you, something that I have never noticed in you before," Deryn responded. "Maybe it was always there, or perhaps ... perhaps something in you has changed."

"Well, something good, I hope," Cal said a bit nervously.

"I cannot say, for I have not yet seen the full fruit of its sprouting determination," Deryn said frankly. "But never you mind what it is that I see, Calarmindon Bright Fame. Salvation and exile await us both, and they ride upon the back of that iron key of yours."

Cal held the key in his right hand and steeled himself for what would happen next. "Come on, then. I will need you to be my eyes outside of these timber walls," he told the Sprite sentinel. "Fly atop the rafters of the granary and tell me when I am clear to make my escape."

Cal fixed his gaze upon his tiny, winged friend. "Be safe ... and stay hidden."

Deryn nodded and then flew off in a blue blaze out the iron-barred window and across the gravel road until he was perched in the rafters of the adjacent timber structure.

Cal reached his hands through timber slats and took hold of the cold, iron lock. He whispered an anxious prayer as he placed the teeth of the key into the keyhole. "Forgive me when I have failed You, forgive me even now if I offend Your will. But I still ask for You to protect me and guide my steps, even if it be willingly into exile." With the last whispered word of his prayer, Cal turned the head of the iron key. The click of the latch sounded, reverberating in his cell as his nervous, sweating hand held the remnants of his iron captor. He lifted the lock off the door, placing it in the corner of his prison hold, and then he waited. His eyes remained fixed on Deryn's location, waiting for the signal that all was clear to flee.

After what seemed like an eternity of silence, the Sprite waved his bright blue blade, motioning to his friend that now was indeed the time to run. Cal pulled open the cell that had held him captive for these last three days. As he did, a wave of nerves crashed over him, bringing his senses to life in the wake of their shockingly cold aftermath. He took a deep breath, steeling himself for whatever might befall him, then quietly exited the prison hold and moved against the wall, low and as inconspicuously as he could manage.

The sounds and noises of the stronghold grew louder as Cal crept further and further away from the prison door. Most of the activity revolved around the departure of the *Determination*, so there was little time and little thought given to guarding the rogue groomsman who was thought to be helplessly imprisoned and awaiting his deportation.

"Deryn!" Cal shouted in a whisper, praying that none would wander close and hear him. "What do you see? Gvidus said he would be waiting by the well. Do you see him? Is it safe?"

The small Sprite flew up once again to survey the colony, and as he did Cal heard the laughter of the large-bellied woodcutter as he drew up bucket after bucket of cool water and clumsily poured them into the larger barrels there in his ox cart.

"I hear him!" Cal said. "He can't be more than half a hundred paces from here."

"Indeed, he is there," Deryn agreed as he settled back into Cal's cloak. "But he is not alone."

"Well then, we will wait 'til he is, and I will walk right up to the back of his cart and hide myself amongst the water barrels," Cal reasoned.

"I am afraid that it will not be as simple as that, my friend," Deryn said gravely. "Tahd and three of his guardsmen are walking this way from across the square. Waiting is not advisable."

Cal thought on it for a moment before he spoke. "Then we must be smart about it. Come on now," he said as he turned around and ran towards the open entrance of the granary. "I have an idea!"

He disappeared into a darkened storeroom and searched the shelves and stockpiles of barrels and burlap until he found what he was looking for. Cal enthusiastically grabbed a large, empty wooden barrel and held it in such a way that it covered most of his face. "This way it will look as if I am but helping my large-bellied brother finish the arduous task of gathering water for the day's work."

"This seems much riskier than I would deem prudent, Cal. But as I do not have a better idea, I suppose you had better be about your task quickly," Deryn agreed. "If the plan fails, I shall do my best to protect you."

Cal smiled a mischievous smile. "Very well, my Sprite guardian." And with that he lifted the large barrel, holding it out in front of him. Deryn flew down into the barrel and hid concealed inside its wooden walls, sword drawn and at the ready. The two of them made their way slowly and deliberately toward the stone well, acting as if they were merely about their assignment and all the while praying that no one would pay them any mind at all.

As they approached the well, Cal could make out the sound of multiple voices. He did not want to risk looking up and over the barrel, exposing his true identity to whomever it was that conversed with Gvidus.

"Deryn, can you see who it is there with Gvidus?" Cal whispered.

"I cannot see a thing!" The Sprite's voice echoed in the wooden chamber. "There are no cracks or holes for me to spy from."

"Let us pray that it is no one too keen, huh?" Cal replied, attempting to hide the nervousness in his tone.

Cal was not more than ten paces from the well when he heard the unwelcome sound of a familiar voice. "*More* barrels? You and your lazy brothers are going to drink this damned well dry before you'll have done half-day's work!" the angry voice growled at the large woodcutter.

"You have never swung an axe, have you?" Gvidus shot back with a bravely belligerent tone. "It takes a mighty large draught of water to quench the thirst that is worked up from felling timber. I'd show you how it's done ... but you would need to have both arms to be any good at it. I wouldn't want to see you miss and cut off your leg too!" he said with a sarcastic laugh.

"Listen here, you fat old boar!" the livid knight yelled. "I've felled a hundred angry outliers with my sword, and they had blades of their own with bloody intentions for my neck. I am sure that I could manage to knock over a few *sticks and twigs* that have no defense at all!"

"Pyrrhus!" Cal nervously whispered into the barrel.

"Well, come on then," Gvidus said as he noticed a familiar pair of legs sticking out from underneath a large, empty barrel that was walking towards the well. "I've got a blade of my own right here in this ox cart. I would like to see how the brilliant *fire knight* does with a double-sided axe, now that ... " Gvidus looked to the bandaged and bloodstained stump of a forearm so as to emphasis his insult. "Now that he's half as *bright* as he used to be."

Pyrrhus pressed close to the large-bellied northman. His oily face caught and reflected the flames of the nearby watch fires, and his sour breath was hot and feverish so close to Gvidus' face. "Do not mistake my wounded arm for weakened resolve, woodcutter. I will tame this Wreath, for the glory of my governor and for the light of my city. If I have to fell every Wreather, every fat-bellied bastard and every damned fool of a groomsman that crosses my way, then so be it! Arm or no arm, mind that I *am* a knight of the Priest King's cavalry."

"Aye, and I am a woodcutter who fells the trees and fuels the flames of your ill-sought glory." Gvidus sucked his teeth with pious satisfaction. "And if I don't get about the business of filling these water barrels, that will be the last ship of glory to sail across the black waters. Now, unless the Priest King's knight wants to give me a demonstration in one-armed axe wielding," Gvidus said with an exaggerated display of his hands, "my brother and I have some water to draw."

Cal had done his best to stay far enough away from the conversation so as to not draw unwarranted attention, but he knew his loitering was sure draw attention itself soon enough. Gvidus, sensing the duel of prides was coming to a close, acknowledged his presence so as to punctuate the dramatics with a closing.

Pyrrhus eyed the young man carrying the barrel with great suspicion. His temper was already blazing hot at the irreverent insolence of the woodcutter, and a new target had now entered his presence. He was just about to deliver a violent lashing of hate-filled words when the brass horns of the governor rang in the dark morning air. "Get out of my way, *water-maiden*," the fire knight grumbled as he shoved the barrel-carrying woodcutter to his knees.

Panic washed over Cal as he lost his grip on the large, wooden water barrel. It fell to the ground and rolled a few feet from his position. *Walk away ... just walk away,* he prayed silently. He stayed on his knees on the dusty earth, averting his face from the knight who was standing over him. In the darkness of the Wreath his features were not easily recognizable, but he knew if a flame was brought near or if his voice were heard, all would be lost.

"There is no cause for that now," Gvidus chided Pyrrhus. "You go, heed the bright brass that calls you, and let us woodcutters heed *our* own calling."

Pyrrhus towered over the kneeling woodcutter, a furious snarl curled on his bearded lips. "You should show some homage to the knights who guard this wilderness, *water-maiden!"*

Cal stayed frozen, afraid to even respond, willing this dog of a knight to leave him be. His mind raced for a means of escape or attack, but he could think of nothing that would not bring too great a risk to his calling yet again.

"What do you say, twig?" Pyrrhus goaded, but Cal remained silent, his face cloaked by the darkness. "*What* do you *say*?!" the fire knight screamed and drew his blade in an emasculated rage. "Answer me, woodcutter!"

The groomsman's breath came fast and heavy, and the hair on the back of his neck prickled at the touch of a sharpened steel point resting just below his unprotected shoulder blade.

"That's enough!" Gvidus shouted. "Save your anger for the real enemy that hides in the shadows of the Wreath, not one of our own!"

"I'll run you both through if that's what it takes to teach some order in this godforsaken colony!" Pyrrhus seethed.

The brass chorus cut the nearly fatal tension with their insistent beckoning. Pyrrhus, hearing the call of his master for a second time, sheathed his steal with a slam and a curse, striding off angrily towards the center of the stronghold like a petulant child.

Cal exhaled a desperately held breath as relief replaced the gravity of the moment. "Is he gone?" he whispered to Gvidus.

"Aye brother, he is," the large man replied.

Cal stood to his feet and dusted himself off before he retrieved the water barrel that had rolled away. "Come on then, I would prefer to not have that kind of encounter a second time," he said.

"Aye, prudence won over passion this time, and I doubt you would have a second chance at the same outcome," Gvidus agreed. "Come on, into the back of my cart with you. When they find that you are no longer behind iron, I want to be as far from these timber walls as I can."

Cal nodded his agreement and climbed into the back of the ox cart. He hid behind the barrels and covered himself with sackcloth while Gvidus shifted the other barrels so as to camouflage his rogue cargo. The large woodcutter climbed atop the driver's bench, and as he did the whole cart swayed and shifted, causing water to slosh from the tops of the open barrels. "You might get a bit wet back there, brother," Gvidus said as he cracked the reigns and urged the oxen onward. "But don't worry, provision enough has already been made for you. Once you're free, you'll have all the time in the world to be dry."

Gvidus sang an old timber song as the twin oxen strode deliberately through the square of the colony and out past the timber gates of the stronghold.

Oh mighty birch and mighty elm,
Oh stately pine and oak
Be not dismayed, nor even afraid,
Of our amber fire and smoke.

You mighty giants tall and green,
With leaf and fur and needle
Will light the night with your sacrifice,
Bringing peace to all our people.

"I thought for sure I was dead, Deryn," Cal whispered to his Sprite friend. "I thought his vengeance would be taken right then and there, and that-"

"I know you did, Cal," Deryn whispered.

"Did you not fear as well?" Cal asked, confused by his seemingly nonchalant reply.

"No, I did not," said the blue-winged guardian.

Cal thought on his tiny friend's words in silent contemplation as the cart bumped and rolled along the rooted and rough roads of the timber trails. Many silent moments passed before he spoke again.

"Why? Why were you not afraid, Deryn?" he asked in earnest. "Was it because you were ready to fell Pyrrhus yourself?"

Deryn let the words linger there in the stifled air beneath the wet burlap that concealed them. "No. Though if our Great Father had deemed it necessary, I would have indeed slain the fire knight."

"What, then?" Cal asked impatiently. "What gave you cause for such disproportionate peace? If I am honest ... I have never been more scared in my whole life."

"Do you think that our Great Father, who pulled you out of the river, who called you deep into the heart of the Hilgari, who gave the mighty blade Gwarwyn, and drew you across the black waters of the Dark Sea ... do you think He would let you perish on the dirty ground at the hand of a short-sighted barbarian without first helping you complete the task which *HE* called you to?"

Cal thought on it for a moment before he spoke. "It is hard to remember the voice of providence when the pointed fangs of death nip at the nape of your neck. It is harder still when those fangs are there because of your own folly. But perhaps ... perhaps you are right, my wise little friend." Cal smiled at the nonsensical confidence of this Sprite companion of his. "No, I don't suppose that He would."

"Neither do I, Cal," Deryn said comfortingly.

They rode in the heavy, hopeful silence, their thoughts in step with the clomps of the laboring oxen.

"But what if I fall? I mean, I have already fallen. I have already gone and made matters worse more than once. What then?" Cal's voice shook a bit in the asking. "Wouldn't He rather use someone else?"

"Our Great Father will use *all*—the upright and the fallen, the steadfast and the stumbling—if they but desire to be used by Him. For my kind has always believed that it is the humility of one's will and the readiness of one's heart, not merely the rightness of one's deeds, that makes one worthy of the greatest callings."

Cal swallowed around the lump in his throat. "It is harder than I anticipated," he finally said.

"He is not surprised," Deryn told him. "The Oweles told you so, that day upon the deck of the ship. Redemption is a complicated story ... just look at this darkened world about us. But its beginning was written long before us, dear groomsman, and its twists and turns will be what will make it worth the telling."

The Sprite's voice held a confidence that nearly undid the heart of the groomsman.

"I will not fear the snarling dogs who bark and bare their weak teeth at us, for I do not believe that their bite will ever be enough to destroy us. Their power lies only in their ability to scare or discourage us, and that is a power that only we can give them."

Cal laughed a whispered laugh. "He is a dog, that Pyrrhus, isn't he? And the worst kind at that."

"Yes, indeed he is," Deryn replied.

265

Chapter Thirty-One

THE WOODCUTTERS OF THE FIRST colony had made light work of the surrounding wilderness. Though their number was barely forty strong, their axes were thirsty and their swing was fueled with a great urgency, both for their calling and for their fellow kinsman. And so it was that the mighty forestlands of the Wreath began to yield to the double-bladed vigor of the woodcutters.

Yasen watched the line nervously, for he did not wholly trust the eerie calm of these mammoth trees. His senses were heightened enough with the aim to protect his men, but all the more so as he waited anxiously for news of Gvidus and his groomsman brother. Yasen's large, black Friesian paced the line of woodcutters, retracing his own steps over and over again as he sensed the unease of his master.

"What's the matter with you, North Wolf?" asked Oren, a tall, yellow-bearded man.

"Aye!" chimed his twin brother, Alon. "Why don't you stop your pacing and put blade to birch so you can work out whatever it is that has you in such a knot!"

"My brother is right, you know!" Oren agreed. "There is not much that can be mended fretting the way you are. Put your mind to rest and put your back to some work!"

"I am not fretting, and my mind is right where it needs to be," Yasen argued unconvincingly. "Today the *Determination* sails for Haven, but my bones tell me that something about today feels fragile, like a young limb about to snap." His eyes had a distant look as he spoke the words, staring back towards the fire-lit stronghold in the eastern distance.

Oren and Alon looked curiously at each other, each searching the other's face for the faintest hint of understanding. "Alright then, have it as you like, Chieftain." Oren shrugged as he picked up his doubled-bladed axe and began to bite away at the massive pine that towered high above him.

Alon stood there, still watching his chieftain, and suddenly the greater dread that masqueraded as worry occurred to him. "You know what I think?" he asked Yasen in a kind tone.

"I have a feeling you're about to tell me," Yasen grumbled.

"I think that Cal will be just fine, North Wolf," Alon said matter-of-factly.

Yasen turned his head back to look at his fellow woodcutter. His darkly bearded jaw was set, but his eyes betrayed his true fear.

"Aye," Alon continued. "The lad has survived far worse than a little exile." He then picked back up his axe and turned to face the same pine that his brother was expertly working on. "Besides, I doubt that the THREE who is SEVEN is quite finished with him yet."

"What makes you say that?" Yasen said guardedly.

"Because his silver horse is right over there, packed and ready," Alon laughed as he buried his blade deep into the white flesh of the massive tree. "And I don't suspect that He is a wasteful deity."

As he spoke, the faint sounds of the governor's horns echoed off the dark morning air, causing the mouth of the mighty North Wolf to go dry in worried anticipation.

"I need a drink," Yasen half-mumbled under his breath.

"Well, *asketh and ye shall receiveth*, or however it goes," Alon chuckled. "I think I see the lights from Gvidus' ox-cart coming up the hill. And that fat old boar better have those barrels full to the top this time!"

Relief washed over Yasen's face as he saw the two swinging lanterns swaying from the rumble of the water laden cart, not a few hundred paces below him at the bottom of the gently sloping hill.

"*Asketh* indeed," Yasen said less anxiously. "That water will do my soul a great bit of good."

"Your soul, eh?" Alon said with a knowing look.

Just then the horns rang out again, bright and hurried, angrily raising the alarm from within the fortifications of the colony.

Yasen wheeled his black Friesian around to face the brothers. "I fear that the limb I spoke of has just *snapped,* comrades. Keep a sharp eye about you, and an even sharper blade," he said as he rubbed at his worried face. "You never know which one you may need first."

"Aye, North Wolf," Alon said. "You let me and my old brother here worry about the sharpness of blades and eyes and such, and you ... well, you just worry about quenching that thirst of yours."

Yasen nodded his head in understanding, and in that moment something akin to true gratitude washed over his dirt-stained body. "Even here on these wild shores, and in this darkened wilderness, home is not far if we look to find it," he said, a bit more sentimental than he had expected.

"Aye," Alon agreed. "Home is where you make it, or so my mother always told us." Alon turned his attention back towards the exposed, white flesh of the massive soldier pine in front of him. "Now, see about telling Gvidus to hurry it up, huh?"

Yasen spurred the Friesian and the two of them rode off with a hopeful eagerness towards the swinging lanterns of the ox cart. "Good day there, Chieftain!" bellowed the round-bellied Gvidus. "How goes the progress of our axe-wielding brothers this fine, black morning?"

"Better now, brother," Yasen said as his horse trotted alongside the ox cart. "Better now." Yasen stared at Gvidus as he rode, almost afraid to ask the question for fear that the answer might not be to his liking. So he raised his dark eyebrows instead, letting their movement ask the question for him.

"Aye," Gvidus said softly. "He is safe alright, though I thought for a moment he would have to relieve Pyrrhus of his other arm to be so."

Yasen breathed a long-anticipated sigh of relief, raising the cold flint to his lips to kiss it in practiced thankfulness. "So it looks as if you will be staying on these wild shores a bit longer now, huh groomsman?"

"Thanks to you, I am," came the muffled sound of the groomsman's voice, out from under the canvas and sackcloth that concealed him. Cal pulled back the covering and, by the faint, violet light of his hopeful illumination, he saw his friend and chieftain riding beside him.

"Did you hear the horns, Yasen?" Cal said a bit nervously. "I fear it means that they have discovered I am no longer held prisoner."

"I fear the same, brother," Yasen replied. "Which means we haven't much time to waste now. Gvidus, pull the cart over there, just to the left of those cutters." He pointed and directed the large driver to where he wanted him to go. "It is there that we must *unload* our barreled bounty and bid farewell to its rather reckless contents," he said with a playful smirk.

"Aye, Chieftain," Gvidus replied, his eyes sparkling with the self-satisfaction of a sweet-toothed grandfather who had just been caught in the act of over-indulging his little heirs.

They rode in tandem for a few hundred paces before Cal broke the silent pregnancy of the moment. "Yasen?" Cal started, pausing in the lingering emptiness of an unspoken question. The consequences of the hour were heavy on the heart of the groomsman, but there was another pressing matter that vied for his attention.

Yasen looked straight ahead as he rode beside the ox cart, his eyes fixed on the flickering braziers of his woodcutting comrades. "Goran is with her still," he said, gaze unwavering.

Cal breathed a sigh of relief loud enough for Yasen to hear. The woodcutter felt, as he had almost every day since his arrival on these strange and wild shores, the lonely leagues of distance between he and his curly-haired bar maiden. "I thought it was the light that you were seeking, the new light of the THREE who is SEVEN at that ... not just the affections of some violet-eyed woman?" Yasen asked, a bit too jealously to wholly conceal.

"Oh, I am, brother," Cal said with a sincere grace. "Never you worry about that, for there is nothing is this wild world that would ever truly sway my heart from its course."

"Spoken easily enough from one who has not had the pleasure of tasting the crimson-lipped sweetness of Aiénor's fairer beauties," Yasen said with a goading smirk. "Mind that you don't find yourself caught in the web of her arms, powerless to seek the light you hope to find."

Cal laughed an understanding laugh, and looked to his bearded friend in hopes that his gaze might convey his true intentions. "It's not that I ... that I don't know what it is that you are warning me of, brother. It's only, well ... that I believe my finding this light, this *new light*, is somehow wrapped up in finding it with *her*."

They rode silently together, save for the clopping of the mighty Friesian's hooves and the creaking and cranking of the iron rimmed wheels over the pitted and wild ground. Finally, at the tree line of the woodcutters, they reached two bridled horses that were tethered to the low branches of a young fir tree.

"Looks as if we have arrived, groomsman," Gvidus proclaimed with a jovial twinkle in his eye. "Now, save your elder brother some trouble and help me with these barrels before you leave us this somber day."

"Of course," Cal replied. The kindness of his smile reflected the gratitude of his heart as he and Deryn leapt down from the back of the ox cart to the moss covered ground below.

"I doubt that there is much time to spare, Gvidus," Yasen said sternly. "Seig's men are sure to suspect our brothers in the wake of Cal's disappearance, and I for one would rather see many leagues between us, rather than see him bound in irons aboard that silver ship again."

Gvidus nodded his understanding and sat back down upon his driver's bench, resigned to a sore night's sleep. "Very well then, young groomsman, when you have found your new light, make sure that you come repay your heavy barreled debt to me," he said with a wry smile.

"Indeed I shall, Gvidus," Cal said in return. "Thank you." The gleam in the eyes of the young man made it clear that he was thanking the woodcutter for far more than a reprieve from moving the barrels.

"Seek the light, brother!" The round-bellied woodcutter cracked the reigns on the team of tired oxen, calling back over his shoulder as the cart creaked to life and rolled off towards the line of thirsty woodcutters. "And mind that you find it!"

Cal could not help but smile as he drove away, and he was smiling still when he met the gaze of the two horses tethered to a young fir tree.

"Farran!" Cal shouted in surprised glee.

The silver-coated horse snorted and nodded his head in agreeable recognition as Cal ran to his companion and wrapped his arms around his broad, muscled neck. "You are a sight for sore eyes, my friend!"

Farran lowered his large head to rest atop the shoulder of the groomsman, saying without words that he too was glad to see his old friend.

The sound of an aggravated snort came from the large chestnut that stood just a few paces away. "And I am glad to see you too, girl," Cal said with amusement as he stroked and patted her soft, dark coat.

The brass of the guardsmen's horns broke the tenderness of the reunion, like a heavy boot upon winter's first fragile frost. "You will have plenty of time for all sorts of pleasantries later. Now you must leave, before those cavalrymen get here first," Yasen urged. "Come, brother, you have to ride like the wind."

Cal could feel the ground beneath him begin to rumble with the sound of heavy hooves swiftly approaching, and he could see the flickering amber of the knight's torches as they closed in on their position there atop the hilled tree line. He halted for a moment, knowing the wrath that might be in store for his woodcutting brothers if their aid to him was ever known.

"Cal!" Yasen urged, a hard edge creeping into his voice. "You must leave *now*, for I haven't the stomach to start a war this dark morning."

Cal nodded, and with a single, fluid motion he put boot to stirrup and mounted his grey horse. He took the reins in his hand and fixed his subtle, violet gaze to the north.

"Thank you, brother," Cal said swiftly. "I am indebted to you beyond what I would know how to repay."

Yasen shook his head, brushing aside the dramatic words of his friend. "If it wasn't me, I am sure that Sprite guardian of yours would have done it," he said with a wink.

Cal looked to the faint glowing pocket inside his coat, the blue light reflecting off of the bronzed-armored chest piece and a knowing smile came over his face. "Perhaps you are not far from the truth, North Wolf," Cal said with a laugh.

"I almost forgot!" Yasen said as he reached inside the roll of canvas affixed to the back of his saddle.

"Gwarwyn!" Cal exclaimed, his voice colored with the hopeful hues of utter relief. "I ... I thought, but how?" he said as he stumbled over his words.

"Never you mind," Yasen cut him off. "Ride, ride now ... ride for the sake of all of us. Seek this new light, my brother."

The shaking of the ground beneath them grew stronger and stronger as the convoy of riders came closer with each passing moment.

"What about Astyræ?" Cal said worriedly. "Where is she? Where did Goran take her?"

"The cave, about a half a league from here," Yasen said as quickly as he could. "The same cave we sent her to before ... before all of this. Ride until the ground turns to the stony banks of the creek bed. From there you will have to ride into the forests a hundred or so paces. If they are safe, that is where Goran was told to meet her."

Cal nodded his understanding. He took a last farewell glance at the woodcutters, and then reached out his arm for his friend. "We, by the THREE who is SEVEN," Cal said, looking at the scarred and patched face of his brother.

"We, by the THREE who is SEVEN," Yasen replied. "Now ride!"

Cal leaned close to the ear of his silver-coated friend and whispered his intentions. "Alright, Farran, let's find her." And then, with a spur of his boots, Cal and the two horses took off northward in pursuit of the violet-eyed woman. His heart was anxious, hoping that all of this imprisonment and exile would not be the folly he feared it might be.

Chapter Thirty-Two

THE STAIRS INSIDE THE KEEP of the prison hold spiraled endlessly down into the earthen soil of Haven's underbelly. Michael and Timorets did their best to help the large, wounded schoolmaster as he took slow, pain-inducing steps down into the depths of the keep. Meanwhile, Fryon and his younger brother went before the rest to make sure that the way stayed clear for their escape.

There was not much light here in the dank and musky corridor, save for a single torch that Engelmann had set ablaze with his magic, and the five men were at the mercy of each grimly lit step that they took.

"Argh!" Celrod groaned as he tripped and stumbled, placing too much of his large frame upon his arrow-pierced leg. "How much deeper can one possibly deem necessary when tunneling into the earth of Aiénor?"

"I think it all depends on the depth of whatever it is you hope to tunnel under," Timorets replied rather matter-of-factly. "It is the mighty Abonris, after all ... and I for one have not plumbed its depths, though I doubt it could be much—"

"Bottom!" Fryon called back up to his trailing companions. "We reached the bottom!"

"See," Timorets said with a self-satisfied smile. "Maybe I should have been the schoolmaster."

Celrod just grunted and shook his head in pained disagreement.

"Hurry now, my boys," Engelmann urged the limping three. "I fear that swiftness ..." his words trailed off as if he were listening to some distant but familiar sound.

"You fear that swiftness ... what?" Michael said, a bit worried. "Engelmann? What-"

Michael and the rest had finally reached the floor of the stony, mold-covered stairs, and by the glow of Engelmann's torch the six of them caught sight of the hauntingly black entrance to the long-abandoned passageway. As if the idea of the tunnel itself were not unsettling enough, two large, partially closed eyes were carved into the stone structure, crowning its black opening.

"The *Menashe*," Engelmann groaned quietly as if remembering a deeply painful moment from his youth.

"Look here!" the younger of the brothers pointed between the massive, ocular carvings. "What is this symbol? What does it mean?"

"It is the mark of Kaestor," the schoolmaster said. "The sigil of the house of the mad king."

"Grief shows itself in all manners of form," Engelmann scolded. "And the reign of Kaestor was the pinnacle of sorrow for Haven. See here, what outlines the great tree?"

"It is a tear, is it not?" Michael asked.

"It is indeed, my boy," Engelmann praised him with a sad smile. "For a powerful man who must bury his daughter might foolishly believe that in burying the rest of the world, he might bring her back from the grave."

"It sounds like madness to me," Celrod spoke.

"And indeed it was madness ... though not *just* madness," Engelmann lamented. "Many prisoners, both criminals and countrymen, walked this path of the forgotten to their senseless doom ... vain sacrifices on the altar of a twisted grief."

"Even the mighty Abonris mourns the deeds of this place," Michael said as he felt the droplets of cold water fall and splash against the stone passageway.

"Let us hope that we too will not meet our demise at the end of this tunnel," Fryon mused.

"Aye," said the brewer in nervous agreement as he raised his flint to his lips and kissed it in search of strength.

"Come on, then," Celrod urged. "Enough about the dead in a place like this."

"Do not dismay too much, my friends," Engelmann said as he reached his leathery hands up to catch the tears of the ancient river; the droplets gathered and rolled like quicksilver in his magical grasp. "For perhaps such absurdity might yet have its redemption."

CLANG! The sound of an iron door crashing against the stone above them rang out in the chamber, bringing a startling end to their conversation.

"Quickly now!" Michael said. "They have breached the keep."

The lot of them moved as fast as they could, limping along in the ancient, tear-soaked darkness of *Kaestor's Doom* by the light of a single torch. The distant echo of boots clamoring down stone stairs urged them further into the passageway, beyond the boundaries of all reason and sensibilities.

"Do you know where this ends?" Fryon whispered from up ahead of the group. "Where the *Menashe* resurfaces?"

"Probably into the very chambers of the bloody Priest King himself," said Timorets. "Wouldn't that just be our luck, huh?"

"Right now I don't mind where it ends," Celrod said through pain-gritted teeth. "As long as we get there before any more points of the Raven Army's arrows reach our backs!"

"The schoolmaster is right!" agreed the younger brother.

The ground beneath them began to rumble, and the six looked at each other's torch-lit eyes for some kind of confirmation that they were not the only one to have felt the tremors.

"Did you?" Michael asked in a nervous whisper.

"Aye, I did," replied the brewer.

"What was it?" Celrod asked the Arborist. "What kind of hells-" he was interrupted as a large drop of water splashed in his face. "What in the damnable dark?" the schoolmaster recoiled a bit too loudly.

"*What?*" Timorets asked. "What is the matter, Celrod?"

The ground shook again, this time more violently than before, and the group of six went sprawling to the wet, stone floor. As they did, the distinct sound of something ripping through the air went speedily overhead.

"They are here!" Michael shouted in a whisper.

WHOOSH! An exploratory volley of arrows bounced and pinged off the stone walls of the *Menashe*.

"Engelmann!" Fryon whispered urgently. "The torch!"

The ground shook again, and this time the tears of the river began to fall in trickling streams of lament, rather than the single droplets of ancient sorrow.

Engelmann breathed his magic over the torch, and the golden flames vanished into a smoky mist of spent illumination.

The sounds of spilling water and scrambling feet urged them to hurry. "What do we do now?" Timorets said as an arrow sailed past him, a mere arm's length from his face.

"We run!" Michael said. "We run, *now!*"

The groomsman and the brewer helped the wounded schoolmaster to his feet, then they pointed themselves to the blackened unknown and ran as fast as they could manage.

"Where are we going?" Fryon shouted back over his shoulder, no longer careful to be quiet.

"Further in!" Engelmann shouted in reply.

The ground shook even more violently, and once again the six went sprawling against the wet stone. Arrows pinged and whizzed recklessly, and the fugitives could not bring themselves to stand. Then, without warning, a most horrifying scream filled the chamber with a wailing lament.

"What is that?" Michael screamed into the utter darkness. "What is that sound?"

The walls shook, and the floor quaked, and the icy-cold blue of the mighty river began to empty itself into the passageway below. Trickles turned into streams, and the horror of the moment dawned on each of them at the same time. The *Menashe* was going to collapse.

"Engelmann!" Michael shouted as he reached and grabbed for his friend. "Engelmann, what is that sound?"

The eyes of the Arborist opened their heavy lids, and the pale, leaf-green kindness that had once lived in the stare of the old sage was replaced with a dim, blue flame. "It is finished," he whispered ominously.

"What?" Michael shouted against the screams and terror of this maddened moment. "What is finished? What do you mean?"

"The light ... it has left us ..." Engelmann said, choking back his emotions. "The tree is dead; the great light is extinguished from Aiénor forever." His eyes closed once again, squeezing out the tears that had collected there. The face of the great Arborist crumpled in pain, and a moaning sound of deep lament and anguish escaped his still parted lips.

The ground shook all the more violently now, and they all knew that this pathway of the forgotten would not hold much longer. The raven-fletched arrows of the invading army split the cascading streams of the river's breach, and the rush of wind across the face of the younger brother woke him from his stunned horror. "They ... they are coming for us, friends, and I for one did not barely escape the tongues of fire just to suffer the tears of flood or the bite of arrows!" he urged desperately. "We must go!"

"Come on, my brother is right!" Fryon agreed as he grabbed Celrod's arm and pulled him back to his feet.

Michael watched his friend and teacher, crouching amidst the assault of arrows and the invasion of the cold Abonris. "It was *their* defilement that broke the heart of the tree for good, but it was *our* complacency that dealt the first blow," Engelmann shouted against the rush of river and whoosh of arrows. "Doom is upon us all now, my dear boy!"

"No!" Michael shouted back in protest. "It was neither them nor us that caused the light of the tree to perish! You yourself read the ancient books of magic; *it was always meant to end this way.* Long have we lived under the knowledge that the end was coming," Michael said, reaching for the hand of his old friend as he willed him to leave this failing, watery tomb. "It's only just now that we have ever dared to notice. The tree might have been doomed to die, but I am not so easily convinced that we will share its same fate."

Engelmann blinked his blue-flamed eyes once, twice, and then seven times more until the saddened fires faded to the leafy-green. "Well, perhaps your fate is not sealed yet, my boy."

BOOM! A chunk of earth fell from the rocky corridor above and crashed into the stone passageway. "Then hurry up and leave this place with me!" Michael shouted, tugging on the hand of the Arborist.

Arrows flew and bounced off the falling rock. Engelmann and the five men trudged as fast as their tired and wounded legs would carry them through the cold waters that filled this forgotten pathway. The further in through the pitch black that the lot of them went, the less fearful of arrows they became.

It was Timorets who noticed it first.

"Do you see that?" the brewer blurted out, a bit surprised to hear his own voice that loud.

"See what, my friend?" Celrod grunted through his pained steps.

"The pathway! The rising water! The whole damned lot of us!" Timorets gushed.

"Of course we do-" Celrod began to say matter-of-factly. Then, the reality of the moment began to sink in. He could see the pathway. They could ... *see*. "What in the damnable darkness?"

"Is there a light up ahead?" Timorets shouted to the two brothers in front.

"No!" Fryon shouted back. "None that I can see."

"How is this possible then?" Michael said to his Arborist friend as he searched the lines of his barked face.

The air around them glowed ever so faintly in an almost imperceptible, violet hue. The lines from the masons' tools could now be seen upon the black rock of the passageway as they caught and reflected the light.

"Is this some magic of yours, Engelmann?" Celrod grunted painfully between chattering teeth.

"No, it is not any magic of my own, though I suspect it is one much deeper and much older," Engelmann said with an awe-struck voice and a wondering gaze. "For I will place my light in the hearts of those who..."

"Hope," Michael said, finishing the hauntingly mysterious line of the great and forgotten prophecy. "Is this what that means?"

Engelmann looked around them. The water was now nearly up to their waistlines and he knew that they still had a great distance to travel in this *pathway of the forgotten* before reaching its point of origin. And yet, the Arborist could not keep the marvel of this development from his heartbroken voice. "I do not know what else it could be, my boy. For hope is the only thing we might be foolish enough to see by," he said with a sad, teasing smile.

"Whatever it is, if we want to see any further effects of this magic, we are going to have to hurry!" Fryon urged them on.

They all agreed with silent nods to put the whole of their remaining strength into moving further into the darkness, which was now unmistakably illuminated by a violet glow. The arrows had stopped some time ago, but the cold waters of the Abonris triggered an uncontrollable chattering of teeth that echoed in a cold chorus off the forgotten walls.

"What I wouldn't give for a few pieces of timber to kiss the sparks of my flint," Celrod mused aloud. "Or even better, a boiling pot of mulled wine to warm me from the inside out."

"Aye, or a bowl of piping-hot stewed lamb," Timorets agreed as they rushed along, trying to occupy their minds with the possibility of life outside the tunnel. "Or two bowls!"

"You can keep your stew, and your wine—just give me a pair of dry boots is all!" Michael told them.

"Shhh! Quiet!" Fryon whispered back to the shivering hovel of waterlogged friends. "Did you hear that?"

The faint sound of the invader's horns boomed into the tunnel through some opening up ahead, and the six of them knew that they must be nearing the end of this wet, cold, forsaken road.

"Look here!" Fryon said as he pointed ahead. "It looks to be a stairwell, and thank the THREE who is SEVEN, it looks to be going up."

"I can taste the mulled wine already!" Celrod mused.

"I'm sure the invaders, whoever they are, have brought plenty to share with you," Timorets said sarcastically. "Or have you forgotten, schoolmaster, that we are under siege?"

"Oh, I have not forgotten, brewer," Celrod said as he pointed to his arrow pierced leg.

"Come on now, let's be quick about this," Michael chided. "The waters are not going to cease their rising, and I for one don't want to spend another moment in this place."

The stone stairs climbed in an uncomfortably narrow ascent, barely wide enough for two men to walk side-by-side. There were no iron torch holds upon these steps, for the cursed travelers who had descended these stones before had neither the need nor the opportunity to find their way back. Up and up they climbed, spiraling higher into fresher air, anticipating the swell of commotion that waited above. It was Fryon who spotted the simple, arched opening first. "There, see? Right there; have we made it to the top, then?"

The small band of soaked and sodden men looked back to Engelmann, desperately hoping that this was indeed the end of this forgotten path. "Yes," he said, sadness coating his words. "This is the end, or ..." He let a nervous chuckle escape through his thin, frowned lips. "Or rather, this is the beginning; I guess it all depends on the traveler's perspective, doesn't it?" The Arborist returned the weighty looks of his friends, and the gravity of double-layered doom hung heavy in the moment. "For our journey, this is indeed the end of *this* road. But there, right there—that is where many an innocent life became truly lost," he said, pointing to the small archway.

"Maybe that is where ours might find its second chance?" Michael replied, the hope in his voice surprising even himself.

"Well said, my boy," Engelmann said, quite pleased with his pupil. "Well said, indeed."

The six climbed the last leg of the stone steps, each pace dimly illuminated by the faint violet glow that had somehow colored the air around them. They passed under the archway, and their eyes slowly widened in sickened horror as the room they were standing in came into shadowed focus. The chamber was rounded and rather snug. All along its stone walls hung the high-strung chains of a half-dozen manacles, their binding irons limply littered about the floor. At the near end of the rounded room leaned a score of spears and halberds, and a few oil-skinned swords, stacked against an iron rack. A smattering of blacksmith's tools was arranged upon a small stone table, although there was no hearth or kiln here within the darkened bastion that would have necessitated such instruments.

"What ... what was this place?" Timorets asked.

"Some kind of prison hold?" Celrod suggested.

"No. It feels much too sad to be a mere prison cell," Michael gulped as he spoke.

"A sad place, indeed," Fryon mused in agreement.

"Do you know what this place was?" Timorets said as he ran his hands upon an oddly placed stone chair in the center of the room, directing his question to the Arborist.

"I do, my boys, I do indeed. This was a place where unanswerable questions were relentlessly asked. A black secret of our shining city, right in the heart of the Citadel," Engelmann answered.

"But I don't understand," said the younger brother.

"Neither did they—and truly, neither did Kaestor," Engelmann said as he fingered the edge of one of the forgotten blades. "Grief often demands answers that honey the ears, even if that is all that they are good for."

GAROOOM came the sound of the invaders' horns, much closer than any of them had dared to fear. The sickly tone woke the fugitives from their sad speculation and sent a freezing shiver of terror down their already cold, soaked necks. The sounds of boots running in formation erupted outside the iron-barred door of the chamber. As the guardsmen above came closer, they began to make out their voices, shouting in hurried tension.

"Fall into formation!" sounded the voice of a commanding officer from outside.

"They seek an audience with the Priest King!" came another.

"What do we do now?" Michael said. "We are traitors to the Citadel, fugitives! If we go out those doors, they will have our heads!"

GAROOM! The horns of the Raven Army sounded again.

"Someone approaches ... a rider!" shouted a gate warden. "Make ready to parley!"

"They must have already reached the Kings' Bridge," Engelmann said as he handed each one of the men a weapon. To Michael, Fryon and his younger brother, he gave the three simple, utilitarian long swords; to Timorets and Celrod he gave a pair of beautifully crafted halberds.

"What do you suggest we do with these?" Celrod said, a bit flabbergasted at the notion of this band of ragamuffins doing anything worthwhile by force of blade while an entire invading army and full brigade of guardsmen waited there on the other side of the door.

"Well, you can steady yourself until that leg of yours is mended!"

Timorets replied. "I, for one, could use some relief from the full weight of your burden."

"Well, then, maybe you could hand me those snips over there," Celrod said, gesturing to the pile of blacksmith's tools, "and help me rid myself of this vile Raven's bolt, huh?" Celrod plopped his soaked, heavy frame down upon the stone chair, grunting back the pain as he crossed his left leg up and over his right so that he might examine the full measure of the wound. "Well, it's not all that bad," he surmised. "It hurts like the darkened hell that it came from, but if I can remove the barb ... come on then, brewer, let's be done with it already."

Timorets handed him the iron snips, and it wasn't but a moment later that the blacksmith's tool did its job, and the curled, angry point of the Raven's arrow clanked upon the stone floor.

"When we find some of that mulled wine you've been talking about, we are going to have to pour it in there," the brewer said sorrowfully. "It's going to hurt worse than when that bolt got itself lodged in your leg to begin with. Here," Timorets said as he handed him the broken, barbless shaft of the arrow. "You might want to keep this so you have something to bite down upon when the time comes."

Celrod grunted unenthusiastically to Timorets, then wrapped up his leg in the torn sleeve of his sodden shirt. He steadied himself as he rose to his feet, testing the strength of his wounded leg. "Alright then, Arborist, since I don't believe that you mean to get us all killed this dark day, what would you have us do?"

Engelmann looked about the room, taking in every detestable device as if it were the first time his eyes had beheld such a sad and sorrowful place. "I do not trust that the poison of fear has not already toxified the good senses of our leaders, nor do I suppose that it will be the last time that hopeless circumstances will make a madman out of a mighty king." The Arborist mumbled to himself, ignoring the question of the wounded brewer.

The horns of the guardsmen cut the conversation in two, and from the inside of the chamber, the men listened with anxious attention for all that might unfold just outside their hiding place.

Chapter Thirty-Three

FOR ALL THE MADNESS THAT had decimated the order and decorum of his great city, the Priest King would not dare to cower undignified behind his white, jeweled walls. No, he would heed the traditions of his forbearers and conference with the invaders as a man of pride and nobility. His royal guard marched in a most disciplined cadence, boot upon pavement in direct defiance of the chaotic happenings around them. They formed an armored column about the Priest King and his Chancellor as they made their slow and wary way down the stone-paved streets of the Capital. In the courtyard of the Capital, the remaining force of Haven stood assembled and ready to defend their city against the enemy that waited for them just on the other side of the Kings' Bridge.

"Lieutenant," the Chancellor summoned as they approached the front lines. "*Who* is this army that dares to desecrate our holy city? Who are these invaders who march under the cover of dragons?" Chaiphus said with a deliberately proud demeanor.

"They speak of a Raven Queen," the lieutenant said, his own face now paled to a sickened, ghostly white. "You must have heard their voices?"

He looked to the Priest King for confirmation, but Chancellor Chaiphus cleared his throat with an angered force. "Ahem! Do not assume what we have or have not heard. Give us your report, lieutenant."

"Yes, of course. The invaders, they have sent a rider to parley, only ... the rider, he is not a man—or at least he is one no longer."

Jhames looked out across the last of his glittering-helmed battalion, past the lowered portcullis of the Kings' Gate. What he saw made his blood run cold with fear. There, at halted attention across the wild waters of the mighty Abonris, stood a vast and menacing legion of the green-eyed invaders. The Priest King took a step backwards, overcome with the terror at the sight of such monsters, and in such great numbers. Grief and despair clawed at his pious throat as the impotence of his defenses became quite evident.

Almost as if they had sensed the erosion of confidence, the twin dragons erupted with a fiery blast. Still perched upon the lifeless trunk of the once great tree, they roared out their green flames in violent, punctuated fury.

"What kind of man or monster leads this army of darkness?" Jhames whispered to his trusted Chancellor. "What magic drives them?"

"Your *Brightness*!" came the distant, guttural, mocking voice of the enemy consort who waited for them upon the bridge. "My queen demands your audience!"

There, atop a ghostly pale steed, sat the herald of doom. The cold, north winds caught his inky, feathered cape; it danced in an eerie likeness of a carrion foul's wings descending upon its wounded prey. The rider's face was unique among the ranks of the invaders; it was only half ashen in color, and only one of his eyes glowed with the sickly, green hue. As for the other, by some twist of vile magic, it was permitted to cling to it former *human* glory.

Jhames looked back and forth from the eyes of his frightened lieutenant and then again to the rider upon the Kings' Bridge. He thought for a moment before he met the gaze of his Chancellor.

"I will not ride out there to speak with the likes of that devil. Make ready the Capital's defenses, we will strike the night with the edge of our flints if we have to!" he said as his voice cracked with the tension of his powerless pride. He whirled around, his long, stately robes flowing behind him. As he began to march himself back through the courtyard and into the relative safety of the royal chambers, the voices of the dragons stopped him in his tracks.

Laughter, sickly and mocking, spewed from the sorceress' twin dragons.

The once-bright Priest King has gone mad, has he?

His mind erupted with their tandem voices as their laughter shook him to his core.

Only a pitiful fool would put his trust in the bite of a blade or the strength of a wall, for there are none who will escape the reach of the Raven Queen, nor withstand the assault of her nocturnal armies. And foolish, it would seem to us, you are!

Jhames clawed at his ears and pulled at his long white beard. He yelled into the black sky, desperate to silence the dragons. "No! You cannot have it, you will not have *my kingdom*!"

"Your Brightness?" Chaiphus asked rather nervously. "Who are you speaking to?"

Jhames looked at his friend and confidant and then slowly raised his trembling arm to point his spindly finger in the direction of the dragons.

The remaining army of Haven watched in horror as their leader crumbled, nearly instantaneously, before their eyes. He fell to his knees and screamed in enraged agony, twitching and writhing as if he were possessed by a score of foul spirits. Though none could hear the words the dragons spoke, they could see that the fruit of their meaning had gone rancid, sickening the spirit and strength of their leader with their bitter intent.

Do not trouble yourself so, Priest King of Haven. There is nothing that demands you to fall prey to our hunger. Your Brightness must simply parley with the general. You might very well save your precious city after all.

Jhames knelt there on all fours, like an animal cornered in the back alleys of Westriver. His greying eyes shone wild in the light of the torch fires, and his chest rose and fell in a pounding rhythm of terror.

There is magic to be found within the darkness of this world; there is power to hold, even still for you, Priest King.

Chaiphus gestured to two of the royal guards to help the Priest King back to his feet. "Your Brightness? Your Brightness!"

"I have changed my mind," he said with wild eyes as he looked up towards the holy mountain. "Order the column. I will parley with the invader." Jhames brushed off his robes and tried to stand tall, but his body was shaking so severely that he could hardly will himself to find any semblance of posture. He swallowed back his tears, nearly choking on the ever-present fear as he forced the defeated words from his parched lips.

The thirty-seven men who made up the King's guard fell into position around him, but Chaiphus was seized by the dread of a more ancient fear. He pushed his way through the guard and up close to the Priest King. "Your Brightness, if I may? What is ... why the change of mind?" he managed to ask without breaking the decorum that he so tightly held to.

Jhames looked his trusted Chancellor in the eyes while trails of blood began to trickle from his ears. "Our hope has failed us. The colony has either deserted us or has been smashed upon the shores of that dark land across the damned Dark Sea. *There is no light coming for us.*" Jhames looked down to his pale hands that would not cease their wild shaking, then back again to meet the gaze of his friend. "Would you have me carry the blood of our city upon my hands as well, Chancellor? Would you have me see to the ruin and destruction of every last part and parcel of the great city of Haven? See its Citadel and its citizens alike devoured by ... by *them*?" he said, pointing a quivering finger towards the green-eyed pair of dragons.

"No, your Brightness," Chaiphus confessed. "But surrender? Without a fight? Our bowmen have yet to loose a single arrow, and our cavalry has yet to ride into their Raven hordes."

Jhames gazed through Chaiphus, looking at something beyond him as if he saw the very scene unfolding in a vision. "Our archers are already lost, and our riders have already done their worst out beyond the North Gate, and the winged serpents still mock our efforts and consume our ardor." His eyes slipped closed for the moment as he envisioned a different unfolding of events. "But if we yield to their request, they promise power anew, Chaiphus. *Magic* ... in the darkness."

The Priest King wiped at his ears with his trembling hands and noticed the traces of bright red upon his pale flesh. He clenched his fist and summoned what resolve was left in his frail and fearful body. Chaiphus looked about the skyline of his city, then over his shoulder to the gathered army of the Raven Queen, then back again to the Priest King. An agreement passed between them there, a half-spoken conspiracy.

"If we are doomed to dwell in darkness," Jhames said, "perhaps we might avoid doing so as slaves."

"Agreed, your Brightness." Chaiphus said with a desperate, reluctant gleam in his eye.

The two turned to face the enemy herald who waited for them upon the Kings' Bridge. "Very well," Jhames called out. "We shall agree to your request for parley."

WHOOSH! The jolting sounds of the dragons' wings buffeted the dark sky as the beasts left their perch atop the dead tree and soared high above the city they presumed to possess. The sound of the pounding wind against their leathery wings left every citizen of Haven with a feeling of utter dread.

WHOOSH! *WHOOSH*! Again and again the sounds came as the mighty serpents circled the city. The guardsmen aimed their drawn longbows high into the black sky as the small convoy of knights escorted the Priest King and his Chancellor past the iron teeth of the massive portcullis and onto the white stone of the Kings' Bridge.

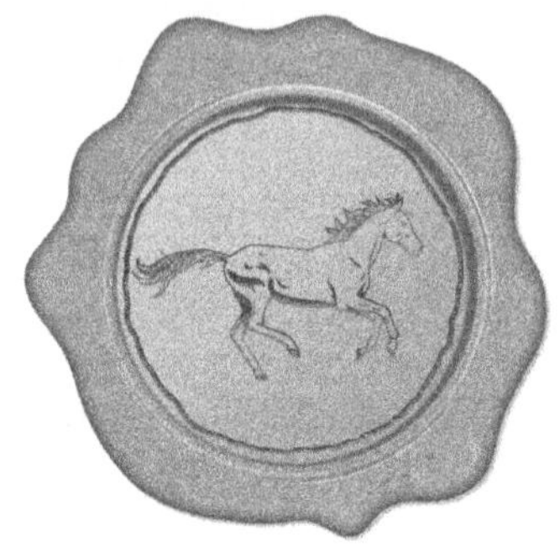

Chapter Thirty-Four

THE SOUND OF THE GROUND beneath the hooves of the two horses changed not long after Cal and Yasen had parted ways; the dull thud of clomping earth transitioned to the stony, sharp, crunch of the iron shoes upon the pebbled creek bank. Cal had not risked the torchlight, but alone, out here in the utter darkness of the wild Wreath, his violet sight was dim at best. He was afraid he would not notice the creek until it was too late, so the sound of the sure shod feet of his silver mount upon the gravel bank woke his heart with joy.

"Oh, bless you, Wielund!" Cal whispered. "I've never been happier to hear the sound of your handiwork than I am right now!"

As he breathed a sigh of relief and tried to get his bearings along the creek, he heard the unmistakable sound of riders calling out behind him. He froze, turning back in his saddle towards the not-so-distant braziers of his woodcutter brothers, and the sight of approaching torches caused his previously elated spirit to feel a knotted pang of nervousness.

"Alright you two, keep it easy here," he whispered to the horses. They remained hidden only by the cover of darkness as he strained to hear and see what the Citadel riders would do with the brothers who had aided in his escape.

"Where is he?" Pyrrhus growled at the chief woodcutter. "Where is that damned traitor?"

"Who *are* you talking about, fire knight?" Yasen said without pause as he continued to bury his double-bladed axe in the white flesh of a massive pine tree. "Who have you lost now?"

"You know well enough who it is that I am talking about!" he shouted at the top of lungs, his frustration echoing through the wild land about them. "And I have *lost* no one ... justice has been *stolen* from me!"

"I am not sure if you plan to be speaking in riddles for the rest of the day or not, but I haven't the time for your tantrums!" Yasen said, annoyance dripping from his every word. "In case you haven't noticed ... the whole of Aiénor has gone dark. So unless you're going to pick up an axe and help ..." He let the insult linger there for just a moment as he freed his blade from the massive trunk. "My brothers and I have some pretty important work to be about."

"What are you going to do with him, Yasen?" Pyrrhus spat in a rage as his horse spun around, clearly feeling the agitation of her rider. "Do you plan to just hide him and feed him like some stray dog, hoping the whole colony will forget what he did and just ... just let him back in?" Pyrrhus held the stub of his arm up and gritted his teeth as he spoke. "I will NEVER forget, *North Wolf*! And as long as there is breath still in my lungs, I will see to it that he— that traitor of a groomsman—*pays* for his injustices. I don't care if I have to run through every last one of you ignorant northmen to find him ... I will have my vengeance!"

The sound of the tree line went silent as every blade was stayed and every eye turned its gaze upon the six riders that towered over their chieftain. The darkness did not conceal the tension in the air as each ear listened carefully to the hostile exchange.

Yasen held his axe up, fingering the edge of his mighty blade as he spoke. "You are but one arm shy of a few guardsmen, Pyrrhus. Our axes and our arms still greatly outnumber your men, so do not be the fool that you are so tempted to be. The war we are waging is one against darkness, and I would just as soon keep it that way. But my brothers and I here, we are prepared to fight fire with fire if need be."

A score of woodcutters with axes in hand came closer to the battle of wills. Their very presence nearly set the smoldering kindling of the situation ablaze, but Pyrrhus' men did not draw their swords. The fire knight fumed upon his agitated mount, but did not choose to wholly test the sincerity of Yasen's threats.

"Now," Yasen said with the authority of one who was finished with the conversation, "don't you have a ship to see about sending off? Groomsman or not, that timber was hard fought and hard won, and our countrymen back home across the waters of the black are expecting this colony to deliver on our promises. We are all responsible to the duty we took an oath to uphold."

"Do not presume to hide behind your calling, or your *responsibility,* as you would have it!" Pyrrhus spat in disgust. "The governor will not be pleased with your insolence, and if I have my way, it will be *you* in the bottom of the ship's hold in place of the groomsman that you released! Perhaps you are the true traitor among us!"

"Well, perhaps the governor himself fancies a swing or two with my axe," Oren, the yellow-haired woodcutter, shouted from within the ranks of his northern brothers. "I'll say it, since my chieftain here is a bit too diplomatic to just go ahead and tell it like it is! If you right and proper Citadel fools can't treat the woodcutters with the respect we deserve, then you'll be felling the trees of the Wreath *yourselves*!"

"You'd better watch your tongue, axe-man," Pyrrhus warned rather harmlessly.

"The real power, the *real* strength of our colony belongs to me and my brothers! Without us, the world goes dark. I am not too sure if you have thought this through yet or not, *fire knight,* but I would wager that a one-handed knight is not going to last very long out here in the wild lands of this Wreath without any light to see by," Oren scoffed.

"Treason!" Pyrrhus seethed through his gritted teeth. "All of you! When the Priest King hears about this, you will see nothing again save the inside of a prison hold!" He wheeled his nervous steed angrily around.

"You tell him!" Alon, Oren's brother, shouted out after the retreating convoy of riders. "You tell him just what traitors we are, and when you do, be sure to tell him by the light of the timber we've sent him, then see what he has to say!"

Pyrrhus and his men spurred their horses and took their offended leave back towards the wooden walls of the colony's stronghold. "I'll have my vengeance!" the fire knight shouted back over his shoulder.

"Well, that went well," Alon said sarcastically as he and a score or so of his brothers watched the six angered knights riding back towards their outpost.

"You sure do have a way of making friends, don't you, brother," Oren laughed as he pounded the back of his younger sibling. "Mother ... she would be so proud."

The men erupted in a burst of satisfied albeit nervous laughter. It was Gvidus that broke the irreverence of the moment with a serious thought. "This isn't over you know, Yasen," he said in an uncharacteristically serious tone. "A proud and angered man is one thing, but he is also a wounded man whose pride has born the brunt of the wound. And, well, those are the kind of men whose cruelty is unpredictable."

"Aye," Yasen said, still in deep thought. "It could be that our welcome here in our western home has run out on us. And if it has not, we need be ever mindful that it could, indeed, in the blink of an eye."

The groomsman and his horses continued to hold their position along the creek, far too close to the exchange for their own comfort.

"They are leaving? Just like that?" Cal whispered to Deryn in a breath of relief.

"Perhaps we should not tarry," the blue-winged Sprite warned. "It would be unwise to wait to see if their minds change."

"You are right indeed, my tiny guardian," Cal said with a chuckle. "Perhaps this reprieve is a gift from the THREE who is SEVEN, huh?"

"Our Great Father uses all manner of emotions to bring about His will; anger, rage, cruelty and chaos do not find themselves exempt from His handiwork. But pride, both the wounded and the wealthy varieties, well ... *that* He uses quite often, though not necessarily in the way one might expect."

"I am grateful for His gift at this moment, no matter what brought it about," Cal replied. "Now come on, my friend, and help me find this cave."

And with that, Cal and the two horses turned westward into the heart of the thick wilderness in search of the lady Astyræ. They clopped cautiously along the stony riverbank for a few hundred paces before the ground beneath them began to slope upwards.

"Do you see anything?" Cal asked his Sprite friend. "The ground is changing, surely there has to be a cave around here somewhere."

"Nothing yet, Bright Fame," Deryn reported back as he flittered and zoomed out in front of Farran's head. "Nothing but trees, stone, and ... wait, just a moment," Deryn said as both his words and his movement came to a halt. "Do you see that over there?"

"I don't," Cal replied. "It just seems to be getting darker and darker."

"Exactly!" Deryn exclaimed.

It took Cal a moment to connect the meaning of his friend's words, but as he did he spurred the side of his horse with an excited, "Come on!" He took off in a charge towards the darkened mouth of the massive cave that stood before them.

As he and the two horses reached the entrance, Cal swung himself down in an almost effortless motion and within mere moments he had plunged into the thick blackness of this wilderness cave, leading the way with Gwarwyn held at the ready.

"Goran! Astyræ!" he shouted in a hushed tone. "Goran, are you there?"

He stopped and peered inside, but the faint, violet light of his hopeful vision barely pierced the darkness before him.

"Goran, Astyræ, it's me, Cal!" he shouted again a little louder. "Are you in there?"

But the cave was silent; not even the echo of his voice could be heard there in the midst of the hushed wilderness. "Goran!" he tried even louder this time, hoping that the riders would not hear his cry.

There was no sound in return, save the noise of the two horses as their iron-shod hooves moved nervously upon the rocky hill.

"Why do they not answer, Deryn?" Cal said, a bit confused. "Is this not the right cave? I mean, we did follow Yasen's directions didn't we?"

"Caw! Caw!" came the eerily haunting cry of a green-eyed raven as it circled overhead and made its landing high above them, perching upon a massive branch.

Farran snorted and Cal shivered at the feeling of being watched. "I do not like this at all," Deryn said as he drew his tiny, azure blade.

"Neither do I, my friend. Neither do I," Cal replied. "That's the same sort of bird from before, the ones with the green eyes-"

Cal was interrupted as the large chestnut snorted nervously at the sound of another pair of raven's wings beating against the darkened air. Cal and Deryn watched as yet another black bird joined his murderous companion, high above them, there upon the mighty tree.

"Look at Gwarwyn!" Deryn said, breaking the tension as he pointed to the leaf-shaped sword in Cal's hand with a stunned expression. "The leaves! They are glowing!"

"What does it mean?" Cal asked, dumbfounded at the very notion of such magic living still within his ancient, tarnished blade. "I have seen its withered, branchlike hilt bloom the silver and the violet, but this ... this magic is new to me too, my friend," he said as he raised the mighty blade of Caedmon and examined it in wonder.

"Something calls to it, Cal," Deryn postulated. "Something nearby knows this blade, or perhaps ... Gwarwyn knows *it*."

"Caw!" called a third raven, and then a fourth.

"Come on, Sprite," Cal said resolutely. "Audiences do not gather for nothing." He turned his gaze back towards the darkened mouth of the massive cave. "Whatever it is those birds wish to see, my guess is that it has something to do with whatever waits inside."

"But don't forget, Cal" Deryn said flitting up to look the groomsman in the eyes. "They are nothing more than carrion foul, and they might very well be gathering to feast upon the bones of the foolish."

Cal gulped back his courage. "They are in there, Deryn, I can feel it. And something ... something is not right." He looked back over his shoulder at the growing murder of gathering birds before he finished. "Let's keep our wits about us then, huh? Whatever darkness drives them, I do not plan to be a feast for crows today."

Deryn nodded and the two of them led the horses to the south side of the cave's entrance, tying them off to a leafless, gnarled locust tree branch before entering the thick darkness of the rock.

"Goran! Astyræ!" Cal shouted again and again. "Goran! Lady Astyræ!" But no sound followed, save his feet upon the cave floor and the echo of his voice.

"You are right, Cal, there is something strange about this place." Deryn's voice had a tone of suspicion and wariness to it that Cal had not heard before.

Cal took one cautious step after the other, with the glittering point of his tarnished blade held at the ready before him. "Do you smell that?" he asked his Sprite friend. "Like old coals, a spent fire?"

"Faintly, yes, I do," Deryn answered as a bit of excitement now began to color his nervous voice.

"They cannot be too far from here, then?" Cal asked hopefully. His eyes were busy scanning the oppressively shadowed cave by the light of his dim, violet gaze and the blue glow that came from his guardian.

"There!" Cal exclaimed as his eyes drew into focus what he had hoped to find. "There it is!" Cal ran towards the small ring of gathered stones and ashen logs. "It is cold, but its scent still lingers. This fire can't be more than half a day old," he said excitedly.

"Where would they have gone, then?" Deryn asked. He flew about the stone room in search of answers, clues to point them in the direction they might need to travel.

"Blast it all," Cal said, frustrated at the suffocating darkness of the cave. "I can barely see a thing in this place. Help me start a fire, will you? I have got to find them! If they are in here still, I don't want to miss their trail. "

Cal bent down and gathered what straw and kindling he could find, placing it back into the ring of stones and hoping that whatever coals might still remain would serve as better fuel than damp wood and green branches. He struck two rocks together, intending to make a spark, but the cold, grey stones would not spark in the least.

"I don't suppose you have some sort of magic that would get these rocks to light, do you?" Cal said rather playfully to his azure guardian.

"Aren't you fortunate that I chose to come with you on this journey, young Bright Fame," Deryn replied with a teasing glint in his glowing, blue eyes. "Where would you be without me?"

The Sprite landed upon the grey stones, and in a wordless song he sung a fire into existence. The air about them prickled and hummed with a holy energy, and within mere moments the ring was ablaze and the walls of the cave were alive, dancing in amber and golden hues.

Cal's eyes shone with wonder at the song and the flame of the Sprite. "Of course," he said with a sincere smile. "Thank you, my friend. And yes, I would be lost, utterly lost without ..."

Cal's voice fell silent as his violet gaze adjusted to the light of the fire. "What in the damnable darkness *is* this place?" His eyes beheld a strange and most disconcerting sight. It appeared to be the scrawling of a mad man, swirling about the walls of the cave in an illegible, maniacal pattern that sent chills down his spine. "What ... what does it say?" Cal asked nervously as his hands traced the patterns. "It seems to be the same thing, written over and over again." Cal reached for a discarded torch that hung against the cave wall, setting its tired fibers to glowing life in the fire that Deryn sung.

"Indeed, it does," Deryn said, overcome with dread.

"What does it say then? *Come on!*" Cal urged, trying to keep the panic from his voice.

"Meus," Deryn told him.

"Meus?" Cal said, rather perplexed. "What does that mean? I have never heard that word before."

"Of course you haven't, Calarmindon," Deryn said as he flew back over towards the markings upon the cave walls. "It is in the forgotten tongue of the once-great city of Terriah."

"Terriah! Of course ... Petros ... the mountain palace, that is where I first found you!" Cal said.

"That it was, dear Cal. Though this is of the high tongue, reserved for and spoken only by the ancient nobility," Deryn said as he flew closer to the painted walls of the rocky cave, examining the maddened penmanship. "I have not heard these words spoken in ages, and I am still but a blossom in the years of my Sprite kind."

"Then how is it that we have found it here? In the middle of this darkened wilderness, half a world away?" Cal asked as he continued to trace his fingers along the swirled lines of script.

"That is a mystery indeed, my friend," Deryn answered him.

"What does it mean?" Cal asked. "And why would someone spend so much time tracing its ancient letters upon this old cave?" Cal stopped short, for something had interrupted his thoughts. "What is this?" he asked. "Is the cave leaking?" The groomsman touched his thumb and his forefinger together. Whatever the wet substance was, it was tacky, sticky between his fingers.

"Meus is Terrian for *mine*," the Sprite answered him. "Though the connotation to its meaning is very possessive, insatiably greedy."

Cal looked at his fingers and then again to the cave wall, and as he put together the reality of the circumstance, his blood ran cold. There on the rock, where he was just moments before tracing his fingers upon the hastily scrawled words, he now saw nothing more than a white, smeared mess.

"What in the damnable dark?" Cal said aloud as his eyes went back and forth from his fingers to the wall and back again. "Deryn," he said nervously. "Deryn, the ink is smearing. Whoever wrote these words wrote them *recently.*"

"What?" Deryn said, completely befuddled.

"Look at my hands!" Cal said with a terrified shudder as he held up his white fingers for the Sprite to behold.

"Help!" came a muffled call from somewhere deep in the cave.

"Did you hear that?" Cal asked his friend.

"Yes, I did. Come!" Deryn called as he shot past Cal in a whir of blue magic.

"What is it? What do you see?" Cal asked as he rushed into the suffocating darkness with a blazing torch in hand.

"It's further in!" Deryn shouted. "They must be further in!"

Cal and Deryn made their way as quickly as they could and with what little light they held; whether by hope, magic, or the crude torch, they saw just enough to continue through the winding caverns ahead of them. Deeper and deeper they proceeded into the eerie cave, each step illuminating the walls enough that they could make out the ancient word that was obsessively and rather frighteningly scrawled upon them.

"Help!" Somewhere, much closer now, a desperate voice called to them again.

"Over there!" Deryn shouted over his shoulder as he flew onward. "The cry is coming from over there!" The walls around him caught and reflected the amber glow of Cal's torch, and it mingled with the azure hue of the

Sprite's illumination. Cal had a fleeting thought that the light was rather beautiful, and that if the circumstances were less perilous, he might have taken a moment to appreciate the mingling light.

Deryn led the way, searching the cavern for sign of danger or distress. Without warning, the rocky floor beneath him disappeared, swallowed up into a pit of utter darkness. By the time the Sprite realized what was beneath him, it was all he could do to turn and shout back in time to save his charge from plummeting to whatever depths lay hidden beneath him. "Stop, Cal! *Stop!*"

Cal saw his tiny, winged guardian, who was not more than a dozen or so paces ahead of him, turn and shout. He saw Deryn hold up his tiny hands, begging him to halt, but before his feet could register what his eyes had seen, Cal had slipped and fallen. His body slid recklessly towards the black opening before him, his momentum threatening to carry him to whatever danger waited at the bottom of this unknown pit. He reached and clawed for purchase upon the dusty floor as his legs slipped over the edge of the cavern, desperately willing his fingers to grip something, anything, while there was still something left to reach for. He let go of his torch to free his other hand before he plunged to the darkened recesses of this godforsaken place, and as he did his fingers caught the jagged edge of the mouth of the pit. He grasped the rock with both hands, forcing himself to hold fast while his legs dangled in the air and sought out a foothold.

"Help us! Help us, please!" came the familiar, silken voice of the violet-eyed woman.

"Astyræ?!" Cal shouted as his feet scraped a rough bit of the cave wall. "Astyræ, is that you?"

"Cal?" she shouted back up towards him with a relieved tremor in her voice.

"Yes! I'm here!" he managed between deep, heaving breaths. "Are you alright?"

"Aye, lad!" came the deep voice of a tired northman. "We are alright ... for the moment."

"Goran!" Cal shouted in excitement at the voice of his friend. "Why in the damnable dark are you two down there, brother?" The groomsman breathed a sigh of relief when his foot finally found a solid ledge to rest on.

The large, bearded woodcutter picked up the still burning torch that had fallen to his tired and weary feet, and held it up over his head to behold his surroundings for the first time.

"My lady? Goran?" Cal shouted back down to them, but neither the large man nor the violet-eyed woman answered, for they were both caught in amazement, staring wild-eyed at what had been illuminated at the dropping of the torch.

"What in the name of the THREE who is SEVEN is this place?" the woodcutter said in an awe-struck voice.

"Goran!" Cal shouted again. "Lady Astyræ, what is it? What have you found?"

"You wouldn't believe me if it told you, brother!" the large woodcutter shouted back.

"Do you see a way out?" Cal asked him.

"No..." Goran answered absentmindedly, still clearly distracted with whatever it was he could now see at the bottom of the pit.

"We have to find a way to get them out of there," Cal said to his Sprite friend. He heaved his body up and over the rough edge of the gaping pit. The metal of his armored chest piece groaned as his midsection rested upon the safe, albeit rocky ground. He quickly spun around, chest still to the cave floor, and peered out over the edge, scouring the walls about him in search of something, anything that he could use to rescue his friends.

"Are you in danger?" Cal shouted back down into the torch-lit chamber, but as he examined the pit from his perch on the ledge, he noticed something odd about the way the fire reflected off the stone walls. "What ... what is that place down there?"

"Cal, over here!" Deryn said excitedly. "I think I found a way!"

Cal tore his curious gaze away from the oddly reflective base of the dark cavern, watching as his winged companion flew in a hurry towards the wall of the passageway that they had just passed through. "What is it, Deryn? What have you found?"

But the Sprite did not speak a single word. Instead, he landed softly and stood triumphantly atop a crudely lashed, birch ladder.

"Well done, my friend! Well done *indeed*!" He stood and brushed the dirt off his cloak, rushing quickly to the providentially placed ladder and grabbing it eagerly. But Cal's joy was short-lived, for as his hands grasped the smooth, birch rungs of the ladder, his ears heard a soul-chilling voice from the entrance of the cave.

Cal stopped in his tracks; he held his breath as he strained to hear whatever or whoever it was that was in the cave with them. "Did you hear that?" he whispered nervously. "Is it Pyrrhus? Did he find us?"

"I don't ..." Deryn said, still straining to hear. "I don't think that is the fire knight."

"Meeeeeuuuuuuussssss," came a long, exaggerated call. The spoken tone of the ancient word sounded almost like a rusted, iron gate, and it sent chills all the way to the fingertips of the groomsman who stood there, listening in the darkness.

Chapter Thirty-Five

"WHAT IS HAPPENING OUT THERE, Engelmann?" Michael whispered in frustration. "Is he giving up the city? Why would he surrender without a fight?"

The chamber at the entrance to the *Menashe* stood right at the outer edge of the courtyard. It was there that the escaped prisoners could hear the words of the Priest King and could feel the tension of all that was happening on the other side of the door that momentarily separated them from the madness.

"Power is a strange and intoxicating poison, my son," Engelmann said. "And I presume that Jhames would rather be a prince of darkness than an illuminated corpse."

"What does that mean?" Celrod asked the Arborist, but when he made eye-contact with his new friend, the blue flames that consumed his gaze gave Celrod a true and unexpected fright. "Arborist? Arborist, are you alright?"

The blue fire extinguished itself in a sudden fury, almost as unexpectedly as it had come upon the Arborist. "We must go ... now is our time!" Engelmann urged.

"Go? Go where!" Timorets puzzled. "The whole damned Raven Army waits just on the other side of the Kings' Bridge!"

"To the sacred mount," Engelmann interrupted. "It is there that you will find your deliverance."

"But what about the guardsmen? The Priest King and the Chancellor?" Fryon said, just before the sound of the clanking iron of the massive portcullis being raised could interrupt his protest.

"Jhames is determined to parley with the Raven Army, and that notion might very well prove advantageous for us," Michael reasoned.

"Yes, my boy!" Engelmann encouraged. "While both the armies of Haven and the invaders are focused upon the parley, we must be swift and deliberate to make our way to the mother willow, and descend into the hall of my brothers."

The bright brass of the guardsmen cut through the dark tension as they announced their intentions to the invading host.

"Come on, now," Michael said. "Grab your blades, and let's make our way to the iron willow while we still can."

Fryon nodded, and with sword in hand he slowly opened the door of the keep, watching as the torch-lit courtyard teemed with frightened men who were steeling themselves for a dance with utter evil.

"Which way, Arborist?" Fryon whispered. "I've never been on this side of those mighty walls. Well, for that matter, I have never been this side of the Kings' Bridge itself, and we will need a guide if we hope to make it to your hall in the midst of this dark night."

"Follow Michael – he knows the way. Be quick, and be quiet; no matter what you see, remember that your deliverance comes from one place and one place alone. Do not give into distraction, no matter how noble it may seem." Engelmann cautioned them cryptically before he opened the door wide before them and walked into the cobblestoned courtyard of the Capital.

"Quickly now!" Engelmann whispered, gesturing to the waiting few behind him. One at a time, the five of them darted out from the door towards the massive bowl-like fountain in the middle of the square. The small band of brothers crouched low, concealing their presence behind the massive water piece. The blaring of the Citadel's trumpets startled them, and they could not help but peer out over the white stone lip of the bowl to observe the unfolding conference upon the water.

"All hail Jhames, Priest King of the city of Haven, and the Lord of the first colony, Proclaimer of the flint and seeker of the light! Kneel, all who enter into his presence, for you shall either receive his favor or suffer his wrath!" The voice of the royal herald rang out in practiced proclamation.

Michael looked on as none, not one, of the invading army knelt in homage before the Priest King.

The world went silent there upon the massive bridge, save for the sound of the pounding wings and the flapping standards caught in the cold, north wind. The brave albeit frightened guardsmen stood their ground, holding their gaze on the green-eyed faces of their invaders. Finally it was Chaiphus that broke the tense silence of the moment with an arrogant reply.

"Homage is demanded! It matters little who you are or what devils you command; all must kneel in the presence of the Priest King!"

"Neither I, nor any blade that I command, will kneel before any other than the sorceress herself," the Raven General said with a haughty tone of unimpressed detachment. "Homage is refused. I will not pay homage to the *unenlightened,* nor will I heed the arrogant words of dead men."

"Who are you, and what do you want?" Jhames spoke before Chaiphus could launch another verbal offense.

"I am Aius, General and commander of her nocturnal army," the massive man announced as his one green eye glowed with a frightening sheen. "I come offering terms that would save your city, lest I raze it to the ground."

"And just what are these terms?" Jhames asked nervously.

"That you forgo fire, timber, torch and flame, and that you relinquish your slavery to its fickle illumination. You will give yourselves wholly over to the power of the sorceress," Aius decreed confidently.

Jhames and Chaiphus looked at each other oddly, for these were not the demands that they had expected of an invading army. "I do not understand," Jhames replied slowly.

The Raven General narrowed his dual-colored eyes at the King's guard and their protected leaders. "Long has your world been dependent on the flames of *His* dying affection. Long have your kind lived hand to mouth, reliant upon *His* singular fire. And where has that gotten you, oh bright Priest King? Has your dedication and flintish piety managed to save the city you swore to serve?" Aius scoffed at the men as he spoke, and in his voice there was an unsettling mixture of both hatred and pity. "*His* great tree has failed, and your *God* has abandoned you to an existence of poverty at the hands of the axe and the tree."

"You are wrong, General. We have been given a spirit and a resolve to make our own light! We but have to strike the dark, and light will burst forth!" Chaiphus retorted brashly, but Jhames quickly and sternly put a steadying hand on his arm, signaling him to be silent.

"But *why*, men of Haven?" the Raven General asked. "Why would you waste your life upon such an archaic way of living, slaves to timber and flame, when what *she* offers is a whole new way to see this darkened world?"

Almost as if to punctuate his words in the most terrifying of ways, the sound of beating wings circled closer and closer, like vultures awaiting the imminent death of their wounded prey.

"Be done with it already," Jhames demanded, the color of life drained from his thin, drawn face. "Our bows are trained and our walls are strong, but you and I both know that our defenses are no match for dragons."

"Your Brightness!" Chaiphus blurted out.

Jhames held high his three fingers, his gaze devoid of patience. "Do not prolong this charade any longer, my old friend," he said as he stared wildly into the eyes of his most trusted advisor. "*I have seen it.* I have seen the razing of our Citadel and the rape of our people. I have seen the corded timber of our determination stolen away from us, carried mockingly on the wind of a cloud of ravens."

Aius stared without malice, his green eye glowing brighter and brighter as the circling dragons came closer and closer to the doomed conference there upon the water.

"Failure, Chancellor," Jhames continued. "We have failed to please the will of the THREE who is SEVEN." Tears streamed in small traces of madness down his bony cheeks. "And it is *HE* that has abandoned us, choosing to banish us into the blackness, a fitting retribution for our failure. Well, I tried, my friend. *We* tried to right this world, one small, stupid mind at a time ... but I will not die for a *failure* that was not wholly our doing! I will not-"

"Have you lost your mind?" Chaiphus interrupted.

Perhaps ... or perhaps he has finally found it.

The voices of the dragons cut through the chatter upon the Kings' Bridge, for they were near, and louder than ever before. They punctuated their sinister words with the resounding boom of their massive bodies landing upon the bridge. The King's guard, who had thus far held to the pride of their rank and the duty of their sworn service, cowered in fear as the twin dragons collided with the floor of the mighty bridge. It was Chaiphus and the Priest King alone who remained standing in the presence of such monsters.

"The sorceress offers the gift of sight to all who would receive it," the general offered, seeming almost amused at their terror. "Have you not been listening? The light is not gone after all, for there is a new light that has arisen from deep within the bowels of Aiénor. It is a light reserved for the darkness alone, a nocturnal fire by which all who receive it shall see the world through *her* eyes."

Jhames and Chaiphus looked around at the sea of glowing, green-eyed Nocturnals whose blackened blades caught and reflected the watch fires of the massive braziers flanking the Kings' Bridge. Time seemed to slow as they gazed at the muted glow, weighing the finality of the decision that they knew they had to make.

"Chancellor Chaiphus," the Raven General spoke again, breaking the long, silent moment with a voice not much louder than a whisper. "One will not have to fear the darkness when one has become a citizen of night."

The last remaining army of Haven watched in fearful curiosity, blades drawn and bows at the ready. They waited, quietly breathless, as they witnessed their mighty Priest King and his pious, unyielding Chancellor kneel before the enormous, inky-black serpents. Then, they watched in horror as the snarled lips of the massive dragons kissed the foreheads of the once mighty leaders of Haven. As scales met flesh, the twin beasts blew an unholy cloud of green fire upon the two kneeling men.

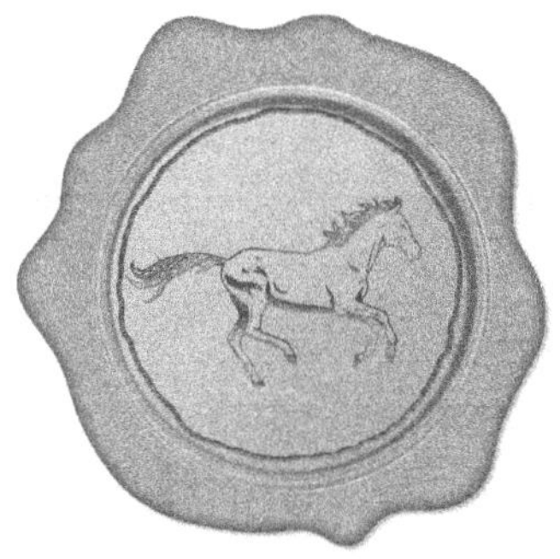

Chapter Thirty-Six

"MEUS, MEUS, MEUS, MEUS, MEUS, *Meus*!" The eerie voice chanted the singular word in a tired, creaking crescendo.

"Hurry," Deryn whispered. "I fear we will find no hospitality from whoever speaks that word."

"Agreed!" Cal whispered his reply as he slowly and carefully lifted the lightweight, birch ladder up and over his head.

"Meus, Meus!" The old voice continued to repeat the solitary word in a haunting cadence, and as Cal listened, he began to make out the sound of footsteps. They punctuated the chanting with a menacing rhythm, sliding along in eerie echoes upon the dusty cave floor.

"Goran! Astyræ!" Cal whispered as loud as he could while lowering the birch ladder into the torch-lit abyss. "I am coming to get you!"

Cal tested the strength of the ladder's first rung with the full weight of his body. He found it to be true enough, so he lowered himself down into the chamber that held his two friends captive. He descended quickly, and before he knew it he was nearly twenty rungs deep into the basement of this cavern before his boots finally reached the subfloor. "Hurry now, someone is coming," he managed to say before the very sight of what lay before him robbed his words of their sense of urgency.

"Have you ever in all your life seen such a place as this?" Goran managed to say while his gaze was still fixated upon the walls of this space.

"I have not seen a wealth of treasures such as this since I was but a child in Dardanos," Astyræ said almost reverently.

"What is this place?" Cal mused. "Where could all this wealth have come from?" They stared in wonder at the tapestries and treasures, armor and arms, jewelry and gemstones that covered the chamber. Then the Sprite flew down in a blue-blazed hurry, and his very presence interrupted the covetous curiosity of the three wide-eyed spectators.

"We must leave, now!" Deryn demanded. "Now! He is coming!"

"Who is coming?" Cal said in a distracted voice, momentarily forgetting his earlier alarm as he stood amidst the light of so many glittering and beautiful things.

Goran whirled around, shining his torch in all the different treasure-laden crevices; searching for something they could use to defend themselves with. "He's coming back?" the woodcutter asked warily. "Arm yourself, brother!"

Goran's alarm woke Cal to the danger of the situation. "Do you know him then? Who is it? What does he want?"

"I don't *know* him, but he must have been the one that dragged us down here in the dead of our sleep to be imprisoned with all of his other keepsakes!" Goran replied angrily.

"Meus, Meus, Meus, Meus!" The incessant, creaking speech continued, bouncing its aged voice off the walls of this forsaken place.

Goran found and reached for a sword hilt with a grunt of relief. The sword was not ornately designed; in truth, it was a rather plain blade, short and made more for thrusting than for cutting one's way through an enemy hoard. "I would prefer to have my own axe, but this one will have to do. Can't be too picky when hoarding magicians—or whatever this mumbling monster is—are after you."

He examined the stunted blade quickly, running his fingers along its edge. His face fell when he saw that this small thrusting sword was nothing more than a token from some king, or some lord of a time long since passed, with no real promise of defense. "The damned thing wouldn't even cut a torn piece of parchment," Goran said in frustrated displeasure. "Let us hope that this hoarder is terrified by decoration, because that is all that this is."

"I still have Gwarwyn," Cal reminded his friends. "It has yet to fail, even once, no matter how grim the circumstances may seem. Perhaps it has a magic of its own that we have yet to see. Look!" he said with a bit of awe as he held the glowing blade before them. "Ever since we entered this place, it has shone with both violet and silver ... all at once!"

"Do you know why, groomsman?" Astyræ asked curiously.

"I do not know," Cal replied honestly. "Though I am thankful for it, and I do trust it."

"That old, rusted relic?" Goran teased. "I'll take my chances with the décor, if that's alright with you," he said with a wink as he reached out and found a bronzed shield, shaped in the feathered form of two folded wings. "At least I can stave off his wizardry with this!" he said to the others, but their gazes were held by something even more beautiful than the ancient, feathered shield. There, hidden behind the discarded piece of armor, rested a long bow made of a luminous white wood and covered with flowering, violet blooms.

"What is that?" Astyræ whispered as a wave of awe washed over the small band that beheld this newfound beauty. "I have never in all my days seen craftsmanship such as this."

"Yes, you have," Deryn said as he flew closer to the ancient bow, his voice thick with emotion. "Though it seems that this mighty weapon of old has not felt the muting of tarnish and patina—or at least, not so much as its counterpart." Deryn looked meaningfully to the sword in Cal's hand.

"What do you mean, Sprite?" the violet-eyed woman asked, almost impatiently.

Cal looked down at his glowing blade. The silver and violet leaves that adorned its ancient hilt were more radiant than he had ever seen them.

"Arianrhod," Deryn said with stunned reverence as he knelt before the still-strung bow. "This was crafted upon the silver wheel of Blodeuwedd. It was he, the very same armorist, who fashioned and forged the heavy blade you hold in your hand now, Bright Fame."

"What? But ... but what is it doing here?" Cal asked, his words both enamored and unsure all in the same moment.

"I do not know that, my friend," Deryn said as he reached forth and grasped the glowing bow with his tiny hands. With great ease, he raised it up and held it in victorious gesture of wonder. "But I do know that this must be a gift, both in design and in discovery, from the providential hands of our Great Father."

Deryn flew towards Goran with the magical weapon held effortlessly out before him. "Here, *Mighty Mountain*, do not concern yourself with mere tokens and trinkets, for the mightiest of all strung weapons has been found this day," the Sprite said as he offered up the bow to the woodcutter.

"No, little warrior," Goran said as he raised his hands in refusal. "A weapon such as this requires more grace to wield than my calloused hands are capable of."

Deryn paused for a moment, but as he considered the woodcutter's words, a dawn of understanding lit in his eyes. "Of course," he said with a smile. "The *Blade* and *Bow* may not be held by the same two hands, save Blodeuwedd himself on the day they were birthed into Aiénor." Deryn recounted the legend as he flew towards the woman. "And so it must be that the *Silver Moon* falls to you, violet-eyed lady of the Wreath," he said respectfully.

Her pearl colored fingers reached out timidly and took hold of the silvery white wood. "Me?" she whispered.

"It is made of the Jacaranda tree, and beauty both mighty and terrible courses through it," the Sprite said with a meaningful glint in his eye. "Use it well."

"*Meus, Meus, Meus, Meus, Meus, Meus.*" The soul-chilling sound came yet again—but this time it was far closer and much louder, and the possessive tone woke them all from their wonder.

"There!" Goran said nervously as he pointed to the space where the ancient weapon had rested. "Grab that quiver of arrows if you plan to do anything more than just look at it!"

Astyræ, still a bit overwhelmed by the relic she held, reached quickly for the white, leather quiver and slung it over her shoulder, preparing with the others to climb up and out to their freedom.

"It is beautiful, Astyræ," Cal said, still a bit in awe. "Do you know how to use it?"

"I am no stranger to the bow. My grandfather used to take me hunting with him when I was much younger."

"Good," Cal said with an appreciative and gentle clasp of her arm. "Alright then."

The group looked to Cal for direction, awaiting the instructions of their unlikely leader.

"Deryn!" Cal ordered, sensing their trepidation. "Fly up first and see to it that the way is clear. Goran and I will go next, and then," he said, turning to meet her violet and yellow gaze. "My lady, you will follow and we will leave this place together."

She smiled the sweetest smile and nodded in agreement while still fingering the ornate vines that seemed to have grown both into and out of the silvery-white bow.

"Are you ready, brother?" Cal asked his large friend.

"We have been down here in this treasure hoard for what feels like days," he said as he placed his hand upon the shoulder of the groomsman. "Aye, I have never been more ready to leave a place than I am at this moment."

Deryn drew his tiny, azure blade. He and Cal nodded their mutual understanding and then, in a wash of bright blue light, the Sprite shot up out of the pit and signaled for the group to begin their ascent.

Cal was first to climb over the ledge, so he reached down to help his woodcutter friend up and out of the glittering prison. As Goran put the soles of his boots upon the dust of the cavern floor, the words of their captor cut through the torch-lit air with a deafening closeness.

"Meus," the hoarder whispered.

The hair upon the back of Cal's neck stood erect in heightened alert.

"Meus," came the satisfied murmur again, too close this time.

Cal turned slowly with the point of Gwarwyn held out before him.

"What have I here?" said the same chilling voice, and the unexpected speech caught them by surprise. "Is this but another prize for my collection? I may be blind, but I know beautiful things when they come near!" The voice, clearly belonging to an old man, sounded as though it were almost intoxicated by the possibility of more to possess.

"I came in search of my friends is all," Cal said loudly to the shifting creature in the darkness.

"Your *friends,* you say?" the creaking voice asked. "Do you also *collect* beau-ti-ful things? Or maybe your *friends* collect beautiful things? Which is why they were trespassing upon my stores?"

"There was no trespassing at all!" Goran roared in protest. "We were but passers by, seeking shelter from the darkness, when YOU captured us and threw us into this treasure pit of yours!"

"I could not see what you were doing in my cave," the hoarder said with an ominous tone as he walked into the glow of Cal's torch. "Only that you were indeed beautiful ... and worth *keeping*."

They could see him now. They both swallowed back a jolt of fear as they saw empty, black holes where once his eyes had been. The man stood tall and lanky; his knotted, oily hair fell in filthy tangles all about his ancient face, and his wild, grey beard covered his sagging skin. His once-white robe was frayed and tattered, hanging heavy upon his bony frame.

Astyræ made her way up the last rung of the birch ladder, peering over the top with a wary gaze. Though they knew he had no eyes to see, it seemed as though her glowing violet and yellow eyes instantly caught the attention of the blind hoarder. He shook violently, then began to rock back and forth in a singsong trance. *"Meus, Meus, Meus, Meus, MEUS, MEUS!"*

"Shut it!" Cal screamed violently at the strange man, stepping in front of Astyræ in a defensive stance. "She is not yours and neither are we!"

"Oh?" the hoarder said smugly. "But you are! Did you not know that it is my right, my *des-tin-y,* to gather, to col-lect the lost and beautiful things of this world?"

"We are not lost!" Cal insisted. "You are mistaken!"

"Oh! It is not I who is mis-tak-en," the old man said gleefully. "You are more lost than you ...

could ...

pos-si-bly ...

see."

With a quick wave of his spindly finger, the hoarder called upon some unknown magic and flung them all through the air and against the wall of the cave. The chamber echoed with the hard thud of soft flesh colliding with the cold stone. With his left hand, the hoarder called forth the birch ladder and slammed it against the chests of the two men and the violet-eyed woman, pinning them mercilessly in place against the rock.

Cal coughed violently for air as his very breath was stolen from his lungs. Astyræ screamed in horror and Goran gritted his teeth. "What do you want with us?" Cal managed to sputter out. "We don't want to take anything from your collection. Just let us go!"

"Ah ah ahh!" said the magician. "That is not how things work in my realm."

"Enough!" Deryn shouted angrily as he darted directly between the hoarder's hungry gaze and his three trapped friends. The man recoiled against the blue light that radiated all the more with the blaze of the Sprite's fury. As he did, Cal was able to free his glowing blade and dismantle the birch shackle that held them prisoner in a single slash of desperate anger.

"What is this trickery?" the hoarder shrieked in wounded disgust. "The tree guardians are *dead*! And beauty ... beauty ... *she* promised that you were no more!" As he screamed his rage, he threw his gnarly hands in a violent fit, sending a shockwave of anger reverberating throughout the cache of hoarded treasures. The collection violently clanked and crashed as the contents were jostled in the wake of his magic.

Deryn stood his ground, blade outstretched in peaceful defiance of the magician's fury. "Let them go! They are not yours to keep."

"But I found them!" he protested viciously. "MEUS! They are MEUS!"

"No, we are not," Cal said with less confidence than his blue-winged guardian had. "We belong to something greater than the mere greed of cursed, blind beggars."

"Do not speak to me about greed, boy," the hoarder said through gritted teeth. "Beauty is mine to hold, to keep, to hide ... and I will have my just due this day!"

With a flick of his hands, a storm of rocks and dust flew up in a messy cyclone of rage and hurled itself towards the three of them.

"Quickly!" Goran shouted as he held his newly found shield out before them all. Cal grabbed Astyræ and held her close to himself, ducking behind the mighty frame of the massive woodcutter. "What do you want from us?" Goran roared as the flurry of rocks beat against the bronzed feathers of his shield.

"Only what was promised me long ago, only what is mine by all rights!" the hoarder demanded.

"The cursed bind themselves to the root of their curse, chained without mercy, prisoner to their appetites," Deryn whispered to them. He zoomed towards the fallen torch that lay burning at the feet of his friends; then he took the fire and held the terrified attention of the hoarder as he flew to the edge of the pit.

"I offer freedom for you this day, if you but accept it," the guardian said before he dove headlong into the treasure pit, fire outstretched before him. The eyes of the Sprite went wild, aflame with the azure hue of his ancient magic as he spoke in his native tongue.

"Sruthán tú fonn meargánta, go dtí go bhfuil gach go bhfanann an deannaigh an fear tar éis titim sular ghlac sé air féin an ifreann."

(Burn you reckless desire, until all that remains is the dust of the fallen man before he took upon himself this hell.)

Deryn caught fire every tapestry and scroll, every wooden chest and woven basket; his words seemed to breathe power into the very flames themselves until even the bronze and gold began to melt and droop in the wake of such enraged heat.

"No! No!" the blind hoarder shouted in heartbroken protest. "Meus! What have you done? *Meus*!"

The onslaught of rock and magic ceased in an instant as the blind man recoiled in agonized loss.

"Run! Run now!" Goran whispered to his friends.

Cal reached back to take Astyræ's hand, but as he did the violet-eyed woman plucked an arrow from her quiver and strung it upon the silver bowstring of Arianrhod, aiming with a fury of her own disgust at the nape of the blind man's neck.

"*Take*," she said through gritted teeth. "Greed! Is this all that men desire? Treasures and trophies? Where has all of your greed and gathering gotten you now?"

The hoarder wept eyeless tears as the labor of his obsession burned in the ruinous wake of the Sprite's justice. He could not answer the woman who threatened him with death, for he cared not to notice more than his precious treasure as it burned to ruin before him. She drew back the string and breathed a steadying breath, but the hand of the groomsman stayed her revenge.

"No! Let him watch, and let us be glad that he does," he said, calming the fire within her. "Besides, we have a long journey ahead of us, you and I. We might just need every arrow in that quiver of yours."

"You do not understand," she said, looking at him through the tears of her vengeance. "I have seen this hunger before. It is the same hunger—the same obsession to serve self, to take and ravage no matter the cost—that ruined my people, that stole my father, and that has raped this darkened world of its true beauty." The flames of revenge still burned in her twice-colored eyes, and Cal could see the depth of both her conviction and her wounds. "*When* will this greed be satiated? When the whole world burns in the fires of the very hells it wrought upon itself?" She pulled back the bow again, ready to end the tangible manifestation of the greed that had so devastated her.

"It was at the hands of the same kind of greed that I lost my family too, my lady," Cal said with a pang of long-lost innocence still raw in his voice. The quiet churning of decision was held there in the tension of the taut, silver bowstring, but Cal held her shoulder with a gentle patience, calming her with his steadying gift. "This greed is ugly and vile, you are right, Astyræ; but I will choose to hope still, that this ruined world of ours is not fully lost, nor is it beyond repair. And I choose to hope that there will be light enough in the hearts of a few of us ruined people to aid in its mending."

Astyræ took a deep breath, and then slackened her pull upon the string. She closed her eyes for a moment, weighing his words against her wounds before she holstered the ancient arrow in its white quiver. "Very well then, groomsman," she conceded. "Show me the way out of this place."

Cal smiled a saddened smile and took her slender hand. They glanced at the broken creature that had once been their captor, but he could not hear the sounds of their escape over the noise of his own mournful wales. The four of them wound their way back and forth through the maze of a passageway, seeing well enough by the slight illumination of the Sprite and the mingled light of their violet hope. At last, they made it to the mouth of the dreadful cave.

"There! There it is!" Goran said, pointing to the cave entrance as the wailing screams of the magician carried his lament in waves of heartrending echoes.

"Come on then, let's be rid of this place," Cal said as his picked up the double-bladed axe of his woodcutter friend. "There is still work to be done yet.

"Aye," Goran said with a smile. "There is still light to seek, ah groomsman?"

"Indeed there is," Cal said as he handed the axe to Goran and slung the satchel of abandoned provisions over his shoulder. "Indeed there is."

Chapter Thirty-Seven

"HURRY!" ENGELMANN URGED. HIS WORDS roused the small band of newly found brothers out of the nightmare they were witnessing.

"But what are they doing, Engelmann?" Michael said. "Why would they kneel? Why would they surrender?"

"Have you not learned a thing from my tutelage, dear groomsman?" Engelmann asked sadly. "For *hopelessness* can lead even a king to bend his knee a thousand different times, making him slave to a thousand different masters without so much as a single clash of iron."

"But this ... this is not just a master," Michael said softly.

"Enough now! Quickly, we have not a moment to spare," Engelmann ordered his friends. "Follow this road. It climbs all the way to the great garden."

The six of them didn't give the Arborist any further hesitation. They wove their way in and out of the once expertly manicured hedges and past the glittering granite statues and high archways of the white stone overpasses. The ornate architecture of the Citadel was silent this dark day, without light and bereft of hope, for her broken heart had found solace in the arms of her enemy. The tales of glory formed and chiseled into her stone foundations could not find the strength enough to tell their stories, and so they resigned to sleep in the shadows of the vague, green evil.

"Nearly there, my boys!" Engelmann encouraged.

The silent night was interrupted with the guttural, sickening tones of the bellowing horns of the Raven Army. Their bowel-churning music stopped the six in their tracks, demanding them to stop and listen.

Behold! The twisted unison of the twin serpents' voices met their ears, hissing in a singsong arrogance. *People of Haven, see the wisdom of your Priest King! See the vision of his Chancellor! For a new light has come, and no longer are you doomed to be citizens of a dying tree whose light has failed you. No longer are you bound to this great darkness. You are now brothers nocturnal, children of the Raven Queen; you may count yourselves as those who walk the darkness.*

Jhames and Chaiphus stood once again, holding out their hands before their faces and examining themselves for the first time in the light of the nocturnal magic. As they looked up, they beheld all of Haven awash in a green hue, bright and sickly but yet somehow nearly as beautiful as she had once been.

"It is true!" Jhames yelled with a frenzied exuberance to all within earshot. "Citizens of Haven, hear my voice, for I can see *all* in the wake of this new light! Our city does not need fall to the innumerable forces of the invading army, for they have brought *true* deliverance as well as sharpened iron."

Wisdom, the dragons hissed.

"Our Queen has come for us," Chaiphus echoed the conviction of the Priest King with his newfound revelation. "And she has brought for us a new life, free from the chains of our flintish bonds!" The Chancellor reached for the elaborately set flint that had hung around his neck for over half a century's worth of time; in one swift and defiant pull, he snapped its gilded chain and held it high before him.

The dragons smiled a deep and satisfied smile, and then without warning a green torrent of un-lit fire issued forth from behind their rows of razor sharp teeth, consuming the once Priestly relic and instantaneously reducing it to a pile of ash.

"My lords?" a palsied voice spoke up from behind the gathered ranks. The guardsmen parted as the elder Arborists of Haven, Ispen and Aspen, worked their way to the front of the king's guard. "Your Brightness," said Ispen with a terrified tremor to his words. "What have you done?"

The twin dragons turned their attention to the aged servants of the dead tree, bringing their maniacal faces uncomfortably close. As the eyes of the dragons narrowed upon the two Arborists, their deep and terrible words spoke nightmarish curses upon the frail minds of these frail men. With little hesitation, the trunk of their resolve snapped and broke, bending their knees to surrender.

"I was once a slave to the silent, failing ways of a silent and failing deity! My fear of the darkness fueled my impotent fidelity; but now I see. I can see in the dark and so I will fear no *God* any longer, nor will I toil tirelessly for *Him*," Chaiphus proclaimed with eyes now aglow in the same sickly green light of the Nocturnal army around him.

"The THREE who is SEVEN has left us, abandoned and besieged by the suffocating black of night." Jhames' voice echoed in an unnatural clarity off the surrounding walls of the city. "I urge you, my people, to lay down your arms; we shall not defend one who has forsaken us in our greatest hour of need!"

"Blasphemy!" came an unlooked for voice from above. "Blasphemy! Blasphemy! Blasphemy!"

"What are you doing?" Michael whispered to the enraged Arborist, but Engelmann would not be deterred. Instead, he left the relative safety of his fleeing companions and walked swiftly, straight towards the danger that awaited him there at the Kings' Bridge.

"Do not be deceived, citizens of Haven!" Engelmann continued to shout in defiance to the words of the Priest King and his Chancellor.

"Engelmann! Engelmann, no!" Michael shouted after his friend and teacher, but to no avail.

"Come on, leave him now; he is gone," Timorets urged the groomsman. "He made his choice, Michael. We have to get to the iron willow before this whole world goes to hell."

"No, he can't be gone!" Michael struggled to contain his emotions.

"Hurry now, lad!" Celrod agreed. "The old spruce has already made a way for us. Let's not let his efforts go to waste."

The Arborist of Haven descended upon the gathered armies at the entrance to the Citadel. "You! All of you who once claimed to know the will of the THREE who is SEVEN—how dare you ascribe such insidious, polluted words to Him *now*?" Engelmann's eyes caught fire with righteous anger as he sharpened his tongue to do battle over the hearts of those caught in the snare of hopelessness. "Do not give way to such lies, such blasphemies, you mighty citizens of Haven! You do not need to exchange your fear of darkness for this *hatred of the light*!"

Abaddon and Angrah seethed in furious loathing of the old Arborist. A thick fog of disgust began to roil and cloud around their massive, inky-scaled bodies; their huge, green-orbed eyes narrowed in bloodlust for one who would dare to resist their plans.

"Do not heed the words of this *traitor*!" Chaiphus shouted in reply as he watched the Arborist, whose eyes were ablaze in a wash of blue flame, march into the thick of the frightened battalion of guardsmen and ever closer to the raised portcullis.

"You DO NOT have to die, nor do you have to lay down your arms! Even if our city is lost to this army of *Nocturnals,* that does not mean that we are abandoned!" Engelmann pleaded with the soldiers. "We must resist! We must endure ... for *HIS* light WILL come for us!"

ROAARR! The angry protests of the twin dragons bathed the black sky in a wash of their fury.

"Look to the North, and leave this place of dying men and dead convictions. Hope will not leave you blind! It was *He* who promised to put *His* light in the hearts of those who will hope! Do not forget the prophecy!"

"But how will we survive this siege, Arborist?" a young officer asked nervously. "How can we compete with dragons and these hordes of Nocturnals?"

"What say you about our homes? Our city? Our way of life?" came the voice of another. "Do you expect us to abandon all of this? And for what? The life of a wanderer? Hunted in the darkness by these monsters?"

As the questions arose from those brave enough to ask them, the air around the gathered guardsmen pulsated beneath the leathery abuse of the twin serpents' wings. They had climbed high above the city, and before anyone knew where they had gone, they crashed down upon the courtyard within the great walls of the Capital.

The soldiers assembled in the square were sent flying as the sheer force of the beasts impacted the stone pavement. Men catapulted in a rippled wave of forced disturbance, striking a new note of terror in everyone who was far enough away not to be hit by the blast. And yet Engelmann stood alone, unmoved by the bullying force, seemingly planted into the ground by an unseen magic.

Foolishness, the dragons seethed as they circled, pacing menacingly around the last caretaker of the great tree. *And you, Engelmann, are the greatest of fools.*

"Engelmann, no!" Michael shouted again as he and the rest watched from the high vantage of the great garden near the top of Mount Aureole.

Engelmann spun round to meet the gaze of his pupil, and as he did he mouthed a single word to his friends.

"Hope."

The dragons let loose a river of green fire over the old Arborist, but the flames of the un-light did not consume him. "Sorceries and counterfeits are no match for Light, true Light ... *HIS Light*!" Engelmann shouted against the blaze. The flames came in a searing conflagration, a deluge of green heat so intense that every human fled even further from the heart of the blast.

As the men of Haven watched, some began to hope for the very first time. Something lit within them as they saw that the flames of the enemy did not burn the defiant Arborist. They hoped that this was indeed not the end of them, even if it was to be the end of what they had once called home.

"Michael!" Timorets shouted to his friend in a wave of panic. "It won't open! The door to the iron willow won't open!"

"What do we do now?" Celrod whimpered. The group was more frightened here than ever before, cornered atop the holy mountain with no foreseeable way of escape.

"Michael?" Timorets shouted again. "What do we do now, groomsman?"

Michael just stared in complete horror as his teacher and friend stood strong and insolently resolute against the mighty tempest of the dragons' fury.

The eyes of the Arborist shone brilliantly, furiously blue amidst the relentless wave of green fire. When the torrent finally ceased, Engelmann addressed the frightened crowd of guardsmen with such conviction and such clarity and such magic that his voice carried far beyond the walls of the Kings' Gate into the outer reaches of the fallen kingdom.

"For *He* will place *His* light in the hearts of those who hope!" the Arborist shouted. "You, remnant of Haven, you must defiantly and deliberately hope! You must choose to pick up your blades and stay your knees from bending to the blasphemies of these winged beasts! *Look to the hills*, for there is yet still beauty more terrible than these-"

His words were stolen from his lips as Abaddon bit the head of the Arborist off with a single snap of his massive jaws. The crowd of guardsmen retreated with a horrified gasp as the burning head of Engelmann was sent careening through their ranks like a flaming missile launched from a trebuchet, landing in a dead-eyed roll amongst their feet.

Engelmann's body stood wavering upon the bridge, still somehow planted to the place where he had made his final stand against the darkness. A bright, leaf-green liquid oozed from the opening atop his neck, and the shock of the moment held everyone who beheld it in a trance of terror.

Do not test the mercy of Nogcwren, the Raven Queen, for she offers sight only to the wise. To those foolish enough to refuse, their fate will be the same as this dead and disgraced tree tender.

The dragons spoke with a satisfied smugness of the victory they had claimed. And with those words, the two dragons tore the lifeless body of the dead Arborist limb from limb in a gruesome display of cruelty. Men vomited, and some ran, while most chose to throw down their arms and bend their knees to the power of the Raveness.

Aius marched through the Kings' Gate as a conquering general; trailing behind him came the green-eyed Priest King and his green-eyed Chancellor. The raven-plumed commander addressed the terrified battalion with emotionless words and a stoic gaze. "Men of Haven, soon the whole of Aiénor will unite under the banner of the Raven Queen, for it is she who will usher in a new way of living, one free of the fickle amusements of forgotten light. It is the traitors and the fools whose blood will water the garden of your dead relic." With that, he nodded to the dragons, commanding them to flight without a single word being spoken. The winged beasts shot into the sky, grasping the ravaged and broken pieces of Engelmann the hopeful in their piercing talons. The gale force of their flight knocked every remaining guardsman to his knees.

"Run! Hide! Quickly!" Fryon ordered his friends. "They are coming this way!"

The dragons rose swiftly into the dark sky, their inky, black wings reflecting the green torches and the yellow watch fires of both the fallen city and its invading armies.

This fool's blood will be the first to soak the deadened ground of your barren god! Their voices boomed, maddeningly loud, inside the minds of all who watched. Michael stood frozen in horror behind the massive, iron statue of a kneeling King Cascarie. Nothing could have prepared him for the pain in his heart as he watched the twin serpents circle overhead, dropping the dismembered parts of his friend upon the once hallowed gardens around him.

Tears ran down his cheeks as leg and limb, arm and torso rained in lifeless thuds, crashing to the expertly tended landscape in an abominable mockery of a life's work. The dragons swirled in victorious rage, lighting up the black sky with their sickly green flames. Finally, when their desecration was complete, they darted back to the general, crashing to the stone courtyard once again.

Michael stood to his feet, his hands still shaking from the overwhelming surge of anger and sorrow. "Engelmann! Engelmann, what have you done? Why have you ... what have you ..." Michael could not finish his whispered thoughts when he beheld a glowing finger on the fallen right arm of his teacher.

"What in the damnable dark?" he murmured to himself.

"Michael!" Timorets shouted in a whisper to his stunned friend. "Michael, what do we do now? The iron willow will not open, and the rest of-"

Michael's mind flooded with the memory of the very first time he entered past the iron mother, whose branches guarded the holiest of soil beneath the burning tree itself. He saw the hand of Engelmann the hopeful as it grasped the leaf-shaped knob of the magical door. It had glowed, he remembered, light green and brilliant; quite different from the sickly hue that hunted and haunted the city of his home. No, the radiance of the Arborist had once been evergreen and full of life, and as he recalled the moment, a wash of understanding overcame him.

"Michael! Groomsman! What do we do now?" Celrod begged worriedly. "None of us have ever been past the portcullis of the Kings' Gate, let alone dreamed of passing through the entrance of the Arborists. Engelmann told us to follow *you*, boy, so show us how we get in!"

Michael stood to his feet, his dirt-stained face streaked with tears as he looked to his still hiding friends. No words passed his lips, but they understood by the look on his face that he knew just what to do. He walked towards the dismembered arm of the last true Arborist of Haven and picked it up gently, holding the horrific mess in his hands. "You have always known what it was that you were doing, haven't you?" he said aloud.

With that, he walked towards the barred entrance of the iron willow and extended the glowing finger to touch the leaf-shaped knob before him. As he did, the leaf began to light in recognition. Without warning, and to the shock of the five who watched, the hand of Engelmann the hopeful reached out on its own strength and grasped the leaf. In a movement steady and practiced, it turned its glowing hold with a final release of magic, giving permission for the iron door to open once again.

"Thank you, my friend," Michael said to both the hand and the memory of his teacher. "Even in death, you still point the way to hope." He choked back the rush of tears and turned to find the dumbstruck eyes of his still watching companions. "Let us leave this damned and cursed home of ours, and go *north*, like the old spruce told us to."

Without a second thought or another word, Celrod, Timorets, Fryon and his younger brother followed Michael. They bowed their tired heads as they passed through the hallowed entrance of the iron guardian and descended its steps, deep into the Hall of the Arborists.

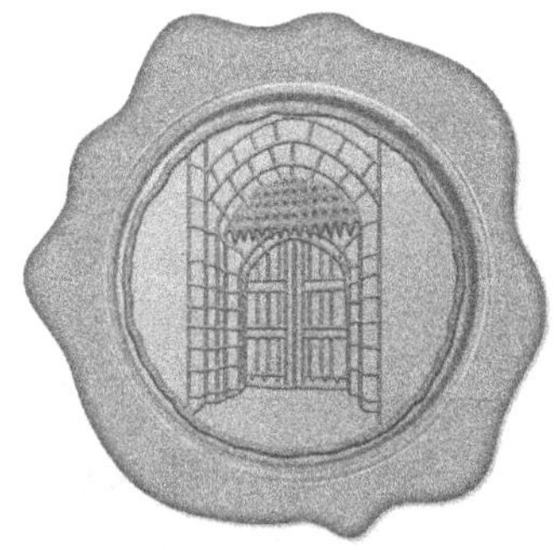

Chapter Thirty-Eight

MARCUM LED THE HOST OF Piney Creek out through the broken Northern Wall just east of the main road. Gone were the landscapes of old, with their towering pines and flowering fields, for the once beautiful northern outlands of Haven were now raped and bloodied, barren of beauty and blackened with the blood of war. The invading army had long since passed by the broken gates, under the terrible wings of the twin serpents, and now the only scenery on the lifeless plains was the wake of their destruction.

When enough distance was placed between the exiled host and their now-occupied homeland, Marcum ordered the lighting of torches. Upon first gaze, he nearly regretted the order given.

"Armas was right," the lieutenant said as he raised his hand to fend off the stench of death. "The black fields, the *Melania,* this place will forever be known to me. So much death, so much destruction."

The road before them was littered with the broken bodies of both man and beast, with arms and armor. Countless arrows rose up from the ground like quills on a sea of angered porcupines, embedded in both dirt and flesh.

"This road seems even more hopelessly long now," a young mother with a nursing babe said as she wiped away the tears from her face.

"What can we do now, Lieutenant?" said a silver-haired carpenter.

"The first thing we can do," the curly-haired barmaid offered as she too wiped the sadness from her soiled and weary face, "the first thing we can do is to arm ourselves. We may be three score strong, but only a third of us have any means of defending ourselves. Out here," she looked about the carnage before her, "there are blades and shields aplenty."

"The lady is right," Johnrey agreed. "But please, be quick about it! I want us to get as far north and as far west as fast as we can."

The host picked through the scorched and pierced remains of their brothers and countrymen, hoping against all hope that they would not find the faces of their loved ones out here in this dark and death-filled place.

When all had outfitted themselves, Marcum gave the order to the weary remnant, and they began to move once again upon the North Road.

"It is too bad we don't have a woodcutter or two in our company," said one of the old men. "Someone who had traveled this road before would sure be a help to us about now. Those cutter carts made many a journey back and forth here with their precious loads of timber."

"Aye, it's a pity," said the miller's daughter. "It would be nice to know where it is we are traveling to. I wonder," she said thoughtfully as she trudged into the death-soaked darkness, "why none of us ever ventured outside the walls of Haven before now."

"Things were different in those days, girl," the old man replied. "Back then ... it was fear that kept us home, behind the high, stone walls. And, now it is fear that compels us as far away from those walls as we can get."

"That doesn't sound so different, with all things considered ..." the miller's daughter murmured.

"My father wasn't afraid!" Keily said indignantly from behind them. "He went out beyond the walls while the rest of you just *waited*."

"Oh, he was afraid all right, lass," the old man said as he shook his head. "But he was even more unnerved to just wait and let his fears hunt him down."

"I wonder which of us are the bigger fools, then," said the miller's daughter. "Those of us who hid and waited, or those who dared to meet this darkness head on."

"I don't think it is really a matter of foolishness," the white-haired corporal chimed in. "Fear will force our hands, one way or the other. Some have hidden and some have run and some have fought. But evil does not seem to give favor to one strategy over another, does it? Its teeth bite all the same."

"Aye. And eventually," Keily said as she finished filling her quiver with spent arrows, "eventually our fears will find us all. We'd best be ready to meet them face to face."

Their conversation ceased as they felt the weight of Keily's words. The group looked upon the carnage on the *Melania*, and the darkness both on the bloodied field and in their discouraged hearts threatened the feeble, violet strength that their vision dared to muster.

"Lieutenant!" came a distressed shout from one of the guardsmen. "Lieutenant! Lieutenant, come quick!"

Marcum nodded to his white-haired corporal, and the two officers rushed to see the forlorn face of the shouting sentry. "What is it, soldier?" Johnrey asked the man at arms. "What have you found?"

The sentry removed his pointed, silver helm, and with heaviness to his voice he sighed, "Oh, Captain."

Marcum and Johnrey looked each to the other and then quickly at the tangled mess of steed and soldier, whose once silver mail was now blackened by the blaze of dragons' fire.

"I had hoped," Johnrey whispered. "I had hoped he had somehow made it back to the city."

Marcum gazed at the dead body of his friend and his captain. The once ruddy face was now a wash of blistered flesh and blackened soil, and Marcum could not help but feel his already broken heart split a little further with each gut-wrenching pang of grief. A crowd began to gather around as the curiosity and nervousness of the remnant grew, and the people pressed in around Marcum and Johnrey to see whom it was that they were mourning.

"Lieutenant?" asked the young voice of a boy not yet ten years of age. "Lieutenant, who is he? Who is this man?"

"Shhh! Hush now!" quieted a woman standing nearby. "That is the lieutenant you are talking to. Let him mourn in peace."

"No," Marcum said, the grief in his face turning almost instantly into a fortified resolve. "No. Death will not be permitted the last word here. Though its toll seems numberless, its victims—our kinsman—they will not be nameless."

Marcum knelt beside his slain leader and picked away the rubble, wiping the dirt from the captain's soiled face with his shaking hands. "This brave warrior is Armas, captain of the Citadel guard—my captain, and my friend."

Keily peered in through the crowd, the understanding of this moment nearly robbing her of her breath. "Oh, Armas," she whispered.

"Should we bury him?" the young boy asked. "Should we bury them all?"

"Aye, son, that we should," Marcum said as he approached the sandy-haired lad and knelt to meet his gaze. "But alas, evil has robbed us of the honor to do so, for the Raven Army is not far from our position and we have no place to take refuge from their advance."

The boy furrowed his brow, deep in thought, his confusion and frustration evident in the wrinkled, smudged expression of his young face. "Well, that doesn't seem fair! None of this does. How can such an army do this to our home, to our friends and families? How can Raven arrows rob us of our warriors and not even allow us peace long enough to bury our wasted dead? Wouldn't the THREE who is SEVEN want us to honor them?"

"You are right, son. None of this is fair," Marcum said as he rose to his feet and addressed the people. "I do not understand the motives behind such bloodshed, nor the fates that have willed them to the theater of this war. I only know that they have found us here." He reached down and held the shoulders of the boy, meeting his furrowed gaze with his own wounded yet determined stare. "Make your peace and your gratitude to these brave, fallen men of Haven, but be quick about it, boy, for I do not wish for you nor any of us to join them just yet."

"The lieutenant is right," Keily said as she wiped away her own tears. "We have hardly begun our trek upon this North Road, and I would very much like to put as much distance between us and those Raven infested walls as we might."

The men and women agreed, and soon packs were slung over shoulders and weapons were brandished. The company slowly began to move northward once again, steeling their hearts for the passage through the bloodied field. The boy did not walk with them just yet, however; he remained with the fallen captain, so moved and yet so disturbed by what he beheld upon the outland fields of his former home. He was fixated on the injustice of it all, and his naïve mind was exasperated by his inability to amend it. Moments sped by as the whole of the caravan passed him there; finally it was the soft touch of the barmaid upon his all-too-burdened shoulder that woke him from his silent reverie.

"Armas would have agreed, you know," Keily told him matter-of-factly. "He was a man of both honor and dignity, even though he was often denied it in return. I think he too would have wanted to do something for his men, even if he knew that he couldn't."

"Then why shouldn't we do for him what he would have wanted for them?" the boy asked.

"Because honor and dignity at the cost of even more lives—that he would have called foolishness," she told him with a saddened smile. "And I never took him for a fool."

The boy looked around franticly, his eyes searching for something more upon the field of war. He surveyed the bloody ground around his feet until his eyes caught sight of what it was that they were after. Keily watched as he found the charred steel of an unbroken sword and carried over towards the fallen captain. He placed the blade in Armas' lifeless hands and then stood to his feet, not quite yet proud of his handiwork.

"He is still missing something," the boy said with both frustration and emotion thick in his voice. "He shouldn't be left like this, not for the ravens to feast upon his flesh!"

"We can't-" Keily tried to say.

"I know that we cannot bury him," he resigned. "But there must be *something.*"

Keily's eyes blurred as she watched this young boy, so overcome with respect and care for a captain that he had not even known. Her own heart ached at the sight of this corpse of a man who had once so deeply cared for her, and she shivered at the thought that he was truly gone. She searched the wreckage of the battle, collecting herself, until she found a singed and soiled cape whose green fabric and silver tree were still reminiscent of their former glory.

"Here," she said. "This will befit the burial of a captain of the royal guard." And with a flick of her wrists she spread out the cape. It fanned into the air and then, in a flutter of short-lived ceremony, it came to rest upon his lifeless body. The barmaid kissed her hand and then held it high in the sign of the flint, saying her silent goodbyes to this defender of the North.

"Yes," said the boy with a sad smile. "It seems better that way, doesn't it?" His eyes looked up at hers with a newfound respect as a bit of trust was born between them. "I am ready now," he said. "Though ... I don't quite know where you are leading us?"

She put her arm around his shoulders and ushered him forward so that the two of them could take up the rear of their exiled convoy. "I don't rightly know where we are going either, but something tells me that out there—somewhere out there—there is still a place for us in this world. A place for those who have not spilled their blood nor bent their knees just yet."

As they walked together in the grief-filled silence, an unexpected and rather unexplainable sound met their ears. Words, distant and ominous, echoed off the cold, northern air. Their origin was unknown to the small group of survivors, but their hopeful meaning was not lost on the wounded and the weary.

"What was that?" Roshan asked. "Some kind of ghost? What does it mean, 'look to the hills'?"

"I cannot rightly say who that was or what he meant by his words," Keily spoke reverently into the dimness. "Though," she managed as she choked back a sudden depth of emotion, "I am glad to have heard them."

They walked in silence for the better part of an hour, following the ravaged and blood-soaked terrain, before the boy spoke again. "What makes you think that?"

"What makes me think what?" the curly-haired bar maiden asked in return.

"That there is a place that is safe, out here in these darkened outlands?" he asked. "Nothing has ever been safe out here! My Pa ... he told me that there is nothing out here but thieves and witches and shadow cats ... and now? Now we know that there are dragons too!" He furrowed his brow and wrinkled his nose; his skepticism was too great for a boy his age. "How can you be sure?"

She let his heavy words roll through her mind, for his simple questions were the same questions that every single one of them were trying either to silence or to answer. A small smile broke her stoic and determined stare, and when she opened her mouth to speak the very air around her seemed to glow and hum with a light much stronger than before. "I know a man, a friend of mine—a groomsman at that," she told him as they walked. "He was sent by the Priest King to make his restitution in the camps of the woodcutters. He saw shadow cats, and bears, and all sorts of dark and horrible things out here."

A feeling of homesickness came over her aching heart as she spoke.

"He did a very brave thing, and saved the life of an even braver man, but he got lost somewhere out here in these darkened outlands. Many of his friends gave him up for dead, sure that he had either been taken by witches, or eaten alive by a brood of foul beasts. But one day he walked back into the Knob, healthy and strong, well-fed and well-kept ... and with a glint of magic in his eye. And that day—well, I knew that there was something more out here than just the shadow cats and the green-eyed ravens. There was something *good*, too."

"Did he tell you where he had been?" the boy begged, the light of this story aglow in his eyes.

"Aye, he did ... sort of," she replied with curious smile. "*Look to the hills*; perhaps that is indeed precisely what we must do."

"Sort of?" he blurted out, the sheer volume of his boyish emotions beyond containment. "Well, what does that mean, sort of?"

"He told me that he had been befriended by a colony of Poets who had made their home in a mountain palace," she recalled to him while she gazed deep into the darkness about them, searching its imperceptible shadows for some sign of this hidden refuge.

"A mountain palace?" the boy said, wonderstruck with the magic of the very thought.

She returned his wide-eyed awe with her own girlish smile, for she too would very much like to see this place that the groomsman had once described to her.

"Is that where we are going now then?" he asked her.

"I hope so," Keily said honestly. "All I know is that he said he came from across the mighty Abonris."

"The Hilgari are even mightier, lass," Marcum interjected. His voice startled her a bit, for she had not realized that her story had gained an audience. "We could search the foothills and base lands for weeks before we find this palace of yours, but we might well starve or freeze to death long before we find it."

"I know, Lieutenant," she said, the youthful confidence disappearing into a distant memory. "I just pray that whatever it was that guided Cal, also guides us."

"Well, we will know soon enough, won't we?" Marcum said matter-of-factly. "The Northern Altar of the Priest is but a half day's march, and I'll feel better about resting our weary people when we have made it at least that far."

"*Then what?*" the young boy asked in exasperation, forgetting who it was that he was addressing.

Marcum looked at him for a moment, not sure whether to be amused or offended. Finally the lieutenant determined that exile does not leave much room for insult or offense when prior formalities are forgotten. "Well lad, your friend here believes that our hope is to the west. I imagine that the Altar would be as good of a place as any to turn and head that way."

Marcum held his gaze for a moment, and the silent words reestablished a bit of order with their unspoken message.

"Yes ... yes, sir, Lieutenant, sir," the child said rather penitently as the weight of his disregard fell heavy upon his boyish candor. "I'm sorry, forgive me."

Marcum just nodded his grace and then returned his attention back to Keily. "We haven't much provision, so let us also pray that whatever it is that is guiding us might either quiet our appetites or stretch what little stores we do have. If not, well, keep your eye out for any brambles of berries or any game, no matter how big or small. Johnrey tells me you are quite a skilled hunter, and that might just be our saving grace."

"Alright," she replied. "I'll keep an eye out, though I doubt the sixty of us slogging along will lean much in our favor of finding anything at all to hunt."

"Just as well," Marcum bantered back. "The THREE who is SEVEN just might go ahead and surprise us all with an answer."

"May it be so," she said under her breath.

"May it be so, indeed," the lieutenant agreed.

Chapter Thirty-Nine

CAL, ASTYRÆ, GORAN, AND DERYN found their way out of the hoarder's cave and were welcomed to the darkened wilderness that expansively rolled out before them. Farran snorted and stamped his worried welcome at the sight of his friend.

"Were you worried, my silver steed?" Cal said as he wrapped his arm around the well-muscled neck of the grey-coated courser. Farran lowered his head upon the shoulder of the groomsman in an embrace of sorts, conveying the relief that he truly felt upon their reunion. "You remind me of a mother Percheron I once had," he said with a wistful smile on his face as he tussled the silver mane of the mighty horse.

"We can't stay here, Cal," Astyræ said as her eyes surveyed the darkened canopy above. "The darkness is fully upon us, and if we do not find shelter we will be hunted by more than just the soldiers of the tree men. We have to keep moving."

"Where will you go?" Goran asked, betraying the notes of worry that laced his deep voice.

"Will you not come with us?" Astyræ pleaded.

"No, my lady. Whatever journey the THREE who is SEVEN has called you upon, whatever roads your feet are draw to tread ... he has not yet released me from my own." Goran spoke with more kindness than Cal had ever seen in the old mountain man. "Besides, the North Wolf would be lost without me! Someone has got to provide our once shining city with timber enough to shine again by. At least until you two find your new light, eh?"

"Thank you, brother," Cal said, embracing the massive man with both arms. "Thank you for keeping her safe."

"Well, I wouldn't say I did that," Goran said with a laugh. "But she is safe enough now, I suppose."

"All the same, you are a true brother, and I, for one, am grateful." The groomsman held the embrace a moment longer, and the woodcutter finally pulled back with a grunt.

"Aye, okay, okay. You're welcome. Don't you go getting all sentimental now, you'll set the woman to crying and then where will you be?" Goran said, his misty eyes betraying his generous heart.

Astyræ raised an eyebrow at the large man. "We don't want anyone crying, that's for sure," she said with a graceful smile. "Are you ready, Cal?"

"Do you know where it is that you are going?" Goran asked again.

"North," Cal said, turning to face the darkened wilderlands. "I don't know where it will lead us, but it's the only true direction I have for the moment."

"Well, here then," Goran said as he handed over the ancient shield with the bronze feathers. "You'll need this more than I will."

"Goran?" Cal tried to protest.

"I have no use for it! Besides, how would you suppose I try to explain something like this to the governor or his yapping dog of a captain? You take it. Use it to keep safe out there ... wherever *there* is."

"Thank you, brave woodcutter," Astyræ said as she rose to her toes to kiss his smudged forehead. "It has been a rare occurrence here in the west of the forgotten world to encounter such selflessness. And yet, here I am, thrice its recipient in less than a week's worth of days."

Goran blushed a deep shade of red, even by the flickering light of his own torch. "If you find this new light, I expect you to come let me know when I can stop the felling of so many trees, huh?"

"I will, brother," Cal said with an amused grin. "I promise."

They watched as the large, bald-headed woodcutter walked off, both torch and axe in hand, back along the stream bed and southward towards the tree line of his brothers.

"I will miss those woodcutters," Cal said to Deryn and Astyræ. "When I first met them, they were not much more than the wardens of my punishment. And now, well ... I am more sad to leave them than I was afraid to meet them."

"I know exactly what you mean," Astyræ said with a sincere smile.

"Come on, then," Cal said as he placed one boot in the side stirrup of his silver horse. "North is still calling us."

Cal and Astyræ mounted their horses and Deryn flew on ahead, illuminating the way before them with a protective glow. They rode in silence for quite some time, not wanting to attract attention to themselves, though there was much that they wished to say. After several hours of making their slow and deliberate way through the wood, the weariness of the last few days took its toll.

"There must be a place we can make our rest," Cal whispered to Deryn. "A cave, or something?"

"I haven't seen any shelter, Bright Fame," Deryn said, and the exhaustion could be heard even in his voice. "Perhaps we should just find a grove and keep quiet in the darkness."

Cal looked to Astyræ, and she nodded her weary assent. The group stopped near what looked to be a small clearing, and hastily made camp against an old tree. Sleep came upon them fast and hard, bringing with it a chance to put from their minds the enormous uncertainties that loomed in the distance.

Cal awoke sometime later. It was hard to tell day and night apart anymore; when he had been with the colony, they had kept track of the rhythm of their days with their meals and their work and their rigid schedule, so night was still distinguishable even without the subtle glow of silver to guide them. But here, in the wilds of the Wreath, with the great tree dead and gone, and no schedule to keep track of, time ran together in an unsettling blur.

Nevertheless, Cal woke to find that Astyræ was no longer resting beside him where she had been when he fell asleep. He jolted upright, worried that she had either been taken from him or worse, that she had left him; relief washed over him when he saw her glowing eyes watching him from just a few paces away.

"My lady, were you not able to rest?" he mumbled groggily, still waking from the heavy sleep.

"I slept well enough. I am eager to be on the move again," she whispered, nodding at the sleeping Sprite who lay atop Cal's cloak. "But we can wait until *everyone* has caught up with their rest."

Cal smiled at Deryn. "It seems as though this one never rests; that cave was not the first time he has saved my life."

"Nor hopefully the last. He is a brave companion, Cal. You are lucky to have him." Astyræ's face grew serious then. "*More* than lucky, I suppose. A Sprite, I don't ... it is hard to believe a child of the Jacaranda is here before my very eyes," she said, and as she stumbled over her words, her eyes filled with unexpected tears.

Cal paused, confused as to the reason for her swell of emotion and equally unsure of what he was supposed to do to comfort her.

A sob escaped her then, and Deryn awoke with a start.

"It's alright, Deryn," Cal murmured as his concerned eyes directed the Sprite's attention to their crying friend. Cal moved towards Astyræ, who was still sitting a few paces away, ashamed of her tears and yet unable to contain them. "My lady," he offered as he placed a comforting hand upon hers. "I ... I don't ... I didn't mean for all of this, I only ever wished to help, from the day when we found you locked in that awful tower. I am sorry for dragging you into a story that wasn't yours to begin with."

She looked at him, and her tears slowed as her expression changed from sadness to confusion. She wrinkled her nose as she thought on his words. "You misunderstand my tears, dear groomsman," she said, wiping the tears from her face. "You didn't drag me anywhere. You rescued me, and more than once at that! No, Cal, do not apologize for anything. I am but grateful for the invitation ... grateful for you."

"But all the trouble, the damned fool of a knight, the hoarder, the mess— is that not why you cry, my lady?" he asked sincerely.

"No, it is not," she said as she took a deep breath to steady herself.

"Then why, lady Astyræ?" Deryn asked as he flitted over to rest upon her lap.

"My sorrow is much deeper than bullying men and fading trees," she told them both. "I fear that I deserve whatever trouble finds me, and I fear all the more that my trouble will become your own trouble, too."

"I don't understand," Cal said. "No one need resign themselves to trouble, Astyræ, that is not what the THREE who is SEVEN made us for."

"That's just it, Cal," she said as a tear rolled down her pretty, pearl cheek.

"What is?" Cal asked again, his brow furrowed in frustration. "I don't understand ... just tell me."

Deryn, sensing something deeper and perhaps darker brooding behind the surface of her tears, flew up from his perch upon her lap and met her sorrow-filled eyes with his own azure gaze. "Go on."

The moment went tense and silent, like a storm of wounds that was about to break. Astyræ swallowed hard. Then, with shame coloring her voice, she began her telling. "Before our city fell to the will and power of Nogcwren, my father was the steward of Dardanos. He cared for many sacred and special artifacts housed in the vaults of the treasury. The most important part of his duties was to watch over our most precious treasure; it was because of this treasure that our city thrived, seemingly unaffected by the ever-growing darkness of this world. We became the object of the malevolent desire of the sorceress, for the brightness of this forgotten magic somehow chased away her shadows."

"A treasure that warded off darkness for a whole city?" Cal asked incredulously. "What could it have been?"

She winced, and then replied. "The last remaining un-ripened fruit of the long-vanished Jacaranda trees."

Deryn looked to Cal in worried wonder, and a knowing expression came across his face.

"My father resisted her offers of power and sight, for he had no reason to bend a knee to her when his people could still see in this darkened world. It wasn't until ..." her voice caught in her throat. "It wasn't until I nearly died that he finally and reluctantly succumbed to her treacherous offer."

Tears began to fill her violet and yellow eyes again, and Cal and Deryn could feel the palpable weight of her grief.

"While I was yet in my mother's womb, she began to bleed," Astyræ continued. "She hemorrhaged for six days and my father grew desperate in his panic, desperate for his wife to be rescued and his child to be spared. Some say that it was the sorceress herself that caused the blood to flow, in hopes of forcing my father's hand. But regardless of the cause, the Raven woman told him how he might save us both."

"What did she tell him?" Cal gently urged.

"That if she, my mother, were but to *eat* the whole fruit of the Jacaranda, the magic of the ancient trees of beauty would heal her wounds and save both of our lives." Her face carried a massive guilt, and it seemed as if her very existence was suffocating right there in the telling of her history.

"My father chose me and my mother that doom-filled day," she told them. "He chose us above the safety of our city. He spoke *her* vile words and my mother ate the holy fruit, and Dardanos ... well, Dardanos was never the same."

"Is that why ... your eyes?" Cal softly asked. "Is that why they are violet?"

"That is also why they are yellow," she responded lifelessly.

The telling of the story settled heavy upon them all, and quiet moments passed as the groomsman and the Sprite considered the meaning and the consequences found in this woman's words.

Finally, Cal spoke with a charming hopefulness. "But love rescued you once already, my lady, and love, even when it has a price, is beautiful. You should not lament your whole story while it is not yet fully told; for perhaps some sort of beauty might rescue you a second time?"

"Why would it ever?" she said angrily. "Dardanos fell one bended knee at a time! We were the last true opposition to the sorceress, and because of me ... because of me, my father Aius, the last steward of Dardanos, surrendered his will to *hers.*"

"Well, I am not going to judge you as harshly as you judge yourself," Cal said confidently.

Astyræ looked to the Sprite in shame, tears flowing all the more now. "And you?" she asked.

Deryn flew to her, and in a great display of costly forgiveness, he took her tear-stained face in his tiny hands and spoke confidently."None of us can know the complete plans of our Great Father. Perhaps your fallen city might yet prove to be a part of them."

"But my father ... the *fruit*." Her eyes filled once again as her voice caught in her throat.

"I do not hold your father's choice against you, lady Astyræ," Deryn told her. "How could I? For it was not your choice to make."

She pressed her lips together in a moment of deepest gratitude. "Your grace is more than I could ask for, my brother," she whispered.

Deryn nodded nobly and flew back to Cal's side. "Tell us, what happened to Dardanos after your father surrendered?"

"It was as if the very marrow of our once bright and thriving city was slowly sucked out of its bones. The walls still stand unbroken, claiming their dominion of the valley, though now only as elaborate grave markers of a dead people."

"The sorceress did not attack the city? I thought you said it fell to her will?" Cal said in confusion.

"Not a single arrow was fired, nor blade colored red. When my father bent his knee, the city was already hers for the taking, for we no longer held the fruit of the Jacaranda. At first it was as if nothing had even happened. He submitted to her will, and my mother lived, and I was born. But over the next six years he became less and less my father and more and more her slave," she told them. "The light in his eyes changed from the pale blue that my mother had swooned over as a young maiden; at the end of it, one eye had turned a sickly green that haunted my mother in the night. I think he fought the magic with the goodness of his heart for as long as his failing strength would allow him to—longer than most—but he fell, as he knew he always would."

"But what about the city?" Cal asked. "How did she take the city without force or show of arms?"

"The light of the fruit was gone, and fear gripped and strangled the strength of my people," Astyræ continued. "She would come often to the city, her caravan encamped just beyond the entrance to the mountain pass. Scores upon scores of people would flock to her for the gift of her *un-light*, for I am not the only one in Aiénor that fears the darkness. And when they would return to Dardanos from the Itzal Valley ..."

"Yes?" Cal coaxed.

"They were slaves to the un-light. No longer themselves. Puppets of the Raven Queen."

Chapter Forty

THE AIR ABOUT THE SEVEN travelers was strikingly cold within the broken, granite bowels of the once hallowed mount, but it was not dark. For although shadows still hung heavy in the passageway, hope itself had lit the air with its ever-violet light.

"Do you know where we are going?" Kahri asked nervously as she held tightly to the hand of a young maiden named Georgina.

"Yes? Margarid, do you know the way?" Georgina asked.

"No," Margarid replied. "I do not, though it would seem that the only way available to us is directly ahead. So I will follow the path that was carved out of these ancient stones and pray that it leads us somewhere safe, somewhere beyond the reach of those dragons."

The path they beheld was little more than a parting of the stone in the middle of the mountain, a crevasse created by the magic expelled from the dying Arborist. It was narrow, wide enough for one or maybe two people to walk through at a time, though it seemed to rise infinitely upward into the hallowed peak of the mountain. Whether by providence, or magic, or maybe just luck, something about their hope fueled a welcomed, violet illumination. For though they knew not what kind of enemy it was that pursued them into these suffocating bowels of the rock, they traversed this Elmer-path with the vision of a refuge in their hearts.

"What of Engelmann? And Michael?" Harmier the merchant asked. "Are we to give up hope for their lives like we have given up hope for our city?"

Portus put his large hand upon the shoulder of his auburn-haired friend, consoling her worried heart as he addressed the frightened remnant. "We cannot say, for there is no way to know what has happened to our friends."

"But we also cannot just wait here in these cold, granite halls, hoping for even more miracles than we have already received," Margarid said resolutely, steeling her teary gaze forward on the path ahead of them.

"But why?" Georgina asked in her still girlish voice that seemed to glide her words up to the calloused ears of her companions. "That is what I hope for: that we will not be alone in our journey, and that Michael and Engelmann will find us soon."

"Well then, I will choose to join you, young lady," the tall tanner said kindly. "For that seems a much more pleasant thing to hope for than the realities that the rest of us have supposed."

The seven of them walked quietly through the cold corridor of the mountain pass. The air about them glowed in a faint violet hue, but their hope revealed very little, for their surroundings consisted of nothing more than the sheer sheets of rock and their glittered veins of failing magic. They continued this way for hours, until finally their feet angered in protest and demanded rest.

"We have been at this trek for what feels like a lifetime of steps," Kahri whined in exhaustion. "We must stop ... we need a rest, we need something to eat."

Margarid thought hard about it, but although she too was weary from the Aureole road, she did not put much trust in the broken, iron willow doors to bar the Nocturnals from hunting them down. "But what if-" she tried to say before the farm girl interrupted her.

"Please, Margarid?" Georgina begged. "I don't know how much longer the path is, but I do know that we must rest if we hope to find its end."

Margarid agreed with the young woman, though fear would not let her wholly relinquish her watchful guard just yet. "I would like to put more distance between us and that green-eyed hell of an army that invaded our home." She sighed as she let go of her pack and released it to the granite floor. "But you are right, Georgina, we must recover our strength."

"Me and Harmier, we will take the first watch," Portus said with gracious conviction. "Please, you five, rest while you can. The girl is right; we have no idea what still lies before us."

The rest of them dropped their packs and eased to the ground, grateful for the respite. As they rummaged through their provisions in search of any food Elmer may have gathered for them, they came upon figs, hard tack, and half a dozen skins of wine, and at the sight of such provisions their bodies nearly groaned in utter relief.

"Oh!" Harmier said excitedly in between mouthfuls of food. "Thank the THREE who is SEVEN, thank Him, indeed!"

"I think that my gratitude is owed to Elmer, thank you very much!" Kahri said, making no effort to hide her disillusionment. "He seems to be the only one who has done anything praiseworthy as of late."

"That's blasphemy!" Harmier retorted. "But this food is too delicious for me to waste a precious moment caring! Go on and thank whoever you like!"

"I am curious," Margarid asked in between her own greedy gulps of wine. "Who do you suppose it was that prompted Elmer to set aside provisions for us?"

"That's easy enough," Kahri said smugly. "Engelmann did! I overheard them talking one night back when we used to meet at the mill. He told him to gather what he could in preparation to leave the city, and my guess is that this is what he had already prepared."

"I guess we owe a lot to them ... the Arborists, I mean," Georgina interjected.

"And who do you suppose it was that prompted those old tree-beards to plan for our escape?" Portus offered up the question, sensing even now where the fiery-haired friend of his was going.

CRASH! A soul-jarring sound of iron against iron rang out in the distance, intruding upon their conversation.

"What was that?" the merchant asked warily.

"I don't know," Portus replied. "But it sounded far enough off at least."

"We cannot rest here, then, not while the *green-eyes* are still on the hunt," Margarid decided with a resolute look about her. "We have to keep moving."

"Come, you heard the lady ... and you know that she is right about this," Portus urged. "Chew your food quickly, for we are not armed enough to properly defend ourselves against a wild pack of kittens, let alone a whole invading army."

"It's a wonder those old Arborists didn't think of that when they made all their *preparations*," Kahri said sourly. "A sword or two would have been nice, Engelmann, EH?"

"Hush now. If they had meant for us to fight an army, there'd be weapons aplenty. Eat your food, girl," Portus chastised.

She nodded sullenly, not offering a further response.

They ate quickly and quenched their thirst happily with the wine that Elmer had provided for them, but their rest would have to wait. The sounds of the invaders reverberated in the distance, echoing between the silent swallows of the huddled remnant. The small group exchanged worried glances back and forth as they focused their attention straight ahead through the glittering, granite passageway inside the mountain.

"Alright, everyone," Margarid said. "We need to put some more distance between us and the entrance to this tunnel. If they are desecrating the whole city of ours, I do not doubt for a moment that they will allow the hall of the Arborists to remain untouched."

Portus nodded in weary resignation and gingerly rose to his tired, aching feet. With his large hands he grasped the hands of his fellow travelers and in turn helped them up from their all-too-brief rest.

"She is right, you know," Georgina said to Kahri, who was staring at Margarid with the most displeased of expressions.

"But how do we even know that we are going the right way? We can't even tell if we are heading *north* when all that we have seen is a sheer edge of granite for leagues upon leagues!" Kahri argued.

"Have you seen another way?" Portus argued back. "If so, please, by all means, lead us there! But only one way was made for us through this mountain, and this Elmer-pass is a gift. No matter how taxing it may feel; it is still a gift."

"But what about tomorrow? What about the next day, and the day after that?" she asked, angry and exhausted. "What if this *Elmer-pass* is nothing more than a granite road to our tombs?"

"Did you not see what we saw?" Harmier asked the maiden with an incredulous raise of his brow. "Did you not see the brave sacrifice that was made to give us this road at all?"

"Easy now, easy now!" Margarid called softly over the eruption of frayed nerves and raised voices. "Tomorrow I cannot speak for; none of us can. But, today? Today, I believe that the best way out is indeed through. All that lies behind us is death, or worse; if that is what you want then not one of us will force your feet any further upon this path." The remnant went silent at the compelling words of this auburn-haired maiden as she poured her own weary conviction into this unexpected moment. "But as for me, I will look with hope towards tomorrow, and the next morrow and the next if that is what this journey will require of me. I trust the hearts of our Arborist friends and I will still pray that we will not be alone on the other side of tomorrow."

With that, Margarid gathered her strength and walked slowly forward, continuing the dimly lit march deeper and deeper into the heart of the mountain. Portus looked the others in the eyes. When his gaze fell upon Kahri, his eyes nearly demanded an apology from the seamstress. Kahri exhaled a reluctantly humbled breath before she obliged the tall tanner.

"I'm sorry, I'm sorry, alright? It's just..."

Portus stared in confusion at his friend, still not understanding why her anxiety had so suffocated her senses.

"I'm sorry, Margarid is right. Let's ... let's just be on with it, alright?"

"That's okay, Kahri!" Georgina said as she reached out and took the hand of her friend. And it was with that gesture of grace that the lot of them followed Margarid off into the mountain, eager to find the tomorrow that she believed in.

Hours and hours passed as the seven of them walked deliberately into the unknown. Their bodies and minds were exhausted, but they were propelled onward by the bumps and clanks that crashed and echoed with a haunting consistency in the passage behind them. The high, stone walls with glittering veins rose upwards on either side of the sliver of a walkway that the seven of them traversed. It wasn't until the granite monotony was interrupted by a vast and empty space that their hope and pace halted.

"What in the name of the THREE who is SEVEN is this place?" Portus said in a stunned whisper. The very pathway that they had marched steadily upon for the better part of a day suddenly terminated at the mouth of a vast and darkened abyss.

"It must plunge for leagues!" Harmier said in amazement. "I cannot see its depths, not with a thousand lit torches would I hope to see its depths."

"Do you see a way across the chasm?" Portus asked the rest. "Look! There must be a way across."

It was as if the very mountain had hollowed itself out here to accommodate this massive pit in the belly of Haven. The stone path ended completely and the ceiling above them rose to great heights while the granite floor plummeted to unfathomable black depths right before their eyes.

"There!" Georgina blurted out. "Do you see it? Right there!" The young farm girl held a wavering hand out before her and pointed towards the other side of the cavern. The group peered into the darkness and before long they could make out the rock face on the opposite side of the abyss with a small, amber, glowing northward arrow carved into the granite walls.

"I see it!" Margarid shouted in excited relief. "Well spotted, indeed!" She grabbed Georgina in a genuine embrace and tousled her hair kindly.

The young lady smiled with a self-satisfied expression, feeling for a moment that she was more than just a child, and that perhaps she too could —and would, in fact—contribute to this new family of hers.

"That is all well and good, but how do you suppose we are to cross this chasm?" Kahri said in fearful defiance. "It has to be thirty paces wide! There is no way to get across!"

"I do not see any way either," Harmier said, defeated. "But there must be one ... somehow."

"I can't believe for a moment that a way was made for us just so that it would end like ... like this!" Margarid said, doing her best to steel the resolve of both her friends and herself. "We must have eyes to see it, we must look harder."

The seven of them dropped their bags, and a few of them plopped to the floor in defeated exhaustion. Though the way through the mountain was barely lit by the violet glow, here at this place of wounded hope, this impasse on the edge of the abyss, the violet light seemed to wane in response to their weariness.

"What do we do now, my lady?" Portus whispered. "I cannot for the life of me make out a way across this ravine, though something tells me that across the ravine is where we must go."

"I do not know, dear Portus. Perhaps," she said as her eyes scanned the downtrodden faces of her fatigued friends, "perhaps our eyes might be more keen after some sleep?"

"Aye, let's hope so, huh?" the tanner said as he rubbed his eyes with his massive hands. "Should we keep a watch?"

"I cannot see it doing much good, can you?" she said as exhaustion overcame her speech. "Not like this, it won't; besides, I doubt a single one of us could keep our eyes open."

Portus nodded and laid himself down, stretching his body out across the entrance to the ravine's great corridor. "Well, if someone does come, they will have to trip over my tired body first," he said as he took a leather satchel and propped it up underneath his head.

"Thank you, Portus," she said with a grateful smile. "Your bravery has not gone unnoticed."

And with those words, it was not long before the massive cavern under the mountain rang out with their heavy breathing. The small remnant slept hard and fast, all save Margarid, for her mind was churning with thoughts of Michael and Engelmann and this impasse that loomed right in front of them.

"What would you do, Engelmann?" she whispered to the dark silence. "What kind of magic would you conjure, what kind of prayers would you pray? What is the answer to this riddle that seemingly mocks our trust? Oh, I wish ... I do so wish that you were here." She spoke to the emptiness as she rose to her feet and determined to look again for the way that could not be seen.

Her mind shifted to Michael, the groomsman that had become her champion, but she swallowed back the lump in her throat as she pushed the thoughts of him aside. She could not dwell long on his absence, so she said a brief prayer for his safety as she began to kick the rocks and pebbles that had littered the ground floor.

Portus awoke at the sounds of her boots meeting the loose gravel of the passageway floor. He realized that Margarid was the only other person awake, so he quietly watched her and listened to the worried prayers of his friend's heart.

"I cannot see anything!" she whispered desperately to the ancient air. " I have tried ... I *want* to see it, I want to see a way out ... a way across. But I have stared half the night away and still *nothing.*"

Margarid continued to pace along the ledge of the ravine, sending rock and stone over the edge of the chasm with each step that punctuated her prayers. "What would you have me do? What would you have us do?" She kicked again, sending a spray hard into the emptiness. This time, unlike each time before, the sound of pebbles and dust landing upon a ledge met her astonished ears.

Portus jumped up at the sound and moved quickly towards her. She felt him approaching and whirled around to face him, eyes wide.

"What was that?" Portus whispered excitedly. "Did you hear that?"

"I did!" she replied as she stood, slack-jawed and speechless. She turned back to face the cavern, and they both peered into the abyss.

"I can see it too. There, right there, floating out in the middle of the cavern!"

"There is a way, Mar!" Portus said, grinning in satisfied approval. "All you had to do was ask to be shown."

There, right out in front of them, a thin line of scattered pebbles seemed to be floating in the middle of the void. It appeared that this spray of discarded dirt now marked a path of sorts across the emptiness. "Quick!" Portus said excitedly. "Follow the line all the way back to our ledge! Do you see where it starts?"

Margarid studied the line for a moment, then repositioned herself. She crouched down and gestured to the starting point of this secret walkway. "Hidden in plain sight! Can you believe that?"

"I think that is the point, is it not?" Portus asked with a sense of wisdom in his voice.

"You have been spending quite a bit of time with Engelmann, haven't you?" Margarid said with a laugh. "All of his wise *riddling* is rather contagious, I think."

Portus smiled as he bent down and examined the thin sliver of rock that protruded to make a narrow line across the cavernous void. He reached out and touched its smooth, granite surface, pushing his weight upon its sliver-like form, doing his best to test the trueness of its strength.

"Do you think we can cross upon it?" he asked nervously.

"I think that is the point," she teased.

"I know it is the point," he said with feigned exasperation. "It is not that I don't think we are meant to cross here. I guess, well, I am wondering if we *can* cross here."

She looked at him quizzically.

"It's not much wider than my smallest finger. And this ravine, from ledge to ledge, has to be thirty paces across," he said with little confidence in his voice.

"This is the way that Elmer made, that the THREE who is SEVEN made for us!" she insisted. "I know it is narrow-"

"Impossibly narrow, Mar," he argued.

"But it will lead us to life!" she argued back. "We have to cross it, Portus. We have to."

As this disagreement brought them to a different sort of impasse, muffled noises came from back in the trench, and the two of them paused to listen in dread as they heard the hurried pounding of boots upon the granite floor. Fear and tension rose at the realization, and the urgency they felt made this impasse seem all the more impossible.

"They are in the passage," Portus whispered.

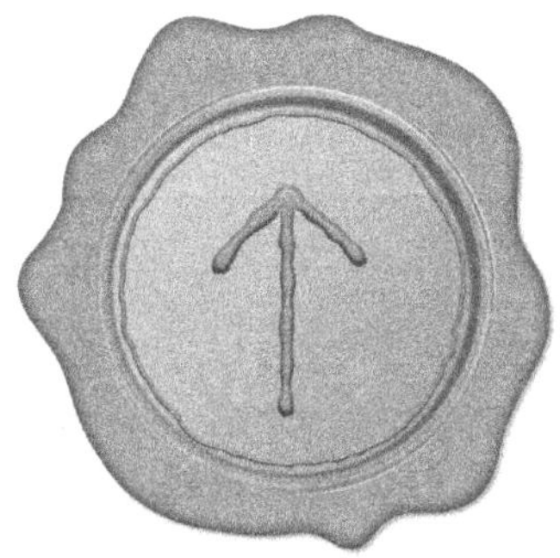

Chapter Forty-One

"THERE IS ONLY ONE WAY, and we have to take it now," Margarid urged Portus with a resolute certainty.

He nodded his understanding, though the very thought of balancing precariously over this abyss on nothing more than a mere sliver of granite made his large hands wet with nervous sweat. Portus wiped them against his dusty pants before he spoke again. "Did he pack us any rope?"

"No," she said, shaking her head. "I already checked the satchels while the rest of you slept."

"Well, then, how do you suppose-" he begged aloud.

"We could just hold hands!" a sleepy voice said from behind them.

The unexpected reply gave the two of them quite a shock, and they turned to find a young girl with wide eyes and a hopeful gaze.

"Yes! We could just hold hands! Margarid could go first, or maybe Harmier could ... yes, probably Harmier," Georgina continued on. "He could slowly make his way, while one of us held his hand, and when they could stretch no longer, then those two would venture out farther while holding the hand of another. And so on and so on ... we can do this until we have stretched across the chasm and reached the other side safely. I think we could cross it that way, don't you?"

Portus looked back at Margarid and studied the eyes of his auburn-haired friend, searching her face for her agreement. At last she answered, brow raised in a bemused wonder at the young girl. "Yes, I think that you might be right, Georgina. Perhaps we can cross it, if we but hold hands?" She directed her question to the tanner whose face was still a bit skeptical.

He paused, but only for a moment, for his ears caught the worrying tones of scuffled rock. "Very well, then," he conceded. "We have not the time to think of anything better. This ... this just might work. This had better work."

The face of the farm girl lit up with pride, and in her excitement she could wait no longer for her tired friends to rest. "Wake up! Come on, everyone! We can cross, we can cross now!"

The remaining four rubbed their tired eyes and pulled at their road-weary faces as they slowly woke to the understanding of Georgina's enthusiasm. "We can cross now, you say?" came the hopeful albeit groggy voice of the merchant. "Perhaps providence has not left us just yet."

"How did you find a way? What happened?" Kahri asked.

"It was here the whole time," Margarid declared. "I just wasn't looking in the right place."

She called the remnant over to the edge of the ravine and pointed out to them the sliver of a passageway that forded the abyss before them. The relief of the moment was stolen as the faces of her friends clouded over with nervousness; the length of the pass and the meagerness of its way did not produce a confidence that this would be at all safe.

"Don't worry, though, we have each other to keep steady," Georgina proclaimed proudly.

Portus and Margarid explained the girl's plan, and soon everyone had cinched their travel sacks and pulled their bootstraps tight, steadying themselves for the peril ahead.

"I'll go first," Harmier said, more unsure than he tried to let on. "That way the tanner can hold on to me from here, so as to keep me from plummeting to my death below."

"And when you get across, we will expect the same." Margarid replied.

Hurried footsteps bounced and echoed again off the passage walls behind them, and their unwelcome reverberations broke the concentrated efforts of these seven. "Did you hear that?" Kahri whispered. "Someone is coming. We have to hurry!"

Fear gleamed in the eyes of the remnant as they listened to their approaching pursuers.

Harmier nodded to Portus, and the men grasped arms in an effort to bring their own luck to this most unlucky moment. "If you fall after several have gone out, I cannot hold you all for long," Portus whispered. "We have only one chance at this, so keep your head about you," he said as he looked back over his shoulder to the echoing mountain pass. "There is no time for fear or second guessing."

The young merchant nodded his understanding, and in an effort of desperate bravery he placed his boot upon the sliver of granite and took his first step. It was Georgina that reached up and took the hand of her friend, and Portus in turn took the hand of the farm girl. They stood facing sideways, ready to shuffle their feet one person at a time as surely and as carefully as they might along this treacherous pass.

"Steady now, just move one foot and then the other," Margarid said as evenly as she could.

"Hurry! Hurry now!" Kahri begged. "The noises are getting closer!"

Portus shot a disapproving look towards the woman. "Shhh! Do not distract them, Kahri! They are moving as quickly as they can."

When the merchant had shuffled down the pass far enough for Georgina to step atop it, Portus squeezed the hand of the farm girl and moved his grip higher up to take her by the forearm. "Alright girl, now it's your turn. Nice and even now."

The two disheveled blonde braids that had once crowned her head flopped in agreement as she nodded to the tall tanner that held her arm.

"One at a time now, alright?" Margarid urged. "First Georgina, and then you, Harmier."

Georgina took her first step, giving the merchant room to take his next step, and as she did, her foot rolled atop one of the scattered pebbles. Georgina let out a desperate cry, her knees wobbling and her heart pounding as she franticly tried to regain her balance. Margarid's breath caught in her throat at the sight, but the strong arm of the tall tanner held firm, and the merchant stood his ground. To the great relief of the terrified travelers, Georgina found her footing again there between the strength of her two friends.

"Are you alright, girl?" Harmier asked, his own voice shaken by the near mishap.

"I think so," she said, choking back her fear. "I ... I am sorry."

"Another now," Portus encouraged. "You are doing well, lass."

The collectively held breath of the remnant eased, though not all of their confidences were restored at Portus' calming words.

And so this slow dance of nerves proceeded; first the girl and then the merchant until the length of their reach was exhausted. Portus remained as the anchor upon the ledge, calmly helping each traveler to join the line. But when the time came for the next of his friends to place her boot upon the granite pass, her distraught fumbling disrupted his concentration.

"Hurry, please! Hurry!" Kahri blurted out as she grabbed Portus' shoulder. Her frantic voice began to disrupt the balance of the four who walked the line. "Let me go now, it is my turn. We have to cross now before they are upon us." Her eyes bulged and her breath came in short gasps as she stared fearfully at the passageway behind them.

Portus looked at Margarid. His gaze begged her to do something, anything, to calm the frenzied woman down. Margarid understood the silent pleading of the tanner's eyes. She firmly grabbed Kahri's hands and held them in her own. "You cannot speak like this—you must control your words," she hissed. "Do you want to cause us all to fall to our deaths?"

"I don't want to die, Margarid!" she said, both her hands and voice shaking under the pressure of so great a fear.

"Kahri!" Margarid demanded, trying to quiet her own anxiety. "Please, *calm down!*"

"Mar, we need another!" Portus said steadily. "Is she ready?"

The auburn-haired woman held the uncontrollably shaking hands of her friend, and she knew that Kahri was not ready at all. She calmed her voice and her eyes, trying to find kindness when all she felt was frustration. "I need you to wait here; you cannot cross like this. You have to steady yourself, first. Please. Just breathe! Please." Margarid turned back to the tanner and spoke again. "How much further do we have to go?"

"Ten, maybe fifteen more paces!" Harmier shouted back to them. "We have passed the halfway mark for sure!"

Margarid nodded to herself. "I'll go next!" she said, knowing the risk she must take. "Calm yourself, Kahri, we are nearly there," she whispered her words to her friend before she turned to take the grip of the butcher's wife who held tightly to Portus' massive hands.

"What are you doing?" Portus asked.

"She cannot go yet, she will bring the whole lot of us down," Margarid said as she reached out and calmly, gently took the arm of the silver-haired woman who waited upon the edge. "Hopefully Harmier can make it to the other side without her, and once he is on solid ground," she looked over Portus' shoulder at the tear-streaked face of the nervous woman. "Then it will be a little easier for her to cross."

"Let's hope that Harmier is not as stingy with distance as he is with his coin," Portus said.

"May it be so," Margarid prayed in agreement. She took a deep breath and steeled herself for the challenge to come, and with great uncertainty she took her first step. Each successive step followed the one before until the whole line had moved a pace. One after the next the steps were taken, like ripples upon the surface of lake waters.

Portus looked at the woman who held herself, pacing back and forth across the cavern floor. Her eyes were wild with fear and although she knew where salvation waited, she could not find peace enough to walk towards it. The footsteps in the pass were growing louder and louder, for whomever it was that hunted them was coming closer and closer.

"You have to come now," Margarid said to Portus. "We are nearly there ... she will be fine for a moment."

He squeezed her arm in agreement and then, like the five who had gone out before him, he too took his first step upon the edge of the granite knife. The ripple of shuffling boots flowed out across the abyss, and the chain of arms stretched and twitched as they yearned for the safety that waited mere paces before them.

"Slowly now, easy!" Portus whispered to himself.

"A few more steps!" Harmier said to the group. "I am nearly there."

The six of them balanced and steadied themselves in valiant fashion; without an anchor to hold to, one false move or over-correction and all of them would plummet to the endless darkness below. A squeeze and then a step, a squeeze and then a step; the rhythm of the remnant propelled them slowly toward their refuge.

"A little more!" Harmier shouted back. "Just a little further!" The group responded with another ripple of forward movement and then at last, after what had seemed like an eternity upon this purgatorious passage, the boots of the merchant fell on the solid granite of the opposite cliff. "We did it! I made it across!" Harmier said with a relieved grin.

A collective sigh could be heard, for though they were not free from danger, at least they had something to anchor their hopes to. "Kahri!" Margarid called back. "Kahri, we are ready for you now."

CLANG! The sound of metal upon stone rang out as something crashed in the passage behind them.

"Never mind that noise, girl, just walk out here and give Portus your hand," Margarid said sharply.

Kahri walked to the edge and placed her boot upon the sliver of granite. Portus was beyond the point of reach now, so she would have to make a step or two on her own without the reassuring safety of the tanner's large hands. Quickly and unmeasured, driven by the fear of the fast approaching enemy, Kahri took one step, and then another and then a third before she crashed into the arm of the tanner with unbalanced force, sending a shockwave down the line of weary and terrified travelers.

"Kahri!" Portus grunted as he flexed his arms and tightened his grip in an effort to absorb—or at least control—the effects of the collision. But it was of little help. Arms began to twitch and shake, trying desperately to regain the control they had worked so hard to maintain. Harmier pulled tightly, preparing for the worst.

The woman flailed and cried, pulling on Portus as she tried to recover from her hasty entrance.

"Kahri, stop!" Portus shouted again, but it was too late, for in an effort to regain balance, the soles of her boots slipped from the thin granite and she began to fall. The tanner grabbed tighter, but gravity had already taken hold of her. She slammed her chest against the sliver of rock, and as she did

Portus released his grip from Margarid's arm in an effort to save both the falling woman and the rest of his friends. The impact of her body's collision against the rock offset his balance, and the tanner too fell sideways along the pass of granite. He kept his hold on her while he frantically grabbed at the slippery rock with his free hand. Screams rose from the other five as they desperately fought for balance while Portus hung upon the rock, grasping with arm and chest and leg, using all of his massive body to keep purchase while yet clinging to the flailing arm of the screaming woman as she hung, maddened and terrified, over the nothingness below.

The shouts of horror and fear were punctuated by the sounds of movement in the passage behind them.

"Hurry!" Harmier shouted. "They are nearly upon us! Pull her up!"

"Kahri, Kahri you have to stop kicking and screaming!" Portus shouted through gritted teeth. "You have to stop!"

But the woman continued her flailing frenzy, and her madness chipped away at the strength of the tanner. "Kahri! I need you to use the wall in front of you, use your feet to find purchase and help me pull you up!"

"Help me! Help me!" she screamed and cried, completely ignoring the instruction of her wearied friend.

"That is what I am trying to do!" Portus shouted back in exhaustion as his hand began to slide upon her slick skin. "Use the face of the ledge! Hurry, you are slipping!"

"Portus!" the desperate woman cried.

"Portus, hurry!" Harmier called with a heightened sense of dread. "I can see their torches in the passage."

Kahri's boot found the face of the rock ledge. Quickly she placed her boot upon its smooth surface and in a desperate effort to propel herself upward, she pushed all of her weight against the stone.

Portus gritted his teeth, willing his strength not to fail him now. "That's it! That's it, Kahri!" he shouted encouragingly. "Climb, girl!"

The torchlight in the passage suddenly lit the whole cavern in a subtle glow, and Kahri looked wildly toward the crevasse to see who it was that came upon them. In the moment that her head turned and her attention shifted, the young woman's boot failed her, slipping upon the slick surface. The force of the jolt and the weariness of both their hands caused Kahri to slip in Portus' grasp. He reached fiercely for her, trying to catch the falling woman, but all he could touch were the fingertips of his friend as she fell, screaming wildly, into the abyss.

"NO!" Portus shouted after her, clinging to the pass as his tears fell helplessly from his bearded face. "Kahri, no!"

Screams were replaced with sobs as the remaining travelers stared in utter disbelief at the empty darkness that had swallowed their friend. None could find the words to express the horror that they felt in the wake of this needless loss. Portus still lay dangerously upon the sliver of rock, his chest heaving in exhausted grief, while the rest of them still stretched both their limbs and their resolve halfway across the abyss, barely aware of the danger that still pursued them.

It was Margarid who first raised her gaze up to behold the torch-lit passage across the chasm. No longer was it empty, for their pursuers had emerged from the cleft in the rock, and as she looked upon their faces she was overcome with a different sort of shock.

"What?" she whispered as she choked back the sadness that had overcome her, "What in the damnable dark?"

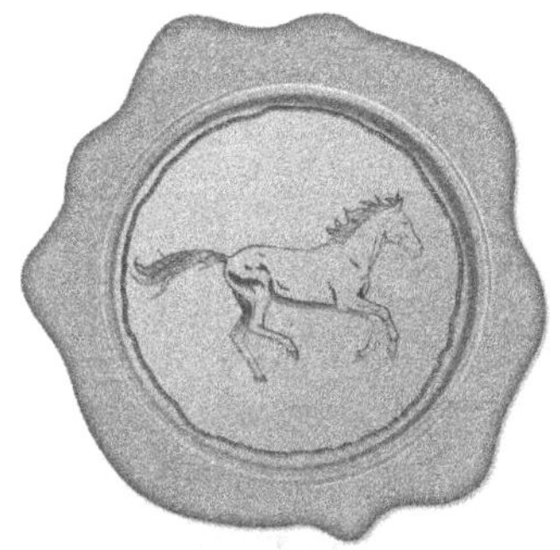

Chapter Forty-Two

THE SOUND OF A CRACKING branch woke the weary travelers from their sorrow-filled reveries. "What was that?" Astyræ asked.

"I cannot say," Deryn said as he flew to the edge of the camp to survey the darkened forest line. "But it is time that we leave."

"Agreed," Cal said. "I fear that the hospitality of this place may have run its course."

"Where exactly are you leading us, groomsman?" she asked. "You speak of light, but do you know where we should begin to look for it?"

Cal thought on her question, for this was the very same question that he had been asking himself since he was a boy. In fact, this was the very same question that all of Haven had been asking since the first branch fell more than seventy years ago.

"Shaimira," Cal replied to the violet-eyed woman. "It is the only direction, the only clue that we have, and if I am honest, I am not really sure where it leads or even what it means."

"The guardian," Deryn answered in reply.

"The guardian," Cal said under his breath, letting the idea run through his thoughts.

"How will we find this *guardian,* this Shaimira?" Astyræ asked as Cal helped her atop the large chestnut of a horse.

"HIM, I imagine," Cal said matter-of-factly as he cinched tight her saddle and adjusted the braided leather stirrups.

"Him?" she asked, unsure of his meaning. "Who is *Him*?"

"The very one who called me across the angry waters of the Dark Sea and led my weary feet to these western shores. The very one whose call to seek the light led me also to find you," Cal said with the brightest of smiles and an effortless conviction in his eyes. "The THREE who is SEVEN, or as Deryn's people call Him, the Great Father."

"And you think *He* will just lead you? Just magically point the direction?" she asked skeptically as she watched him mount the silver courser in a single, fluid motion.

"Hasn't He already?" Cal told her as he tapped his boots to his horse's flank and clicked his tongue, signaling it was time now that they made their way from this place.

Astyræ just sat there atop the mighty horse, still and stunned, her mind reeling at what this groomsman, this tree man, took as truth. "Wait a moment!" she yelled after him, but Cal and Deryn continued their ride.

"Groomsman!" she shouted, and then tapped her own heels upon the horse's side, following after him in frustration. "You are not suggesting that the writing on the wall and the northward arrow were placed there by the hand of the THREE who is SEVEN; are you?"

"Yes, actually," Cal said as he turned with a grin. "That is exactly what I hold to be true. Nothing is ever wasted in this world of ours, is it? I happen to believe that even the worst of the travesties and terrors wrought by the hands of men will yet have their illuminated redemption. The men who made those markings upon the walls of that prison tower sought the same light that I seek." He stopped, remembering that it was not *just* he who heeded this great call; he was no longer alone in this quest. "That *we* seek, even now. It cannot be reduced to chance that I found you there in the bowels of the tower Enguerrand, retracing the very steps of Illium himself."

Astyræ rode in silence for a moment, considering the depth of his words.

"I have known magic in this world, Cal, though the benevolent kind only ever existed in childish fables and in the minstrels' song of heroes and legends," she reasoned.

"Well, perhaps that is precisely where we have found ourselves," Deryn suggested to his companions.

"Ha ha!" Cal blurted out in a laugh. "I'm sure that He would have chosen someone much more *heroic* than the likes of us. I'm not too worried about legends and lore, but I do want to see *His* new light. I want that for us all."

They rode alone in silence for a while before Astyræ spoke again. "You are a peculiar one, groomsman." She shook her flaxen hair and smiled in amused wonder. "You believe in your heart that the THREE who is SEVEN is guiding your every step, leading you with magic and intercession on a perilous quest, and yet you do not find yourself—nor will you dare to call yourself—heroic?"

This time it was Deryn who laughed, and the laughter of the fruit of the ancient trees of beauty was almost musical, both whimsical in nature and bright of tune. His traveling companions could not help but smile in merriment at the sound of his genuine amusement, and as they shared this moment of levity, the bonds of their shared calling drew the three of them closer together.

"Alright, alright," Cal finally said in mock annoyance. "I hear what you are saying, my lady." Cal looked out before them, surveying the richly forested highlands of this foreign wilderland, all by the faith light of his violet hope that burned bright in this jovial moment. "We still have a long road before us, and though I am certain we are not left to our own devices to traverse its hidden pathways, I am not certain I will always act heroically upon the journey." His face turned solemn as he spoke. "So, no. I will not confuse myself with a hero. I am, rather, a hopeful sojourner, who is both grateful enough to have been called and frightened enough to not dare travel alone."

She smiled a kind smile, a knowing smile, her eyes aglow more violet than yellow at this very moment. "What kind of groomsman ponders such possibilities? None that I have known, and my father was once a lord with many horses."

"Where was his kingdom?" he asked, doing his best to shift the subject away from such flattery. "Your home, I mean? You said he was the steward of

Dardanos before it fell to the sorceress. Is that ... I mean, was it nearby? I would like to see it."

Astyræ's smile faded a bit. The longing for her home was still fresh in her heart, even after all of these years. "No, not so near to where we are now. Dardanos is south, behind the marches of the Greywood Forest, nestled in the heart of the Itzal Valley."

They continued riding northward as she spoke. "Those few who did not bend their knee to the *un-light* of Nogcwren were forced to abandon the walls of our homeland; she would give no sanctuary to those who resisted her. Some packed their mule carts and horses and rode north, seeking to make a home for themselves here in the thick of the Greywood. But her ravens—her damned, greened-eyed spies—flew throughout the forests, leading her warlords right to their camps. Others sought out refuge in the foothills and highlands, reduced to living like thieves."

"Is that where you lived all these years? In the foothills?" Cal asked again. His curiosity about the Wreath was overshadowed only by his curiosity towards this magical, golden-haired woman.

"Yes," she answered. "On the eastern fingers of the Hekate'. A mere forty of us dared to defy *her* power and escaped to a safe and hidden place. I have lived among them, though I have never wholly been welcomed. For though I, too, chose not to take the offer of the un-light, I have seen plainly enough the blame that my people still heap upon my head."

"But how could they blame you? You were in the womb of your mother, innocent and helpless!" Cal reasoned, flabbergasted at the very notion of such reasonless accusation.

She smiled sweetly at this naïve defender of her honor. "My eyes betray my origin, groomsman. For it was the fruit of the ancient Jacaranda that once bolstered our conviction and held back the darkness. The sacrifice made to save me bred contempt, and how could it not? A reckless decision to save but one, when the whole of our people depended upon its magic."

"Is that why they locked you away in that old tower?" Cal asked.

She grew quiet for a moment before she replied. "No, Cal, not completely," she said quietly. "Though I am sure their contempt sharpened the sword of their justice. But if you mean, as you have already said, to seek this light together ... then please do not ask me to tell that tale to you now, groomsman."

Cal rode in silence, not answering the request of his violet-eyed companion, though his curiosity threatened to boil over in speculation. "Very well, then," he agreed. "I will not ask it of you. But if you choose to tell me one day, I hope you will know that I would not damn you for deeds done before our paths even intersected." A wry smile crept across his bearded face. "One day I would very much like to hear about whatever this folly of yours was that just so happened to become this fortune of mine! Alright?"

She laughed at his presumptions, but could not help but to be taken aback by them too. "We will have to wait and see," she replied coolly. "Perhaps we should be more worried about finding this Shaimira-"

Her words caught in her throat as Cal raised a finger to his lip, begging for her silence.

"What is that? What ... what is this place?" he whispered nervously as his widened eyes darted back in forth, surveying the absurdity of what he beheld.

"I have not been here," she said as she gulped back her emotions, "since I was but a little girl."

"How is this possible? This makes no sense to me!" Cal blurted out his whispered questions without waiting for any answers. "We are at least a league—if not two—from the shores of the Dark Sea. How could something like *this* be *here*?"

"I cannot say," Astyræ whispered as a flood of memories washed over her.

Cal could not wholly believe his eyes, for there, laying crookedly upon its battered hull in the forest clearing before them, rested the withered and rotted remains of a once mighty sailing ship. "There is a small stream five hundred paces south of us, and that is the only water I have seen all day long. How is it that a ship of this magnitude has found its way here? What kind of devilry can drive a full-masted sea treader across the forest?" Cal marveled in whispered disbelief.

"Tell me this, groomsman," she demanded of him. "Why must it be devilry? I mean, magic, of that I am sure it must be; but devilry? Did you not mere moments before dare to argue that nothing in this world is wasted, but rather it was used by the will of your THREE who is SEVEN to guide you on this quest of His?"

"I ... yes ... I did say that," Cal said, quite a bit more unsure now. "But this, this does not make much sense. This is impossible!" He pointed demonstrably to the large sailing ship that loomed eerily out of place before them.

"I sense that the tracings of our Great Father's handiwork course ever and through this peculiarity," Deryn said, interrupting the battle of words.

Cal and Astyræ stopped to watch their winged companion, taken aback by his sudden sense of doom.

"Whose great vessel was this? Do you know, my lady?" Cal asked.

"Yes, of course I do. All of Dardanos once revered the lore of this place, though we did not wholly believe it," she told them. "This is the great ship of the tree men, and a mighty ship it once was when it first appeared in this wilderness; or so my grandfather said."

Cal was stunned; the very breath seemed to freeze inside his lungs as he beheld quite possibly one of the greatest mysteries in all of Aiénor. "You are telling me this ship belonged to *Illium*? But how do you know this? How can you be sure that this was his ... Illium's ... the tree men's?"

"My grandfather and even my own father told many tales of its discovery. Although none know how it came to be here in the forests of the Greywood, there can be no mistaking its mariners," she replied.

"I have to see it ... closer, I mean," Cal said, stumbling over his words with an all-too-boyish excitement. "What if ... what if?" His words trailed off as the groomsman of Haven spurred his silver horse and took off with great haste towards the forgotten wreckage of these royal ruins.

As he neared the fabled ship, he leapt from his horse and approached it reverently. "See! See, look, look right there!" he blurted again. "Do you see the sigil? It is just like the one in the prison tower. There is no flint marking the trunk of the great tree." He was overcome with wonder as his own two hands traced the forgotten, splintered remains of this ghost of legend. "Deryn!" he exclaimed, his excitement barely contained. "Deryn! What can you see up there? Will you look, please? I must go inside."

Deryn smiled at the youthful curiosity of his friend. "Yes, Cal, I will fly, and I will observe all that I might and happily bring you word." And with that the Sprite shot the fifty or sixty hands it was up into the curved hull of the aging relic.

The violet light by which the groomsman beheld this treasure of forgotten hope shone all the brighter as his fingers traced the aging wood on the belly of the mighty ship, *Wilderness*.

"Oh what a gift, what a gift indeed!" Cal prayed aloud.

"A gift?" Astyræ said, confused at the very idea. "How does one call this wreckage a gift?" she asked him with sincere curiosity.

Cal's hands found the hull's ladder, and a wry smile grew across his closely bearded face. "I have worried and wondered; I have both despaired and daydreamed over the fate of this very vessel. And now? Now, my lady Astyræ, I will climb its fretted hull and consider those long-sought answers resolved."

Her brow lifted in a bemused expression at his flowery speech, but she could not help but feel a bit of exhilaration in the wake of his own.

Cal put one hand atop of the other, and with a bright and hopeful light in his eyes, he climbed his way along the leaning belly of the wooden beast until his boot found purchase atop its ancient deck. "Come on now, your turn!" he yelled down to her.

"Is it safe?" she asked playfully.

"I cannot say if it is indeed safe, though I must confess it is rather wonderful!" he shouted down to her.

She smiled and shook her head, and then began the curved assent along the wooden spine of the ladder.

"Look!" he shouted as he held onto the deck railing while climbing his way to the wheel deck. "Illium, our King—he must have stood *right there*, steering his brave ten towards their doom. And there!" He pointed. "The masts, are they still whole? Look, they are still unbroken after all these years."

She reached the top of the hull, and she too felt a bit of the wonder that Cal had found. "The Dardanian people did not trust this place, for there is unknown magic all about its timbers, and we cannot be certain of whether or not it is good."

"Not trust it?" Cal asked as he continued to explore the depths of the deck.

"Yes," she said with great conviction. "My grandfather said that with the coming of the tree men came great suspicion; those who had been brothers and kinsman for generations turned hostile in the wake of their very presence."

"Why did your people mistrust them?" Cal asked intently. "Did they do ill towards them? I cannot imagine the great King Illium of Haven would not act with respect and care for the people of your land."

"It was in the time of a meaningful season for our people. The elders and the leaders had begun the great white hunt of Dardanos, the *Leuktherao,* as it was once called," she said, looking out into shadowed forest that surrounded this marooned enigma. "My grandfather was young in those days, and my father was just barely a man. They had chased the White Stag into this very clearing ... but when they were nearly upon the beast, an arrow was loosed from the bowstrings of the tree men. Its iron barb pierced the flank of the mighty stag and though it did not smite it, the beast was startled and fled the men of the hunt."

"I am sure the tree men meant your people no harm," Cal reasoned with her.

Astyræ looked long into the shadows as she remembered aloud. "Perhaps not, but our elders and leaders never found the body or the blood of the hunted one, and the White Stag was never again seen in the forests of the Greywood, though many a hunt has been made to seek it."

"Cal!" the voice of Deryn interrupted her sad tale. "Cal, lady Astyræ; I think you will very much want to see what I have found."

"What is it, dear Sprite?" she asked him.

"Come on," Cal said taking her slender, pearl colored fingers by the hand. "Let us find out, huh?"

She smiled an almost sad smile, but nodded her head in hopeful agreement, for she very much wanted a reprieve from her saddened memories. The two of them followed the azure glow of their winged friend down the stairs of the main deck and into the vast hold of the royal ship.

The hold was empty, with not much else save rotting rope and split barrels. The iron hooks where the crew's bedding once hung held nothing but the ghosts of thread that refused to release their purpose. The storerooms were stripped bare, and as they surveyed the emptiness, it felt as though the very essence of this once magnificent ship was merely a carcass whose flesh had been picked over by a host of carrion.

"What have you brought us down here to see, Deryn?" Cal asked rather uneasily, as if he were trespassing the floor of an ancient tomb. "What have you found?"

Astyræ held tightly to his muscled arm, all the more nervous here in the shadows of this cursed place. "Is it near? Are we near? For I do not feel safe in the bowels of this ... of this place."

"Just a bit further in, and then we must go up," Deryn urged.

They walked precariously through the remains of the once great hold until they came upon another set of stairs with an elaborately carved, pearl inlaid railing which led one to believe that *these* steps were meant for someone with great status. "Does this ... does this lead to where I think it does?" Cal asked hopefully.

Astyræ looked to him, not sure what it was that he was suggesting, but Deryn answered for her. "Yes, to the captain's chambers, the very quarters of the-"

"*King!*" Cal said interrupting his companion with his eagerness. "Well, come on then, I would very much like to see this place."

Cal and Astyræ held tightly to the intricately carved railings as they climbed up the steep set of stairs at a most awkward angle. The boards beneath them creaked and groaned under the almost forgotten weight of boots upon their now brittle surface. They reached the top and came upon a double-framed door that now hung limply broken, splintered and off-keel after sixty years of non-use. Cal put his hand to the masterfully carved door and pushed on it with a dramatic flourish so that he and his companions might behold the seafaring dwellings of the last King of Haven. The room shone gloriously in the violet light of so much hope and so much excitement.

The windows were shattered, and whatever stores of armor and weaponry that had once lined these richly paneled walls had been taken from their rightful place, but to Cal these dwellings seemed as if Illium himself still chose to abide here.

"I never in all my days thought for a moment that I would be standing in the King's quarters of the mighty ship *Wilderness!*" he blurted out to his friends. He plopped down hard upon the aging, wooden deck as a potent mixture of wonder and humility overtook him. His gaze traced the royal chambers in wide-eyed amazement. "Why me, Deryn?" he asked in stunned disbelief. "Why do I get to behold such history, such fabled lore? What did I ever do to warrant such a gift as this?"

Deryn smiled, though he did not feel compelled to answer the question-laden musings of his friend. Deryn knew in his heart that no spoken answer would ever suffice the unanswerable wonderings of one who has beheld the glimmers of his own destiny.

"Do not tarry too long in the land of wonderment," Deryn said playfully. "Or at least, not just yet, for boyish fantasies must still give way to a calling fully wrought, and there is more to discover here than history."

"What is it, then? Huh?" Cal laughed. "Out with it, my riddle-speaking Sprite friend!"

Deryn came to rest upon the writing desk of the king, and as he did the azure glow of his wings illuminated letters etched in black, hasty runes upon its wooden surface.

"What is that?" Cal said as he slowly rose to his feet.

"A voice still calls out from the *Wilderness*, dear groomsman," Deryn said.

Cal walked closer to the angled, wooden writing surface, and grasped one hand upon each side, looking very much like the great, priestly orators of Westriver. With an awestruck voice he spoke the old, ruined words aloud.

Barkas,

If you have made your way back here, you will find that we have departed. We have gone north after a most encouraging discovery. Payam was sent to find you, though he has not returned. We have heard whispers of a guardian called "Shaimira", and it is said that safe in its keeping are the hidden secrets of a great magic. A way has been prepared for you, so look to the north, for that is from whence I perceive our help will come.

Seek the light, warrior of Haven.

~Illium

Cal stared silently at the ruined writing table, reading and rereading the words over and over again. This last message of the King himself was carved into the very surface of the desk, and Cal's fingers traced the indentations of the script as he thought long on its meaning.

"What does it mean, Cal?" Astyræ asked him finally. The groomsman did not answer her. His hands gripped the side of the table, doing their best to anchor his balance while he steadied his thoughts. "Cal? Cal, what do these words mean?"

He looked up from the desk, his eyes filled with joyful tears. "What does this mean, my lady? It means that the King was not lost at sea, nor was he run aground upon the shores of the Isle Dušana, nor did he perish behind the bars of Enguerrand!" Cal choked back his emotion and boyishly wiped the tears from his eyes with his forearms. "It means that the story of the King still lives, that he did not die here. It means that he didn't give up on finding the light, that he went northward just as we thought, and that at least ... at least once upon a time, a way was prepared for someone to follow him. And perhaps ... just maybe ... that way still stands."

"Ever north we go then, groomsman," she said as she reached out with her soft fingers and wiped away his heavy tears. "How, though, will we know the way? The Wreath is wild and vast and I have never heard of such a place as this Shaimira."

"Of that I cannot say, though I don't doubt for a moment that we will recognize this way that has been prepared when we do, in fact, find it." He spoke with a kind smile, his own large hand meeting hers upon his cheek. "Ever north we go ..." he said in a singsong voice.

She smiled deeply, for his faith—despite its absurdity—compelled her ever to him. "Come on, groomsman," she said playfully as she slid her hand from his bearded face. "You'll have to lead the way."

He smiled at her and then turned to his winged friend. "Do you think Barkas ever read these words?"

"I hope he did, Bright Fame. But either way, it appears that the King left some clues about the way to Shaimira, and I think we had best make our business about finding them," Deryn replied with a wry smile of his own.

Chapter Forty-Three

MICHAEL COULD NOT BELIEVE HIS eyes at what he saw there before him. The groomsman stood stunned, silent with horror and yet overwhelmed with gratitude.

"Hey!" Timorets shouted out into the distance. "Are you alright? Wait there! Don't move—we are coming for you!"

The group of escaped prisoners ran the short distance to the edge of the abyss, staring into its depths with the wonder and dread of the moment.

"I cannot believe it!" Michael murmured in a shaky voice, looking at the group that appeared to be suspended over the chasm. "How is this possible? How in the name of the THREE who is SEVEN is this even *possible*?"

"I think you answered your own question there, groomsman," the large schoolmaster answered. "Do you know these travelers?"

"Yes!" he said as he put his arm around his rotund friend. "Yes, indeed, I do!"

"Brewer, are you steady on your feet?" Fryon asked his friend as he surveyed the dangers both below and out in front of them.

"Aye, I am," Timorets said reassuringly. "Though I am going to need both you and your brother to steady me while I help."

The three of them held tight, each to the other, giving a much-needed strength to the task at hand. "Friend?" Timorets said calmly and reassuringly to the large man barely hanging onto the ledge. "Whoever is lost, is lost; but you need not follow in her footsteps. Come, give me your hand, and let's all be done with this terrible place."

Portus looked up. The strong face of the tall tanner was indeed defeated with the weariness of his failed strength and the loss of his friend. "She fell —she would not stop kicking ... I couldn't ..." he faltered.

"You gave your strength, sir, and nearly lost your life too. Come on, give him your hand and we will see you safely across," Fryon said to the large man.

"But how ... how will I stand without falling?" the tanner asked as he took account of his perch. "You cannot lift my full weight."

"Grab my hand, and use it to turn yourself up to a sitting position," Timorets instructed firmly. "Once you are seated upon the ledge, you can grab the lady's hand there and the two of us will help you stand. Careful now."

Portus nodded his understanding, and grasped the brewer's hand.

"Steady!" Timorets grunted as Portus pulled heavily. "You all better hold tight!"

Celrod and Michael anchored themselves with as much strength as they could muster, grasping the brothers, ready to heave the brewer back to safety if the worst happened. Michael winced as Celrod's grasp closed over his burnt hand, and he steeled himself for the inevitable pain he would have to endure. Everyone stayed silent and focused as the men positioned themselves, and to their great relief, Portus was able to sit upon the ledge in momentary safety.

"What about the green eyes?" Portus asked, worried that soon the enemy would be upon them all. "Did you stop them, how far are they behind you?"

"No, friend, we did no such thing," Fryon said. "It will take more than a few convicts to stop whatever hell it is that drives that nocturnal army."

"But we did not see them along the pass," the brewer said reassuringly, nodding at Margarid to take Portus' other hand.

"We heard them coming," Portus muttered as he glanced at Margarid's offered hand.

"Easy there, Portus," came a familiar voice from the ledge of the ravine. Michael had stepped away from the group enough to look the tanner in the face. "We are safe enough for the moment—let's just worry about getting to the other side for now."

"Michael?" Portus said in hopeful disbelief.

"Aye," the groomsman smiled. "Come now, stand up—can you?"

Portus glanced at Timorets and Margarid to check for their readiness. Then, carefully, he gathered himself and slowly rose to his feet. "Aye," he said with a nod and a sad smile.

"You are a sight for sore eyes, old friend," Michael said. "Now come on, and I'll greet you proper on the other side."

Before Michael stepped back at the end of the line, he caught the tear-filled eyes of his auburn-haired affection staring back at him in grateful amazement. "My lady!"

She sent the fullness of her thoughts across the ravine in a single smile, and then quickly looked back to her tanner friend. "Alright, Portus, let's be done with this place."

"Alright, Mar," he replied with a tone of wounded hope. "Let's be done."

Eleven they were now, and with frayed emotions and new strength they slowly all made their way across the mountain pass onto the solid safety of the other side. The remnant collapsed in an exhausted heap once the last of them had stepped off the pass, feeling both victory and defeat at such a crossing. Margarid flung herself into Michael's arms, and he was glad to receive her. They kissed and embraced, careless of those who watched them, for the joy of this reunion would not be swayed even if it were in the presence the Priest King himself.

"Where is Engelmann?" she asked him as he wiped away her tears. "Was he not with you in the prison hold?"

Michael looked back to the four with whom he had traveled under river and fire and mountain; their grief at the loss of Engelmann showed heavy upon their faces.

"He has gone to the eternal lands, my girl," Celrod said sadly. "I've never seen such a deliberately foolish sacrifice in all my days."

"He is ... *gone*?" Margarid whispered.

"Yes," Michael said in an exhausted exhale.

"That makes, I mean, that ..." Portus had a hard time gathering his thoughts and forming them into words. "That they are both gone? Both of them?"

"Both of them?" Timorets asked.

"Yes," Georgina lamented. "Engelmann and Elmer."

"Elmer? But why?" Michael said, stunned at yet another loss.

"It was through his death that this northward pass was even made; he made this for us," Harmier answered.

"Do you see the glowing marker?" Margarid pointed. "After he was consumed in the death of the great tree, the arrows have appeared all along this Elmer pass, pointing the way for us."

Michael stared at the amber arrow, carried away by thoughts of all that had passed and all that had been lost. "The Arborists are gone, the city has fallen, the Priest King himself has taken the un-light from *dragons,* and the people have followed him. There is almost nothing left to hope for."

He spun around, tearing his gaze from the glowing icon and meeting the eyes of his weary friends. "And yet something still pulls at me! Something is not yet final. Something makes me think that *all* is not lost, at least not yet."

"And what is that?" Fryon asked.

"It seems as though the magic of the Arborists may have passed from their bodies, but not wholly left this darkened world of ours," Michael mused aloud. "And that ... that cannot be mere coincidence or happenstance. No. That must be done with some other design at hand. It has to be."

"He is right, you know?" Georgina assured the group. "Have you noticed just how much brighter this passage has gotten since they have joined us? There has to be a reason for that too, doesn't there?"

"Why, I do think the girl is right!" Celrod said, looking around the cavern.

"But what about Kahri?" the butcher's wife asked. "Was *that* of some higher design, too?"

"I cannot presume to account for her loss, nor whatever other miseries await us all," Michael responded honestly. "But I do not believe any piece of our journey to be meaningless."

"Should we pray for her?" Georgina asked sheepishly. "I know it seems silly with all the loss the world has felt this day, but I do wish someone would speak the words over her."

"Yes. Yes, of course we will," Michael assured her as he tousled her flaxen hair. He looked to Portus, silently asking the broad tanner if he wanted the closure of speaking this final prayer for Kahri.

Portus looked out over the cavernous abyss behind them, then nodded to Michael. *"May bones and breath be born again, in limb and tree and light. May flint and flame your soul reclaim ..."* his voice trailed as a lone tear travelled down his cheek.

"And dawn break through your night!" Michael said, finishing the ancient ritual for them, only this time he added his own words to the ancient prayer. He clasped Portus on the shoulder and the tanner nodded his thanks.

"May it be so," came the gathered voices in unison. They embraced each other, this new remnant family, and wiped away their tears as they picked up their packs, knowing that the time had come for them to leave this place.

"Do you know where this leads?" Celrod asked Margarid.

"North," Portus spoke for her. "That is all he said to us."

"Then north it is," Michael told the group. "Let us hope that wherever this mountain pass lets out, it is far enough away from the Raven Army ... and the dragons."

"Dragons?" Margarid said in disbelieving horror. "There are dragons?"

"Twin beasts, winged fire-serpents," Celrod told her. "Like the drakes of legend."

"It is worse than we thought," she sighed in resignation.

"Aye, it is worse alright! Whatever evil lives inside of them, my lady; they are consuming any who oppose them with their green fire. And their damned voices—they will chill your blood cold," Fryon grumbled as he slung a pack over his shoulder and grabbed the wooden shaft of his halberd.

"Is Haven gone?" Harmier asked. "I mean ... is it gone for good?"

"Her bricks and walls may still stand," Timorets told him. "But her heart is broken, raped and soiled by the nocturnal fire of the mistress of the dragons."

"Haven as it once was, as our home—that's gone," Michael said grimly. The mood of his friends darkened under the heaviness of this truth, and even as he spoke, the voice of his teacher bubbled up through the mire of his lament and he thought better of his words. "But here," he continued as he tapped two fingers to his own brow. "Here is where we will begin to build Haven again. Our city is gone, but a new Haven has already begun."

Margarid beamed a proud smile at this groomsman of hers, truly hopeful even in the midst of so much destruction. "Do you think that we are all that is left?" she asked him.

"Haven was a big city, and I am sure that we are not alone," Michael said confidently. "And besides, we aren't the only ones who still have hope. For just as the magic of the Arborists leads us north, an even greater magic called my cousin west; and if anyone is going to find that *new light* of King Illium's, it will be him."

Michael smiled as he thought about Cal. In all of the madness of the last few weeks— the prison hold, the fire and dragons, the death of his friends, and now this mountain pass—he had almost forgotten that there were still other purposes at work in this world. "No, we are not alone, not at all," he said with a chuckle. "Now come on, there are glowing markers for a reason. Northward they lead ... so northward we will follow."

The eleven took up their packs and weapons and passed under the amber arrow into yet another vein that flowed out from the heart of Mount Aureole. Fryon and his brother took up the van at the front of the line, and with torches in hand and a hopeful, violet glow about them, they blazed the trail for the rest of the remnant.

"Where do you think this pass will end?" Celrod asked the brewer.

"The schoolmaster comes to me now, does he?" Timorets teased. "Well, I *have* always been rather keen on the matters of maps and geography."

Celrod rolled his eyes and Michael couldn't help but laugh out loud as the sounds of their camaraderie bounced and echoed off the granite walls.

Timorets grinned and offered the only answer he had at the moment. "I would say that based on how many steps we have taken and accounting for the innumerable more that we have yet to take, we will end up someplace significantly colder than where we left."

"I hope these friends of yours, Michael, had the sense enough to pack some coats or furs or something thicker than this Westriver attire of ours," the heavy schoolmaster said.

"So do I, my friend." Michael agreed. "So do I."

The remnant carried on, traversing the passageway for hours upon hours. The only change in the scenery was the glittering sparkle of quartz and gemstones that ran in swirled waves throughout the black stone. They walked until their legs could go no further, and there in the granite halls they collapsed in exhausted heaps as sleep came fast upon them. For the first time since the sickening, guttural tones of the enemy's horns were heard upon the wind, these eleven rested peacefully. They slept a dreamless sleep, and when they awoke, their hearts and their feet were ready to continue their northward journey.

The morning continued much the same way—endless trudging past glittering veins of rock—until the shouts of Fryon and his brother rang out in excitement.

"Another arrow!" they shouted back to the caravan following behind them. "We found another arrow!"

The sound of boots upon the stone quickened as the group rushed to see this glowing marker in the rock floor, but before they could fully celebrate the discovery of the arrow, a dread-filled wonder overtook their senses.

"What in the name of the THREE who is SEVEN?" exclaimed the butcher's wife as she looked up and into the passage before them. "What is this?"

The pathway opened before them into a domed chamber. The fragrance of this place was both metallic and sweet, and it hummed with the soft rustlings of a syncopated rhythm. The eyes of the group found the floor, and they beheld the shimmering, pulsating waves of silver.

"Have you ever in all your life seen such a sight?" Harmier asked as he reached his hand out towards the silver that flowed across the floor "Butterflies! Thousands and thousands of them!"

"What is this?" Portus asked aloud. "I have never seen this many before, and never any with silver wings such as these! And why do they not fly? Instead they lay here as but a carpet upon this cavern floor."

"I don't know if you should touch them, Harmier!" Margarid said, worriedly placing a hand upon his back. "Let them be, something in me says not to disturb them."

"But see the way their wings ... they shine?" Harmier marveled. As he bent down, the merchant was overcome with their beauty. "I have traded in the finest of goods, and I have beheld riches that I might never even dream of possessing, but I have never in all my life seen something as breathtakingly strange and beautiful as this."

"Do you not see?" Georgina said, the worry in her voice barely constrained. "This is not our home, this is not *our* mountain! We should not disturb what is not *ours*!"

"But there are so many, girl, and I, for one, think we should appreciate the pretty things in this darkened world of ours," the merchant argued. "Besides, the Arborist made this way for us, did he not? So maybe they *are* for us, after all?"

"Harmier!" Margarid shouted, and as she did, the cavern floor pulsated in waves of disruption.

Michael stepped forward and pulled Margarid back. "I think the girls are right, Harmier ... I do not think we should disturb them."

The merchant could not help but marvel in wide-eyed amazement as he knelt and examined the tiny, silver-winged butterflies. "Oh to have one of you for my very own, for my pleasure, to be *mine*." His slow, whispered speech took up a possessive tone. "Come, perch upon my finger, and help me forget the evils that have invaded my life, little one."

"Harmier," came the calm, even-toned voice of the tall tanner as he placed his large hand upon his shoulder. "He has given us their beauty already; you will need only recall the memory and possession of these silver wings will be yours. But I, too, fear that anything more," he gulped back his nerves as he tried to speak, "anything more will come at a price too severe to pay."

The merchant stared a few moments longer at the butterflies, then blinked his eyes and rose to his feet as a tear traced his smudged face. "If we are not to disturb these winged treasures, tell me, how then do we hope to cross this place?" he said as if waking from a dream.

The group of them looked about the domed space. Its entire floor pulsated in silver reflection, a sea of dangerous beauty that stood between them and the doorway beyond.

"I don't know what difference it would make," Harmier grumbled disappointedly to himself.

"My ma always told me that a guest should keep in mind that they are just that: a guest. Whether honored or not, welcomed or not, a guest should be a guest," Georgina said as if she were playfully scolding the merchant.

"Look!" Fryon said as he pointed across the room. "Another northward arrow ... it glows there atop the passageway. And yet this arrow ... this arrow at our feet ... it isn't pointing, north, is it? It points over there, toward the arrow above the passage. Is it a trick?"

"I do not think that the THREE who is SEVEN would waste the lives of His Arborists for riddles, do you?" Margarid asked.

"No, I suppose not," Fryon replied.

"Indeed. What gain would He have by confusing the matter?" Michael said as he focused his determined gaze on the prize before him.

"What do you mean by that?" the butcher's wife said in confusion. "All the arrows have pointed north until now."

"I think it means, my lady," Celrod said as his mind connected the pattern before them, "that we should trust their direction, and follow it carefully."

"Perhaps if we *are* guilty of disturbing these winged creatures, the THREE who is SEVEN will know that it was done only in an effort to follow His direction," Margarid said aloud.

"I will go first this time," Michael said to the group. "Mind that you stay close," he let out a nervous exhale, "and that you do not deviate from our course."

"Aye!" Portus agreed.

Michael put the sole of his boot directly upon the glowing, amber arrow and inhaled a steeling breath, hoping against all hope that this was what they were supposed to do. One step, and then another, until he was not but a hairsbreadth away from the silver-winged creatures.

Michael raised his boot and held it out before him. As he put the weight of his body into his forward step, the ground beneath him erupted in a whirlwind of winged fury. A wave of movement pulsed through the resting butterflies, revealing scattered bones and little brass bells, hidden beneath the canopy of butterflies. They stopped and stared in a strange sort of fascination as a wave of silver rolled away and the pathway before him became clear.

"Are those ... *bones*?" Georgina asked with dread.

"What kind of place is this?" Timorets whispered to the travelers. "Where bone and bells lay unburied?"

"I have felt dread in my stomach from the moment we first stepped foot into this winged cathedral," Portus agreed.

"Follow my footsteps. The way is clear before me, and I do not wish to tarry long," Michael told his friends.

With each step, a shockwave rippled through the ranks of butterflies, and yet they hovered without attack or consequence. Whispers were all that any of this company were willing to speak, for it seemed that any sort of noise fed the agitation of the congregated insects below them.

"Michael?" Celrod tried to whisper as he carefully took his next step, not taking his eyes from the boots that walked in front of him. "How much further must we go?" His deep voice carried and bounced off of the rotunda of granite, and a single butterfly flew up in front of his face, passing the layer of whatever invisible magic it was that had kept them at bay.

"Brewer?" Celrod asked nervously. "What is it doing? Why did it-"

But even as he was asking the question, the silver-winged creature landed upon his large nose and robbed him of his voice, mid-sentence. Celrod's eyes went wild in panic as he desperately tried to make a sound, but nothing save gasps of breath would come from his lips.

The schoolmaster whirled around wildly in a wave of panic, and as Timorets beheld his friend's state, he too could not stop the frightened words from escaping his lips. "What in the damnable dark?"

No sooner were the words spoken than the sound of an ill-timed sneeze crashed through the hush, like a boulder hurled from the grasp of a mighty trebuchet. The clamorous noise woke the herd, and without warning the tide broke in upon them. The otherworldly butterfly creatures began to swarm angrily around the frightened travelers.

"Run!" Michael shouted. As soon he spoke the word, the very next word he tried to say was devoured before it was completely uttered.

The magical insects engulfed the eleven travelers in a writhing, hungry cloud of angered indignation, and though the remnant ran towards the glowing northward marker, the silver swarm easily overtook them, stealing voices and paralyzing strength. Their eyes were wild in panic as fear overwhelmed their senses. They ran as hard and as fast as they could in the maddened wake of the silver-winged assault, but they could not escape the suffocating horde. Within mere moments, the eleven were completely covered by the weightless, silver bodies.

The chaos ceased once the covering was complete, and then not a sound was heard, although countless muted screams still rang loud in the minds of the eleven. The violet light that had shone brightly just a handful of moments ago waned, and the hopelessness of the moment threatened utter darkness amidst the silver silence.

After what seemed like an eternity of aborted purpose, the deafening silence that had forced their surrender gave way to the presence of a great wind.

WHOOSH, WHOOSH, WHOOSH came the pounding of wings upon the silent air.

The dragons have found us, Michael thought to himself. *We have failed; it is finished.*

This is holy ground to you who have been born from the dust. A wise, old voice reverberated in their thoughts. *You have tread thoughtlessly upon its hallowed space, waking the wrath of the Danatace. Were it not for HIS great compassion, I would not have intervened. But alas, a greater purpose awaits you, travelers, and so I impart HIS mercy.*

And with that last word, the wind of the great wings pounded throughout the chamber. The silver insects fluttered in its mighty wake, releasing at last their muted prisoners to remain willfully speechless in the presence of so great a magic.

There, hovering motionless save the beating of its mighty, red-tipped wings, flew a beast more terrible and more breathtaking than they could have described. An Owele, with violet eyes that saw deep into the hearts and minds of man, peered at them warily. His talons shone in violent beauty and yet anger could not be found on his feathered face.

"Forgive us, my lord." Georgina spoke with tears catching in her voice. "We did not mean to offend you."

I am no lord. The Owele spoke kindly to the farm girl. *I am but a servant.*

"Who are you?" Celrod asked, his curiosity outweighing his frayed nerves.

I am Remiol—a watcher in the night, whose sight is set upon the coming dawn. The mighty bird screeched his answer inside their minds.

"What would you have of us?" Michael asked penitently. "What does ..." he fumbled over his words, unsure here in the presence of the Owele. "What does *HE* want from us?"

Follow, Remiel screeched. *It was mercy that made this way for you, remnant of Haven, and it will be mercy yet again that you might keep it. So by this mercy I bid you follow, follow until the remaking of the whole of Aiénor."*

As soon as the last of his words were spoken, the pounding of his wings sent the holy bird backwards, his violet gaze still holding their stare until the Owele was out of sight, beyond the passageway and the glowing marker.

"What in the name ..." Harmier began to speak, but the heavy hand of his tanner friend silenced him. "Let's not disturb them a second time, huh?" he whispered.

The merchant nodded his understanding, and in a single line the eleven passed through the silent judgment in grateful awe at the unlooked for mercy they had received.

Chapter Forty-Four

THE THREE LIGHT-SEEKERS SET out from the ruins of the ship *Wilderness* with new vigor and an air of wonder that seemed to fuel their violet hope all the more. They rode north, in and through the massive columns of soldier pines where not a sound could be heard save the crunch of the two horses' hooves upon the floor of the wild Greywood. They rode for what seemed like hours, while Cal recounted all the lore and legends of the Lost King to his violet-eyed companion.

"For decades—*decades*, Astyræ—not a living soul in all of Haven had heard even a single word of Illium's whereabouts ... and now this! This is overwhelming to say the least!" he gushed in disbelief.

"Tell me this, groomsman," she said with a hint of mischief in her voice. "Why does this matter so much to you? Why do the ruined words of ruined men move your soul in such a way?"

He thought about it for a moment before he spoke, as the clop of the heavy-hooved horses counted the moments of reverie. "Haven is not what it once was, much the same way your city, Dardanos, lost her true heart. And now, the thought ... no, the reality that something of the old Haven—the *true* Haven—yet lives in this darkened world, even if it is buried beneath all of this wilderness ... well, that moves my soul, alright, my lady. That *matters*, more than I can quite say. It makes me want to ask even greater questions, I think."

She smiled her understanding and then turned her head to meet his gaze. "And what questions would those be?"

"What else have I not yet dared to truly hope is possible?" he said quietly as his eyes fixated on something moving off in the distance.

"Well now, that is rather poetic of you, isn't it?" she teased, but whatever it was that had caught his notice had now indeed stolen his attention.

Cal did not respond to her compliment; rather, he remained absorbed with something just out of sight.

"Cal?" she asked, a bit worried at his silence. "Cal, are you alright?" She looked at him hard and then followed his gaze out in front of them, but beyond the shallow, violet illumination, she could not see anything except for the suffocating darkness of the forest. "Cal!" she said, rather unnerved now. "What is it? You are starting to scare me! Speak to me ... please?" she pleaded as she reached over to take Farran by the reins. The groomsman's hands fell slack as she took the leather from him, and his face was expressionless, as though he had altogether departed from his very self. "Where did you go, groomsman?" she begged as she reached a hand up to his forehead. "Cal, please!"

Without warning he gasped hard, drawing in air in deep breaths as his eyes widened in wonder and shock.

"What happened to you?" she said as she let go of the reins. "Where did you go? You scared me!"

"You sound like my aunt," he told her as he rubbed at his eyes.

"What?" she puzzled.

"After my parents ... after they died, I would stare off from time to time. The healers just thought it was sadness of mind, but I would see things, dream of things. Things that were not sad at all, come to think of it. But no one ever really believed me. It's strange," he said softly, looking at her with a sense of realization. "The trances, they haven't been happening to me nearly as often as they used to."

"Is that what just happened now? You fell asleep and dreamt, right here while riding with me?" she asked him.

"No, it isn't like that at all!" he tried to tell her. "It's not sleeping; it's a sort of magic, I think. Anyway, I saw something, Astyræ. White, ghostly white, out there, off in the distance." He pointed as he explained. "And I swear to you I heard it calling to me, calling me straight ahead!"

"What was it that you saw?" she asked him, trying her best to temper her wary thoughts.

He struggled to find the words to explain himself. "I don't ... I can't really say for certain. It was bright though, and my heart tells me that it can be trusted. That it is good."

"Perhaps this is why people had such a hard time believing you there, groomsman," she playfully teased him with a raised brow and a half-grin, doing her best to lighten the air of the moment. "You're not making much sense, you know."

"Fair enough," he said, his eyes alight with a self-deprecating smile. "But I don't think that is why they never believed me."

"Oh?" she asked, all the more curious now.

He rode for a beat or two, staring off into the darkened distance, willing whatever light he had just glimpsed to show itself to him again.

"Cal? I'm only teasing. Please tell me why," she said sincerely.

"Honestly?" he said. "I think it was because they were afraid to hope that maybe, just maybe, I was right. That there might indeed be something bigger than themselves out in the wild, unknown places in this world. They were *afraid* to believe me."

She stared at him as they rode, his eyes fixed on the horizon and her gaze fixed upon this blonde tree man who had rescued her from her own darkened fate. "I understand. I promise I do."

"Oh?" he returned the playful teasing.

"I do," she said as a wave of shame washed over her pearl complexion. "I do."

"Well, why don't you tell me then," he said, concern now coloring his previously playful expression, as he motioned Farran closer to the large chestnut. Cal was about to press the question when Deryn flittered up to meet his gaze. The Sprite guardian shook his head with a grace that Cal could not help but silently understand. He nodded his reply and the blue-winged Sprite came back to rest upon the front of Cal's saddle.

Cal placed his hand upon her slender shoulder, and his eyes did their best to read the history that was so illegibly written upon her saddened face. She reached up and covered his hand with her own for a breath of a moment, then blinked away the gravity that held their gaze captive to each other, looking instead towards her horse and swallowing the words she might have spoken. He sighed, and brushed her golden hair behind her ear before returning his gaze to the forest in front of them.

The three of them rode in silence as the untold narratives of their own stories held their tongues captive by the power of their own disgraces. The innumerable trees with their massive trunks seemed to pass by without ceasing, for the strength of the Greywood was mightier and more vast than any of the forests of Haven, and Cal was grateful for such a monotonous distraction.

"Do you remember what these lands were like? Before the sorceress came to power?" Cal asked her finally, breaking the quiet.

"I don't, no. But I have heard stories; the elders loved to tell them," she said with a sad smile. "This part of the world was once illuminated with a beauty all its own—or at least that is what I heard as a little girl."

"You mean ... a light?" Cal asked.

"Yes. The light of the Jacaranda. They say that Deryn's kind once protected the borders of Aiénor, and that their violet trees held both evil and ugliness at bay," she recalled aloud. "Dardanos was young then, not much more than a wandering tribe who had sought to make a new life in the cleft of the Itzal Valley. Our ancestors were befriended by the Sprites; even the High Queen Éimhear once blessed our forefathers, speaking great words of life and of powerful magic over our people."

"I can only imagine what this world must have been like, with my kin free to bestow great deeds of love upon this wild tapestry," Deryn thought aloud.

"It was paradise," Astyræ blurted out. "Or, that is what the legends say. My grandfather would tell me of the great flowerings, when the mighty Jacarandas would grow ripe and give birth to swarms of Sprite children. Such a feast the High Queen would hold in their newly winged honor that all the kingdoms of men could not help but pay homage to these great protectors of beauty."

"Do your people ever speak of such histories?" Cal asked his blue-winged guardian.

"They do," Deryn replied. "Though their words are laced with much more sadness and longing. The song of the *Sleth Aodh;* the voices of the heralds can still be heard singing its ancient lament throughout the bowels of Islwyn. For the betrayal of Niniané, daughter of the High Queen, sister to my own Queen Iolanthe, was what first set the course of Aiénor upon this dark and bloody path."

"I am sorry, Deryn," Astyræ said earnestly. "I did not mean to bring up such pained memories for you. I merely ..." Her words trailed off as the weight of yet another failure threatened to imprison her voice.

"It was not your failure that brought such woe, nor should you take responsibility for it," he said with a kind smile. "The death of so many of my kind will always carry for me a deep and utter grief ... but that does not mean that we were not once great in number and stature and strength. It is good to remember the good; both things and times, my lady."

"Were you there?" she asked curiously. "When the High Queen blessed my forefathers?"

"Long have my days been in Aiénor, but alas, my half-sister; I am not nearly that old," he said with laughter in his eyes. "I was born in the grove within the mountain alongside the daughters of the Queen, well after your people had built their great towers."

"Did you ever know the High Queen?" she asked.

"I did, once," he said slowly as the gravity of that recollection watered his luminous eyes. "I was but very young in the years of my kind, and her daughters Niniané, Iolanthe, and Gormlaith had taken me for a playmate. *Brave,* she called me that day; a brave little bird. And ever since that moment I have done my best to live up to her assessment of me."

"Well," Cal said confidently. "I think that the High Queen would have been proud of you indeed, my winged friend. I do not want to know where I would be without your bravery."

"Three daughters?" Astyræ said curiously. "My grandfather never mentioned any children, let alone three."

"Yes, indeed," Deryn confirmed. "The fruit set apart. Éimhear tended to the three blossoms herself, and by the blessing of our Great Father the three princesses were given to us."

"Well, this is strange," Cal interjected with an intrigued expression. They stopped the horses, looking around them at a most unexpected sight: a great clearing in the midst of the massive forest. "What is this place?" Cal asked the violet-eyed woman as his eyes beheld the oddity of this glade. Here, in the very heart of the rich soils and heavily timbered forestlands of the Greywood, was what seemed like a barren scar on the landscape.

"Have you ever seen such a place?" he asked Astyræ as she slid off the large chestnut and walked to the center of the clearing.

"Yes, groomsman, that I have. My people call these places the Ágoni gi, *the beautifully barren*. My grandfather told me that in the rape of the Sprite trees, as the monster Šárka feasted upon their burning bark, the earth wept in tears of glass." She reached down into the sandy soil and let the teardrop-shaped shards of woe fall through her fingers back down upon the ground.

"What do you mean? Are you saying ... do you mean a Jacaranda once grew *here*?" Cal said, trying to make sense of her mournful words.

"Yes, groomsman. One of the violet trees of beauty once flourished here in this very place; that is, until it burned."

Deryn flew down from his perch atop the silver steed until he rested his leaf-shaped boots upon the glassy soil, reverently surveying the unsettling sight.

"Long were we known as Sprite friends!" she said as she knelt down to console her little companion. "And even now the few of us true Dardanian who remain in this darkened world would still honor the winged brotherhood of our past. I cry your pardon for this atrocity, Deryn."

"It is said that Éimhear herself is buried beneath the glass of the fired remains of the royal tree, *Fionnuala*, entombed at the very site of her royal birth," Deryn whispered. "I have been hidden away all these ages, never to see the aftermath of such insatiable evil, such reckless destruction. Now that I have beheld this, I know that the High Queen left her reflective mark of beauty, even in her death."

"I am sorry, my friend," Cal said as he dismounted Farran. "Perhaps one day, before all of this is said and done, we will find your Queen and tell her that all was not lost in the death and the fire."

The blue-winged guardian looked up from the ravaged landscape, the shimmering fragments in the crystalline soil now the only traces of the ancient trees of beauty. He met the gaze of his friend, and his silent, sad smile said a thousand unspoken words. Cal returned the soundless kindness with his own.

"Are there many more places like this one?" Cal asked Astyræ as he beheld the paradox of the glittering beauty upon such a wasteland, noticing how the veins of glass spread in the pattern of long-consumed roots from the dead Jacaranda.

"There are. My people thought them to be both sacred and haunted, so for the most part they have been undisturbed," she told them. "My grandfather never once took me to see one; I had to do that all on my own. He said that he had never met a Sprite in all his days and he surely never wanted to meet one of their ghosts." She spoke with a wry smile, doing her best to lighten the weariness of the moment, and then ... then another thought caught her mind. "The whole world does not believe that you or your kind exist anymore, little Deryn," she said suddenly, her emotions caught up in the compelling implication of this notion. "And if that is true, then perhaps ... perhaps *she* doesn't know, either."

Cal's face registered just what this violet-eyed woman was suggesting, and he snapped his head quickly around to look at his friend. "Perhaps it is I that should have been guarding you all this time?" Cal wondered aloud.

Deryn grew uncomfortable with all the attention, and he shook his head defiantly in response. "No, my friends," he said as he flitted up to meet their star-struck gazes. "Our people, my kind—we are tasked with the tending to and the defenses of *beauty*, not power! Do not bestow upon me a deference that is beyond my kind, for our Great Father has long known the truth of our fruited purpose."

"But what if you were hidden for such a time as *this*?" Cal wondered. "To exact your revenge on the evil of this world and reclaim the lands of your people!"

Deryn smiled a kind smile as he met the excited gaze of his charge. "No, Cal. My people haven't any lands to reclaim, or vengeance to unleash—though I do not doubt that we were indeed hidden for such a time as this."

"What do you mean, Deryn?" Astyræ asked him.

"I mean that my purpose is not to defeat the sorceress—though if given the chance I will surely fight her—nor is it to remain hidden and protected any longer. My purpose now is only to point the way to beauty and to protect those who choose to seek the light ... those who dare to hope. For it is by the light of beauty that hope might yet be revealed." He spoke with a depth of understanding, as his tiny, azure eyes grew wet with conviction. "It is hope, hope that helps us to believe that this darkness is indeed not the end of Aiénor. Hope that compels our feet to keep pursuing, to keep searching, to keep *dreaming* that there is yet a light to be found, hidden somewhere in this world of ours. Hope that reminds us that pain and evil, lust and death, will not, in the end, consume the heart of our created identity." He flew down and grasped one of the teardrops of glass in his tiny hands, and then in a whir of blue he flew back to punctuate his message. "Why else would evil have struck its first blow upon the trees of beauty, my friends? If you rid the world of inspiration, what hope would we dare to live by?"

The light seekers stood for a moment, enraptured by the truth, caught up in the gravity of the Sprite's words.

"But it would seem, wouldn't it, that even in its death, beauty still reflects the light of its purpose," Cal said finally as he held out his hand and bid his winged guardian to rest. "Look about you, Deryn. The light of beauty still remains, it still dances and colors this wild place, illuminated by the violet light of our collective hope."

"So it does, Calarmindon Bright Fame." Deryn smiled a true, satisfied smile. "So it does, indeed."

"Come on now," Cal urged them all. "This is as good a place as any for us to make our rest. I do not think that we will stumble upon the halls of Shaimira today, but we have indeed found a good place."

"Agreed, groomsman," Astyræ offered.

The three of them sparked a fire on the rim of the Ágoni gi and tethered their horses to a great laurel tree whose branches hung low to the ground, making for themselves a place to rest. High above them, in the boughs of a massive soldier pine, perched a violet-eyed Owele, Edur, taking watch over the hopeful company as they slept. Off in the eastern distance, an angry storm began to brew. The Owele could hear the sounds of deathly screams and ominous thunder as it began to roil and grow under the haze of a black cloud of hatred.

Soon, Edur spoke silently in the wind. *None will be safe, and evil will invade once again. May you rest and recover, light seekers, your hearts washed white in the peace of HE who is calling you further.*

That night Cal dreamed in visions of old, of the destruction of the mighty Jacarandas and the death of so much beauty, and he wept in his sleep for a loss he had never himself endured.

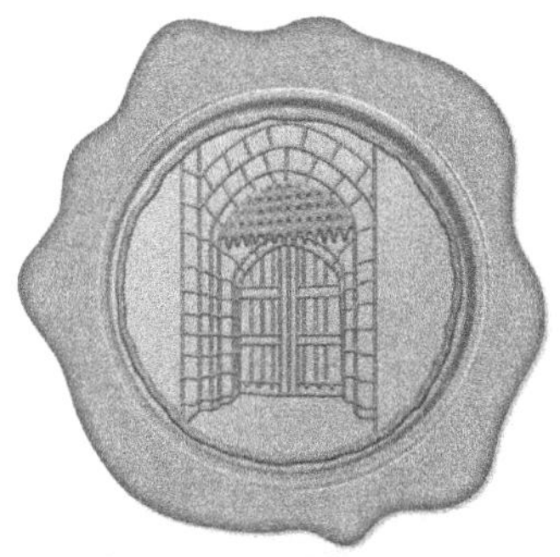

Chapter Forty-Five

THE REMNANT CONTINUED THEIR NORTHWARD march while the wind howled a cold song about them. The ground, though illuminated by the violet light of their faint hope, yielded not much more than scrub brush and willow grass. The trek along the war-littered road threatened their sprits, but as they remembered the fallen bodies of the brave guardsmen on the path behind them, they knew that they must continue onward.

Scouts positioned themselves a few hundred paces beyond the main body of the host, but they could not venture much further than that, nor could they scout alone, for the strength of their fragile violet vision lay firmly in their proximity to each other. The closer that they were together, the brighter their hope lit up the darkness about them. As the scouts ventured further away from the group, their hopeful resolve could not help but wane in the silence of the solitary.

"Do you know how much further the altar is?" Keily asked the white-bearded corporal. "In all my days hunting these lands, my father would never permit me to venture this far away from his thirsty patrons."

"It is hard to say, my lady," Johnrey replied. "The lands about this road have changed greatly over the years, and it has been quite some time since I have been on a scouting detail."

"I hope it is soon enough," she said. "I don't know how much more stamina this group has in them today; we could all use some place safe to rest our weary bones."

Johnrey turned and looked behind them. The siege fires of the enemy were still burning off in the distance; their green and amber hues danced in the north winds and reflected their devastation in his old eyes. "Even when we get there, I am not sure I will feel safe enough to rest at all."

"Well, we have to rest, whether we feel safe or not," she told him. "Let's just hope that there is some place we can find some cover from whatever hells lurk here in these outlands."

"Lieutenant!" came shouts from the scouts. "Lieutenant, I think that we have found it!"

A rumble of curiosity rose through the remnant, for it was doubtful that many—if any—had ever left the safety of the walled city, let alone traveled the North Road to the foothills of the Hilgari.

"What do you mean?" Marcum asked. "What do you mean that you *think* that you found it?"

"Well," the guardsman paused, searching for the right way to explain himself. "You will have to just see it for yourself. It's there, just on the other side of that hill."

"Secure it, then," Marcum ordered. "Take a dozen bowmen and form a small perimeter, make sure that it is safe—or, at least, safe enough."

The scout looked unsure of himself, but nodded his understanding and left to carry out his orders.

"Johnrey," Marcum said, beckoning his last remaining officer over to his side as they continued their march towards the altar. "Prepare the men for a few more hours of duty, see that they have some strength left within them this day. Let them know that once we have made a camp and secured it, we will make sure they all find a bit of rest ... for we all will need to rest if we ever hope to make this next leg of the journey."

"Yes sir," the old officer agreed, the exhaustion thick upon his raspy voice. "I'll make sure the men are ready enough."

Marcum and Johnrey reached the top of the hill and looked upon the Northern Altar of the Priest. The remnant of Haven who stood closely behind them gasped in audible shock as they saw the horror before them. Where there once stood a monument to honor and duty—a sacred relic of the Priests and their flints— now stood nothing less than a *monster*, a defilement, a mockery of Haven.

"What in the damnable dark?" Marcum murmured as he beheld the large, black raven's wings that protruded grotesquely from the holy altar. Words foreign to the eye—but sinister nonetheless—were hastily painted in white overtop the inscription of the edifice, and there at the base of the monument now lay the capstone of the altar itself, as though its very head had been decapitated.

"I won't sleep here!" shouted an older man from the group. "I would rather take my chances back on the bloody battlefields!"

"What kind of evil does such a thing?" asked a nursing mother.

"The same kind of evil that sacks a city and devours her strength!" came the nervous voice of an archer.

"It's just intimidation, sir," Johnrey said to the lieutenant. "Pay it no mind. It cannot hurt us."

"Oh, it is more than *just* intimidation, Corporal," Marcum said aloud. "It is desecration, and if we are not careful, it will rob us of our fortitude."

"How dare they!" Keily seethed between gritted teeth. "They break our walls and sack our lands ... and now this, too? What sort of hatred must they have for us?"

"It is just stone, dear," said the old corporal. "There was nothing particularly holy about it, nothing more magical than whatever we told ourselves it was. I would suspect that the only thoughts to cross their minds were of conquest, and a carnivorous victory. "

She looked up at the gratuitous mockery of this once-glorified shrine, and she knew that the white-haired, old soldier was right. "It's just—I don't know—salt on an open wound. I can hardly bear to look upon it."

"I know, girl," Johnrey agreed. "But whether this altar be broken or not, the way of the flint was never confined to any stone, not even the ones that once hung around our necks." He noticed a score of eyes now looking at him, hanging onto his words, desperate for some kind of reassurance. "We can still strike the night, we can still bring forth a spark that births a light so bright that neither raven nor dragon can withstand it."

"But how?" asked a voice from the crowd.

"Yes, how, Corporal? How will we do this?" came another.

He thought about it for a moment, running his dirt-stained hands through his snowy beard. "I don't know how just yet, but I do know that we won't create any spark at all if we give way to bullying threats and sacrilegious mockery."

"The corporal is right. And I, for one, needed a bit of reminding," Marcum said to the people as he clasped Johnrey's shoulder in a gesture of gratitude. "We can start by getting some rest. I fear that we still have a long journey ahead of us."

"A long journey?" asked an old woman. "Where are we going?"

"Do you know where the mountain palace is, Lieutenant?" The young boy who still stood near Keily's side spoke up innocently. "Do you know the way?"

"A palace?" questioned a voice from the crowd.

"What palace?" asked yet another.

Marcum stared intently at the outspoken child, reading his foolish forwardness and finding it bereft of malice. His gaze then shifted to the curly-haired bar maiden, but all she returned to his silent inquisition was a proud and rather bemused smile.

"Tell me, boy," Marcum said rather sternly. "What is your name?"

The young boy's expression changed from an honest curiosity to an ever-so-subtle clouding of self-aware shame. He lowered his gaze at the sharpness of the lieutenant's questions before he answered. "Roshan, my lord," he said meekly. "My name is Roshan."

"Well, Roshan," the lieutenant said in reply, his words intended for both the young boy and the gathered crowd. "No. I do not know where this ancient mountain palace lies, nor if one even exists in this darkened world of ours. But a reliable witness has said that it lies to the north and the west. So, perhaps, if the THREE who is SEVEN wills it, we might yet make our refuge within its ancient walls."

"May it be so," came the sound of a collective, whispered prayer and nervous kisses from all who looked on.

"There may be some truth to these rumors of a place that still offers hospitality for the likes of us, though we will still have to find it," Marcum addressed the remnant. "Come now, gather your things and prepare to make camp on the north side of the first foothill, right at the base of the Hilgari," he said, gesturing to the north.

The people nodded their agreement, sensing that the time for group discussion had come to an end.

"Corporal!" Marcum called.

"Aye, my lord?" Johnrey replied.

He walked with Johnrey a few paces away from the gathered crowd. "I do not want to be taken unawares, nor do I want to expose the whole of our position if, by chance, we are overrun. It would be better if some of them have the chance to flee than for all of our people to perish out here," Marcum said as he rubbed his tired and weary eyes.

Johnrey stood strong, nodding his understanding.

"Take a dozen, maybe a score of your bravest," the lieutenant thought aloud. "Set up a defense there, right there at the Altar. I will take the rest of the host a few hundred paces towards the mountains, and in a few hours I'll send another dozen or so to relieve you."

"Yessir," the white-bearded officer said. "There is no cover here ... so if we are spotted by the Raven Army? Or if we espy them—what would you have me do?"

Marcum thought about the heaviness of this question, and his shoulders slumped ever-so-slightly with the weight of his response. "Well," he sighed. "Do you still have your horn?"

"I do," Johnrey answered.

"If you are overrun," he said with great solemnity, "then for the love of the THREE who is SEVEN, please use it and we will come to your aid. If you but spy the enemy, or any movement whatsoever, then use your flint. We will signal back with the silent spark of the flints when your relief has come; three flashes to be answered by seven if all is clear."

"And if it is not?" Johnrey asked his leader.

Marcum looked up to the grotesque abomination that stood mockingly overhead. "Do not risk your spark, and neither will we."

The corporal crossed his arm over his chest in salute, and the lieutenant returned it before the old officer turned to leave. When he was just a dozen paces out, Johnrey called back to Marcum.

"We will find it, you know," he said with the confidence of a man who had to believe in this long shot of a hope. "We have no other choice."

"Yes, right, of course we will," Marcum solemnly agreed.

"This ravenous siege will not wholly consume us, Lieutenant. It can't. It mustn't," The old corporal went on. "We will find this mountain palace, and perhaps ... perhaps somewhere within the ancient rock, salvation will yet still come for us."

Marcum smiled and nodded in exhausted agreement. "I do hope you are right, Corporal. I do so hope you are right." And with that he turned and walked to the main body of the host.

Johnrey gathered his men, choosing twenty to position in two flanking points on either side of the North Road, hoping to make it appear as if his line was significantly longer than it really was. He gathered his men and as he was giving them their orders, the curly-haired barmaid interrupted him in a whirl of offended indignation.

"Why did you not choose me?" she demanded, her gaze fixed accusingly at the white-haired officer. "I am a better bowman than any of these guardsmen of yours. I should be staying here with you. I should be part of the first watch."

"I am sorry, but you do not have any armor, you have not been seasoned in combat-" Johnrey tried reason, but she cut his words off with her own fury.

"Was my time there upon the wall not considered *combat*?" she seethed. "Did my arrows not pierce the same raven flesh as these men? How can you say that, how can you-"

Johnrey held his hand up to silence her. "Keily," he said with stern authority, his face first hardening at her outburst and then softening a bit with respect for her courageous spirit. "We cannot afford to lose you so soon if we are overrun. It was you who gave us this flickering hope of a mountain palace, and it will be you who will have to lead us there."

"But I can *fight*!" she argued.

"And fight you will, girl," he granted her. "Fight for their freedom, fight for their survival, fight for the lad, Roshan, and all the others who need you to endure, to withstand these damned raven assaults." He took her by the shoulders and looked at her with fatherly affection, his eyes pleading for her understanding. "But do not fight me on this, girl. Now, go and see to it that our people find whatever rest there is to be had out here in this damnable darkness."

She stared at him hard, her pride bruised even though in her heart she knew he was right. She turned and left without so much as a word in response, walking swiftly through the thousands of stumps and bramble weeds that stood as markers to a once thriving forest.

Keily followed the remnant of Haven across the plain and down the embankment that Marcum led them to. "Here now, rest well, and rest quickly. We will take watch in shifts, for I do not trust the darkness about us. And when we have rested, we shall make our way in search of this mountain refuge." Marcum's confident voice gave the people enough courage to believe that they had found a safe enough spot to rest, so with this order they dispersed and found whatever places they could find to make their camp out here in the exposed darkness of this cold land. They found fresh water from a fen of the mighty Abonris that had fingered its way in and along the rolling lands. Shallow pits were dug, and small dried knots of willow grass and elderberry bushes were used as fuel to feed the shallow fires of this cold, new family.

Keily looked around at all the people huddled among the fires, desperate for some kind of relief from the north winds. She very much missed the Gnarly Knob, with its great, river stone hearth and her big iron cauldron of stewed mutton and the smell of freshly baked bread. She missed her father; she even missed the patrons and their brash compliments. But mostly, she missed Yasen.

"He would know what to do out here," she whispered to the darkness around her. "He would know where to look."

"Who would know?" asked the curiously innocent voice of the little, sandy-haired boy.

"Yasen would," she stated.

"Who is that? Is he one of the guardsmen?" he asked her.

"What? No! No, he is much braver than any guardsman," she whispered conspiratorially to him. "He is chief of the woodcutters, sent with the men of the first colony to the Western Wreath, but he knows these outlands here like the back of his axe."

"Is he your husband?" Roshan asked.

"What?" she said, surprised at such a question. "Husband?" She sighed longingly. "No, he is not my husband, but he does have my heart." Her eyes smiled back at the boy. "Perhaps one day, Roshan, he will be; and if so, I'll be expecting you to be the light bearer for me."

He smiled and blushed a bit at the thought of so great an honor. "Well, then, I wish he were here, too," he said with boyish conviction.

"You need to rest, you know," she told him.

"I know," he said. "But ... can I rest here, with you?"

"What about your mother? Or your father?" she asked. "Won't they be worried?"

"My mother and father never made it out of Piney Creek," he said as he, too, stared longingly at the darkness in the distance. Keily placed her arm around the boy's shoulders, pity overcoming her own bereaved heart. "Well, in that case, please, please come rest with me. I could use the company."

He looked up at her, his eyes still wet with sadness. "Alright, then, thank you."

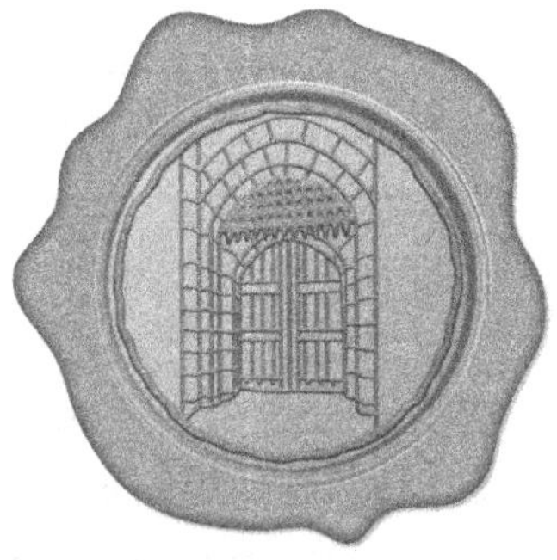

Chapter Forty-Six

A FEW HUNDRED PACES AWAY, Johnrey and his men kept watch over their kinsmen as they rested. The corporal had dug in behind the desecrated altar, while another ten of his men huddled behind an outcropping of stone that flanked the North Road. The men were more than nervous, exposed as they were to the comings and goings of the nocturnal invaders.

"Do you think there are any more of them out here?" one of the younger archers asked.

"How can there be? Did you see how many of them filed in through our broken gates?" another guardsman replied. "They must all be in the city."

"Oh, I don't doubt for a moment that more will come," said another. "They may have broken Piney Creek, but they still have the barracks of Westriver and Abondale to deal with!"

"Don't forget the jeweled walls of the Citadel!" grunted another.

"That's right, and they are-" The archer's voice stalled out in his throat as the flash of flint sparked in the darkness from behind the stone.

"Shhh," came the whispered orders of the white-bearded corporal.

"Someone is coming." He ordered his guardsman to signal back their receipt of the message, and they all waited and watched in breathless silence.

Off in the distance, advancing towards them from the eastern darkness, pounded the sound of boots upon soil as they marched in numbered unison. The small group of soldiers watched with sinking hearts as the sickly, green torches came into view, flickering at the vanguard of the nocturnal formation. Their standard, a white raven on a field of black, flapped brashly in the cold, north wind.

"Steady now, lads," Johnrey whispered. "Keep your wits about you."

The men were nervous. Some fingered their blades and nocked their bow strings, while others held their breaths and wrung their hands, attempting to stay out of sight of the company of green-eyed monsters advancing closer and closer to their weak and vulnerable position.

Without a word, the legion of the Raven Army turned their gaze upwards, towards the defiled Altar of the woodcutters, their heads all snapping to the right in an almost involuntary fashion as their un-lit eyes beheld the desecration. The motion of their march stopped instantly as the enemy officer's hand raised into the air, and with a soul-chilling silence the soldiers halted in homage before the winged mockery.

"It would seem that the General has served the Raveness well, does it not?" thundered the deep voice of the company's leader.

"Yes, Commander Črotmir," came the whispered response of the entire legion.

"Soon all of Aiénor will see by the un-light that we have been privileged enough to be given," the hulking commander boomed. "It falls to us now to ensure that *all* subject themselves to the will of the sorceress."

"Yes, Commander Črotmir," the Raven soldiers whispered again, eerily as one.

"Though Aius may have taken the city for her, *we* will keep it for her!" His words resounded across the plain, colored with yellowed hatred.

Johnrey and his men watched and waited in nervous silence as the invaders continued to gather from the east. Their bows were drawn and at the ready as they hid behind the sloped mound of earth that the altar crowned.

The rest of the road-weary remnant huddled quietly in the distance. They had been startled awake from their all-too-brief rest by the thunderous voice of the Raven commander. The small bramble fires were quickly covered with soil and the guardsmen went to arms, cautiously climbing the bank of the hillside to see what terrors awaited them. Now all they could do was remain hidden and silent, praying that the legion would advance toward the city and pass them by. Marcum, Keily and the other archers and guardsmen formed a small defense between the invading army and the fearful exiles of Haven.

CRACK! The sound of crunched kindling rang out in the near distance, behind their position. "What was that?" Roshan whispered to Keily, his eyes wide. Keily raised her finger to her lips, motioning for the boy to go back and wait with the rest of the hidden remnant. He scrunched his nose and held to her skirt, stubbornly refusing her silent request. She shook her head in frustration, then pulled an arrow from her quiver and nocked her bow, drawing it back and aiming it into the darkness, beyond their violet vision.

CRACK! The noise came again, as if something heavy was trampling the brittle underlayment of this dead forestland. "What is that noise?" he whispered to her. The unsettling sound came again and again. Her bow was drawn tight, her breathing even and calm, though her heart beat wildly with fear of whatever it was that crept in the shadows behind their camp.

The world around them was silent, desperately listening in the darkness, hoping for mercy and favor. All of a sudden, the sound that they had hoped most not to hear met their ears. A bright brass trumpet of the Citadel cut through the heaviness of the moment, causing their very stomachs to retreat frighteningly into their chests.

"They have spotted Johnrey," Marcum said with a resigned fortitude. "To arms!" he whispered.

Keily turned to see the nervous tension, men and women everywhere huddled with blade in hand or bow trained on the ridge line above. She forced her eyes back ahead of her, determining to not be distracted by the ominous sounds still crunching in the shadows behind her.

The noise of battle collided with the dense silence of these darkened lands. The *thwang* of bowstrings and the clash of iron ravaged the stillness as thuds and screams erupted on the plain, a mere two hundred paces from their position. Keily winced as she thought of Johnrey and his men being slaughtered, just to buy the rest of them a few more moments of life.

"Make ready to fire!" Marcum whispered his orders.

"Keily?" Roshan said nervously, but her attention was focused on the assault. "Keily?" he pleaded to her again.

"What *is* it, Roshan?" she spat out, more harshly than she intended.

"Something is coming!" he said nervously. "Something is behind us, close ... too close."

"Are they going to flank us?" she whispered in dread.

CRACK! This time the sound could not be ignored. The barmaid whirled around, tearing her attention from the ridge line and peering west into the darkness. "Get behind me, quickly now!" she ordered the boy as she trained her bow at the unknown noise.

"Keily, what is it?" Roshan asked again.

The brass horn of Johnrey rang out again. Whether it was signaling for help or warning the rest to flee from danger she did not know, but its call beckoned her heart to turn and take notice.

She glanced at the ridge line above, where the last score of guardsmen made their defenses. "Steady now, men. Wait and be ready to fire," Marcum said in a frantic whisper as he gazed in pained horror at whatever was happening near the altar.

The cracking sounds drew her attention again, and she turned back towards the camp. As she did, she beheld a figure in the shadows making its way into the violet vision of the huddled remnant. "What in the damnable darkness?" she said as she peered at the approaching wonder through the sights of her bow.

"A horse!" Roshan shouted, his boyish excitement overpowering his prudence to hide their position. "Don't shoot it, Keily! It is just a horse!"

Črotmir turned his gaze sharply to the hillside just beyond the North Road, for he had heard Roshan's small voice ring out from within its darkened folds. "Over there!" he ordered as he pointed to the rolling expanse.

"What is a horse doing out here?" Keily said in bewilderment as she watched the tired looking beast wander into their encampment.

"I'll get her!" Roshan announced as he took off after the still saddled animal.

"Roshan, wait!" she whispered after him, but it was too late. The boy was determined to rescue this wandering steed.

"Make ready!" Marcum whispered his order while the archers drew their bows in practiced unison. "They are coming this way!"

Roshan had finally reached the horse, and when Keily caught up with him she did not quite understand the mix of worry and sadness in the boy's eyes.

"Keily?" Roshan asked nervously. "Keily, what happened to her? Is she going to be alright?"

The barmaid saw now what had upset the boy so much. There, decorating the dirty, dun-colored face of this mare were the most angry and violent looking scars she had ever seen upon the face of such an animal. The eyes of this beast were still kind, though her frame seemed gaunt and her markings terrifying enough to strike a gasp in the breath of even a seasoned groomsman.

Time slowed to a standstill for Keily as she beheld the face of this horse. Her breath caught in her throat as the familiarity of the scarred lines awakened memories of a young groomsman and the first time she had met him. "What in the damnable dark?" she whispered. "How can this be?"

"Are you okay?" the boy cooed as he ran his tiny hands along the neck of this noble horse. "There now, you are safe with us."

The horse snorted her understanding and nodded her weary, scar-ridden head. Tears pricked at Keily's eyes at the tender way the boy spoke to the horse, and at his naïve promises of safety in the very moments before death claimed them all. As the sounds of blood and battle reached her ears, she determined to try and make good on the promises of the young Roshan.

"Run!" whispered the lieutenant down to the exiles below. "They are coming now, and we won't be able to hold them off for long. Scatter now! Make for the hills and save yourselves!"

The host of frightened people tried to flee as quietly as they could; men and women who could not hope to truly fight grabbed what they could and ran for the mountain's base.

"Fire!" shouted Marcum from above, and scores of arrows were loosed in volleyed succession upon the company of Nocturnals that had come into shooting range. "Take out as many of the green-eyed bastards as you can, men!"

Keily looked up at the carnage above, and what she beheld struck fear into her brave heart. The thin line of their defenses, though valiant and desperate in effort, began to crumble almost immediately under the maniacal attack of the green-eyed enemy.

"Keily?" came the frightened voice of her young friend. "Keily, what should we do?"

She stood frozen for a moment, watching her panic-stricken people flee, watching the falling forms of the arrow-pierced guardsmen as they tumbled down the hillside in a heap of blood and armor, watching the horrific host of Nocturnals closing in to butcher the rest of them. Her heart pounded in her ears and her mouth went dry with fear; it wasn't until the hand of the young boy tugged at her tunic that she engaged the madness swirling all about her.

"Keily?" he begged her as the tears fell from his own frightened eyes.

She looked down at the frightened little boy and knew that she must do something to protect him. She looked into his eyes and determined her course of action. "Come on now," she said with a calming order. "It is time to ride, Roshan!" Keily helped him atop the dun-colored beast, and then ran her hand along the mare's smooth, soiled coat.

"Are you not riding with me?" he asked her, even more nervous now as the remnant fled in wide-eyed terror about him.

"No, Roshan," she told him as she cinched the saddle and handed him the reins. "I know this horse, and I knew her rider. You must let her take you far, far from here."

"But, Keily?" he begged.

"We haven't the time!" she said as the screams and grunts of battle echoed overhead. She took the horse's head in both of her hands, examining her kind albeit sad eyes. "Take him west, and keep him safe! And if you find help, *Dreamer*, please lead it back to us as fast as you can!"

Dreamer snorted her understanding while Keily handed the boy a large knife. The sound of the Raven's arrows cutting through the fading violet sky gave her all the motivation she needed.

"Ride fast, and find us help!" Keily told them both, the horse and her boy, and then smacked the hindquarters of the mare and yelled after them as they fled. "Yaw! Ride swift, and may the THREE who is SEVEN guide you safely!"

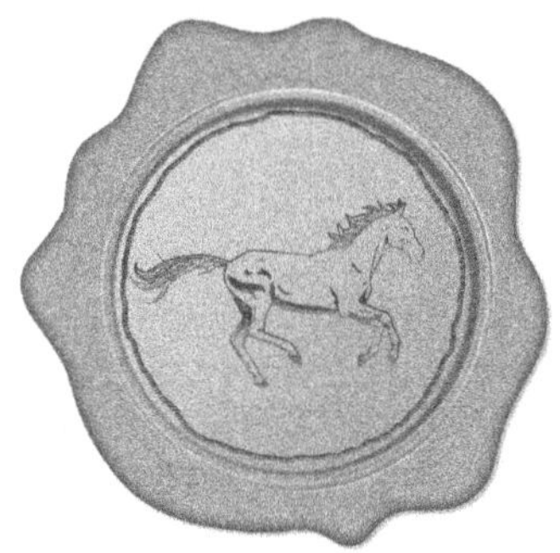

Chapter Forty-Seven

"CAL!" DERYN WHISPERED NERVOUSLY. "CAL, Cal, wake up!" The Sprite guardian did his best to quietly rouse his sleeping friend. "Now is not the time to slumber so heavily!" he grumbled to himself.

The Sprite flitted over to the sleeping woman who lay close to the smoldering fire. "My lady, please ... please wake up!" he whispered again.

The sound of boots and the clanking of metal off in the timbered distance made the Sprite's tiny throat dry with nervous anticipation. Deryn shot up to the tree line, doing his best to conceal his azure wings in the thick foliage of the evergreen canopy above them as he watched the band of green-eyed Nocturnals below.

"What is the hurry, huh?" came the grumbling, gurgling voice of an ashen-faced soldier. "The whole damned world is already hers!"

"Are you really going to complain about the will of the Raveness?" said the tallest of the enemy scouts.

"Not complaining," the first Nocturnal backtracked in his reply. "I am merely wanting to understand."

"Understand?" came the voice of their leader, growling out a loud bellow of disproval. "Understand!" He pulled a small scythe out from his black, leather belt and held it to the throat of his underling. "If the Raven Queen wants them hunted," he paused, letting a seething calm come into his voice and linger for a moment, "then we who are her servants ... will ... indeed ... hunt."

"But there is no one left to stand against her," said the first Nocturnal, unflinching at the bite of the razor-sharp edge. "Why would she bother with nomads and leftovers?"

"*Why* is not our concern," the leader said between barred teeth. "If you would like to ask her, then by all means, go ahead. But don't blame me when you become food for her dragons!"

The moment hung there, tense, as the remaining four Nocturnals watched their captain hold his blade to the throat of one of their own. "Do any of the rest of you care to ask another question?" he queried with a piercing gaze.

The heads of his subordinates shook their answers, and before he could exact his anger all the more upon the lone grumbler, something else caught his attention.

"Captain?" one of them asked.

The captain turned towards them in a sharp movement, the disgust of his answer all too evident on his face. "Do you smell that?" Almost as if on cue, the six of them began to sniff the air, their gaunt noses pinching as they took in the scent in question. "Someone is out here; someone is close." Their captain grinned a sinister smile. "I can smell their *fire*."

"Is it them?" came the question of another.

"Don't be foolish!" spat one of the six. "It is probably some Dardanian dog, or some smudge from *Clarus*."

"Regardless of who it is," said the captain, "whether it finally be the prize of our hunt, or merely some *un-enlightened* beggar, we will see to it that there is none left still breathing who refuse to take the *un-light*."

Deryn had heard enough. In a bolt of blue light that he prayed the soldiers would not see, the guardian Sprite shot from the cover of the mighty tree limbs and perched himself upon the nose of his friend. "Wake up!" the Sprite hissed, before leaping from the face of his friend to that of the lady Astyræ. "My lady, please!" he begged, as urgently and as loudly as he dared to risk.

"What is the matter, Deryn?" Cal said groggily and a bit too loudly as he woke from his exhausted sleep.

"Shhh! Quietly now," the Sprite warned.

"What is it?" Cal asked, the anxiety of his friend quickly sobering up his drowsy thoughts.

Deryn flitted up to meet his gaze as he spoke. "There are Raven soldiers, Nocturnals, six of them, just there beyond the Ágoni gi!"

Cal reached over to the sleeping beauty beside him, gently shaking her pearl-colored arm to wake her. "Astyræ? Astyræ, you must listen now, my lady."

Cal watched her as she stretched, her disheveled, golden hair framing her soft, pale face in such a way that he could not help himself but to stare, overtaken for the moment with her waking grace. "Is everything alright?" she cooed sweetly, as if she were waking upon the bed of some far-off refuge.

"The Raven's kind are here, just out beyond this clearing," Cal told her, quelling his attraction and turning to the seriousness at hand.

"They are hunting something, or someone," Deryn reported.

Quickly, Astyræ rose, the fog of sleep now vanished as she reached for Arianrhod. She slung the white leather quiver over her shoulder, fitting one of the silver-winged fletched arrows to its silver bowstring. "Have they followed us?" Astyræ growled her question as she aimed her arrow at the clearing. "Is it us they are after?"

"Even if they had followed us, we were on horseback," Deryn answered her. "And these green-eyed monsters are not mounted."

"How long were we asleep, then?" Cal asked his Sprite friend.

"A few hours, maybe, if that."

Cal unsheathed his ancient blade, and the smattering of silver and amethyst leaves shone brighter than ever before. A jolt of wariness pulsed through the groomsman as he realized the danger that they were in. "However it is that they have come so close, we cannot just wait here and let them find us." He walked over to his sleek, grey courser, and held his strong head with his left hand. "Whatever you do, Farran, keep quiet for me now.

You too, girl," he said as he patted the flank of the massive chestnut.

"Where are you going?" Astyræ whispered to him.

"There," he pointed with the glinting end of Gwarwyn. "Right where he spotted them. Deryn, stay with her, near the horses."

"No, groomsman, it is I who should run sentry for you," Deryn protested.

"I am not so sure of that," Cal said absently as he peered off into the darkened thick of the surrounding forests.

"Cal, don't be foolish-" Deryn continued to argue, but Cal cut him off.

"Please!" he shouted in a whisper. "Just stay here with her."

"Very well then, Bright Fame," Deryn said with a wounded disappointment. The Sprite and the violet-eyed woman watched him walk cautiously beyond the glassy, barren clearing and into the thick mass of birch and pines and thick, climbing ivy.

"How many were they?" she asked the Sprite, distress coloring her words.

"Six, or at least that is what I could see," he told her as he watched nervously for his friend. "He won't be able to overpower them all."

"I hope ... I hope that he will not try. I don't think that they are looking for us," she said. "I don't think they would even know that *we* exist in this darkened world."

"Who then, my lady?" Deryn asked, his eyes still trained on the trees before him. "Who would they hunt?"

"Once my father fell, and Dardanos was hers, the sorceress sought only to conquer and command any who would resist her. The *Amaian* they were called, the last, the end of all people." They heard a crack in the forest, and she drew her ancient bow tight, training its pointed, silver barb on the noises before them. "Oh groomsman, please do not do something foolish," she whispered. A tear of worry and a tinge of hurt clouded her vision and her thoughts for a moment.

Deryn rested his hand on her shoulder, sharing her distress. "The *Amaian*?" he prodded, turning her mind away from the powerlessness she was feeling.

"The rest of us had to move, to never settle; we were nothing more than wanderers, nomads," she went on to explain. "But lore had it that somewhere in the depths of this wilderness there is a protected land, where we who refuse the un-light of the Raveness might yet make a new home for ourselves."

CRACK. The sound of twigs breaking added to the quickening thump of her beating heart.

"Is that who you believe they are hunting?" Deryn asked. "These *Amaian*?"

She nodded her answer. "Yes, though I cannot say if *she* would know about the return of the tree men from Haven to these shores. The Great Father knows that *my* people certainly didn't know."

CRACK. CRUNCH. The sounds came again, this time closer than before. Then, before they could pinpoint the source of the noise, a low, guttural, gurgling sound joined the chorus of breaking branches and crunching footsteps. Deryn drew his tiny blade while Astyræ held her bowstring taught.

Cal had made his way a mere twenty paces into the thickness of the forest when he heard the group of Nocturnals just off through the trees. *Protect me, please, guide my steps so that I might yet seek Your light,* he prayed silently as his hands wrung the hilt of the still-tarnished sword.

The sounds of the soldiers came even closer, but when they were nearly upon him, the most unlooked for of all noises filled the spaces of his mind. *SCREECH* came the sound of an Owele off in the distance, and Cal was instantly frozen. Before he could struggle against the constraints on his body, he beheld a radiant, white figure of light, leaping and bounding like an eerie dream through the forest, ever closer to him. He tried to move his hands, to ready himself to strike a fatal blow to the Nocturnals that crept closer and closer to his position there behind a thick, knotted, oak tree.

Not now! *Not now, please*! he pleaded, but his voice had once again failed him. He was helpless, prisoner to the moment, motionless and powerless while those who were hunting him and the lady Astyræ were nearly upon them.

The bright light wove in and out in ghost-like fashion until it stopped not but forty paces from the frozen groomsman.

"I can see the glow of their light," one of the Nocturnals growled as they paused just before the very same oak tree that Cal was helplessly concealed behind.

"If they refuse the un-light, we will feast upon their flesh," their leader seethed. "You three, go north forty paces and we will go south. I do not plan to let them escape this day." Without hesitation, the band of Nocturnals moved into their positions. Cal stood there, frozen and helpless, watching and hearing it unfold before him.

Deryn. Astyræ! he shouted in the echoes of his thoughts. *No! Please, no!*

Once the band of Nocturnals was in position, their captain looked through the darkness as if it were as bright as when the great tree was still shining, and nodded his green-eyed command. The Raven soldiers crept from the tree line like savage hunters, their muted, iron blades held above their beak-helmed heads, circling in on the smoldering fire there in the glassy wasteland.

Why will you not let me protect the people I care for? Cal shouted silently, the madness of memory flooded his mind as he recalled the moments when the demon bear nearly took the life of his woodcutting friend. *Why won't you let me come to their aid?*

Just then, the very light that had seemed to bound its way like a glimmer through the thick darkness of the forests took shape there upon the Ágoni gi. The blurred edges and morphing shapes sharpened and solidified, and a white stag stepped forth in the middle of the clearing, right in front of three of the Nocturnal soldiers.

Watch out! Move away from there, Cal begged the brilliantly lit beast. But the Nocturnals could not see it, and indeed they passed right *through* it as if it had not existed at all. *What in the damnable dark is this?* Cal said to himself.

The Nocturnals paused after they had stepped through the stag, blank and confused looks suddenly coming over their faces. Just then the sounds of loosed arrows and clashing metal woke up the heavy sleep of the forest, and a small, blue blur of light dove in and out between the stupefied Nocturnals in the clearing.

Do not be afraid, Calarmindon Bright Fame.

Cal heard the deeply resonating voice of this beast, whose luminous face was crowned by a massive array of glowing antlers. The stag's coat was as white as snow, and it stood nearly twelve hands high, but it was the three-pronged crown of obsidian antlers that sprouted like black ice out of both the sides and the base of the beast's massive head that caused Cal to forget to breathe.

Your friends are yet safe for the moment.

Cal stared in utter amazement, for this stag blazed with light, the very same light that had haunted his dreams just two days ago. *Was that you I saw? In my dream?*

Indeed, it was, the animal replied as his burning, violet eyes met the groomsman's gaze. *Tell me true, Bright Fame, what is it that you seek?*

Cal was held in a most familiar motionless state, prisoner to the will of this magical creature, helpless to either his kindness or his wrath. He thought long about his words in the muted silence of this holy conversation. *The light.* At last, he answered the white stag. *I have come across the black waters, at the bidding of the Oweles, to seek the light of the THREE who is SEVEN.*

The giant cervidae snorted his understanding and shook his mighty crown. *Indeed, it was foretold, and indeed, you have been called across the depths, and indeed, in your seeking, a new light awaits.* The beast stamped the ground and snorted majestically before he finished his words. *Though in truth, light is not* all *that compels you in your quest, offspring of Ádhamh.*

Cal's eyes dropped, crestfallen under the judgment of this deep magic. *I do not know the way to this light, nor do I wish to find it alone. Forgive me ... if I have betrayed my calling?*

It is not wholly good for the offspring of Ádhamh to be alone, though it is not wholly without a different sort of wounding in the togetherness, the stag surmised with a puzzling mix of grace and pain. *No. There is not a trace of betrayal to be found, though there is a troubled destiny that shadows your journey.*

Shame seemed to lift from Cal's mind as quickly as it had settled, and his youthful curiosity could not help but ask awe-filled questions of this mysterious creature. *Why have you come for me?* he asked, as his eyes ran over the beast from tip to tail. It was when he saw the jagged scar along the flank of the white stag that he knew just what creature it was that held him. *Why have you haunted my dreams? Why have you met me now, here, amidst the enemy's wilderness and while my friends fight for their very lives?*

Anger seemed to burn violet-bright in the eyes of the mighty cervidae, and he stamped and snorted, shaking his antlered head in rebuttal. *This is not the enemy's wilderness*! His voice bellowed adamantly in Cal's mind.

Cal recoiled, not meaning to offend this servant of the THREE who is SEVEN. *I'm sorry, I only meant-*

All of Aiénor is but a garden of His great pleasure, and though weeds and disease have invaded its design, beauty is even now and ever always being restored, the beast interjected. *Do not give authority to the dark trespassers, for though His light is hidden, this world and all that is in it is still His own.*

A beat of a moment passed as the groomsman considered the words of the great stag. Then the scurried sounds of his friends' struggle woke his attention with a jolting call into the forest. "Cal!" he heard Astyræ shout as she nocked another of her silver-winged arrows on the ancient weapon. "Cal, where are you?"

He could see her there in the clearing, but his position was still cloaked to them, and he ached with the powerlessness to rush to her aid. Although the first wave of attack appeared to have been repelled, the other Nocturnals were now upon his friends.

Deryn darted in and out of the three still standing, his tiny, blue, Sprite blade aglow in an azure wash of fierce protection as he slashed at throats and dove in and out of the path of the enemy blades. The Sprite managed to stick his blade in the gullet of the first of the Nocturnals, but it had gotten momentarily lodged there, and it was only by a hairsbreadth that he managed to free his weapon and miss the crushing swing of another's jagged mace.

"Where is he, Deryn?" Astyræ pleaded from the tree line as she dispatched another arrow, which merely glanced off the armor of the Raven soldier. "Have they taken him?"

"I do not know where he is," the Sprite said as worry colored his fury. "But something unsettling is afoot." He dodged yet another blow from the Raven blade.

"Cal!" she cried out again into the darkness.

I have to help them, please! Please let me help them! Cal begged.

You cannot help them now, Calarmindon. It was you who left them, the Stag said bluntly. *Yet ... you are still meant to seek the light with them.*

Cal listened to these heavy words, and the weight of their meaning fell upon his shoulders. *But I don't know where I am going,* he said shamefully.

How can I take them somewhere that I have never been, let alone some place that no one has ever been to?

This, Bright Fame, is why I have been sent. The gaze of the beast held Cal's, unmoving. *You are to retrace the ancient paths, and I am to guide you on your foretold quest. For a way has long been made for those who would but seek it.*

Will you come with us, then? he asked the white cervidae.

A burst of short, agitated snorts came in heated blasts, the indignant breath visible in the chill of the atmosphere. The stag was angered and yet sorrowful; a knowing weariness could be seen in his burning eyes. He broke his stare, his tri-crowned head turning to look upon his own scarred flank before returning to meet the eyes of the groomsman again.

I am.

And with those two words, the massive white stag turned its head sharply and leapt off in the direction of the clearing.

The instant the creature left him, Cal's body released from the strangling hold of the holy beast, and he dropped to his knees. His chest rose and fell, heaving great, labored breaths. Cal forgot momentarily about the ambush of his friends; that was, until the sounds of clashing iron and frenzied commotion woke him from his respite.

"Deryn, Astyræ!" he whispered to himself, and in a flash he was up again and on his feet, the point of the ancient blade of the dragon slayer held thirstily out before him. He was nearly to the edge of the clearing when he heard the *THWANG* of a loosed bowstring.

Cal broke through the line of thick pines, and as he did he saw the fierce glow of her eyes, both yellow and violet, staring focused and ready to fire, zeroing in on him. "Astyræ!" Cal screamed, begging her not to shoot him. "Astyræ, it's me! Are you-" he began to say, but as he beheld the impossible aftermath about him, his own words caught lifelessly in his throat.

"Cal?" she yelled back her worried question. "Are you alright?"

But all the groomsman could do was stand and stare at the bloody mass that lay lifeless on the clearing floor.

"Oh, thank the Great Father that you are alright!" she said, relieved as she hurried towards him.

"Cal?" Deryn asked, feeling the growing tension of the moment. "Cal, where were you all this time?"

But Cal did not answer; his eyes were locked and his mouth slack-jawed at the horror that lay bleeding out in front of him.

"Cal?" Deryn said suspiciously as he wiped the black blood from his tiny blade. He flitted over to his charge and pulled at his shortly-bearded jaw, examining the shock in the eyes of his friend. "Cal? Cal, *answer me,*" Deryn asked again, his worry unbridled now.

Cal slowly looked up, peeling his horrified eyes from the bloody mass before him and meeting the gaze of his guardian.

"I ..." His mouth suddenly went dry and his voice was now altogether unsure. "I was talking to him," he said lifelessly as he pointed to the arrow-pierced flesh of the dead White Stag.

Astyræ lowered her bow, the threat of the Nocturnals now gone for the moment. Her mind raced, and her fears, her soul-quaking fears began to shake and threaten the respite of the small victory that she and Deryn had just won. "Cal?" Her voice was uncertain, her question disproportionately heavy to the singularity of the word.

A single tear rolled down his weary face as he looked in shock at the majestic and magical servant of the THREE who is SEVEN who now lay lifeless, devoid of power, there upon the clearing floor. Cal swallowed hard, doing his best to choke back his emotions as he beheld this woman, this beautiful distraction who held in her slender hand the instrument of destruction. "*What have you done?*"

Chapter Forty-Eight

THE MOOD OF THE FIRST colony was tense at best. The rift between the guardsmen and woodcutters threatened the fragile civility of this wilderness encampment with nearly every interaction between them. Stockpiles of freshly hewn timber began to accumulate in great mass along the stronghold's eastern wall as the North Wolf and his men waited for the mighty ship *Determination* to return with her empty holds from the harbor of their homeland. The governor watched Yasen and his men with great suspicion, for though he relied upon their sharped axes, in his heart he suspected betrayal from the northmen.

Days had turned into weeks since Tahd and Captain Means set sail from the rocky shores of the Western Wreath in search of glory, bearing the fuel of hope for their countrymen beyond the Dark Sea. Hope, however, had quickly turned to worry, for in the last few days the rumblings of a great and violent storm grew louder upon the winds. Guardsmen and woodcutters alike could not ignore the streaks of sickly green lightning as they woke the darkened skies of Aiénor with enraged fury.

No rain had fallen, but still the haunting wrath of the storm moved slowly, lingeringly, towards them. The distress over the last great ship of Haven setting sail through such a tempest evoked bloody memories of brothers lost and the *Resolve* shipwrecked, which only added to the tensions of the fractured colony. Woodcutters and guardsmen both did their best to continue their assignments with fervent conviction, but the charade was haunted with the sinking suspicion that they were indeed lost to these western shores, that the last ship of Haven might never again return.

"Is it ready yet?" Yasen asked the nervous smithy. "That timber is not going to fell itself, you know."

"Yes," Wielund answered rather exhaustedly through a wash of sparks as he pedaled the sharpening stone. "I am nearly finished, sir."

"Thank you, Wielund," Yasen said kindly.

The smithy pumped his legs in concentrated silence for a few moments more. His brow was furrowed with questions, but he was unsure of just how it was that he was supposed to ask them. "Have you ... have you seen him? Talked to him?"

Yasen just stared at the young man, his one eye doing its best to bore a hole through any ill-gotten meaning. "Seen who?" he asked.

Wielund just let out an exasperated sigh, and then stopped his pedaling altogether. He wiped the dripping sweat from his face with a filthy rag that hung from a nail on one of the rafters nearby. "You know who," he said in defeat.

"I do know who it is that you inquire about," Yasen said matter-of-factly as he held a burning piece of kindling to the simple, carved bowl of his pipe. "Though I am not quite sure your motivation for asking?"

"He was my friend too, you know. He saved my scrawny hide from the depths of the black waters," Wielund said, his words thick with both emotion and defensiveness. "Though we didn't see eye to eye on things, it doesn't mean that I wished him harm."

"No, perhaps not," Yasen said through a haze of fragrant smoke.

"So, have you?" Wielund demanded. "Have you seen him? I am ... rather worried about him," he admitted as he rose from the sharpening wheel and walked over to pump the bellows and stoke the glowing coals.

Yasen looked behind him before he chose to answer the smithy's questions, and when he perceived that there was in fact no one in earshot, he exhaled his plume of smoke and answered him. "If I *had* seen him, I am sure he would be wasting no time at all, seeking what it truly was that he came here to find," he said as he smiled a knowing smile.

"I don't know if I understand it all, this talk of new light and deeper magic," Wielund said.

"I don't know if I do either, smithy," the North Wolf agreed. "At least, not completely. But I do know it is real enough, whether I understand it or not. And the groomsman? The groomsman seems to know that he is here on some sort of greater assignment."

"Greater than this? Greater than the colony of the Priest King? Greater than harvesting the light for our people?" Wielund whined, his pride bruised at the notion of something more important than the station he had been graciously appointed to.

"Aye!" Yasen puffed. "This is all just temporary, you and me, and all of this, this is all dependent on blades and backs, governors and greenhorns." He pointed with the tip of his carved pipe towards the stockpiles of timber on the eastern wall. "What Cal is seeking ... he *believes* that it is beyond himself, somehow. Beyond all of this. And I, for one, pray that he is right."

"Why?" Wielund asked as he pulled a glowing metal horseshoe from the coals of the massive forge.

"Why what, smithy?" Yasen said. "Out with it, go on!"

"Why would you pray for that?" he said, genuinely confused at the notion. "Wouldn't that mean that you were wrong? That all of this was *wrong*?"

"Wouldn't you rather be wrong if what he hopes for is indeed right?" Yasen argued. "I believe in what we do. I have pledged my life to the service of Haven and to my brother woodcutters. But I don't really want to strive under the weight of darkness forever. There are other things I would rather do with my hands, other labors I would rather devote my life to!" he said with a wry smile as he thought of the beautiful barmaid of Piney Creek who had captured his heart when she tended to his wounds.

"I don't rightly know if I ever thought about it like that," Wielund said in between the strokes of his hammer.

"Thought about what?" came the mockingly suspicious voice of the one-armed fire knight.

"I – I just ... I was merely talking about-" Wielund nervously tried to stammer out.

"Are the shoes ready, smithy?" he demanded through indignant disgust, cutting off whatever explanation the smithy was trying to formulate. "I've been waiting for you to shod my steed for days now, and somehow I now find you in here wasting whatever vigor you still have on the likes of this *wood rat?*"

"I had to ... I had to sharpen his axe!" Wielund reasoned.

"And which of these tasks do you think that the governor would say was more important?" Pyrrhus seethed.

"Should we ask him?" Yasen replied. "Or perhaps ... perhaps we should write a correspondence to the Priest King himself and see what it is that *he* would rather us pour our resources into: the timber for his entire kingdom to see by, or whatever phantom enemy it is that you are so bravely defending us from?"

Pyrrhus just stared at the one-eyed woodcutter, his rage roiling under the surface in wounded fury. His hand flexed open and closed, as if he were barely restraining himself from reaching for his own blade and ending this once and for all.

"Mark my words, *North Wolf!*" the fire knight growled in anger. "This Wreath is not all oak and pine, and its natives are not all golden-haired maidens. There is something darker in these lands, something much more sinister than mere shadows, I know it in my bones; I can feel it. And while you and your northmen are all off on whatever holy war you think this is, who do you think is going to defend the very timber you fell?"

"Chase whatever ghosts you like, Pyrrhus. My men and I, we will carry out our orders," Yasen said as he thumbed the blade of his freshly sharpened axe. "Thank you smithy," he said with a nod of courtesy before turning his dark, bearded face to meet the enraged stare of the fire knight. "Your work is swift and sure, as always."

The horns of the watchmen sounded suddenly, breaking the battle of prides with their startling tones. Pyrrhus and Yasen met each other's eyes with a wholly different concern on their faces. "The watchmen signal," Yasen said. "Perhaps the ship returns with your captain?"

"Not likely," Pyrrhus arrogantly argued, reaching for his sword as he thundered away from the smithy and towards the commotion.

The square of the colony's stronghold was buzzing with curiosity, as woodcutter, Priest, and guardsmen alike poured out from their barracks so as to see what it was that the watchmen heralded.

"Pyrrhus!" called the authoritative voice of the governor. "What is it? What do your men see?"

The fire knight looked over his shoulder to spy his men there upon the palisade walls. It was then that he saw his two night watchmen pointing to the east. "The east?" he said under his breath, sure that the alarm would be for something much more sinister than the return of the great ship.

"Did you say the east, Pyrrhus?" Seig asked, approaching the fire night with a purposeful stride.

Pyrrhus stood there dumfounded for the moment, trying to wrap his mind and his pride around all that this could mean. "Yes, yes, Governor. The east. My watchmen signal something in the east."

"Tahd!" Seig exclaimed. "My captain is returning, and with him the glory we have fought for, and so rightly deserve!" He slammed his massive hands upon the shoulders of the knight. "This will be a day for celebration Pyrrhus! Glory for me, for all the men of the first colony! And for you, reinforcements!"

Pyrrhus thought on what the governor had just said, and the small wound of pride he felt at the absence of an enemy was quickly replaced with the swelling of power he felt at the arrival of men to command.

"Yes, indeed, my lord," Pyrrhus said as a proud smile spread across his thinly-bearded face.

"Gather your men, for we will go to the shoreline to greet our captain and brothers returned!" Seig ordered, now nearly drunk with excitement. The governor leaned over and whispered to his attendant; as soon as the words were finished he took off in a sprint towards the center of the commotion.

The horns erupted in a cacophony of brass as the notes of the watchmen yet again demanded the attention of all who gathered. Everyone looked to the center platform where the tall, dark-haired governor stood, seeming somehow even taller here in these anticipatory moments.

"Men of the first colony, today is a bright day indeed. For our watchmen have espied the lamps of the *Determination* sailing upon these black and angry waters, and they are nearing an arrival upon our western shores!" the governor declared victoriously, with fist held high.

The gathered crowd let out a relieved cheer, patting shoulders and embracing each other with great joy. "See!" said Alon the woodcutter to his brother. "I told you this was not all for naught!"

"You told *me*?" Oren said, with great offense in his voice. "If I remember right, it was I who told *you*!"

Seig raised both of his hands in an effort to silence the jubilee of the men. "We will make ready ourselves to greet our brothers, those returned and those new to these wild lands of the Wreath. Banners will be unfurled and we will give our fellow colonists the welcome of heroes! Pyrrhus!" the governor ordered. "Make ready the knights and the guardsmen for our trek to the shoreline. Fresh water and ale are to be brought to the beach, for our brothers are sure to be thirsty, and we will not meet them empty-handed!"

Gvidus elbowed Goran and whispered to his large brother. "And just what do you suppose that they would have *us* to do on this fine day? Huh?" He looked to their chieftain, whose patched face was still resolute in the uncertainty of the moment.

"Governor?" Yasen shouted out over the commotion of the announcement, but Seig went on congratulating himself with all of his fellow guardsmen, and paid no attention to the request of the chieftain. "Governor!" he shouted even louder now. "Governor Seig!"

"Yes, woodcutter?" he said, feigning his sudden acknowledgement.

"What of us, then? Of me and my men, what would you have us do to aid in the welcome celebrations?" Yasen asked, already presuming the answer.

"It would seem prudent to me—right even—that you and your *brave* woodcutters should continue to pursue what it is that you have come for." His words were dripping with mockery as he spoke them.

"And what would that be, Governor?" Yasen said, unaffected by the belittlement intended. "Glory?"

"*Timber,*" Seig replied, his words hanging long in the air. "We would not want you to waste much time on festivities, now, would we? Not when our great city is waiting for your men to bring them their light."

Yasen nodded in silent assent, bridling his anger as he strode towards his brothers. "All of us—not a single damned one of us—will be in this stronghold when the captain and his new charges arrive. If it is timber that they want, than it will be timber that we will give them."

"But, Yasen?" Oren asked. "What if there are more of our brothers aboard the ship?"

"Aye, shouldn't we be here to make sure they find their way through these sword-wielders?" Alon agreed with his brother.

"I doubt that Hollis was given the luxury of sending any more northmen to aid in our cause," Yasen argued back. "Not when it was Tahd who brought the report to the Chancellor and the Priest King."

"Besides," Goran interjected. "We had better make friendly with this new lot of them if we hope to keep this whole mess from boiling over. And by make friendly, I mean avoid any sorta conversation whatsoever!"

"Aye!" Gvidus spat. "Their sorry excuse for a *celebration* doesn't interest us anyhow, I doubt there will be enough ale to make it worth our time, North Wolf! To the trees and the timber!" The woodcutter raised his axe with a wild-eyed grin.

Yasen shook his head, grateful for those brothers who had not only made this journey with him, but who had remained true to their first assignment here upon this foreign Wreath. "Alright then, gather your axes, your wineskins, and your water barrels. Make sure the horses are fed and the timber carts well oiled, for we will not return 'til we have harvested a bounty of timber the likes of which the governor will not so easily forget!"

"Oh, but mind you now, lads!" Goran said, only half-seriously. "We won't have our *friend* the fire knight to keep watch over us, so maybe you should think about bringing a little something extra to keep you safe out there!"

The men erupted in laughter as the woodcutters agreed and went about the task of gathering all the supplies needed for a long day out on the tree line. Not quite an hour had passed, and the company of northmen gathered at the massive timber gates, their carts sloshing fresh water while their prides still healed of their offended indignation.

"Move aside, *woodcutters*!" Pyrrhus gloated. "The governor and his men are coming, and we have an errand that will wait for no man."

Yasen raised his brows in mock deference, bowing slightly to the fire knight and gesturing down the path towards the shore. "Say hello to the captain for me, brave guardsmen of Haven."

Pyrrhus narrowed his eyes with annoyance at Yasen's sarcasm and the nonchalance of the woodcutters, who went about their preparations without so much as a jealous look at the procession that passed them by. Yasen shrugged and turned his back on the knight, clenching his fists while willing his rage to dissipate in the action. Though he would never let Pyrrhus see his anger over such an insult, he could not help but feel the sting as he and his men once again suffered the forced humiliation.

Seig and his men rode forth, their green banners lit and their newly polished armor glinting by the burning torches they carried with them. The parade was brief, but their arrogance was great, and it was all the woodcutters could do to refrain from hurling jeers at the rival kinsmen who tried to demean them.

Finally the procession passed the outer walls of the stronghold and made its way down the sandy road towards the shore.

"Watchman," Yasen shouted up to the guard above them. "Close the gate after we make our leave. We shall leave the stronghold protected and in good hands while we are away at the tree line!" And with that last order, Yasen and his woodcutter brothers made their way past the gates and off down the well-worn cart paths, through the torch-lit blanket of darkness towards their timbered fate.

Two massive braziers had been constructed on the beach of the Wreath, specially purposed for the arrival of the *Determination* back to the shores of the colony. Pyrrhus had ordered one of his knights to ride on ahead of the governor's parade, and as the procession reached the halfway point on the trek to the black waters of the stormy beach, the two enormous watch fires were lit, one after the other. The light and the heat that issued forth from the twin braziers woke the shoreline in a false daylight that seemed to beckon the storm-drawn vessel ever faster. Seig took up his spyglass but could barely make out the shadowed outline of the mighty ship. He peered into the tempest, and slowly the lamps of the vessel came into view, rocking and swaying violently from the highest masts of the *Determination*.

"Here she comes!" he called out with glee.

Lightning cracked and splintered overhead, sending a wave of startled shock through the twenty armored guardsmen that followed behind Seig. Gusts of wind began to buffet their faces as they approached the shore, each stronger than the last. With every brilliant green blast of lightning, the hairs on the arms of the men stood erect in frightened anticipation for what would happen next. The ship seemed to gather speed; faster and faster it cut through the punishing waves of the Dark Sea, driven by the ever-quickening winds. Lightning cracked again, and this time the silhouette of the seven-masted vessel could be made out clearly and ominously upon the water, hurling towards them at an unfathomably fast pace.

The mouths of the watching guardsmen went dry.

"See!" Seig shouted in between the rolls of thunder, oblivious to the fear that had awakened in his men. "The THREE who is SEVEN cannot help but to deliver our great glory and grand aid with *determined* haste!" The ship careened through the waters, and the white, cold foam of its spray parted oddly in the wake of its furiously driven keel. "Have you ever seen such a magnificent ship sail with such speed?" Seig said, beaming with pride.

"Never," Pyrrhus offered hesitantly. "It is rather ... *unnatural*."

The sounds of the storm were fierce and thunderous, yet not a drop of rain could be felt or seen. The mood of the men, which mere moments ago was jovial and triumphant, turned dark and suspicious. The green banners of the Citadel whipped and pulled atop their long-handled spears, and a few tore free in the wake of such a violent wind.

"Welcome to the Wreath, my brothers!" Seig shouted against the furious gusts like a maddened victor. "Welcome!"

Just then, an enormous bolt of green lightening cracked above them, and as it lit up the darkened sky, it illuminated the body of the mighty ship, which was now only half a league from the shoreline.

"What in the damnable dark is *that*?" Pyrrhus said in horror, forgetting his decorum and snatching the governor's spyglass.

"It would seem that our *Determination* is chasing the storm, my friend!" Seig reasoned.

"Or rather, it is driven by it?" Pyrrhus offered. "There, look!" He pointed. "A massive black cloud is at the bow!"

"It will anchor soon, Pyrrhus, and then all shall be without worry," Seig tried to reassure him.

"Anchor?" Pyrrhus blurted out. "It is not slowing in the slightest! At this rate it will run aground!"

"Nonsense!" Seig bit back. "Tahd would never allow it!"

The sandy ground around them began to quake with each rolling boom of thunder, and the massive watch fires were caught in the fury of the wind. Their amber flames stretched and grew at an alarming rate, fueled by the bellows of this unnatural storm.

"*The trees!*" came a panicked shout from one of the guardsmen. "The trees are on fire!"

Pyrrhus turned in horror as the forest line, which was thought to be a safe distance from the massive braziers, erupted in a devastatingly wasteful blaze.

"The trees, my lord!" Pyrrhus said to the governor.

"It is but fanfare to our glory!" Seig cackled, his flame-lit eyes bereft of all reason.

"It is not stopping!" came the shouts of another guardsmen. "The ship! It is not stopping!"

The lightning came even quicker now, charging the air with a current of terror. The illumination of the brazier and the now burning trees cast an amber glow, but somehow this once hopeful color seemed poisoned by the punctuations of the sickly green streaks of lightning.

"What is that?" Pyrrhus heard his men gasp.

When he turned his head, he beheld the bowsprit of the mighty ship bearing directly towards them, less than a hundred paces away. "Move!" Pyrrhus shouted desperately to his men. "She is headed straight for us!"

"What kind of devilry is this?" Seig puzzled with a sobering sort of terror in his voice.

There, standing madly upon the bowsprit, was a massive figure, arms outstretched in front of him, looking as if by some dark magic he held the cloud before him at bay. The ground shook again and the soul-chilling sound of birds, cawing ravens, was heard between the cracks of lightning and the roiling booms of thunder.

"Draw your swords!" Seig ordered. "Bowmen at the ready!"

"We haven't any bowmen!" came a shouted reply.

Pyrrhus reached for his flint and kissed it, and as he did the keel of the mighty ship crested the sandy shore, plummeting through the dunes and the sea grasses, sending sprays of splintered Greywood and sand raining through the air.

"Draw your blades!" the governor shouted against the rage of the storm.

The horses reeled in terror, sending their riders crashing to the ground. The guardsmen along the shore lost their footing in a quake that heaved the very ground beneath their feet. Not a single man stood before the display of power that had beached itself upon the shores of their new homeland.

There, before the unbelieving eyes of the colony of Haven, the green-eyed driver let out a scream that reminded Pyrrhus of a great bird of prey. His ashen-colored muscles rippled with exertion, for he held to hundreds of tiny leather thongs that saddled *thousands* of green-eyed ravens, and the strain of their pull tore at his skin.

"What in the-" Pyrrhus began to say, as he pulled himself up and to his feet, but his words were eclipsed by the soul-chilling voice that interrupted him.

"Men of the dead tree," it said with bellowed malice. "Behold, your salvation has come, and it rides on the wings of the *Raven Queen*."

Epilogue

THE MOOD OF THE POET colony had gone grim these last weeks, for rumbles and rumors of war had reverberated their bloodthirsty threats all throughout the bowels of the ancient mountain palace. The Sprites and aging Poets all felt the weight of the coming battle, yet none save the Queen seemed to know how to prepare for it.

Queen Iolanthe had remained enthroned upon the white seat that stood in her great hall, deep within the ever-flowering Jacarandas. Islwyn was buzzing with activity ever since she had ordered Faolan, her captain of the host, to arm all of her children for whatever war befell them.

"Before the rape of the trees of beauty, our kind paid little attention to the instruments of battle, though we were ever-skilled in their making," she told the Poet woman, Klieo. "We crafted them more for their shape and their magic than did we for their letting of blood."

"What happened, my Queen?" the old historian asked.

The Sprite Queen stared off into the violet shadows of the hidden grove, as if she were reliving the atrocities of her people all over again. "Some were valiant and defended our people bravely, but our strength was cut short with every tree that was consumed by *her* sorcery. For the flowering fruit of the trees of beauty are nothing but a sad song apart from the branch and the bough of their birth."

"And those of you here?" Klieo asked. "Is it because these trees were hidden? Is that why you still remain?"

"Our Great Father whispered His secret wisdom to my mother, Éimhear, and before I had even blossomed into this world, she had planted these hidden seeds in preparation for the fall of beauty." Iolanthe smiled at the very idea of her noble mother, the High Queen, stealing off into the night, pregnant with a hidden hope as she flitted her way to the falls of Sarangrael.

"I, for one, am thankful for her conspiracy," Klieo said with childlike honesty.

"If beauty still lives—if it still dares to exist in this darkened world of ours—then we will have a second kind of strength to defend and care for each other by," Iolanthe said as her tiny hands held the wrinkled face of the Poet.

"Oh?" said Klieo.

"Yes, my child," she said wisely. "For duty, and fear, and even vengeance will compel the heart for only so long, for only so far. It is inspiration that sets it on fire anew each darkened day, with a dream of life restored."

"Your majesty?" interrupted the voice of Ardghal, the herald of Islwyn. "Your presence is requested in the great halls of Terriah. Our Poet friends are in urgent need of you," he said as he bowed in reverence.

She read the concern on his face and stood to her feet, smoothing out the violet seams of her silken gown. Just then a shower of violet leaves began to fall ever so purposefully down from the high boughs of the Jacarandas above. They did not fall to the floor of the dais, but rather swirled about the Queen in a tingling wind of holy magic. The eyes of the Queen went luminous in violet power as the wordless wind of her Great Father spoke in a silent storm of discernment. Klieo bowed her head, an overwhelming feeling of unworthiness causing her to avert her gaze, while Ardghal knelt in practiced reverence for these hallowed moments.

Finally in a whisper of a last breath, the wind words spoke for all to hear. "*Tá sé tar éis tús curtha.*"

"It has begun," the Queen said, her voice laden with a deep sense of coming doom.

"My Queen?" the herald asked. "What would you have of me?"

The violet eyes of the Queen shone all the brighter here in the presence of the spirit of the Great Father, and it was with both holy power and great conviction that she made her request known. "Summon Faolan, and assemble the host, for the time has come for our kind to bid farewell to the safety of this cleft of stone."

"May it be so," the herald said in a wing-splayed bow of obedience. Then, in an explosion of silver magic, the herald of the Queen shot high into the air of the grove, pursing his lips to his silver trumpet and giving forth sound with such a breath that the Poets high above the ground were said to have heard his call to war.

"Let us go and speak with your Poet brothers and sisters, shall we?" Iolanthe said with a gracious and genuine concern. "For Faolan still has much to make ready, and the urgency of their request is not lost to me, dear Klieo."

"May it be so, my Queen," Klieo said with a clumsy curtsy.

By the time Klieo and the Queen made their way into the great hall of Petros, a rare commotion had begun to swell amongst the Poets of Kalein. "Tolk? Clivesis?" Klieo asked, nervously now. "What is going on here? What is all the fuss about?"

"Queen Iolanthe," Tolk said with great affection as he slowly and rather painfully knelt before this ancient, winged nobility.

"My dear Tolk," she said as she gracefully flitted to the old Poet leader. She held his wrinkled, round face in her tiny hands, and saw the worry hidden behind the crown of white, bushy eyebrows. "What is the matter, my friend?"

"Your majesty?" spoke the worried voice of Elder John. "I found something ... or rather, I found *someone*."

"Oh?" she said, unsurprised. "Tell me, Elder John, who have you found that has caused you and your people such distress?"

And at that very question, the sea of anxious Poets parted before the gaze of the Sprite Queen, and she beheld the blood-stained shirt of a young boy, who lay upon the large, stone table of Kalein. Meledae held a blood-soaked bandage to his chest, imploring the Sprite Queen with pleading eyes to do something to save the boy.

The Queen's face shifted from distress, to worry, and then almost instantaneously back to steady resolve. "Klieo, send for Eógan; we will need his mending arts if we hope to save this child."

Klieo did not wait to respond, but took off in the direction of the great library so as to do the bidding of the Queen as quickly as she might.

All eyes were on Iolanthe as she watched the young boy before her. "Where did you come across him?" she asked.

"Ransom and I were hauling in the day's catch, when I heard hooves upon the riverbank. I thought to myself that I must be going mad, but when I looked up over Eiluned's rocky cliffs, I saw him," Elder John recounted. "He was barely clinging to the face of a scarred, young mare." The Poet looked at the ground, not sure if the Queen approved of him bringing such an outsider into their sanctuary.

The face of the Queen tightened, deep in concentration as she heard the Poet retell his story.

"You said we would aid the remnant, and ... well, he is the first remnant we've come across. I think." Elder John offered.

"Where is the horse that bore him to us?" Iolanthe asked him.

"She is with Moa," Meledae answered for him. "She was wounded, too. I found a skin of liniment on her, and gave her a bit of tending to. But ..."

"Yes?" the Queen prompted, urging Meledae to continue.

"There's something about the horses, your Majesty. Moa took to taking care of this young mare as if she *knew her*, somehow." Meledae's voice choked with emotion at the tenderness she had seen in the horses.

Just then Eógan, shepherd of the weary, flew up in a great haste of purpose.

"Ah, Eógan, see what you can do for the boy," Iolanthe instructed gently.

Eógan nodded proudly, "Of course, my Queen. It is my honor."

"The horses?" Iolanthe asked Meledae again.

"They are bonded in a kindred way, I think. Perhaps they shall mend each other."

Iolanthe pondered the thought as she searched Meledae's face, sensing the truth in her perception.

"My Queen!" came the small, excited voice of Eógan, echoing through the great hall. "My Queen, the boy ... the boy is awake!"

The boy rubbed at his eyes as if he were in a splendid dream, his wounded and weary face alight with wonder. "I found it! The palace! I found ... wait, who are you?" he managed to whisper at the hovering figure before him.

"My name is Iolanthe, Queen of the Sprites, and you are safe now, dear one," she told him with great kindness to her words.

He smiled for a moment, and then the reality of his memory came crashing into the joy of his discovery. "No! None of us are safe now! The Raven Army has taken them!" he said as boyish tears began to stream from his eyes. "You've got to help them! You've got to help my friends, please! *Please!*"

INDEX

Caution: This index contains spoilers for Book Two.

CHARACTERS/ THINGS

Abaddon: dragon of the **Nocturnal** Raven Army with byzantium colored scales, vile green eyes, and a serpent-like body; moves and talks in symmetric synchronicity with his sister dragon, **Angrah**

Ádhamh: the first man of **Aiénor** sent by **The THREE who is SEVEN** to sire the people of **Terriah**

Aius: General and commander of the **Nocturnal** Raven Army; previously was the last steward of **Dardanos** and father of **Astyræ**

Alon: woodcutter of the **Western Wreath** colony; yellow-bearded; brother of **Oren**

Amaian: group of people who refused the un-light of the Raven Queen; now live in a protected land deep within the **Greywood**

Angrah: dragon of the **Nocturnal** Raven Army with byzantium colored scales, vile green eyes, and a serpent-like body; moves and talks in symmetric synchronicity with her brother dragon, **Abaddon**

Arborists: tree-like stewards of the great burning Tree of Light and keepers of ancient magic and prophecies

Ardghal: Sprite, silver-winged arch-herald messenger of the Queen, *"Herald of High Valor"*

Arianrhod: ancient magical bow given to **Astyræ** *"Silver Moon"*

Armas: Captain of the Capital Guard, leader of **Haven's** Northern forces against the **Nocturnal** Raven Army

Aspen: Arborist, brother of **Ispen**

Astyræ: beautiful, mysterious woman from the **Western Wreath**

with violet eyes and yellow pupils who accompanies **Cal** on his quest

Bakaren: old woman from **Asier**, member of the council of elders

Barkas: Captain of the Capital Guard during King **Illium's** reign; crew member aboard the ship *Wilderness*

Benhiram: guardsman dispatched to the Capital by **Armas** to report on the war in the North

Blodeuwedd: Sprite, armorist who made both the sword, **Gwarwyn,** and bow, **Arianrhod**

Brádách: woodcutter who walks with a limp after he buried his axe in his own foot

Branwen: raven-haired, beautiful wife of **Caedmon**, the dragon slayer; the evil of **Šárka** corrupted her and turned her into **Nogcwren**, the Raven Queen

Caedmon: hero dragon slayer of the ancient Kingdom of **Terriah** who wielded the magic sword, **Gwarwyn**; his wife was **Branwen** before she became the Raven Queen

Calarmindon Bright Fame: goes by **Cal**; groomsman who is called by **the THREE who is SEVEN** to seek a new light for the Kingdom of **Haven**; he was given the sword **Gwarwyn**

Cascarie: past King of **Haven**, father of King **Illium**

Celrod: round-bellied schoolmaster of **Westriver**, fellow imprisoned cell-mate and escapee with **Michael**

Chaiphus: Chancellor to the Priest King **Jhames**, pious and arrogant

Clivesis: Poet of **Kalein**, he is the keeper of wisdom and stories

Črotmir: Commander of a company of soldiers in the **Nocturnal** Raven Army

Deryn: Sprite, blue-winged warrior who is **Cal's** companion and guardian on his journey to find a new light

Determination: three-masted, silver-sailed ship that brought the first colony to the **Western Wreath**

Dreamer: Cal's first horse; she was attacked and scarred by an **Owele** which set **Cal** upon his quest, but she ran away into the wilds of the North

Edur: Owele who guides and protects **Cal**, "*Snow*"

Éimhear: High Queen of the **Sprites**, mother of Queen **Iolanthe**, **Niniané**, and **Gormlaith**; now entombed at the site of the royal tree, **Fionnuala**

Elder John: Poet of **Kalein**, humble fisherman helped by his mule **Ransom**

Elmer: Arborist, green-haired and leafy-bearded brother of **Engelmann**

Engelmann: Arborist, green-haired and mossy-bearded teacher of **Michael** and leader of the hopeful remnant in **Haven**, "*The Hopeful*"

Eógan: Sprite, golden-winged healer, "*Shepherd of the Weary*"

Erik: Corporal in the Northern cavalry under Captain **Armas**

Farran: Cal's dapple-grey courser horse that he rides on the **Western Wreath**, "*Iron*"

Faolan: Sprite, silver-winged Captain of the Host, "*Little Wolf*"

Fryon: older of two **Westriver** brothers imprisoned unjustly, fellow escapee and companion of **Michael**

Georgina: young farm girl of **Haven**; follower of **Engelmann** and remnant companion of **Margarid**

Goran: woodcutter of the **Western Wreath** colony; mountain of a man with a big heart and a big appetite

Gormlaith: Sprite, daughter of the High Queen **Éimhear**

Gvidus: woodcutter of the **Western Wreath** colony; large-bellied and jovial man

Gwarwyn: magical, leaf-shaped sword rescued by **Cal** from the depths of the Falls of Sarangrael; the hilt blooms as he performs valiant deeds, *"Beautiful Dawn"*

Harmier: merchant of **Haven**, follower of **Engelmann** and remnant companion of **Margarid**

Hollis: Chieftain of the Northern woodcutters; wears a white lion fur and wields his great axe named **Viðarr**; fiery-haired uncle of **Keily**

Illium: King of **Haven** at the time the first branch fell; sailed to the **Western Wreath** to find a new light 73 years ago and never returned, *"Light Seeker"*, *"The Lost King"*

Iolanthe: Sprite, violet-winged Queen of the **Sprites** who are hidden underneath the **Hilgari Mountains** in the North; daughter of the High Queen **Éimhear**, *"Violet Flower"*

Isme: herald of the Raven Queen, ashen-faced nobleman who threatens the council of **Asier**

Ispen: Arborist, brother of **Aspen**

Jhames: Priest King and de facto ruler of **Haven** who will do anything to retain his power and position as ruler, *"His Brightness"*

Johnrey: Corporal in the Northern cavalry under Captain **Armas**

Julen: Lord of the amber city of **Asier**, leader of the council of elders of **Asier**

Kahri: seamstress of **Haven**, follower of **Engelmann** and remnant companion of **Margarid**

Kaestor: past King of **Haven**, father of King **Cascarie** and grandsire of King **Illium**; went mad after his daughter **Talfryn** died; *"The Mad King"*

Keily: barmaid of the **Gnarly Knob** tavern in **Piney Creek**, courageous archer in the Northern militia, daughter of **Shameus** and niece of **Hollis**; love interest of **Yasen**

Kemen: young hunter and messenger of **Asier**, nephew of **Zuriñe**

Klieo: Poet of **Kalein**; historian and keeper of the library

Marcum: tall and long-haired lieutenant; second-in-command of the Northern forces under **Armas**

Margarid: also **Mar**, one of the first pupils to follow **Engelmann**, auburn-haired leader of remnant of **Haven**, love interest of **Michael**

Means: Captain of the first colony ship, *Determination*

Meledae: Poet of **Kalein**; healer and horse caretaker

Michael: cousin and closest friend of **Cal;** pupil of **Engelmann**; leader of a prison remnant of **Haven**; love interest of **Margarid**

Moa: Cal's black Percheron horse he rode while at the northern woodcutter camp, *"Mother"*

Morana: evil sorceress of the **Isle Dušana** who lures men in to take control of their bodies and then devour their souls, was once the **Sprite** princess **Niniané**

Nasrin: citizen of **Westriver**; the wild rose woman

Niniané: daughter of the **Sprite** High Queen **Éimhear,** she was betrayed and became **Morana,** the evil sorceress of the **Isle Dušana**

Nocturnals: green-eyed servants in the **Raven Army**

Nogcwren: the Raven Queen, evil sorceress who desires to enslave all of **Aiénor** to her un-light; controls the Raven Army of Nocturnals; was once known as **Branwen,** the wife of **Caedmon** the dragon slayer before evil corrupted her, *"Raveness"*

Oren: woodcutter of the **Western Wreath** colony, yellow-bearded brother of **Alon**

Oskar: Northern Woods woodcutter who died on the journey to the **Western Wreath,** best friend of **Goran**

Oweles: large owl-like watchers and servants of **the THREE who is SEVEN;** protect and guide **Cal** on his quest

Payam: mariner aboard the ship *Wilderness* and fellow explorer on King **Illium's** quest

Poets: rival religious sect of the **Priests,** they believe in the powers of beauty and hope; live in the **Poet** colony of **Kalein** hidden in the **Hilgari Mountains**

Portus: tanner of **Haven,** follower of **Engelmann** and remnant companion of **Margarid**

Priests: ruling religious sect of **Haven,** they believe in the powers of resolve and piety and live in fear of the great tree dying and the loss of light

Pyrrhus: knight of the **Western Wreath** colony, arrogantly loses his arm as **Cal** is defending Lady **Astyræ** from his cruelty, *"Fire Knight"*

Ransom: Poet Elder John's mule

Remiel: Owele who guides and protects the **Haven** remnant, *"Mercy*

of God"

Resolve: two-masted, amber-sailed ship that sunk during the first colony's trip to the **Western Wreath**

Rolf: woodcutter of the **Western Wreath** colony, older man with a strong work-ethic

Rolph: citizen of **Piney Creek**; friend of **Shameus**

Roshan: young lad from **Piney Creek**; northern battle survivor companion of **Marcum** and **Keily**

Šárka: sorceress of the ancient Kingdom of **Terriah** who destroyed the Jacaranda trees by burning them; her evil corrupted **Branwen**, turning her into **Nogcwren** (the Raven Queen)

Seig: Governor of the **Western Wreath** colony; exhibits bravado and seeks glory; overall leader of the colony's guardsmen and woodcutters

Shameus: owner of the **Gnarly Knob** in **Piney Creek;** killed by **Nocturnals** in the far north while on a scouting mission to defend his home; father of **Keily**

Sharon: young lass from **Piney Creek;** dies trying to escape **Nocturnal** Army with **Keily**

Silvus: Northern Woods woodcutter; commands **Yasen's** riders in his absence under **Hollis**

Soren: Chief of the Watchers and member of the council of elders of **Asier**

Sprites: magical, fairy-like race born from the last remaining Jacaranda trees of **Aiénor**

Tahd: Captain of the guardsmen of the **Western Wreath** colony; obediently serves as second-in-command under Governor **Seig**

Talfryn: daughter of King **Kaestor**; died while traveling to the **Bay of Eurwen**

The THREE who is SEVEN: God of the world of **Aiénor** who gave the world the tree of light; sent the Oweles to help **Cal** seek a new light, *"Great Father"*

Timorets: long-bearded brewer; imprisoned cellmate and fellow escapee of **Michael**

Tolk: Poet of **Kalein**, leader and eldest member; present at **Cal's** baby dedication

Wielund: blacksmith of the **Western Wreath** colony; friend of **Cal**

Wilderness: ship that carried King **Illium** and his crew to the **Western Wreath** to seek a new light

Yasen: Chieftain of the woodcutters of the **Western Wreath** colony; lost one eye to a demon bear; has an eyepatch that his love interest **Keily** made for him, *"North Wolf"*

Zuriñe: old man, member of the council of elders of **Asier**; uncle of **Kemen**

PLACES:

Abondale: southern borough of the city of **Haven**

Abonris: mighty river that runs through the city of **Haven**

Aerebus: dark castle on **Western Wreath**, birthplace of the dragons **Abaddon** and **Angrah**

Ágoni gi: areas within the **Greywood** where the Jacaranda trees died, leaving teardrop-shaped shards of glass in the barren ground, *"the beautifully barren"*

Aiénor: the known world in which the Kingdom of **Haven** resides

Argiñe: river that flows next to the city of **Asier** on the **Western Wreath**

Asier: once great city on the **Western Wreath**

Aureole: mountain on eastern edge of the city of **Haven** that contains the hallowed, great burning tree in a garden at its top

Bay of Eurwen: bay south of the city of **Haven** where the men of the first colony set sail

Bright Harbor: town south of the city of **Haven** where shipyards are located

Capital: the royal homestead castle and keep where the Priest King resides

Citadel: towering structure within the **Capital** that houses the important officials of Haven

Clarus: once a city on the **Western Wreath**, now home to nomads, wanderers, and leftovers

Dardanos: abandoned city on the **Western Wreath;** located at the southernmost point of the **Greywood** and within the heart of the **Itzal Valley**; childhood home of the Lady **Astyræ**

Dark Sea: cold, deep sea surrounding the Kingdom of **Haven** and separating it from the **Western Wreath**

Eiluned: calm pool surrounded by the rocky cliffs of the **Hilgari;** where **Elder John** likes to fish

Enguerrand: long abandoned prison tower in the **Greywood** where **Cal** finds **Astyræ**

Fionnuala: the royal Jacaranda tree that birthed the High Queen

Éimhear; buried beneath the glass of its crystalized remains, **Éimhear** is is said to be entombed

Gnarly Knob: tavern in the northern borough of **Piney Creek**

Greywood: wilderness forest in the central part of the **Western Wreath;** the men of the first colony landed here to bring back firewood for the citizens of **Haven**

Haven: walled city containing the great burning tree

Hekate': mountain range in the southern part of the **Western Wreath**

Hilgari: mountain range located north of **Piney Creek**

Isle Dušana: island in the **Dark Sea**; home of the evil sorceress **Morana**

Islwyn: hidden **Sprite** home in the heart of the **Hilgari** containing the last remaining Jacaranda trees

Itsaso: ancient name for the **Dark Sea**

Itzal Valley: valley that houses the abandoned city of **Dardanos** on the **Western Wreath**

Kalein: Poet colony hidden in the **Hilgari**; part of the palace of **Petros** in the forgotten kingdom of **Terriah**, *"Beauty is Calling"*

Maris: ancient lighthouse situated at the southernmost point of the Kingdom of **Haven;** guards the mouth of the **Bay of Eurwen**

Melania: field of battle outside of the Northern Wall; renamed for the soil that was defiled by the blood of battle and by the dragons' fire, *"Black Fields"*

Menashe: damp tunnel going under the river **Abonris** from the **Citadel** to the prison keep, *"Kaestor's Doom"*

Northern Territory: land north of Haven where **Hollis** and his band of woodcutters harvest the last trees of the Kingdom of **Haven**

Northern Altar of the Priest: stone monument at the terminus of the Northern Road

Petros: stone palace and royal residence of **Terriah's** past kings, now inhabited by the **Poet** colony of **Kalein**

Piney Creek: northern borough of the city of **Haven**

Sarangrael: falls and pool found at the ending of the **Abonris** River that nourishes the Jacaranda trees within the hidden **Sprite** home of **Islwyn**

Shaimira: location of hidden secrets of great magic, *"Guardian"*

Sleth Aodh: the Sprite song of deepest lament for the loss of the trees of beauty

Terriah: ancient ruined city north of the **Hilgari** where the **Oweles** live

Western Wreath: forgotten wilderland across the **Dark Sea;** encircles the Kingdom of **Haven**

Westriver: western borough of the city of **Haven,** home to **Cal** and **Michael**

ACKNOWLEDGEMENTS

This project would not be possible without the amazing team of friends and fellow Lost Poets who have given their hearts, their time, and their incredible talents in pursuit of this entire dream. I am and will be forever grateful for all the hard work and sacrifices, so here are some clumsily articulated gratitudes to people who truly deserve the most eloquently penned thanks.

To the best partner, protector, red-penned arguer and editor that a grammatically challenged author could ever ask for: Melody, Haven wouldn't be half the story it is today if it were not for your tireless work and care.

Chris Farrell, thank you so much for channeling your inner dragon! Your voice work and video productions are, as always, first class.

Thank you to Rob Stainback for the inspired cover and map design!

A special thanks to the amazing proofreading team! Brandon Greenwalt, Richard Kesky and Jennifer Morel: your attention to detail and your excitement over this book are a blessing to me in so many ways.

For tackling the painstaking task of compiling the ever-growing index, Richard Kesky, you are a scholar and a gentleman. Thank you, sir.

Grant Radebaugh and Jordan Thurmond, thank you for letting me flesh out the very early (unedited) versions with your two sets of eyes!

Thank you to Brandon Hyde for the early on conversations about this story. Though our worlds and schedules have changed much over these last few years, I am still thankful for your encouragement, brother.

A second round of thanks to the talented Amanda Farrell for her beautiful sigil work.

To Stephen Ross, thank you for all of your energy, your enthusiasm, and your encouragement as we share this story with the world.

I am grateful for the eager ears of my beautiful wife, Katie, as she listened along the way to my over-excited initial drafts performed in my poor British accent. You may not have known about all that marrying me might entail but you chose to journey with me anyway ... and for that I am daily grateful.

To my kiddos, Annsley and Gabriel: I cannot wait for you to read this! Seek the light, you two adventurous hearts ... always seek the light.

To all of you fans, readers, and even those critics out there: thank you for giving this story both your imagination and your time. I pray that you have adventured well ... and that you could sense the bigger epic happening right in the midst of this smaller one.

Gratefully,
R.G.

MORE FROM R.G. TRIPLETT

Begin the adventure with
The Great Darkening
Book One in the Epic of Haven Trilogy

Available on Amazon:
https://www.amazon.com/Great-Darkening-Epic-Haven-Trilogy-ebook/dp/B00I8DVQUO

Go deeper into the allegory with
Seeking The Light
Editorial companion guide for *The Great Darkening*

Available on Amazon:
https://www.amazon.com/Study-Guide-GREAT-DARKENING-Triplett-ebook/dp/B01F7E7K9C

www.ingramcontent.com/pod-product-compliance
Lightning Source LLC
Chambersburg PA
CBHW070813190726
48292CB00006B/1996